G.T. Foster

THE BOYS ARE NOT REFINED

Butt Naked Publishing
Pasadena, California

Copyright © 2024 Butt Naked Publishing

All rights reserved. No part of this book may be reproduced or transmitted in any form or by any means, electronic or mechanical, including photocopying, scanning, recording, or by an information storage and retrieval system - except by a reviewer who may quote brief passages in a review to be printed in a magazine or newspaper - without permission in writing from the publisher. Your support of the author's rights is appreciated. Any member of an educational institution wishing to reproduce part or all of the work for classroom use, or anthology, should send inquiries to:

permissions@buttnakedpublishing.com.

Cover and book design by Christopher Askew ε

ISBN: 978-1-949713-41-1
Library of Congress Control Number: 9781949713411

Butt Naked Publishing
Pasadena, California

Dedicated to my brother, George Spencer Foster, a 20-year vet, and to the men and boys sent to fight unpopular wars.

Acknowledgments

Thank you is owed to the dozens of Merano Writers who read the story and commented "show me don't tell me" including Jackie Chou, Mari Sloan, Jane Hallinger, Bernie DePaolis, Chris Cressey, Seven Dhar, and Sky; but particular shout outs to: Bob Phen who insisted I begin at the beginning then immediately demanded 150 pages be cut because it wasn't part of the war story; Mike Riherd who said "this book is going be a best seller;" Kitty Kroger for an early edit of the manuscript; Lynda Crawford for editing and insisting the work be published as a whole rather than in 3 parts; Chris Askew for editing comments, the layout of the manuscript, posting various Google Docs, and all kinds of technical support. And Tish Eastman for more than words can say.

Preface to War

Dave and I met in March of 1966 in a class at the Standard Oil Cadet Training Academy in Berkeley. Graduates of the 3-day training program were guaranteed immediate employment. Starting pay began at an unheard of $1.65 per hour. These were the highest paying gas jockey jobs in America.

We both completed the training and were hired. I was assigned to the station at Ashby and Telegraph Avenues. Dave worked at various locations, but began his employment at that small training station on Shattuck Avenue.

My Emeryville-Oakland friends referred to him as White Boy Dave. We often drove to Stinson or Agate Beach to guzzle beer, smoke reefer, and sing "99 Bottles." We both bought used Austin-Healeys. Dave proceeded to perform a custom job on his. He replaced the original four-cylinder engine with a Chevy 289.

My Healey was a more recent model and came factory equipped with a straight six-cylinder engine that ran as fast as the Devil carries off a soul. But not fast enough to avoid a war.

Dave was inducted six months before me. Part way through his tour in Vietnam he was granted a Recreation and Relaxation Leave. His Berkeley girlfriend got a ticket on an airplane from San Francisco to meet him in Hawaii. There he shared with her a VC-courier-Da-Nang-barmaid-delivered case of high-grade VD.

I hope the gentle reader understands, we were young boys and men. We came from the core of the nation's 17-, 18-, and 19-year-old population. We had only recently lost our adolescence—freshly popped cherries the lot. Forgive us our willingness to exchange our wild oats for bowls of their delicious sticky rice.

Specialist Forest is mostly me. This memoir is mostly true.

> G.T. Foster
> Pasadena, California
> August 2023

THANK YOU

to my family who encouraged,
nourished, added perspective,
and showed the patience of Job.
I want to thank Robin
my wife of over 50 years, who has heard
these stories over 50 times.
A special thank you to my daughter, Julie
for tons of advice, encouragement
and always having time to help
and to my daughter, Damali
for her respectful silence.
And thank you Damali and David
for Dylan and Marley
my wonderful grandchildren.

Study Abroad Pro...

On January 12, 1968, in the mid-morn... months after my induction, our troop plan... Thailand's Don Muang Airport. Before we disem... ...an army sergeant said, tongue-in-cheek, "Soldiers, keep your seats. It is my duty to warn you that the nature of your mission dictates you will, no doubt, be laying Thais with the natives. Boys, there is a danger there. There is danger in getting laid anywhere in this country."

The subtle joke slowly registered, then brought the expected laughter, and the sergeant continued, "Eyes front and center! Okay, Specialist, run the film."

So we sat and watched a sordid, Technicolor War Department film on the various types of venereal diseases readily available for contact and transmission in Southeast Asia. The filmstrip depicted cases so severe we were told, "Those poor, careless GIs will be quarantined for the remainder of their shortened lives."

I thought, "Is this fact or more government propaganda?"

Mind you, my thoughts included caution, yet I remembered earlier spiels by government-approved representatives and flashed back to a seventh-grade classroom visitation by a lady from the local chapter of the American Cancer Society. She brought with her a former naval seaman.

The ex-sailor told his personal tale of addiction. How he had innocently started by smoking cigarettes. How he had

...s like cocaine and morphine as a ...medical staff, and how before long he ...eroin.

...ty-minute nutshell, the Cancer Lady and the ...man, at least in their own minds, had proved in no ...ain terms cigarette smoking leads to heroin addiction. ...t—there had been a leap there somewhere, and by seventh-grade I had abandoned my policy of freely distributing credulity. I sat and reasoned that the navy man must have had other issues, for I knew far too many cigarette-smoking adults who were not drug addicts. I could not buy the pitch.

When the film ended, the sergeant introduced a US government official. The man, neatly dressed in a light blue seersucker suit, identified himself. "I am the cultural affairs officer assigned to the American Embassy in Bangkok." He explained a few do's and don'ts to remember during our stay.

"There are cultural courtesies and taboos, gentlemen, like removing your boots or shoes before entering homes or a Thai temple. Small things really, remembering to never, ever touch a Thai person's head. That is probably the worst thing you could do. It would be considered very rude and offensive."

A few guys paid attention, but most seemed to blow the whole thing off.

By the time we exited that TWA plane it was 1) a.m. Despite the brightness of the Asian sun moving across a stark blue, cloudless sky, there still lingered an early morning coolness. It was January, the tail end to the mildest of Thai seasons. But the season was changing; another few weeks would bring on the heat.

An army sergeant led us across the tarmac to a waiting olive green military bus where we retrieved our duffle bags. They had preceded us. With my worldly possessions secured inside, I grabbed mine and I sat on an unshared bus seat.

The journey from the airport to the city center was about 12 miles but took 30 minutes. It was plenty of time for my fellow soldiers-in-arms to expose their egotistical lack of compassion. It was not subtle and was openly expressed in their raw, uncensored banter.

"My God, would ya get a load of that . . ."

"Hey, guys, look at that fuckin' legless guy!"

"Beggin'!"

"What the fuck else he gonna do? He's got leprosy."

"Leprosy?"

"No shit?"

"No shit!"

"Holy shit!"

"This fuckin' dump looks like Mexico," said another. "Did you getta load of them lizards back at the airport?"

"Crawling up the walls, man!"

"This is my second tour here. Wait until you guys see that hole in the ground they call a toilet."

"Hell, this shit-ass place smells like Mexico, too," another said. He slid the bus window closed, while others laughed.

"Aren't we the pretty bunch. We need only set one foot on the ground to be fully qualified, ready, willing and able to judge an entire people and their culture. Shame, shame, you should hear yourselves. You sound like a bus load of 'Ugly Americans.' Have you never seen a San Francisco street rat?"

I looked back at the soldier who had spoken. He was courageous; it was always easier to follow the herd. Ashamed of my prior silence and emboldened by a fellow-in-arms, I piped-up, "Teach, brother!" although the speaker had been white. "You know he's right. Is the hole any worse than my aunt's outhouse? I bet the flies here are smaller."

A brief silence followed. The resumed chatter was more subdued and private. No doubt each of us was at his own state of high-alert. There was an undeniable stranger-in-a-strange-land quality to the whole thing. Awe and alienation was to be expected but why the haughty American and his prideful superiority?

"I didn't mean no disrespect," apologized a soldier sitting across the aisle from me. "Hell, he's right. We was bein' critical. My granny calls it, 'small, narrow-minded'." He extended a hand across the aisle. "Brown," he said.

"Shoot, ever gagged at the smell from a nearby factory or packin' house back home? I'm from just outside Milwaukee and I sure the heck have."

I smiled, shook the hand and said, "Forest. Milwaukee? You a Braves fan?"

"Heck yeah! I love Hammerin' Hank. Best hitter in baseball!"

"I'm a Giants fan. Give me my Mays! I'm from Emeryville. California. It's a small community on the east side of the San Francisco Bay. It's really nothing more than a tax haven for corporations and factories like Shell and Standard Oil. Local radio and print advertisements describe the town as 'A few blocks of industrial parkway surrounded by Berkeley and Oakland.'"

"Boy, Oakland, that seems like a week ago."

"Man, I tell you, residents of Emeryville breathe the stink and polluted air of that little town every day. You'd swear at a certain time every afternoon they cook cat shit." Looking out the window I noted, "Shoot, I've been to places in California just as rural as anything I see outside this bus."

"Really?"

"Yeah, really. And I've seen those rats that fellow was talkin' about wandering the street gutters of San Francisco. They are bigger than any crawling lizard you can imagine."

"Yeah. But you got to admit there's some strange sights out that window."

"Yeah, I admit. It's new!"

The Boys Are Not Refined

I rode the remainder of the way mum, determined to keep an open mind and if at all possible enjoy the new experience of an entirely different world.

A Room Key

For our overnight stay in Bangkok, the country's capital, we checked into the American, a towering, thoroughly modern, air-conditioned hotel with large black and white checkered tiles on the spacious lobby floor. Shimmering chandeliers hung from high stucco ceilings and wide stairwells led to both second and third floors, with elevator option to all floors. Most important of all, as if in happy negation of my worst nightmares of life in a Third World country, every room had running water and a flushing toilet.

The hotel personnel dressed in white shirt or blouse, brownish orange jacket with pants or skirts depending on gender. The majority of the guests appeared to be white European or American. Once in civilian attire, except for their generally shorter haircuts, military personnel were indistinguishable from businessmen or civilians on holiday.

In my hotel room I occupied myself with the three S's (shower and shave among them). I changed into civilian clothes and left the room. Within the hotel I found a stationary store where I purchased a pocket-sized notebook. I vowed to immediately begin to record and learn a few words each day. I left the safety of the hotel and walked in an eight-block square to see the sights, hear the sounds, and feel this new and fascinating place.

Upon my return to the hotel I realized I had left my room key in my room. I went to the front desk to seek assistance. Unfortunately, the young lady behind the counter spoke little or no English. My explanation and pantomime only brought a confused look to her face.

"Key...," I repeated, "key. I left my key in my room."

She looked across the lobby, pointed and said, "*Hong-naam.*"

I turned in the direction of her gaze and followed her finger. I looked past the check-in/check-out crowd toting luggage and shopping bags to the opposite side of the lobby to see the Gentleman and Lady neon signs.

"No," I said, shaking my head in negation. I pointed up toward the ceiling. "My room."

Frowning, she turned and walked through a door but quickly returned with a male clerk.

"May I help you?" he asked in very clear English.

"Why, yes!" I replied. "My key, my room key. I think I left it in my room."

He smiled and chuckled softly. "Oh, I see," he said. He turned to the pretty clerk and spoke in Thai. *"Jaao mai ja bpai kee." "Kao kor luuk gan-leh."* They both laughed.

He returned his attention to me and said, "She misunderstood. She thought you want restroom." He paused and gestured to the door across the wide hotel foyer to which the pretty clerk had tried to direct me. "You see," he continued. "In Thai *kee* mean same as you say in USA, 'caca.' You know, shit."

"Oh," I smiled. We looked at each other and then the three of us shared the laugh. He pulled open a counter drawer and handed me a spare key. I then took out my notebook and phonetically wrote down my first Thai word, "key."

All Aboard

The next morning in front of the American Hotel I joined troops waiting to be transported to new duty stations. Private, commercial buses had been chartered to carry us to various bases. Most of the waiting men were Army personnel. A few went to Takli, others to Sattahip, or Nakon Phonom, but most, like myself, to Korat and Camp Friendship.

Our bus arrived, and the driver with two helpers assisted as we boarded, each GI carrying his duffel bag of worldly goods. I chose the first seat on the right. They drive on the opposite side of the road in Thailand, and their vehicles are constructed accordingly. I sat directly behind the driver.

Once all the soldiers were seated, the bus slowly headed out of the city. It was early morning and both town and countryside were already alive with activity.

The left side of the bus had two sets of doors, the vestibule door nearest the driver and a rear side-door. One of two helpers stood in the stairwell of each door. From time to time one or the other, holding onto a hand bar with his right hand, would lean outside the open door and wave his left arm to direct traffic and assist the driver in negotiating in and out of lanes.

Our driver had reached the frontage road on which we had traveled into the city from Don Muang Airport the previous day. We were ahead of all north-bound traffic catching one green light after another. On the outer edge of the city limits we approached what was the final light before a clear, uninterrupted highway.

Thirty-five yards before the intersection, the driver pumped the clutch and shifted the transmission into the next highest gear. As he did so, the light changed from green to yellow. For a brief moment the bus decelerated. A nanosecond later it lurched sharply forward as the driver, having set his mind, down-shifted and floored the accelerator in a vain attempt to make the light.

From my front row seat all action seemed to move in slow motion. I could see the cross traffic waiting at the intersection. Clearest in my focus were the motorcycle and rider in lane one and the Japanese pickup truck in lane two, both waiting for the light to change; and change it did.

Without hesitation or a glance in our direction, both vehicles, with the light now in their favor, entered the intersection. There was a terrible clank and thud as we struck the motorcyclist. For him, it was horrific. For us it was like swatting a fly, as he came hurtling toward the wide windshield. He landed first on the hood then ricocheted over the top of the bus. Instinctively, I turned my head from the sight upon impact. Voices attached to more attentive eyes shouted:

"Jesus Christ . . . !"

"Look out!"

"What the fuck!"

"What the hell . . . ?"

To this day I have no idea how we managed not to strike the driver in the Japanese pickup truck. Our driver immediately hit the brakes, and the next moments were chaos. Even before the bus stopped, flames had engulfed the hood.

"Fire! Fuckin' fire!"

The bus doors swung open. I slid my right arm through the straps to latch and shoulder my duffel bag, bolted from my seat, and scampered down the steps. I was first off the bus.

"Move it man! God damn it, move!"

"Outta my way. Outta my way!"

As some soldiers followed me out the front, others exited through the rear side door. Other GIs were at unopened windows, all fingers and thumbs, frantically pressing the slide-release mechanisms.

"Don't fucking panic!"

"Shit man, move it!"

"Jeez!"

"Get off my fucking foot!"

Still others tossed duffel bags out open windows while the most anxious clambered feet-first through the gaps. There was the palpable fear of being trapped inside an inferno.

Someone yelled, "Back the bus up! Back up the bus!"

Was it the driver, one of the helpers, or a quick-thinking GI who took action and responded by backing up the bus? I don't remember. But after the initial confusion it was apparent that the flames were coming from the gas tank of the motorcycle pinned beneath the bus.

When the bus was backed away from the flames, a semblance of order was restored. However, across the intersection to the south a crowd had gathered around the poor, unfortunate motorcyclist. No one seemed to move to give first aid or comfort. It sounded as though the crowd was chanting.

Suddenly, a Thai policeman in a khaki shirt and pants with royal purple trim, appeared in the midst of the chaos. His revolver drawn, he was looking for the driver of the bus. We watched wide eyed and aghast as he cornered the two helpers at gunpoint and questioned them. But the driver was nowhere to be found.

As army luck would have it, there was a hired Thai native interpreter on the bus with us. A sergeant asked him, "What is going on?"

The interpreter explained, "The driver disappear. Best for him. According Thai custom life must be taken for life.

You see? Now, poor motorcyclist, him die already. It be policeman's duty to take driver life for payment. Then case close."

But in this case, he explained, having fled, the driver could now go to the district police office and turn himself in, and quite possibly, be allowed to assume certain social and financial obligations on behalf of the victim's family.

Later I would come to realize that this same custom of social obligation had discouraged anyone from giving aid or comfort to the dying motorcyclist. For it seems that if the victim dies in your arms, you are also responsible for the welfare of the victim's family.

Onward to Korat

Once the policeman was satisfied that the driver had indeed absconded, we reboarded the bus. One of the helpers became our new driver, and our journey continued north to Korat. From the outskirts of Bangkok we traveled due north for sixty miles to the Sri Nakon Ayuttaya junction.

My visual senses were now on high alert to this strange, foreign place with ways far different than mine. Outside the window the terrain was flat. There were new mixtures of color in the immense rice paddy fields in varied stages of production.

People, mostly women, were carrying buckets of water to certain plots of the field to irrigate plants. Men labored in repetitive rise, bend, and plant motions. All were dressed in sarongs and shirts. Their often-clashing colors seemed chosen from the rainbow. The men's sarongs were folded and tied around their waists and thighs, just so.

Alongside the road we passed numerous carts being pulled by oxen or buffalo. However, the bicycle was easily the most popular mode of local travel throughout the towns and villages we traveled. Yet, even subtracting the earlier, unfortunate rider there were many, many motorcycles along the way.

I was filled with sudden waves of dread and apprehension despite my best efforts to keep a stiff upper lip and optimistic world outlook. What exactly was my situation? All I knew was what I had heard, and unfortunately, I had heard very little.

The Boys Are Not Refined

While home during the holidays, I had spent three nights at my cousin Lucretia's San Francisco Haight-Ashbury apartment. Her boyfriend, Melvin, was ex-military.

"Yeah, I was in Thailand. But I was with the Air Force at Utapao. These big lizards would crawl up the walls of buildings and homes. People would just ignore 'em. They was plain as the nose on yo' face but people just looked the other way. And some of them people eat these big ole flying bugs. Look like giant flying cockroaches to me, man. It was damn different all right."

He had warned, "You know they squat and take a damn dump into a little hole?"

Jesus, I had thought. *But it's got to beat 'Nam!* "What about the army base? You were in the air force. What about the air force base?" I asked.

"Pretty rough, but some of the sites were getting indoor plumbing. But we had these latrines they had dug out. Be sure to take a smoke with you. There's apt to be five or six others doing their business. We had this one guy read the *Stars and Stripes* every morning, rise and shine. In the fuckin' shitter!"

"Oh, well . . . Anything beats 'Nam."

And now, this was that anything.

On the outskirts of Sri Nakon Ayuttaya our driver stopped near a roadside kitchen and declared through the interpreter a twenty-minute break. We could get refreshments, stretch our legs, or use the toilet facility to the rear of the dining area.

Most of us remained aboard. However, the bus was soon surrounded by vendors and beggars of all types. Many came to the windows, and a few, in turn, climbed the first steps of the bus to offer their wares. They were selling watermelon and pineapple slices, roasted meats on kabob sticks, nuts in a bag, and cold bottled sodas.

A woman squatted and cooked on a wok outside the main dining area. Hers was a separate and independent enterprise. A legless leprosy victim scooted along under the traction of his fists and forearms. He begged with pleading eyes and by lifting a tin cup tied around his neck. Numerous children were among the gathering.

"GI give *baht*."

"Number one, GI. GI number one."

"GI can do. GI give *baht*."

"Five *baht* GI. Five *baht*."

"What is *baht*?" I asked the interpreter when he returned to his seat aboard the bus. He now sat across the aisle from me in one of the forward seats.

"One *baht* is worth about an American nickel," he said.

"Thanks," I said, and wrote *baht* into my notebook.

After leaving Nakon Sri Ayuttaya we rode north by northeast, rising on a winding two-lane highway into the mountains. Our journey was continually delayed by the necessity of sharing our lane with heavily loaded, slowly creeping logging trucks. Our driver had to wait for the proper stretch of clear road to make his pass. It was during these passes the bus helper showed his true skill and value to our transport as he leaned and waved us in and out of traffic.

We stopped briefly at the village of Sara Buri to refuel. We then traveled east-northeast as we descended the mountains and entered onto the Korat Plateau. The distance from Sri Nakon Ayuttaya to Nakhon Ratchasima (Korat) and Camp Friendship was approximately 100 miles.

The entire 180-mile journey from our Bangkok hotel to camp, including one fatal traffic accident, had been about five hours.

Arrival at Friendship

When we stopped at the entry gate to Camp Friendship our driver showed his papers to the military police guards. Satisfied, they raised the two long-poled barriers and the bus drove onto the army encampment and parked at Ninth Logistical Command Headquarters.

This was the final destination for the majority of us. Even the soldiers assigned final duty stations further north in Khon Kaen and Nakhon Phonom needed to stop here as part of their in-country processing. We grabbed our bags and got off. The bus made a U-turn and exited the camp.

Sorted into alphabetical lines, we danced the "hurry up and wait" processing shuffle in its raw staccato-static rhythm. As we moved along with our orders, pages were switched, creased, or stamped. Somewhere along the line, in response to someone's inquiry about this or that regulation, one fed-up clerk barked the mysterious acronym, "FTA, god-damn it! FTA!"

Having completed the long, although less-than-arduous task of all 19th Battalion personnel, three of us assigned to the 21st Transportation Company were gathered together. The office clerk of our new company had arrived, and we loaded our gear and our three bodies into a ¾-ton truck, were driven to company headquarters and turned over to the master-sergeant.

He took our orders and looked us up and down. Having finished his inspection he rose from behind his desk and said, "You men follow me."

He led the way across the room through an open door into the inner office of the company commander. "These are the first of the replacement troops, sir. Privates Forest, Henry, and Johnson. Men, this is Captain Cousins, your company commander."

The three of us came to sharp attention and saluted.

"Stand at ease, men, and welcome to the 21st Transportation Company. The short-timers will be happy to see you boys. The master-sergeant will assign you men quarters. Take your gear, get settled in, and then go chow at the Mess Hall. Spend the rest of the day getting orientated. Be at the motor pool at 0800 hours for battalion orientation."

"Yes, sir," we responded, almost in unison.

"Master-Sergeant . . . "

We left the captain's office, and the master-sergeant gave us a brief orientation of his own. "You fellas just try to do your jobs and get along. Keep your noses clean. Learn what you are supposed to do and do what you're told fast, quick, and right and we all will get along just fine. We got a fine company of men here. Most are short-timers. They've done their job and gotten along and will be going home soon.

"Follow the book and things will go well for you. Now, one more thing; after the first ten days, we have a very open pass policy. You want to go downtown? Just sign out, take one, and sign back in upon your return to camp."

He thumb-pointed to a wall sign that read: Sign-In/ Sign-Out. An arrow had been drawn beneath the sign. It directed our attention to the open book on the tall table below. A second sign read: Take One. Next to the book and beneath the second sign sat a stainless-steel bowl. It was filled with dozens of condoms.

"And be smart, " he smiled, "use it. Specialist Sasse!"

"Yes, Master-Sergeant?" replied the company clerk, who had transported us from Battalion Headquarters.

The Boys Are Not Refined

"Specialist, show these men to the barracks and have Leggett bunk 'em."

Company Mascot

Specialist 4th Class James Sasse escorted us across the street and a barren half-acre field to a set of two-story structures on the adjacent lot. A washroom was set squarely between the four buildings. One of the four buildings on the acre lot was our barrack. We approached the west wing entry stairwell to our second story barracks from the south side.

Along that side stood a small, rectangular, wooden structure mounted on long legs about three feet off the ground. Seen from the front it was obviously a cage. Stenciled over the cage door in red paint was the warning: DON'T PET THE MASCOT.

Sasse stopped before it and pointed at the black stripped golden orange feline, "That's the Captain's pet. It's an ocelot tiger."

"Why, it ain't no bigger than a fat alley cat," said Private Henry.

"Some cat—don't!" Sasse shouted. "Can't you read? Don't even think about petting it or giving it food! Easiest way in the book to get yourself an Article 15. And that will cost you money. That would be in addition to an emergency trip to the base hospital to try and save your arm."

"You're kidding but I get it," grinned Henry.

"I'm not kidding and you obviously don't get it. An ocelot is no joke. The Captain has a permanent reminder on his left arm that runs from here to here." He traced a line with his finger that ran from the bottom of his palm toward his elbow a length of six or eight inches.

"It was a mess," he continued. "Blood everywhere. They couldn't get it to stop bleeding. Thought he was going to lose his hand for sure. You see? It's our mascot but don't be so foolish as to try to feed or pet it. No pet, no feed."

"Yeah, Specialist. I see."

"Just wait, if you should be so lucky. You'll see, you'll see. The Captain will buy one of those live monkeys right there in the big Korat market and bring it back. Then watch him feed the monkey so to speak. You ain't seen nothing until you watch one of those monkeys howl his last."

"Jesus, man. Must be something." I could envision the raw savagery of the cornered, scrambling, and shrieking monkey's wide-eyed final moments.

"It really is. It really is." Sasse turned away from the cage. "Well, up the steps we go," he said and led the way.

It was a two-story prefabricated structure attached to steel frames and our barrack was on the top floor. Like a dream come true, it had painted white interior drywalls and beige linoleum floors throughout except in the latrine-shower area, where black and white tiles covered the walls and floor with its ten toilet stalls, a like number of urinals and a row of several face basins mounted beneath a long wall mirror.

The barrack, very much like the ones we had inhabited during Basic Training at Fort Bliss only newer, was an improvement over the living quarters at Fort Huachuca, Arizona in every way.

The platoon leader, Sergeant Albert Leggett, was introduced. He was from Washington, but not the state, rather the District of Columbia, although you never heard him call it that. It was always "D.C." Being from California and the west coast I noted it as an east coast view of the world.

Activated with his reserve unit, he was a former high school and junior college football star. His sports background produced noticeable leadership traits that served him well in the army. He was an E-6. As platoon leader he held the power of work assignments and was therefore the object of many a brown nose.

Each of us was assigned a new home—one-half of a shared living space consisting of a wall locker, a top or bottom bunk bed, and a footlocker.

Then he said, "Listen up. Tomorrow morning, report to the dispatcher's room in the company motor pool. Don't worry about any formation. Eat your chow then report there at 0800 hours. They're going to orientate you, explain our mission and battalion policy. So I'm not going to go into that now. Just unpack and find your way around."

He turned and called, "Lem, *maa nii.*"

A young Thai national I judged to be my age appeared and joined us. "This is Lem. He's our houseboy and keeps the place clean. Lem, this Private Forest, Johnson, and Hayes."

Lem extended his hand to each of us and I took it in turn. He was being polite but his limp hand and weak shake betrayed his lack of fully understanding the gesture. It was a western thing.

Leggett continued. "You don't have to make your bunk or worry about laundry. We have women that do that. If you need your shoes or boots shined, set them out on top of your footlocker. Lem will take care of it from there. That's part of his job. Thanks, Lem. Chow is served from 1700 until 1900 hours. I'll see you boys tomorrow morning in the motor pool after your orientation. Welcome to the jungle that is Thailand."

I placed my duffel bag on the lower bunk to unload. I was twenty years old. Looking around the barracks I did not see any man younger. The two other new troops were no younger and those we were replacing were noticeably older. Not one among them would I judge to be less than 24.

As I hung my civilian wardrobe in the wall locker, Lem passed pushing a dust mop. He pointed, saying, "GI no need. Berry, berry hot. GI no need." He referred to my purple cardigan sweater. It was wool and preppy. I had purchased it at a Telegraph Avenue shop one block from Cal.

"Maybe you give Lem."

"Maybe," I replied. "But not today."

But Lem would prove to be patient.

G.T. Foster

Revelation of the Unknown

That evening after the mess I stood on the western balcony stairwell landing of our second floor barrack and scanned the grounds of Camp Friendship. I could see the honing runway lights of the adjacent American Air Force base. Jointly, the two facilities covered five square miles and formed a vast military complex. Do forgive me, but what was not to question? How had all this come to be?

The hindsight of Cold War history neatly explains it all as part of the larger State Department domino game begun by Truman, expanded in theory by Eisenhower, buttressed by Kennedy, and passed on to Johnson. That night it was impossible to connect the dots knowing nothing of the forces that had guided the process.

But then again, in 1968, how many Americans had heard of the Rusk-Thanat Memorandum issued by the State Department on March 6, 1962?

Mission Orientation

The next morning after a mess hall breakfast I recognized a couple of company members and followed them to the motor pool. The motor pool yard was easily a spacious acre of hard-pan ground. Parked side-by-side in four rows of ten were most of the 40 five-ton, dual-axle, dual-fuel, (optional diesel or gasoline) fifth-wheel trucks assigned to our Camp Friendship-based company.

There were another two rows of empty flatbed, stakebed, and refrigerated trailers. There were few loaded trailers in the motor pool. Most cargo had been delivered prior to the drivers returning their assigned vehicles to the pool.

There was an open front maintenance and repair area. It was constructed with a corrugated steel roof that shaded the space from the intense sunshine and sheltered it from the heavy monsoon rains. The floor held three concrete, six-foot deep, four-foot wide, and eight-foot long trenches used to make transmission repairs or to inspect the vehicle undercarriage parts such as steering tie rods, fuel lines, crankcase, drive shaft, or rear end. The building also had a driver rest and relaxation area and an assembly room-dispatch office.

I proceeded through the dispatch office to join two other new arrivals seated inside a small inner-office assembly room. One of the other two asked no one in particular, "Is this going to be another round of hurry-up-and-wait?" His fingers drummed the back of the unoccupied chair in front of the one he selected. On each chair was a small notebook and pencil. He picked them up and sat.

"I'm thinking the sooner we begin this in-country orientation rigmarole, the sooner its ends," I said and took the chair next to him.

And indeed, the room quickly filled and we began. "Good morning, soldiers, and welcome to Thailand." The speaker was a tall, 30 plus, thus over-the-hill looking soldier. "My name is Officer Lewis. I am 19th Battalion Chief Warrant Officer. The post commander, General Black, insists that all army personnel under his command get a proper understanding of their unit's mission."

He scanned the room, then said, "You boys are all new and are assigned to the various companies that make up the 19th Battalion. By show of hands, how many of you have been assigned here, at Camp Friendship, with the 21st Company?"

I digested the question, raised my hand, and looked around the room. Besides the hands of Privates Henry and Johnson one other was raised.

"Remember this. There are two types of companies within the battalion. We have type A and type B." He paused for effect then asked, "Did you get that?"

There was silence.

"What are the two types?" he asked, in required redundancy.

"Type A and type B, sir," most of us managed to mutter back.

"Okay, those of you with the 21st are in a type B company. In fact, most of our companies are type B. How many of you, show of hands, are assigned to the 69th Transport Company at Khon Kaen?"

Again I scanned the room. Two hands went up.

"You two soldiers are either the fortunate or the unfortunate. We'll let you decide. But you have been assigned to the battalion's only type A company."

Two hands quickly sprang into the air.

"Yes, soldier," said the warrant officer, recognizing one of the two hands.

"Sir, what's the difference? I mean, what is an A-type company?"

"Well, although I had hoped you would, I thought you'd never ask." His answer drew the intended chuckles and he continued. "Gentlemen, boys and girls, the difference is an A type company is an American only company."

There was silence. Then without raising his hand a soldier blurted, "But if we are not American only . . . I mean, if we belong to some kind of mixed company, what does that mean?"

"You didn't make All-American, dude!"

There was laughter.

"Straight fucking A."

The remark was followed by more laughter.

"Okay, okay! Pipe down! No, that's not it. Every one of you is an All-American, Private. You are confused and I'm sorry. I should have explained better. Under the terms of our agreement with the Thai government, within our so-called mixed companies, the type B companies, for each American soldier assigned to the company as driver, vehicle maintenance worker, machinist, or mechanic, the same number of local Thai nationals must be hired."

Some faces, mine included, reflected either confusion or a lack of clear understanding. The warrant-officer took note and continued, "Simply said, for every American soldier assigned to the line to drive or to work repair there is a Thai National under contract to perform the same work . . . more-or-less. These are our Type B companies."

A hand was raised.

"Yes, soldier?"

"Yes, sir. Sir, you said that these . . . these, these B companies . . . You said that these B companies have Thai Nationals?"

"That's right, Private."

"Well, are these Thai Nationals military or are they civilians?"

"Oh, right. Quite the right question to ask. Yes, a very good question. But they are civilians, of course. It makes it less complicated." Then he added a second thought, "In some ways."

The officer droned on, naming the other companies and units that comprised the 19th Transportation Battalion and checking assignments by a show of hands. There were apparently five full-strength companies and a couple of platoons embedded in camps at Sattahip, Bangkok, Charn Sinthrope, Korat, Khon Kaen and Udorn. They logistically spread from the Bight of Bangkok to the Laotian border.

The company and platoon names — 53rd, 260th, 55th, 13th, 69th, and the 33rd — meant no more than the names of the various camps from which they operated: Vayama, Samae San, Charn Sinthrope, Khon Kaen, and Foster.

He spoke proudly of the types of cargo the battalion moved. "We haul bombs, land mines, general goods and merchandise, foods stuff, petroleum, and frozen foods and meats. 90% of everything that is unloaded into this country off American ships is transported to its destination by our drivers." Although he seemed to go on for hours, in truth it was about fifteen minutes.

He was concluding and asked, "Are there any questions?"

I looked at my notepad and raised my hand. "Yes, sir, I was wondering, all kidding aside, what's a 'reefer'?"

There were loud snorts and laughter. I looked toward the sound then back to the podium and said, "You said there was a Reefer platoon . . . ?"

There was more laughter.

"Alright, at ease. Can the corn and calm down! That's a legitimate question. What's a 'Reefer', anyone? And you had best not say marijuana or joint, if you know what's good for you. Anyone?"

"It's a refrigerated trailer used to haul frozen food."

"That's right and thank you Private . . . James."

"But Sir, they never taught us that at Huachuca. We're going to be hauling trailers? Our entire training was behind the wheel of three-quarter ton trucks. We received no training on anything else, yet this entire motor pool is filled with Mack trucks!"

"Five-tonners, Private."

"Well, five-ton tractors with fifth wheels. Sir, call it what you will, we weren't trained on anything but 1-ton trucks."

Someone muttered loudly, "FTA!"

"Fuckin' right, FTA!" another seconded the notion.

"At ease! Private, you should have been trained. At any rate, you will have plenty of opportunities to practice around the yard before your first assignment. Are there any other questions or concerns?"

He looked directly into each of our newly arrived faces. Seeing the nothingness, he knew. Very little of what he had said made any sense at all to us. But given a little time, it would all begin to take its own shape, and things would fall into place. The general gist would soon clarify itself. So, he concluded, "Then you are dismissed to your units."

"FTA," intoned the tall black soldier next to me rising from his chair.

I read his name tag as I, too, stood to leave. Having fully realized I had seen this popular acronym alongside the famous World War II epitaph "Kilroy was here" on the walls of the Oakland Army Depot while awaiting my Southeast Asian flight, I asked, "Pvt. Bryson, FTA? What the heck does that mean?"

He turned a grinning face to me and said conspiratorially, "Fuck the Army."

I snorted and repeated, "Fuck the Army." I extended my hand and said, "Private Nigel Forest, US5678156, Oakland, California."

He shook it. "Michael Bryson, Seattle, Washington, and as you can see, I'm a US draftee, too."

We walked out together.

Time for Sergeant

The rest of my week was spent under the direct tutelage of Sergeant Leggett. He was responsible for melding me into the company. I became his second shadow and made three hauls, driving for short stretches but, essentially, riding shotgun.

On our third haul we had stopped to lunch at a roadside establishment. It was the same place we had stopped that sadly fatal second morning leaving Bangkok for our duty stations. It was, Leggett explained, a common stop-rest-check point.

As if part of my in-the-field training and indoctrination, Leggett had repeatedly admonished, "Never ever take a single item from your assigned cargo!"

As we parked, we were swarmed by young children vendors, some selling meats, sweets, and flowers; others simply begging. Legette exited the driver's side and went to the rear of the trailer. I exited from the door on my side, stood aside and watched. He untied the tarpaulin cover, climbed onto the top of the load, and pulled back the tarp.

"GI, GI give me cigarette."

"GI number one."

"GI number one, give American cigarette."

"GI give me *baht*. *Baht* GI, *baht*."

"GI number one can do."

"GI, GI . . . "

Leggett then took a pocketknife, cut open a large cardboard box, and pulled several smaller boxes from within. These he tossed to the boys below.

"C-rations," he explained. "GIs don't eat this shit!"

I liked Leggett very much but couldn't help but think, Yeah, right. That's what they all say as an excuse for misappropriation of this or that item.

Mental dishonesty? No, the world is not black and white.

His actions seemed to torpedo his earlier admonition against pilfering, thereby making the warning nothing more than a do-as-I-say, not-as-I-do behavioral footnote. But Leggett was vindicated, first by his lack of pretext. For him it was a Good Samaritan act, pure and simple. He received nothing in exchange except happy laughter, smiles, and a few "thank you GIs."

Furthermore, what he said was true. GIs in Thailand didn't eat that shit. One year I would spend in-country and never see an American soldier eat the can rations. There were far too many better dining options. Yet the rations kept pouring into the country.

Where did all those crates go? Who was eating all that government-issued larder?

Over There and Yankee Music

Call it fresh boots on the ground, but the policy of the 21st Commander was a no-pass first week, so my nights were spent on post. Even without the restrictions there would have been no pressing urge to visit downtown. The base had its own delights.

Off-duty the second night and still dressed in olive green fatigue, I watched the movie *To Sir with Love* starring Sidney Portier in the camp cinema. Afterwards, hungry, I walked to the enlisted men's club for a hamburger. Besides food and drink, the club had pin-ball games, slot machines, and music with live bands.

Reaching Camp Friendship's Enlisted Men and Non-commissioned Officers Club (EMNCO Club), I entered the diner and placed my order. Food in hand, much to my delight and surprise I spotted Private Bryson seated alone in the main ballroom. On the table lay a pack of Kool cigarettes. He sat smoking, watching, and listening to the band on stage.

"Bryson, right?"

"Right. Forest, right?"

"Right . . ."

"Join me?"

"Right!" I said and placed the plastic basket containing my hamburger with an order of extra crispy fries on the table as the band began a familiar tune. The instrumentation was well done. But the female vocalist sang words that were indecipherable in the context of their new phrasing:

"If you go in to Sa Fra Ciko . . ." she belted!

"What the heck is—" I blurted, turning around to face the stage.

"That ain't bad. You should have heard her earlier. I've listened to them close to thirty minutes, half-hour of top-twenty tunes without the vocals even once being close to their original sound. This really ain't a half-bad rendition."

". . . we are floor in you haa . . ."

"Well, the music is somewhat familiar," I said with a mouthful of burger.

It was a popular song and was well received by the mostly homesick GI audience. Upon its conclusion, despite the fact the singer had mispronounced half the lyrics and was without a clue to their meaning, the grateful soldiers warmly cheered.

It was the last song of the group's set and as they began to clear the stage, a soldier lifted a mug to me in greeting and recognition, and proceeded toward our table. It was Specialist Sasse.

"That's our company clerk, Sasse. I think he wants to join us. He's white but he seems like good people."

"Man, I'm cool with it. I'm cool with everybody. Besides, it's smart to get to know the company clerk."

"Don't I know it? I feel the same way. I just didn't want to make anybody uncomfortable."

"I'm good."

"Sasse," I said but remained seated.

"Forest."

"This is my friend Bryson. Care to join us?"

"Thanks," he said. "I hate to drink alone. There's a good band coming up next. James Sasse, I didn't catch your name." He extended his hand.

"But it wouldn't take that good a band to top that bunch," Bryson said half rising and shaking the proffered hand. "They couldn't sing to their own tune, which is too bad because they can play. Michael Bryson. I'm with the 33rd Reefer platoon."

"Oh, yeah, your barrack is right next door to ours? Are you in building C-2, on the bottom floor?"

"Yeah, that's right, twice. So where is your barrack? C-1?"

He pulled a chair from the adjacent table and sat down. "That's right. We're in C-1, top floor. These guys are good, I promise you. They're on a par with Johnny Guitar, The Cats, The Kinks, Son of P.M. or any of the other great little rock bands coming out of Bangkok."

"I'm sure we'll have to take your word for all that. I've never heard of any of them. I've only been in country a week. I just got back from my first haul to Bangkok today. But I've been sitting here the last hour listening. Where do these bands pick up on American and British top tunes so quickly? These are current hits."

"These bands are almost all good cover bands. They listen to the Beatles, Elvis, Ventures, and other names of the day. Few play anything of their own. Some do. When they do the sound is a kind of Thai-American fusion. I like it."

"How come you know so much about it?" Bryson asked.

"Hell, he's a company clerk. They always seem to know which end of the base is up," I said only half in jest.

"That might be part of it. But really, I've been here six months. I love it. I got a Thai girlfriend. She's teaching me to read and write Thai. So I extended my enlistment two years with guarantee of a Thai duty station for another year."

"What! You re-upped?" I asked.

"You got to understand, I got nothing going back home, even with a college degree. I'm thinking about after the war, too. Look, I got good duty. So I've got it licked, at least, for another year."

"Jesus, yeah, but re-up?" said Bryson in true draftee disbelief of such a possibility.

"Even with this stinkin' war going on? Well, I guess it takes all kinds. Sasse, turn your head a little bit more toward the light. I want to get a good look at you."

Sasse looked at me smiling but quizzical. Grinning I said, "Come on man. I'm just poking fun. Relax." Changing the subject I asked Bryson, "Did I hear you right? You've already made a haul? Did you drive or ride shot-gun? I mean—I was being honest when I told the officer during orientation that we hadn't driven five-tonners. Where did you do your A.I.T., anyway?"

"I trained at Fort Lewis, Washington. I got lucky. I did basic at Fort Ord and was shipped back home for A.I.T. It was like going just up the street from my house. Heck, we had almost a week behind the wheel of these exact same Kaiser trucks. Sure did."

"So you qualified 64B20?" asked Sasse

"Yep. What about you, Forest?"

"No way, I'm 64B10. That's light-vehicle designation. I checked."

"What can you say but FTA."

"FT fuckin' A," I said!

The band began a tune and several GIs cheered approvingly to the opening notes. "What can you say? That sounds familiar," I said as I turned to face the stage.

"Hey, that's Booker T. and the Mgs. It's Green Onions," said Bryson, naming the tune. He began to scat the song.

The female singer voiced a Thai lyric; then several of the soldiers moving wildly on the dance floor attempted to sing along in chorus.

"*Po-so sang pan haa loy si piu yai lee dtai glong bprachum . . .*"

"That's *Piu Yai Lee*," said Sasse. "It's a song that makes a joke of the governments' habit of making top-down policy decisions that people below have to follow. The village head, Mister Lee, rings the gong and reads the edict to use diversified farming methods. It orders the villagers to domesticate ducks and pigs. But the official document uses Sanskrit terms including the word for pig: *suwan*. When Mister See, one of the gathered villagers, asked, "What is a *suwan*?" Ignorant of the term, Mister Lee, the bumpkin village head, replies, "A *suwan* is a common, small dog"

"Yeah? How come all these guys know the song?"

"Couple of years ago, this American girl, Louise—Lois Kennedy, I forget, she's some kind of expatriot — rumor says she was a niece of President Kennedy, anyway, she made a recording. They played it all over the place. American radio, Thai radio, hell, Armed Forces radio; it was a big hit. They tell me there are other versions of the song including one in Indonesian. But this Kennedy girl was an instant classic. The Thais love it when you try to sing their songs and fit in."

He joined those GIs singing, *"Ma noy ma noy tamadaa."* They even gave it a distinct American flavor. In the dead space between the repeat of the choral refrain they barked, *"Wroof, wroof"* and ended the song singing, *"piu yai lee, sawatdii, cha cha cha."*

After the song Sasse ordered a round of beers. As we drank our chosen brew he gave his back-story. "I graduated college and came home for the summer and bam, bang they got me. It wasn't like I had graduated cum laude and had the world by the balls. Hell, I was nowhere near the top of the crop. College had been too much fun for that. But with my typing and writing skills, bingo, I'm an administrative clerk. And, look Ma, no hands — Thailand to boot!"

Sasse proved to be a very knowledgeable and valuable source of information as to who was who, and what was what, not only in the camp at Friendship but in Thailand in general.

G.T. Foster

The House Boy

The house boy was hired to sweep, dust, mop, and wax the entire barracks, and shine shoes, and also, to clean the latrine, and restock toilet paper and paper hand-towel dispensers. The house girls made the beds but the house boy gave them an assist with any heavy lifting, and he passed on to the house girls any special instructions on GI laundry like heavy or light starch or the sewing of name tags and insignias of rank after promotion, or heaven forbid, demotion.

Our boy, Lem, a young man in his early twenties, wore his hair in a pompadour, read Thai popular fan magazines, and listened by transistor to Thai radio-station music broadcasts. Watching me unpack, he had spied my cardigan sweater. Purchased in Berkeley from a Telegraph Avenue men's clothing store, it was purple and preppy.

"Thailand too hot, GI no want."

"No, Lem, GI want."

Such had been our first encounter. But Lem was nothing if not persistent. Day-two he immediately noted my interest in the Thai language.

"GI For-as, maybe I help you talk Thai. You not know *kam* ... word den I teat you word. You give sweater. I tell anytime. Good deal GI For-as."

"Maybe."

"I help you talk *keng* same-same black GI before. Him *piu dam puut keng*. I help you same."

"How do you say, 'Can do'?"

"*Bpen dai.*"

"*Bpen dai*, huh?"

"*Chai* For-as, *bpen dai*."

"How do you say, 'No way, impossible'?"

"*Bpen mai dai*."

"Okay Lem, me give you my sweater *bpen mai dai*."

"*Mai chai GI mai chai*. GI kin do. *Tom dai*. Kin do!"

"Maybe later. Now I *bpai* chop-chop."

"See For-as, see? I kin help you. No kin say chop-chop. No be Thai word. *Mak-mak* GI say, *bpai* chop-chop. Thai people no say. Thai people say *bpai gin kao*—Go eat rice."

"What—no *bpai* chop-chop?" I asked.

This was a shocker. Throughout the first two days at mealtime I had heard many GIs in the company tell their Thai companion drivers, "I go chop-chop" or just as often "I *bpai* chop-chop."

I had assumed it was the one Thai expression everyone knew, connected the dots, and wrote the expression into my Thai language notebook; only now to learn it wasn't a Thai expression but rather some form of Thai-glish, a coded system created from a twisted interplay of Thai and American boy-soldier communications.

"No chop-chop. I help GI. Korat too hot. You not need sweater, I promit, GI For-as. Lem no *go-hok*."

"Maybe, Lem. Ask me tomorrow." I paused, then repeated, "No chop-chop?"

"No, For-as. *Puut, bpai gin kao*."

I smiled, shook my head, and chopped up the thought. My own English expressions contained a few possible links to its mysterious origin. I thought of Chop Suey, chopsticks, and chop-chop. Two were language crossovers from Chinese, the other Pidgin English meaning without delay: quickly. I also remembered the colloquial expression, "chops" and imagined how it came to be.

My mind sketched an image of an American soldier repeatedly telling his Thai counterpart at the lunch and supper hours, "It's time to feed my chops."

Over time, trained and as sensitive as a Pavlovian pup, the Thai driver would look to his own watch and ask, "You *bpai* chop?"

"Yes, I go chop. *Bpai* chop-chop."

I shook my head and thought, "Chop-chop not Thai! What a hoot!" Then I walked to the Mess Hall.

★★★

On the third day Lem sealed the deal. Upon my afternoon return to the barracks he retrieved from the washroom a beautiful bolt of black and blue hued Thai silk and laid it on my bunk.

"For-as my mom sista make for you shirt or suit from dis, For-as. No charge you, For-as. No charge you."

"Wow, Lem, it's very nice cloth. Thai silk?" I asked as I rubbed the shimmering fabric with the back of my hand. "It's really smooth."

"Thai silk number one. You will like . . . "

"Enough already, I was already going to give you the sweater as reward for your chop-chop lesson. You don't have to give me this. She doesn't . . ."

"No, For-as, *krap*. It be good deal. I want. It be tray for you and me. She have chop at *talot* in Korat."

I opened my wall locker and took out the sweater. I laid it on the bed and folded it, then handed it to Lem.

"I write her chop number here." He handed me the paper. "Anytime, For-as. Tell her Lem. She know. She know. Tank you, GI. Tank you, For-as."

It had only taken him parts of three days to obtain the object of his obsession.

The Boys Are Not Refined

Marking Time

It was my eighth day in-country. I was sitting on my bunk reading when Leggett entered from the eastern door, stopped and asked, "Have you been downtown yet?"

"No man, I haven't," I said, shaking my head. "I've only been in-country—"

"Forget that. You want to come down with me? My wife has just gotta have a gown made from Thai silk. She sent me a pattern and everything, and now it's ready. What you say? I'll show you the marketplace and maybe we can get a bite to eat."

"Sure," I said. "I'd love to."

After a shower and change into civilian dress, I walked to headquarters with Sgt. Leggett. He signed his name in the off-post roster then initialed my own sign-out. He grinned and took a prophylaxis from the adjacent bowl. I followed his lead. That evening I was wholly unaware that over time sign-out would become a small detail blown off by eighty-five percent of company personnel.

We walked to the NCO Club and hired one of the taxicabs parked out front. At the gate the MP marked the taxi license plate number on a clipboard and waved us through without an identification check of any type. The driver drove the four miles to town and dropped us into the middle of the civic heartbeat of Korat: the marketplace.

It was a fascinating place filled with new smells and neck-twisting sights. Tables, tents, and booths filled the central plaza square. Vendors sold a vast assortment of meats, fish, fruit, animals, clothing, jewelry, cameras, radios, furniture, arts, gadgets, and native craft items.

"Monkey balls, GI? Monkey balls!" barked a young Thai entrepreneur wearing shorts and sandals. "Bery good, bery delicious."

"Hey, *oui! Oui puchai*. Gimme two of those." Leggett took two dollars from his pocket to complete the transaction. Leggett handed the boy the money and the kid gave him two sticks of skewered meats, then walked away, continuing to hawk his sizzled treats.

"Monkey balls, monkey balls . . . !"

Leggett handed one to me. "Eat," he commanded and bit into a steaming ball of rolled flesh.

I took a bite. It was heat hot. *Hmm*, I thought as I chomped. *This is very good*. I chewed, swallowed, took another bite and began the tasty process all over. And still that initial *hmm* continued to gnaw.

Didn't he say . . . monkey's balls? Finally a thought, almost loud enough to be heard by others, reached my mind and muttered, "Shut-up already and eat."

Which I did, and they were delicious, indeed. The urchin hadn't lied. A bit greasy but perfectly seasoned.

As we ate the monkey, Leggett led the way to the tailor shop and the stitched-to-size, ready for pickup gown. Along the way he pointed out the silk shop of Lem's aunt, so I could return at a later date. The business was in the same neighborhood, one corner and a few doors away from Leggett's tailor.

After inspection, as we waited for the merchant to wrap the gown, Leggett confessed, "I don't come downtown much anymore unless it's to come here to the *talot*, the central market-place. Most guys get themselves a *tealok*."

"*Tealok*?" I asked. What's a *tealok*?

"It's Thai for girlfriend; a steady. One you see regularly. You ain't supposed to be seeing anybody else and neither is she. Take my word. It's safer in the long run."

"Thai women are jealous, huh?"

"Nah. It's not that. Although some of these women . . . Don't be fooled by their smile. Hell," he chuckled. "You can say the same about Thai men. Don't be fooled by the smile. But it ain't that. It ain't that at all. It's VD, man. VD. The venereal disease around here you don't want."

"Oh, I see."

At a nearby storefront stall, three Americans in civilian clothing were examining long walking-sticks. A clerk stood in the shop doorway barking sale offers to passers-by and quickly identified me as fresh meat.

"GI, I have for you," he said, handing me a jet black, six-foot-long wooden pole, heavily shellacked with a high-gloss Asiatic sumac varnish. On its top was an intricately carved head of a black panther.

"It's heavy."

"I think it's mahogany and I think it's expensive," Leggett informed. *"Taa lai, krap?"*

"Twenty dolla' US. It be good price."

The stick was quite striking, even magnetic to the eye. Etched or burnished into the wood were various scenes from the panther's life and evolution within its jungle world—contending with other animals of the wild, finding a mate, and raising little black, panther cubs.

"Too much," Leggett responded and made a counteroffer. "Fifteen, *krap*. Fifteen dollars US money."

"Mai dai, mai dai. Twenty dolla'. GI can do. Twenty dolla' fair, GI. Twenty dolla'."

Curiously I asked, "You have two?"

"No. No have same-same. Eat one different. Dis one." He took back the long black stick. "Only one."

"Okay, okay. I like it. But twenty dollars? *Song . . . song sip? Song sip mai dai.* No can do. Sorry. Fifteen? I can do fifteen. *Sip haa. Sip haa* dollars, US."

For a moment, he silently shook his head no, then he began to nod yes and said, "For *piu kao* GI I neba do, but okay, GI, I do for you. *Piu dam* GI *kon dii*. I like black sol-ja."

Later Leggett took me to a little Thai cafe. He referred to the owner/cook as *mama-san*. She prepared us each a plate of the house special *kao pot*—my first of many journeys into plates and bowls of Thai fried rice.

As we waited I confessed, "Initially I felt guilty, conflicted about buying one." I glanced at my walking calendar as it rested against the cash register counter.

"Why?"

"Well, it's not like we're in Vietnam. There the friggin' reality is so scary I'm sure a brother thinks twice before tempting fate. I mean superstition or the unpredictability in how anything comes out. You know what I'm saying?"

"I'm listenin', man."

"What I'm saying is, if you're on the front lines, there is an absolute inherent possibility of injury or death. Daily! It's like the sword of Damocles hangs over the transformation process of each individual stick. That's what gives them value. They're from the war zone. They're the genuine article, the Real McCoy. The short-timer sticks I see when I look around our barracks are like night and day. You know what I'm saying?

"It's like comparing General Custer's Little Bighorn battle sword to a dime store, Mattel toy replica. Really, no offense, I'm just being honest."

"None taken, Private. Go on."

"That's all. I bought it, sure. But I'm still kinda mixed. Is it heavy, beautiful, and ornate but—ultimately, hollow? I'm not trying to sound like some deep thinker. I see all the short-timers in our company with them, almost to a man. And even here ... look over there, and both those guys. Where's the grim, gallows spirit that is attached to their meaning in Vietnam?"

"Damocles, transformation process? Speak English! What you talking about?"

I started to try again to explain, but he raised and wiggled his hand's index finger to silence me and continued, "I get you man, but hold on a minute and get your head out of your ass. *Don't let what you don't know color your opinions.*"

"That's what my grandmother always says."

"And you know what? She's a wise woman. Guilty, you feel guilty? Hell, Thailand's got plenty of danger of its own. You want gunfire? There is a significant insurgency in some of the very northeastern provinces we drive through."

"Really?"

"Last year at least three of our battalion convoys came under fire or were struck by bullets near Sakon Nakon."

"Where is that?"

"I hope you don't find out anytime soon. I'm not kiddin'. You feel like you need to earn it? Join the Corps of Engineers. They still slash jungles. You'll see them out there. Diggin' trenches and tunnels for sewage and communications. Is snake bite dangerous enough? I can get you reassigned."

The waitress brought our steaming plates of fried rice, each topped with half a hard-boiled egg and slices of cucumber, and set them on the table. Then she swiveled and took the soon to be ubiquitous small condiment rack of dried, ground red chili, sliced chili with vinegar, and sliced chili with fish sauce—*nampla*—jars from an empty table and placed it on ours.

"Wait a second. You want chopsticks?"

"Yeah, sure, I've used them before."

To the waitress, Leggett said, *"Kor gip song thuay, krap."* Although his accent was American and his pronunciation halting, I was quietly impressed by his bilingualism.

She placed a napkin, fork, and chopsticks next to each plate and left. Picking up my chopsticks and returning to our conversation, I defensively said, "I wasn't complaining."

"Could've fooled me. Sure sounded like it. Be patient, young blood. By the time you leave you will feel you've earned everything you get. There will be times you bivouac with nothing more than mosquito nets. And when you go to Phanom, which by the way is our most frequent run, you will live in one of the screened huts you seem to crave."

"Come on, Sarge, I said no offense."

"None taken. I have an Air Force buddy here from back home. We go out from time to time. Kid we drink with—he's also Air Force — least was. His Friendship based plane went down on a mission. He was one of the forty-three pilots and Electronic Warfare officers reported killed or missing from Friendship last year; one of forty-three.

"They probably lost close to fifty planes. Look around. Most of the Americans you see are airmen; our next door neighbors, so to speak. They ain't in Vietnam, but I'm sure they don't want it no hotter."

Finally, he cracked a smile and said, "I guess for you it's going to take you shaking loose a few hemorrhoids, and gulping down a belly full of bumpy road dirt dust.

"Look, nobody's claiming to be a hero. I got a cane. Am I under siege? Hell, nah! But I'm ritualistic. I notch off a piece every month on the 28th, the numbered date of my ETS. Hell, yes, I count down to my return to the World and normalcy. I swear, when that day comes I will never, ever again in my life squat to shit through a hole in the floor."

We both laughed.

★★★

The Monday following Leggett's two-week mentorship and orientation I reported to him in the motor pool. He was standing in the maintenance shed area with a Thai national.

Formally introducing me to my assigned Thai co-driver, Leggett said, "Private Forest this is Rien. Rien, *krap* meet Private Forest."

"Glad to meet you," I said extending my hand. Instead of embracing my hand to shake, Rien cupped his own hands into a *wai* and raised them before his smiling face. "Fo-rest, *krap*," he greeted in a good attempt at correct pronunciation.

"Private Forest, from now on Rien will be your new best friend. You will share transport assignments. Wherever you go, Rien will go, but if not Rien then some other Thai national, but mostly Rien. Got that?"

"Yes, Sarge."

G.T. Foster

A Distasteful Night

At the end of my second week in-country, I began to take more after-duty trips to Korat. A café downtown specialized in steak sandwiches. It was owned and run by a black American Air Force sergeant and his Thai wife. The steaks were thick and the sandwiches delicious.

The first bite was always followed by a tongue-tied idea. Similar to the proverbial "The emperor has no clothes" it was a question none dared ask, "Where are they getting the meat?"

The steak was either buffalo or beef. If buffalo it could readily be purchased at the local market place. However, they did not have the gamey taste one expects in buffalo. But if the sandwiches were beef, the beef undoubtedly was of military origin and had been purchased at the back door of either a Friendship Army or Air Force mess hall.

No one ever asked, "Are these buffalo steak sandwiches?" Nor did I ever hear anyone inquire, "Are these beef steak sandwiches?"

They just sat there and ate the sandwich and returning at a later date ate another, because they were so darned good. You assumed the proper Thai and military authorities had been paid their fees, fines, and graft cuts, and therefore the enterprise was permitted to operate as a legitimate business.

On my first unaccompanied visit I ate the sandwich, drank a Singha beer, and went to check out the nightlife scene.

The Boys Are Not Refined

The first establishment I came upon was clearly the most popular American bar in downtown Korat. However, the place made no bones of the fact it catered solely to Caucasian military personnel. Outside, two mini-skirt-and-boots-attired Thai *gully* girls (prostitutes) inculcated with the ideas of their clients, spewed racist slurs and slanders about black men in a bilingual street theatre act.

The first, speaking in Thai, held one hand on her hip as she gestured with the other, "*Mai yaak piu nang see dam. Piu dum mii leung yai muan gan ling soong. Puying Thai lek-lek. Mii gloor, mii gloor!*"

Then her sidekick translated into highly intelligible English saying, "Dis bar no want any black men. Black men have bery, bery large dick. Dick like a monkey tail. It too big. Thai girl no hab big body. Thai girl be bery small. We be afred *jing-jing*. No want black GI!"

Staring incredulously I said, "Damn, wait just a minute *puying. Mai dii!* I didn't come here for this. Jesus, why do you do this?" I'd had it. Frowning, gritting my teeth, and shaking my head I angrily turned and walked back down the street. At the corner I waved down a taxi and rode back to base to seethe.

"Coon"

The morning following my visit to downtown Korat I admittedly was still agitated. The *gullies'* remarks were still ringing loudly in my mind's ear as I walked to the motor pool. I replayed the scene outside the bar while I silently completed the truck maintenance check with Rien.

Finished, I headed to the Dispatcher's office and then I heard it, again. I had thought I heard it a few times earlier but had simply ignored it as a paranoid impossibility. But this morning I clearly heard the first driver I passed say it and now another had boldly repeated the slur.

"Coon."

Well, I'll be damned, I thought. I turned my head toward the driver who had called the epithet and glared. Instead of stopping to confront the prick, I continued toward the dispatch office just as the smiling interpreter, the person I wanted to see, came out.

Somchai was an interesting guy. Soon after we met, he confessed he had been a commercial bus driver and a former heavy-and-constant *ganchaa* smoker. He warned me about the potentially addictive quality of Thai *ganchaa*, especially when smoked through water-pipes.

He told me how his own thirst for the next bowlful to the next high had been so intense that he would salivate like a trained dog just thinking about it. Working hours were impossible to tolerate. He began taking detours along his assigned route in order to drop by the homes of smoking friends or his local drug dealer. There he would park and enter while the bus and its cargo of bewildered or agitated passengers were forced to wait out the unscheduled stop.

It had finally cost him his job. He was now clean and sober yet was no born-again prohibitionist. He introduced me to his friend Vim, who drove for our company. Vim was capable of filling any of my *ganchaa* needs.

In 1968 the expression "going postal" had yet to enter the American English lexicon so I said, "Damn it, Somchai, the next person who calls me a coon is going to get smacked. I swear I'm going to smack 'em upside the head."

"*Sawatdii*, Forest, *krap*. Please, excuse me. Repeat da problem, please," requested Somchai calmly.

"Damn it, Somchai! They had best stop the bullshit. I didn't come ten thousand miles around the world to be called a fucking-ass coon or any other fucking honky name. I'm just warning you and you better tell them I said it."

"Calm down, calm down Forest, *krap*.

"I am calm. I am just calmly warning you. I'm tellin' you, no more coon! I'm not turning any cheeks!"

"But Forest, *krap,* you misunderstand. Da Thai drivers like you. When . . . "

"They have a strange way of showing it."

"No, no. You see, *kun* not mean that. *Kun* just mean you. Dey only calling you. 'You!' Like dey say, 'Come here, come here.' You understand? You see?"

"Oh," I said in surprised embarrassment as my hand jerked reflexively to cover and censure my mouth. "I'm sorry. I'm really sorry."

"*Mai bpen lai*, it's okay," he said. "No big ting."

"But you need to understand. In the United States many white people call blacks ugly names like monkey, crow, gorilla, tar baby, nigger, and coon. A coon is a . . ."

I paused as I took my notepad from my fatigue shirt pocket and turned pages to the entry. "Animal, *sot*," I said. "A coon is a *sot*. It isn't a nice thing to be called."

"I understand *kun*, Forest, *krap*," Somchai smiled. "I know."

As I walked to my truck I wrote *kun* on my notepad.

The Bridge

My muses must have been at work on my duty sergeant Leggett and the dispatcher. That afternoon I was given my first haul, unaccompanied by another American. Rien and I were to deliver goods to Camp Foster, a new post being carved from the jungle forest, 75 miles west of Bangkok.

The camp was located five miles outside of Kanchanaburi. The provincial town borders the Khwae Yai River and is the sight of the infamous crossing bridge, part of the "Death Railway" built by Allied prisoners-of-war and Asian forced-labor crews during World War II. Thousands lost their lives, as the ill-equipped prisoners struggled before Japanese military rifles under appalling conditions to complete the 250-mile railway that linked Burma and Thailand.

I drove the stretch from our motor pool at Friendship on the Korat Plateau through the mountains and down to the Sri Nakon Ayuttaya rest stop. There we paused for refreshments. I drank a bottle of cold Pepsi chilled in a tub of ice. Rein ate a plate of *gang-nuu*, a beef stew spread over steamed rice. Upon our return to the truck, Rien drove.

I was doubly relieved. Our route took us smack dab through the heart of Bangkok's legendary streets, a tangle of Japanese pick-up trucks, logging trucks, buses, taxis, motorcycles, bicycles, *samlode* tri-wheel vehicles propelled along by the manual pumping of a driver's huge calves and thighs, putt-putts, cars, tankers, vans, military vehicles both foreign and domestic, and more Honda, Kawasaki, Triumph, and BMW motorcycles.

East, west, north, and south, traffic snarled and swirled around the mid-city intersectional circles; converging then splitting to optional streets. There were few traffic lights. Right-of-way seemed based upon politeness, or lack thereof. In such cases, it became a matter of size and bull-strength.

Rien down-shifted and chugged along through one-way and two-way jams chock full of every make and model vehicle the industrial world had produced. Although all vehicles contributed to the carbon monoxide fumes, the diesel busses and trucks seemed to emit more than their fair share. Their gagging black plumes of exhaust gasses created the odd spectacle of monks in beautifully bright orange saffron robes wearing non-matching handkerchiefs, bandanas, or scarves around their necks or drawn over their faces to filter their breaths as they stood on sidewalks waiting for busses to pass.

They could not have been waiting to catch the bus, could they? Are monks allowed to ride public transit? Are their lives not dedicated to self-sacrifice and suffering?

Rien sang as he drove:

Yak ja bpai bpai si chan bpai
puying muan Thai mii mak nak naa
bpai lin bpai lai dtaw bpai piu-saa . . .
chan kong ja haa mea mai dai dii.

We crossed some of the city's numerous *klongs*, passed the racetrack and stadium, and finally the bridge over the Chao Phraya River. Along this river the 18th century city and royal palace were first established. The waterway formed a defensive backdrop.

Once through the city we made good time and delivered the shipment to the camp in the early evening.

Camp Foster had been recently carved and staked out from forest jungle. Although the living conditions and accommodations were bivouac, Rien and I were issued bedding and assigned bunks for the night in one of the two camp hooches. The next morning we began our return to Korat.

Re-approaching the bridge as we passed through Kanchanaburi, I felt a sudden rush of confused feelings—a mixture of quiet somberness and excited jubilation.

I gently nudged an elbow into his right arm and pointed, "The Kwai River; the river Kwai." I smiled broadly, but the river did not hold the same fascination for Rien. He nodded his head in affirmation and drove on.

"No, no, no! Stop! Please, stop!" I insisted. "We take *nit noy* break, okay?"

The Bridge Over the River Kwai had been one of the defining movies of my youth. It was a film about loyalty, friendship, and common bonds. It was about the power of unity and the dignity of work. And oh so many soldiers had died!

I was jubilant because I was really here; at this time, at this place! I was here! It was still my rookie month in-country and everything was new and exotic, and I experienced the constant apprehension of the unknown. But on that day it all melted into the sheer joy of being at that spot on the planet:

Da da, da Da da da, da, dah

Da da, da Da da da, da, dah

This was where Alex Guiness and William Holden held their torrential battle for leadership. Both men wanted to lead the war prisoners and give them dignity and purpose in the midst of Japanese oppression. They had the same goal but vastly different beliefs on how best to achieve it. Which was best practice against an enemy who gave no quarter and responded with two kicks for every tactical error, the path of submission and non-violence or violent resistance?

The blown bridge and rail track had long since been reconstructed. Some of the original side spans remain. Rien pulled over and parked the truck near the bank of the river. I stripped to my green army undershorts and waded into the water.

Rien shook his head negatively and said, "*Ngo, ngo.*"

I responded, "Yeah, it really is very cold, but you get used to it."

I swam and floated from one bank to the other—from what I thought was Thailand to Burma and back, again. I dressed and we continued our return journey. Leaving Kanchanaburi, we passed the only cemetery I ever saw in the whole of Thailand. It is the final resting place for many POWs from the WWII prison camps.

Later I learned from Lem that *naao* is the Thai term for cold. *Ngo* means snake and the Khwae Yai River is a favored habitat for many of the most poisonous varieties. I also learned that although I had reached the far side of the river, I had been nowhere near Burma, which was another forty miles beyond.

May God protect babes and fools.

The Boys Are Not Refined

Language Development

Despite being handed a dunce cap and sent to a self-imposed idiot's corner for misunderstandings, *(ngo* and chop-chop), I had continued my daily effort to learn a new word or expression. Not surprisingly, sprinklings of vulgar words, including *hee* (vagina) and *yet* (fuck) made their way onto my tongue to join *kee*.

But I also learned to count. The Thai number system is a marvelously simple ten base: *nung* (1), *song* (2), *saam* (3), *see* (4,) *haa* (5), *hok* (6,) *jet* (7), *bpeet* (8,) *gaao* (9), *sip* (10), *sip-et* (11), *sip-song* (12), *sip-saam* (13), *sip-see* (14), *sip-haa* (15), etc. until *sip-gaao* (19), then repeat the pattern, again beginning with *yii-sip* (20), *yii-sip-et* (21), etcetera to *saam-sip*(30), *see-sip* (40) etcetera, until *nung roy* (100) and then etcetera, etcetera, etcetera ad infinitum.

It was easy, man; pretty darn easy and simple. In addition, my two-week list of learned Thai would include the following terms and expressions:

Sawatdii: hello, good morning, good day, goodbye (very flexible expression)
bpen: can, is;   *bpen dai:* possible
bpen mai dai: impossible;   *bpai*: go
bpai gin kao: dine;   *gin:* eat
kao: rice;   *mai*: no;   *dii*: good
mii: have;   *baan:* home
hong: room;   *hong-naam*: bathroom
puying: girl, female;   *puchai*: boy, male
chai: yes

pom, chan: I, me; *naam*: water
kee: feces; *meen-kee dom*: to stink
mai mii: to not have; *dii mai*: is it good?
mai dii: bad; *ma noy*: little dog
maa: come; *duey:* also, too
kun: you

The one basically Thai expression, as ubiquitous as the bastardized *chop-chop* every GI on post could more-or-less recite spouted from the tongue of American television's *Get Smart* character, Agent 99 who was forever apologizing for one error or another with the inane "Sorry about that, chief."

GIs at Friendship could forever be heard saying, "*Sia chai duey kee*" which translates, "Sorry about that shit!"

Red Alert: Tet Offensive

I had been in the country twenty days, less than three weeks, when hell suddenly broke loose in Vietnam. We went on full alert at Camp Friendship. Non-duty hour, off-base passes were canceled. Our evening recreational activities were confined to those on camp, and we were told to be prepared to join the fight.

I went to the cinema and watched *In the Heat of the Night*, but the film's slow, southern pace did not blot reality and achieve normal Movieland suspended disbelief. Real time events had intruded. When would the retreats and evacuations stop? Would we really (troops in Thailand) have to enter the fray?

January 30th had marked the beginning of Tet, the traditional New Year. It had previously been observed by both sides as a cease-fire period. But that was then and this was now. In 1968, the holiday marked the beginning of the Tet Offensive, the simultaneous and coordinated countrywide attacks by the North Vietnamese Army and their Viet Cong and Viet Minh allies.

The second night I had a steak and potato supper at the NCO Club. The television images were upsetting. What the hell was going on? It was supposed to be a search-and-destroy jungle war. Our soldiers had taken the fight into the field, always worried about snipers, booby traps, and underground tunnel fighters who popped from concealed earth, killed American squad members, and vanished into the jungle canopy. That had been our training.

The Viet Cong now came literally popping out of the doorways and from around street corners. They attacked five major cities, most provincial capitals, and at least fifty hamlets. In Saigon, desperate battles were fought at the governmental palace and the Army Headquarters of the Republic of Vietnam while the United States Embassy grounds were overrun by Viet Cong; the Marines had been forced to give ground and evacuate.

Evacuate the Embassy in downtown Saigon?! This was urban guerrilla warfare, a citywide street fight from building windows, rooftops, and corners. After five years of war and promises of victory we seemed suddenly to be caught totally off guard, our pants down and unprepared.

Although quick military response recaptured most of the lost or evacuated territories within a week, the ancient capital city of Hue took nearly a month to recapture. There the Viet Cong held on until February 24th.

But by then the real damage had been done through international network broadcasts. Worldwide news telecasted picture after picture of United States military forces under serious duress. These were different than the Hamburger Hill photographs of weary, war-worn, and fatigued soldiers of the November and December 1967 clashes. Those had been battlefield images of two armies locked in a death struggle over a strategic body of land.

These exhibits were worse because the enemy seemed to come from everywhere. Vietnam was beginning to look like a bottomless, man-eating pit. Strategies were again revised. Commanding General Westmoreland wanted to activate the Reserves and bring in an additional 200,000 ground forces.

★ ★ ★

In Korat, after the initial shock and awe of the offensive, the reality of the military situation in Vietnam was reevaluated and the garrison stood down from its high-alert status. Overnight passes were reinstated and our focus returned to our mission in Thailand.

Even though for North Vietnam the Tet Offensive was a military failure, the images delivered a political and psychological victory of great magnitude to the Viet Cong and North Vietnamese government. They dramatically contradicted optimistic claims by the US government that the war was all but over.

.

G.T. Foster

Our Daily Cornbread: the Motor Pool

The day really began after Reveille and breakfast. The 0700 morning formation in the motor pool was the official start. It was then that the daily agenda of dispatch and battalion updates were pronounced. Yet there always seemed to be ready excuses for missing this daily event.

For example, any driver who had returned from the road the previous day after 1600 hours (4 p.m.) was exempted by battalion order. Under this standing policy, any return to Camp Friendship could be timed to qualify a goldbricker for the exemption. However, the less innovative but more widely used method was simply to report to sick-bay in the base clinic.

The company formation was followed by a joint American and Thai driver policing of the motor pool grounds. The drivers lined up shoulder to shoulder across one end of the motor pool, then slowly walked to the other end of the yard, picking up any trash, debris, or cigarette butts that had been carelessly discarded.

We then broke into our driving teams to conduct the tasks of first-echelon vehicle PMCI (Prevention-Maintenance-Care-Inspection). Although very crucial for the prevention of untimely breakdowns and stranded vehicles, it was tedious monotony. It required each team to check the truck from top to bottom, inside and out—the engine and generator fan belts, the oil, fuel, and water levels of the engine, transmission, overdrive box, rear end, radiator, gasoline tank, and braking system. The fifth-wheel must be greased. The windshield-wiper blades, radiator hoses, air-brake hoses and connections,

The Boys Are Not Refined

as well as brake, tail, parking, and turn-signal lights must all be checked or tested and replaced when necessary.

Drivers inspected tires but the Americans repaired all flats on their assigned trucks. They also had to repair flats on the cargo trailers they hauled; invariably, on these dual-axle freight boxes, the flat would belong to the inside twin and necessitate the removal of both tires.

It was the same stuff every day, the same tasks without the benefit of a pair of teasing mini-skirted legs on the other side of the windshield. No pretty smiling face on which to raise an eyebrow with the sexual innuendo buried in, "May I help you with anything?"

Man, but it was boring! Its completion brought the relief of 9 a.m. dispatch orders. Left without assignment, the remaining men would break into various groups of friendship or interest to hurry-up-and-wait-out the remainder of the morning and early afternoon, or during lulls in bombing raids and subsequent drop in convoys, the entire day. They formed smoking circles, played (Thai) checkers, kick-boxed, told stories, and sang songs.

G.T. Foster

The King's Drivers

Although each American driver in the 21st Transportation Company had his Thai counterpart, in the way of their world, our non-military co-drivers held very special jobs. Favors and bribes had been paid to secure them. Men had paid men, who in turn had paid other men, and so on and so on . . .

The drivers came from every part of the country and its frontiers, and were from all ranks and social classes of Thai society. Most had been professional drivers previously. Some had been mechanics, others soldiers, laborers, farmers, fishermen, or vendors. One had been a boxer. Their ages varied. The youngest of the drivers were about twenty-five (to be honest, I had a poor track record on guessing Thai ages), the oldest about thirty-five—all high-testosterone years.

Thai males kick-boxed from the time they could stand until they walked with canes as broken adult men. It is the national sport, as Thai as baseball and apple pie are American, and in that sense, beneath the widely advertised land of smiles there is a major machismo.

I soon discovered every village has a brothel; male only of course. Yet, our drivers openly flirted with all unmarried girls and women. Passing through villages, drivers, even Rien, often shouted, *"Sawatdii, puying cheng-ga dii"* out the truck window to walking or bicycling village girls going to or returning home from school in their black and white uniforms.

Drivers explained again and again the concept of *mia yai*—big wife and *mia noy*—small wife. "Thai custom—a man can have as many wives as a man can afford." As United States employees our drivers did not lack for cash.

At the time I thought, yeah sure, and simply saw it as serial shacking-up, a couple cohabitating without a serious commitment to permanence or marriage, a variation of the common male-female partnerships practiced among many blacks I knew.

However, in America, if the relationship should last seven years, the woman earns common-law-wife status. But what if the relationship sours or the male Thai has a change of fortune and can no longer afford multiple wives? What becomes of the *mia noy*? Seemed to me she would be just plain SOL.

G.T. Foster

Singing for My Supper

Initial communications were in grunts and pointing gestures. I was eager but my Thai was too limited. Rien wanted to teach me about his country, people, and culture but possessed only a broken and limited English. Nevertheless, from the day of our introduction, he began to teach me to say in Thai the few English phrases he knew.

On one of our first hauls, he was driving and said, "Forist, *krap*," in his best approximation of my name. "*Puut*: '*Pom bpen hue*'; I be hungree. *Puut, puut*."

I tried to echo the phrase. "*Pom bpen hue*." But Rien didn't think it was good enough. He modeled the expression three more times. Each time he waited and listened, until I'd finally met his approval. Next we worked on *kor gin kao*: I request to eat, or, more literally translated, I beg to eat rice. Both expressions proved very handy at our truck stops

Although I initially understood barely a mumbling word, Rien constantly sang Thai songs and soon began to teach me a snippet from a popular *Luk Thung* song, "*Puying Tii Suay Yang Kun*". Thais compared the *Luk Thung* genre of music to our American Country-and Western style.

My sixth week in-country, Rien and I drew a pickup assignment that was waiting at the Phanom switching station. Pulling an empty trailer, I drove from Friendship to the official battalion cafe rest stop on the outskirts of Sri Nakon Ayuttayah.

The roadside diner sat at a juncture where two major highways converged into a single B-line toward Bangkok. The road we traveled, designated Friendship Highway #1, led back to the Korat Plateau and points north and northeast. The other roadway led to the northwest toward Uttaradit, Chiang Rai, and Chiang Mai.

I parked and we walked to the cafe. Rien was convinced I was ready. At the entrance he lagged behind a few feet whispering, *"Leung pleeng, leung pleeng"* (Sing the song, sing the song).

Inside, two women worked delivering customer-food plates and clearing tables, a third, older woman, whom I recognized, was either the owner or the manager of operations. She was seated near the cash register so I approached her, drew my hands together into a *wai* and said, as I had been taught, *"Sawatdii, kon suay dii, saawadii. Pom bpen hue mak-mak. Kor gin kao. Pom leung pleeng dii."*

The two Thai waitresses had stopped serving tables and turned to listen. All three faces of the women broke into smiles. The seated customers, including two 21st Company driving teams returning to Korat, looked on with smiling faces of either wonder or bewilderment. But even before the women had nodded their heads in approval, I began to sing:

Puying tii suay yang kong
tamboon wai duey arai
ching suay naa pit samai
naa rak naa krai pim prao...

It was a song about a pretty girl and that's all I knew. Although I've translated it since, at the time I only understood a few words like *suay;* pretty and *puying;* girl. But my heart was racing in a high, anxious joy under the magical rush of performance adrenalin.

Upon completion of my single verse, I was rewarded with applause from the waitresses and patrons, a plate of *gang-ga*i chicken stew; and an ice-cold bottle of Pepsi.

G.T. Foster

The Drivers and I

A couple of the Thai drivers who had seen the performance must have told others. Upon our return to the Friendship motor pool many gave me congratulating words or grinning glances of approval.

A couple of afternoons later, during an unusually long, hurry-up-and-wait for dispatch, several Thai drivers had gathered in the shaded shed area. They were in various groups within the space smoking, playing Mah Jongg, or Thai checkers.

As I passed among them, Yut, a former Bangkok taxi driver, nodded his head at me, smiled and broke into what he later explained was his favorite song, a 1950s version of *"Kor Hai Muan Duan"*, "I Beg to Be Given the Month Again":

Gon ja gan kuun nan song lao
Nap saao saao kor pa bpra paa
Tii lom wan lam baam lom
Ter hai chit chom . . .

He sang the first verse and might have continued with the second but before he could, Bie grabbed his grubstake, rose from his Mah Jongg squat, and applauding with money still in both hands, said, *"Dii mak* (very good), *dii mak. Pom chop fang Naao Ja Dtaai,"* and began to sing his song "The Cold Shall Die":

Naao ja dtaai yuu leeo
Nong geeo yai mai hen jai baang
Rap rak pii noy naung naang
Hen jai pii baang tert mee kun . . .

The spontaneous sharing of songs spread like a spark-set wildfire. When Bie finished the verse, Cak, an ethnic Cambodian-Thai, shouted, "*Leung pleeng Kon Baa. Kon Baa!*" He turned to me and said, "All GI like dis song, *jing-jing, kun* For-it, *krap.*"

Cak was handsome with a sharply pointed nose and square chin and at 5'10" considerably taller than most other drivers. He was no older than twenty-five, still young enough to be aggressive by nature and he loved to kick-box.

Grinning, he waved his hand to beckon and shouted across the shed, "Sakwan, *Leung pleeng Kon Baa!*"

Summoned, Sakwan left his checker game to join the motor pool troubadours, and in a rich baritone sang what sounded largely like a Buddhist chant:

Pom baa ganchaa
Jon huu dtaa laai . . .

Before Sakwan had finished the verse, Cak stepped to center and ordered a halt. "*Pak leeo* (stop), *pak leeo*. Then he said, "*Muan-gan et tii* (Do it again). Cak, again, turned to me and said, "I tell *Ankit* . . . Englik word, you, GI."

As Sakwan sang:

Pom baa ganchaa jon huu dtaa laai
Hen moo dtoo dtao kwaai
Oo duan ngai
hen bpen duan kwan
Ok eurie plaat leei
bpai sia tung sam
Dut ganchaa
naa ying dum . . .

Cak explained, "I am crazy from marijuana. I see things. I see a rat; it seems be water buffalo. I see morning dawn but it be setting sun. You, GI *dut ganchaa;* you be black face, *naa ying dum.*" Cak laughed. "You see?"

I didn't really, but he quickly answered his own question. "You *dut ganchaa* forget shave face. Too much *ganchaa*, too much hair on face. GI see? *Naa dum*. GI see?" He made no attempt to conceal his joy at the joke.

Then Sabaht said, "*Pom chop* Surapon Sombatcharoen *ja pleeng Mong* (Stare)." Seizing the spot he began to sing:

Mong
Ter saao ter suay chan jeung dai mong
Haak ter mai suay chan ja mai mong
Haak ter mai jem chan ja mai jong
Chan ja mai mong hai hua-jai dten . . ..

In the middle of Sabaht's performance I was summoned into the dispatch office and given a bill-of-lading for a cargo of ball bearings destined for the air base at Takli. Subsequently, the drivers taught me several idioms and proverbs like *yak luu samii hai mong naa pan-rayaa*—if you want to know the husband look into the wife's face. And *muur dai gaa dtam tam bpra teet Thai Siam gaa dtam tam duey*. Whatever Thailand does, Siam has to do, too.

The songs were effective ice-breakers and were also an excellent tool for developing my budding Thai language skills. I could actually understand a few words and from time to time a phrase or two. The lessons were acts of kinship. Through language I was being granted admission into circles designed to mystify outsiders.

A Visit with Sombaht

"You go wit me," Rien said as we exited Camp Charoen Sinthrope's comparatively small motor pool. It was one of my early trips over the rutty roads to the southern-central switching-station. Here, we were south of the Khao Yai National Park, closer to Cambodia than Laos. Grape vineyards had been planted in much of the area.

Time had made him more comfortable with his English. Rien pointed to a structure visible from the camp gate, about a quarter-mile away. "We go dere. It be *baan puen pom*, me frien," he said. We crossed through a field of five-foot high reed-like plants and then the short distance to the house was clear.

His friend stepped down from the veranda, and cupped his palms in greetings. "*Sawatdii*. You Rien friend, you my friend."

It was the first Thai home I had ever visited, and it was also Rien's first visit to Phanom since the home's completion. Its owner, Sombaht, was assigned to our battalion staff and worked at the switching station. He was Rien's oldest and closest friend. He was as proud of his house as a first-time parent. "You, come, come," he said, waving us to follow.

Both Rien and I removed our shoes outside the door. Since the same inside space is used to play, eat, and sleep, the floors are touched only by clean hands and feet. Walking with clean feet in such a space is culturally correct and wholly functional. Shoes are never worn inside.

Sombaht, a native of the region, gave us the grand tour and pointed out various aspects of construction. He had planned and built the house, and now wanted our approval. He repeatedly asked *"Dii mai, dii mai?"*

Like most homes throughout Thailand, in preparation for the annual flooding in monsoon season, it was built on stilts that raised it well above four feet from the ground. It was wooden and had highly polished Neem floors, a heavy wood that repels termites and other pests. The roof, although often wooden and sometimes bamboo, corrugated steel, or tile, was tiered, arched, and thatched. It was made from palm fronds tied to big, strong bamboo poles.

It had a wrap-around terrace porch that circled the entire structure. Adjacent to the main house was a roofed open gallery area that Sombaht used to entertain his guests. Large ceramic jars and vats stood nearby ready to catch fresh rain-water run-off.

Hey, what did I know about Thai architecture? Criminy Christmas, I was twenty-years old. But it seemed to me a display of utilitarian genius. Constructed by the owner himself it seemed to optimize all available space, large or small.

Space was convertible and could serve varied functions. Hinges, shutters and tracks were utilized on windows, doors, walls, and rooftops. Tracks and hinges allowed them to be raised or lowered or to be slid or swung, open and closed. Even portions of the roof could be quickly folded or rolled back to present the sun and open sky or, as easily, battened down to keep mosquitoes and other flying insects at bay.

Sombaht practiced the ancient custom of chewing betel nuts, the seeds of the betel palm tree. The basic betel chew or *paan* consists of pieces of betel nut eaten with lime and betel pepper leaf. Chewing results in a distinctive red staining of the mouth, teeth, and salvia. It is about as pleasurable to watch as people dipping snuff or spitting tobacco. Like American "chaw" the effects are said to be stimulating and energizing, but over the long term carcinogenic.

We had been there only fifteen minutes when Sombaht asked, "You want try some homemade *lao*? Wit-key?"

"Sure, why not," I replied.

He went to a tall palm coconut tree. From the tree there hung a long rope. Attached to the rope and raised high above the ground was a black sack. He loosened the rope and lowered the sack from its twenty-foot high, dangling position. Once lowered, he reached inside the black sack and took out a coconut with a small plugged hole. He removed the plug, found glasses and poured three shots. He gave one glass to Rien, another to me.

"Kup kun mak," I said. It had the look of watered-down milk. The aroma was uninviting, more a smell than a bouquet, but the Marco Polo in me said, *"Drink."* So, I mouthed the dose and swallowed.

Rien gulp-drained his glass and Sombaht did the same. Both men responded with a mildly affirming, "Ahh."

I could barely refrain from a retch. It was the worst tasting liquid-excuse for an alcoholic beverage I have ever dared to encounter.

"Mak-gwaa iik, krap?" Sombaht asked, lifting the bottle in offer of more. I politely waved him off and handed him my glass. Rien consented, and he and Sombaht shared second shots.

Rien and I stayed the evening through dinner and spent the night on Sombaht's living room floor. That night and later, whenever I stayed in Thai homes, whether for an evening's visit and supper or for an overnight sleep-over, I followed Rein's example. I took off my fatigues or civilian clothing, washed, and accepted a clean sarong to wear into the interior space.

I mostly refrained from using the toilets during my visits. The few I used were located in a detached, non-elevated structure to the rear of the house. There into a brick or tiled floor was constructed the dreaded squatting hole, a small, cylindrical well into darkness. On such occasions I often philosophically wondered where, after its dropping, all the serious business ultimately landed. Was there a cesspool somewhere?

And what of that great city, Bangkok, called the Venice of Southeast Asia, many homes are constructed along and above the numerous *klongs*. Where does it all go? There is plumbing there, right? What kind of sanitation and sewage system runs throughout the city's underbelly?

Growing a Seventh Sense

I was at high alert most of the time. The unusual never seemed that odd. For something extraordinary to happen was almost to be expected. After all, we were the outsiders. The alien stranger, foreigner, with limited tongue, unable to express himself, marginalized.

The visage was that of an American soldier in his olive-green uniform, driving his five-ton truck, contrasted against the yellow-brown, semi-desert topography of the Korat Plateau region. We were always on mentally reactive haunches, beneath the hot Southeast Asian sun or the evening moon and stars; whether walking, driving, riding, or seated, always listening, observing movements, and sensing colors and smells and the sounds of landscapes and fields, buildings, plants, rivers, lakes, canals, reptiles, insects, and people. Very little of this new world was familiar.

There were regions that held haunting similarity and rhythm that reminded me over and over of growing up in a San Joaquin Valley farming town. Visual flashbacks of the back breaking farm work of picking cotton, tomatoes, peaches, or grapes were encapsulated in the planting, growing, and harvesting of rice. In places where water was plentiful, side-by-side one could observe brown muddy fields ready for planting, green fields of rice almost ready to harvest, straw yellow fields of cut stalks waiting to be plowed under, and mounds and mounds of brown rice drying.

Each day sees a water buffalo pulling the plough Deere-tractor-like through sludgy brown fields or an ox lugging a cart down the road. And in the good ole USA there are no orange sarong monks, lotus sitting in roadside tree shade with *baat* alms bowl in their laps.

Traffic in the larger towns consisted mainly of motorcycles, bicycles, taxis, and mini trucks, and perhaps a police or military jeep or car. Fewer private cars were seen. A smaller village might only have one car, belonging to a policeman or government official. The main mode of local travel was by foot or bicycle.

On the roadways throughout the country there was a defined hierarchy. First and foremost were the American Army drivers wielding their five-ton trucks made of the finest United States workers' Grade #1A cast iron and tempered steel. Other drivers, for the love of Buddha, please, yield right-of-way!

Next were the petroleum tankers and logging trucks. Before the American intrusion, they had been the kings of the road. On the next level were the commercial buses. These were of substantial size and in all collisions save those with higher class US military vehicles, civilian petroleum tankers, or logging trucks their outcome was favorable.

But collisions of all types continued to occur at alarming rates. Their aftermaths became common scenes. The worst were between trucks and passenger buses. The solid steel structure of the trucks would hold, but the beautifully painted sheet-metal-and-aluminum structure of the buses would render them virtual rolling tombs.

Wreckage would be strewn for yards along the roadway, a mangled front axle detached from the frame, the passenger cabin smoldering or aflame. The rear axle would finally come to rest across the roadway in a flooded rice patty.

I often wondered, what became of the staggering and sitting injured survivors?

Lucky Seven Club Korat

"My sitta like you."

We were seated across from each other at a table in a club that catered to all races, but the bar's musical fare was Soul. She had a golden olive complexion and long, black, untethered hair draped over her shoulders and back. Her crimson lips sipped from a glass of Seven Up over ice, leaving a kiss on its rim.

I drank slowly from a cold glass of bitter beer. "But I like you, Nong."

"No way, GI. Not possible. I hab boyfren already. He come beck."

"Maybe."

"I pregnit wit' him baby."

"I see that. You are very pretty. You have . . . a glow."

There was a pause while she considered the word.

"Glow? What mean, glow?"

"Your face, it is alive. It's beautiful. You shine."

She smiled and placed her hands on her little roundness and assured me. "He come beck. I wet for him. You go wit my sitta."

She'd said it again, her sister. There had been a total disconnect in the gene pool: the girl looked nothing like her. Her sister was very light-skinned, more Chinese in that way. She was also round and plump. Not fat but lacking a defined shape. The high, tight Thai-buttocks was absent, and although her eyes sparkled when she smiled, her face did not intrigue.

"What if he never comes back?"

"He come beck. For sure. I wet."

"Swell. Maybe he will come back. But right now it doesn't really matter. You are here and he's there and…you are very pretty."

"Lit me explain GI, I lub my baby faada."

"But he is not here. Like the song says, love the one you're with.'"

"No…tank you. As you say in America, tank you, but no tank you. You go wit my sitta."

"I could make you happy."

"Yeah, sure, GI, dat what dey all say."

"Really, I'm not joking. I think you are very pretty and I would like to get to know you."

"Sure, GI, I belieb you. But I not kidding, too. I going wet for my baby faada to come beck Chi-cago. You go wit' my sitta."

"But if he does not come back? What then?"

"But dat neba happen. He number one *jing-jing*. He come beck."

"Maybe a big mistake?"

"Not be mistake. You make mistake, not go wit my sitta."

Was Jonesy really coming back? How many American service men held true to promises they made to these women? She unquestionably believed her lover would prove different. She was lovely and spirited, which made her the more desirable. But a blind man could see nothing was going to happen.

I puckered my lips and with the fingers of my right hand made a kiss-off gesture of friendly surrender, then turned to her sister and asked, "*Kun chua arai?*"

"Nit," she said. "GI *puut Thai dai.*"

"*Nit noy*, Nit. *Nit noy.*"

"*Kun chua arai?*" she asked.

"*Pom chua* Forest, *krap.*"

The Boys Are Not Refined

"GI want go wit' me do boom, boom? Five dolla' short-time, ten dolla' all night."

G.T. Foster

Kee Mao in Korat

Lyrics from a *Luk Thung* song popular in 1968:

Tung mee pii nii ja kee kao
Chan pii gin lao diao kao mao mak

My big brother drinks whiskey,
then he is very drunk.

One particularly furnace-heat hot night the combination of a steak sandwich and a tepidly chilled Singha beer took its toll. Well, truth be told, there had been a toke or two, no more than three. Okay, there had been three tokes from a high-grade, commercially packaged, marijuana cigarette, *Nam Tok*.

Apparently and despite the nation's draconian drug laws, the Falling Rain Cigarette factory was being reopened in an after-hours operation by a staff member or other employee. *Ganchaa* was being substituted for tobacco and loaded into bins. A few revolutions and presto—stamped and sealed packages of twenty-one marijuana cigarettes.

They were perfect replicas of legitimate cigarettes and were readily available on the streets of Korat. But the packaged contents produced a totally different odor, taste, and effect. Un-like the phony 5th Avenue "Rather fight than switch" claims of the American Tareyton cigarette, this Falling Rain was a brand truly worth a brawl at breakfast, a mix-it-up during the morning brunch, scratch-an-eye at lunch, duke-it-out at dinner, and slap someone for a late-night snack. The taste and buzz were that good.

The Boys Are Not Refined

At some point, someone had passed me a joint and I topped the evening meal with a smoke. I then entered a split-level bar and dance hall. The barroom occupied the first floor.

Upstairs was a dance hall featuring a live band. I went upstairs, chose a partner and began dancing to a fast, hard-driving, trumpet-blaring, bass-thumping, rock-and-roll song. Halfway through the song, the heat, meat, beer, and *ganchaa* cocktail began to spark. I blacked out while still on my feet. I was no longer dancing. Instead, I found myself leaning against a wall.

My dance partner was asking, "You o-kay, GI? You! You o-kay?"

"Yeah," I lied. "I'm okay. I just need some air."

I used the wall for support and inched to the stairwell. Holding the railing I descended the steps to the first floor and out the door into the furnace heat. I felt groggy and clammy. I was sweating freely from my forehead, neck, and underarms.

I hailed a taxi, flopped into the rear seat and said, "Camp Friendship, *krap*."

The driver made a U-turn and headed toward the camp road. However, upon reaching the junction between the highway and the camp road, I yelled, "*Pak leo! Pak leo!*"

The driver stopped the vehicle and I opened the rear door, leaned out, and vomited. I reached into my front pants pocket and pulled out a handkerchief, blew my nose, and closed the door. Leaning back in the seat, I moaned and muttered softly, "*Bpai leeo, krap. Bpai leeo.*"

The driver gave me a disgusted look. He shook his head and said, "*Mai dii leui! Kee mao, kee mao mak-mak!*" He was right. It was not good and I was very, very drunk. Turning his eyes back to the road, he drove onward.

In the back seat I continued my moaning and groaning all the way to the post, as the toxic mixture of food, alcohol, and *ganchaa* tobacco traveled through my abdominal tract.

But thanks to the driver's lucky Buddha, I didn't throw up in the poor fellow's car. That would have necessitated a big apology and an even bigger tip for the god-awful lingering smell.

Outside the barracks I paid the cabbie and exited. But suddenly I felt the need and rushed up the stairs and inside to the nearest bathroom stall, loosening my trousers as I went. I reached a stall and its toilet seat in the nick of time. A thundering flow was released.

But no sooner had I answered one call of the wild than a second urge was duly noted. The need to sit gave way to a need to spit. Diarrhea receded into the limelight as nausea stole the spot. I was barely able to make the tail-to-head switch and avoid puking a partially digested steak sandwich onto the cold tile floor.

My moaning and groaning grew more intense as I promised the great God almighty anything, everything for relief. "Jesus," I moaned. "Jesus, sweet Jesus . . . Just make it stop. Please, lord. I won't drink anymore."

By then the contents of my stomach were emptied but the retching continued with dry heaves. I hadn't offered enough!

"Okay, okay," I thought. "My god, I feel so bad. Yes, I was hedging. I'm sorry, Lord. I'm sorry. I won't smoke anymore, either. I promise. Oh, God, just let me feel better. I promise. I promise. I will not smoke marijuana ever again. Only please, please, make it stop."

And that is how I gave up smoking weed—the first time. After a few days, I realized that I had been extremely hasty that night. Although I had made what at the time seemed like a heartfelt vow, I now thought of the closing lines of Ossie Davis' *Perlie Victorious* when Perlie declared, "I ain't never in my life made a promise I didn't mean to make come true—someday."

Now, to me, this is important because although never directly spoken to like a great and fortunate holy man, I never doubted the existence of a Greater Power or Source. But again, I thought I had not only been hasty, but had been drunk when I took the oath. What god would accept or even want such a vow? Now a devil, on the other hand, would hold your feet to the flame and demand his pound of flesh.

My God is Noah's visiting God of *Green Pastures*, who allowed Noah, after much discussion, to take a single keg of liquor aboard the Ark for so-called medicinal purposes. As for marijuana, I asked myself what great harm is done?

And even more cynically I begged the questions: Has it not been proven that alcohol does greater harm to the body and far greater harm to others while the individual is under its influence than under that of marijuana? Is there an inherent link between marijuana use and criminal or immoral behavior? Isn't the government just simply wrong here?

Colony of Korat Khmer

About a week later, after duty hours, Bryson and I had agreed to meet Cak in Korat for dinner and perhaps a bowl or two of marijuana afterward to begin the evening's frolics. In front of the NCO Club, Sasse, who maintained a girlfriend and an apartment off-post, was waiting for a cab and quickly accepted an invitation to join us. The three of us shared a taxi to town and the restaurant.

Cak stood smiling in the doorway and led us to our table where we had a dinner of amazing flavors. The five main dishes were mutually agreed upon by Cak and Sasse, who continued to stun me with his knowledge of so many things Thai. My favorites were the *Prik Kung* which was a spicy chicken and string bean platter and a red curry soup.

After dinner our party increased with the addition of another Thai driver. I didn't know him but he knew both Cak and Sasse. He invited us to his home. We agreed to go, walked a short distance across a field and entered a housing compound. Inside was a small colony of ethnic Thai-Cambodians living in a connected square of apartments, room adjoining room.

We five were assembled in a squatting and sitting circle with a few of the compound's other residents in an outdoor inter-quad communal space. Sasse, Bryson, and I were the only GIs present. Our host, the other driver, had cut *ganchaa* with *yah*, a medicinal tobacco, and placed it in a bowl before us. As I sat waiting for the pipe, I took a cursory look around the compound.

The Boys Are Not Refined

The circular rotation of my vision was disturbed by something in one of the rooms, and I swiveled my head back to the sight. Through a doorway, its privacy neglected by undrawn curtains, I gazed into a dimly-lit room. I saw a man dressed in a sarong but naked above the waist. He sat on the edge of the bed. Standing before the man and poorly illuminated by the flickering candle light was the shocking and haunting image of a naked six-year-old girl.

Repulsed, but not wanting to stare, I shook my head and turned away. Handed the water-pipe, I took a deep toke and passed it to Bryson sitting next to me.

He, too, took a deep draw, held the smoke in his lungs and passed the pipe. As he slowly exhaled, he muttered under his breath, "That dude's . . . molesting that . . . girl . . . over there."

"I saw that," I said in a whispered reply. "But what can we do?"

The pipe came back his way. He took it, filled it, hit it, and passed it to me. "Nothing," he said. "Not a damn thang."

I, again, inhaled the water-cooled smoke from the amber burning *ganchaa* and held the content in my lungs for as long as I could, exhaled, and still whispering said, "That's fucked, man. That is really fucked!"

I rose to my feet. "I'm sorry," I said in Thai. *"Kor tort."* I made a *wai* with my hands and said for the benefit of Cak and our host, "*Pom bpai tiao."*

Bryson also stood saying, "*Pom bpai, duey."* He, also, cupped his hands into a *wai* salute and we left. Outside the compound Bryson said, "That was fucked. That old man was her grandfather or uncle or something. Didn't the others see? Didn't they know?"

"Sure they knew," I said in disgust.

"That's fucked," he said. "Sex is a bigger commodity here than rice, soybean, or damn cotton."

"Hey, guys... wait up!" We turned to see Sasse. He made a quick dash and joined us.

"Man, did you see that old man pull that little girl into his bed? Then he came and squatted down in the group. He was grunting in such a way I thought he might have a heart attack—the bastard!"

"I was just saying how big the sex industry is here. It's part of the economy. They're registered."

"Who?" I asked in momentary confusion.

"The prostitutes; they have those health cards. That's regulated. The girls must have regular medical exams to get the government's stamp on their card. It's like they're giving them a USDA stamp to show that it's all good, approved meat.

As we walked on Sasse said, "Yeah... but that's all on the legal side. What we saw was the dark side of the business, the criminal side."

"You god-damn right, the criminal side. But fuck, where's the police?"

"Yeah, man," agree Bryson. "It was not like they were trying to hide it. I mean, anybody looking..."

"That's what I meant about the criminal side. It's more like the dark side of the business. They sell orphans. Poor peasant parents sell their children."

"That's bullshit." I was unable to grasp the chilling notion.

"No man, I'm afraid it's real. There are stories told too many times to simply discount. Especially about white girls, American, European, Russian, Aussie it doesn't matter."

"She was no white child. That was a little Thai girl."

"One of those orphans?"

"Probably, that's a part of the business. But white girls or white women sell for crazy sums of money in Asian slave markets."

"Slave markets?"

"Yeah, man, slavery. Supposedly, women held captive in those markets can be used in . . . any way by their enslavers. But mostly they're just sold. You know, who wants damaged goods? That's what saves them."

"Some saving."

"Yeah, some saving."

The Major's Driver

A week before his Estimated-Time-of-Separation date, Leggett and I sat in the motor pool sheltered rest area at a small table, as he taught me to play Thai checkers. Resetting the board with eight black and eight red pieces he asked, "How do you like riding with Rien?"

"Great. Rien is good people. Even though he speaks very little English, he has a way of getting me to do whatever it is he wants me to do."

"Which is usually the right thang?"

"Yeah it is. It is usually exactly what I should be doing."

"Yeah, Rien is a good man. Look here, have you met Major Garrett?"

"Yes, I have. I saluted him here in the motor pool. It was just last week."

"Yeah, did you talk to him?"

"Well, yeah, but it was a short chat. Where are you from? What are your plans? You know; chit-chat."

"What do you think of him?"

"Well, he was . . . pleasant." Then I thought about it and asked, "Why, Sarge?"

"Well, he's as new to the country as you are. His current driver will ETS soon." He chuckled and said, "You caught his eye and were mentioned as a possible replacement."

He paused for me to comment but I was all ears. So he continued, "You would be re-assigned to Battalion. The major was impressed by your relationship with the Thai drivers and how quickly you fitted in. It was smooth. He thought you were one of us, a short-timer!"

"Well, thank you . . . What's his driver do?"

"Well, first off, young blood, he is promoted in grade to sergeant E-5 right away. That's one grade below me."

"Sergeant E-5?" I asked in surprise. "That's two pay grades higher than my current status."

"Yup. Just like that. It's necessary because of the grade classification. A hard E-5 is an NCO and can command troops. It's mostly technical, don't sweat it. You would be on a twenty-four hour, seven-day work week. But it really ain't that bad. The major travels all around the country and always gets the best available quarters, so, how bad is that?"

I'm thinking, Why not? If not an officer, then an officer's man? "Don't sound bad at all," I said.

"Cause it ain't. Plus, it sure would look good on a civilian resume," he laughed encouragingly. "Anyhow, it ain't official. Keep it under your hat.

"Look," he continued. "I'm going to be out of here soon. This idiot, Sergeant Powell, will be rotating out soon, too. Captain Cousins had him on a long-term temporary assignment in Bangkok. He's a fuckin' troublemaker. Just keep clear of his bullshit. He got a young brother from Los Angeles busted out on a general behind his bull. Just stay clear."

"I will, Sarge. And thanks . . . for everything."

"Forget it. New game. Smoke before fire; your move."

G.T. Foster

Replacements

The 21st Transportation Company had been a Reserve unit prior to 1965 and the attack at Pleiku. The unit had been markedly unlucky. It was one the few Reserve units activated over the course of the 10-year war. It was originally deployed to Thailand in October 1966.

Now, with so many soldiers ending their tours, our company was a gold mine of opportunity for the Army Recruitment officers. Recruiters came to the motor pool, made drop-in calls at the barracks, or without invitation sat down to make quick pitches at Mess Hall tables. They came prepared with personnel files and re-enlistment forms.

"What do you say, soldier? There is a $1500 bonus, just waiting your signature."

Some with special skills, enticed by money re-upped for the reenlistment bonus. Perhaps, they completed a second enlistment then returned to civilian society. But civilian life was not in the cards for everybody.

Between enlistments many deceived themselves with mental games: almost every soldier I knew spoke of getting out. They carried the same plan; to leave the army, become a civilian, find a nine-to-five job, and buy a home.

The dispatch sergeant, Wayne, had 15 years of service. One night as I sat in the barracks after work reading, smoking, and listening to music, I asked him, "Why would anyone re-enlist?"

"I re-enlisted the first time out of sheer spite," the sergeant said candidly. "Hell, I was married when they called me up, I had a wife and daughter. My plan was to do my tour, get out and go back to my old life. But when I came home, after a year in Korea, my wife was six months pregnant! She made a big deal about me having gonorrhea, but she was pregnant! So, I re-upped and went to Germany."

"Did you divorce her, Sarge?" asked Leggett. His smile said he already knew the answer.

"Nah, man, it is much cheaper to keep her."

You kidding me? I thought, That's loser's action and has nothing to do with staying married or not staying married. That was a different issue. But reenlisting? That sounded like an excuse, an act of cowardice.

Sasse was the exception; open and honest as to why he had re-enlisted. True "Lifers" lied to themselves and they knew it. The recruiters saw it. There was a hedge in their eyes; doubt about the outside, about themselves. Many were submissive followers and the recruiters knew that, too.

The Army reenlistment officer would ask, "What the hell are you going to do on the outside? Who's going to hire you? Your ex-wife has remarried. She don't want you. And your kids are doing well enough without you."

And if the Regular Army soldier, at the end of his enlistment, continued to waver the reenlistment officer would ask, "And while you are looking for work, who's going to pay the child support if the government allotments stop?" Then the steely recruiter would knowingly stare into the eyes of the Regular Army soldier holding out a pen and repeat, "$1500."

I saw them do it in the motor pool. The guy just crumbled and signed the next four years of his life away. Hell, before guys like that know what happened, they have re-upped twice, then three times, leaving themselves no other smart choice. They become "Lifers" and go for twenty years and the security of an Army retirement check.

The Army gave the recruiters bonus pay for each resigning. The Vietnam era retention rates were very low. But bonus or not, on February 28th Leggett, having completed his active-duty service obligation, left Camp Friendship headed to Bangkok for a return flight to the continental USA and civilian life.

Leadership

If there was some principle behind the shuffling and reshuffling of army ranks it was neither effective nor efficient. And so, without fanfare, the General Staff sent a young Officer Candidate School graduate, First Lieutenant Donald "Duck" Fisher to Thailand to lead the 21st Transportation Company.

In the mode of the Vietnam conflict, they just slid him into the slot, without a hand-salute hello or a head-nod goodbye. One day it had been Captain Cousins at the formation head, the next it was First Lieutenant Fisher. The net effect was that of a pussycat replacing an ocelot.

Fisher was from Florida and spoke with a regional drawl that seemed overdone. His blond-hair was thick and the face was cheerful, but he had a weak, round chin. His blue eyes exposed an uncertainty—he usually avoided looking anyone squarely in the eyes, and if he did he didn't hold the gaze. At about 5'8" and 155 pounds, he was fit. He had not been in the military long enough for it to have been any other way. At twenty-two he was a little older than me.

He always fell back on the book of Standard Operational Procedure. It was safe guidance. He probably did it more out of timidity than from a truly staunch conservative nature. He would manage to repeat this favored mantra, "Make the best of it," during any conversation. Lieutenant Fisher was either a fish out of water or a fisherman out of his depth.

He reminded me of a childhood cartoon that adorned the walls of the train terminal, both the Greyhound and Continental Trailways bus lines, Woody's Shoeshine Parlor, the 17th Street soda fountain shop, and many of the local bars and boardinghouse lobbies in the downtown business center. The cartoon's popularity came from our proximity and interconnectedness with Castle Air Force Base. Its B-52 Strategic Bombers were a daily reminder we were all trapped, boxed-in and tightly clamped between the talons of the American eagle and the claws of the Russian Bear. Prisoners of the Cold War.

The cartoon, in four panels, depicted a man following the final instructions as to what to do in case of an Atomic Bomb attack: 1. pull down your pants; 2. bend over; 3. put your head between your legs; and 4. kiss your ass good-bye!

The Boys Are Not Refined

Trouble—the Ides of March

Leggett had warned me about Sergeant Powell. He had said Powell had been sent, through Temporary Duty Assignment, on permanent loan to the Bangkok petroleum-tanker unit. But now the sergeant was "short" and had reported back to Camp Friendship to his official unit one month prior to reassignment and his next duty station.

Something had been bugging me since his arrival. Initially, its nature was vague and without form. Despite never having met, there are things we carry with us into war: baggage of formative years; memories of youth. Customs and habits are hard to abandon.

The Confederate flag to a California boy does not necessarily hold the same meaning as, say, to a boy raised in the segregated South, black or white. As a kid in my backyard I had planned Civil War battle stratagems and given them epic names like Bull Run, Vicksburg, Shiloh, Gettysburg, Antietam, and Manassas Junction. The Northern soldiers were represented in dozens of red, silver, and blue Pepsi Cola bottle caps. The gray rebel forces of the South were objectified by a shoe box full of silver and red Coca-Cola caps.

The flag had represented, not slavery *per se* but rather, more sadly, an overmatched underdog who attempted to make up with heart what he lacked in material strength. That it had evoked such sympathy rather than hate was a by-product of a great brain-washing that had allowed the quick rehabilitation and veneration of treasonous military leaders like Robert E. Lee and Stonewall Jackson. Their rebel names are as famous as that of Ulysses S. Grant, the general who ultimately saved the Union.

However, the flag attached to a tackle rig and hanging over a barrack's bed was here and now. It did not represent a kid's game. Suspended from a ceiling in Thailand, it was the personification of the injustice, bigotry, and oppression of slavery, and inequality of Jim Crow to boot. Here it was an international problem and had been previously tied to a vague incident concerning a black soldier's less-than-honorable discharge.

The evening of March 15, while passing his bunk and the flag, I stopped. I felt the need to put a face on what I had previously heard. The face was hard, alcoholic, and ruddy-red. The owner, Sergeant Powell, seated on his footlocker, was either reading a magazine or looking at its pictures.

He felt my boring eyes and raised his head. "Look here, rookie soldier, you got a problem with my flag?" A noticeable southern regional drawl accompanied his words.

"No. Not really. Not yet."

"Well, stuff it. We've been all over that already. Let me recite the Department of the Army memorandum on the subject, and I quote: 'Only official flags are authorized to be displayed in accordance with regulations.' End quote. I suggest you learn both United States history and army regulations. My flag is the state flag of the noble state of Mississippi. I am proud and I am protected."

"That's mighty nice and you might truly be proud," I said, baiting him. "But you, dear sergeant, I have recently learned, are not from Mississippi at all. You are from Pennsylvania. So how do you justify that?"

"I don't 'cause I don't have tah. I have adopted it as my symbol. Ya'll boys got that Rapp fella and that guy Carmichael talkin' 'bout black power and stuff. Well, this here's white power. End of conversation." He stood and turned to his wall locker.

"You and your kind are still fighting the wrong war. You lost. Get over it already."

He opened the wall locker door and fiddled around inside with his back to me. There was nothing more to say. I walked away; smiling but not happy.

G.T. Foster

Private Mad-son I Presume

Three days later we were finishing the morning maintenance routine when suddenly several of the Thai drivers erupted into shouts of "Mat-son, Mat-son." They left their duty stations to surround a tall, black soldier. Uncharacteristically exuberant, they shouted questions in Thai. He responded with wild hand gestures to aid his answers, which were also delivered in Thai.

Suddenly, Cak yelled, "*Ii haa ni*i," and took a classic Muay Thai boxing stance.

The soldier shouted, *"Pom bpai kaa mung sot!"* and assumed the same fighting posture. Over the next three minutes the American soldier and Cak, the native Thai driver, made child's play of a kick boxing exhibition.

"Mat-son, Mat-son," the Thais cheered and encouraged him.

"Mat-son come back."

"Mat-son number one GI"

"GI say come back, no come back. Mat-son, him come back!"

Moved by a miraculous event they shouted their approval. "Mat-son! Mat-son!"

It was the content of legend. The black American soldier, Stanley Madson had been true to his word. And, true to the well-worn prior description, he could, indeed, *"Puut Thai keng"* or in plain English he spoke Thai very well.

And unlike other American soldiers before, he had come back. With words of departing regret and expressions of unabated love, many before had promised, but none had returned . . . until now.

He had finished his first tour in December 1967 and returned to the US of A. In Los Angeles he ultimately made up his mind and re-upped, renewing his army enlistment for another three years on the promise of an immediate return to Thailand for a second tour. After almost 90 days of a stateside Relaxation and Recovery and the necessary travel time, he had come back to a reception far more heart-warming than McArthur's staged return to the Philippines.

The black kettle now seemed set on constant boil.

Cease-fire

In the evening, a fortnight later, Bryson and I walked from our adjacent barracks to the NCO Club. Inside, it was a cool, dark contrast to the glimmering hot furnace heat of the outdoors. Back in the real world, it was only March 31.

"I want a cold beer," said Bryson.

"So do I. But I really want a hamburger and some good ole extra crispy fries. Get two beers and a table. I'm going to the kitchen and order. You want anything?"

"No, I'm good. Oh, oh, what lie is he fixin' to tell?" Bryson pointed to the overhead television hanging from the ceiling, suspended by chain and cable. On the screen was the Commander-in-Chief seated at his desk in the Oval Office. The camera slowly moved to a close-up as he prepared to speak.

I turned to look at the TV screen. "I can fill this one in without even listening." I said in my best Texas drawl, "'My fellow Americans, I would give every stolen dime I own not to be here today as your President.' Or better yet, he's going to cross his fingers and repeat my all-time favorite from '64: 'We are not about to send American boys nine or ten thousand miles away from home to do what Asian boys ought to be doing for themselves'."

"Give it a break and have some respect." An old barfly soldier had been irritated by my well-perceived irreverence. "That's burnt bacon and spilt milk. Be a soldier and quit the gripe."

I gave Bryson a knowing smile, shook my head, and headed to the kitchen. "On second thought," he said, "bring me a burger, too. Only make it dry—no spread or mayo."

President Lyndon Baines Johnson proceeded to deliver a few stunners. Two minutes in, he expressed a willingness to talk peace and announced the halt of attacks on targets inside North Vietnam as part of actions to "de-escalate the conflict."

Soldiers in the bar and dining room reacted as if a permanent cease-fire had been announced.

"Finally, this shit is going to end."

"It's about damn time."

"We'll be home for Christmas!"

"Fucking A!"

"Thank God, finally!"

"This war's over!"

Upon my return to the table he had selected, Bryson handed me a beer and asked, "What do you think, Forest? You think it's over?"

"I don't know, Bryson, I don't know. I sure the hell hope it is."

The room had lost its jubilation. The blind optimism that had moments earlier freely bounced through the room was bashed by the President's final remarks. The gravity of his voice, which had been undeniably compelling, took us on an emotional drop down an elevator shaft.

He shockingly declared, "I will not seek nor will I accept the nomination of my party for reelection for a second term."

"Man, is that desertion in the face of the enemy or what?" I quipped to Bryson.

"He's Commander-in-Chief but he don't want the job?"

"What is that all about?"

"Man, that's heavy."

"Man, that's deep. Is he going home to Texas and calling off the war?"

The room broke into pockets of grumblings as news of the special-delivered telecast spread. It seemed some pinnacle had been reached. De-escalation meant less danger. The end felt much closer.

The President's surprise announcement to halt the bombing of North Vietnam and his expressed willingness to talk peace had immediate effect. On April 3, 1968, Radio Hanoi announced that the Communists were also willing to talk.

But far from promoting peace, the two proclamations and the subsequent politics involved only intensified the fighting in the mountains and jungles of Vietnam as both sides desperately fought to gain military advantages that could be used as leverage and/or bargaining chips during the upcoming May 13th opening of what came to be the Paris Peace Talks. Thus, 1968 would be marked as the bloodiest year of the entire conflict.

The Boys Are Not Refined

The Arriving Whirlwind

So many soldiers in the company had finished their one-year Thai tours together that by the end of March, the empty barrack bunks were noticeable. It was a 19th Battalion-wide problem. To quickly replenish our and other battalion vacancies, an entire company of medium-duty drivers was transferred from Vietnam and attached to the 9th Logistical Command in Thailand.

One platoon of that unit was allocated to the 21st Transportation Company and relocated to Korat. Imagine their relief upon arriving at this new duty station. Imagine also the wild and untamed spirit they brought into Camp Friendship. Their April 2 arrival was memorable.

Boom! Boom!

I was within the quadrangle area between the barracks tossing a football with Bryson and Private Johnson. We looked to the southeast sky as two F-15s began their landing decent, having jettisoned their unused 500-pound MK-82 bombs onto the dumping field range. It was a common but wasteful safety practice.

An instant later, our attention was again diverted. This time by a marching song before we spied the singing soldiers in formal traveling greens at the rear of a ¾-ton personnel carrier:

The boys I mean are not refined
They go with girls who buck and bite . . .

The truck parked at the curb in front of company headquarters. The driver exited the cab, walked to the rear of the carrier and lowered its gate. Soldiers, lugging their duffle bags, climbed out of the transport rear. The marching song continued:

They do not give a fuck for luck
They hump them thirteen times a night . . .

The ditty had been divided into couplets, each assigned to discernibly different voices:

One hangs a hat upon her tit
One carves a cross in her behind
They do not give a shit for wit
The boys I mean are not refined . . .

The Master-Sergeant came out of the office. The men smartly fell into formation, and he spoke. "We all know this ain't you boys first company picnic, so I'll make it brief. You were each transferred into this unit with at least one year of service time to your credit. Good, it makes it easier for the lot of us. Tomorrow at 0800 hours there will be a short battalion and company orientation meeting in the motor-pool conference room. For now, Specialist Sasse will show you to your quarters. Platoon dismissed!"

As if on cue they began again with their boundary-busting chant accompanied by the sound of cadenced boot steps as they marched in place. An open expression of self-identification, it was as refreshing to hear as it had been to see brothers perform the Stockade Shuffle for the first time:

"They speak whatever's on their mind
They do whatever's in their pants . . ."

After finishing the ditty the new troopers fell-out, and began following Sasse into the barracks. Bryson threw a spiral toward me but one soldier broke from the pack and, despite the duffle bag on his shoulder, intercepted the toss. He was about 5' 9" tall, with a slender yet hard muscular frame, had a receding hairline, and would later claim a bi-racial,

The Boys Are Not Refined

Seminole-and-black heritage. His US number identified him as a draftee.

"Specialist Fourth Class, Raymond Lloyd," he said and cast a grinning smile. "Football's my fame but not my game. I still got a shot at baseball." He smiled widely and exposed perfect teeth except for the left front one. He had obviously lost it twice and now wore the hole proudly. "I'm from Miami, Florida."

"It doesn't matter," chimed Bryson. "We all come from the same ancestors. Yo mammy's my mammy, but where in the hell did you learn that chant?"

"Ah, man, that was taught to us by our college white-boy, Bobby Henshaw," said a toothpick-gnawing second soldier. Lloyd tossed the football back in perfect spiral to Bryson. "This is my pal, Green," he said in introduction.

"Green Derby Green," said Green, draftee Specialist Fifth-Class. "Stilwell, Oklahoma. Why don't ya'll guys come on in and introduce yourselves?"

"Hum," I thought, "Oklahoma; Green Derby—that's the same name as my grandfather."

We followed the new arrivals up the steps into the barracks from the west end stairwell. Inside, Sasse led the way pointing out assigned spaces. Trailing, I watched as one of the new boys halted, dropped his duffle bag in the aisle at the head of Powell's bed next to the flag and began to sing.

"Johnny Yuma was a rebel . . . " It was the tune from the '60s television series, *The Rebel,* starring Nick Adams. The soldier stopped after the first line and asked, "Or was it Johnny, your ma was a rebel?"

His fatigue nametag identified him as Ruffin. He pointed to the confederate flag suspended from the barrack ceiling and asked redundantly, "What the hell is that, Specialist," he read the name tag, " . . . Sass-say?"

Speechless, Sasse raised his eyebrows, hunched his shoulders, turned his opened hands palms up, shook his head, and continued into the east wing with his bunk assignments.

Sergeant Willis Bolt was Leggett's replacement, and his cubicle was directly across the aisle from Powell's bunk. Ruffin turned and looked him in the eyes for an answer, but unlike the D.C. sergeant who he'd replaced, Bolt was a losing "Lifer". He turned his head to glance at the offending flag but gave no answer.

I answered, "Oh, that. That just means the doctor is in, or, in this case, Sergeant John Powell, our resident racist is back."

"I got to sleep with that?" Ruffin asked Bolt. He turned and questioned others within earshot, "That don't bother you none? And it don't bother none of you other brothers neither?"

Bolt now had something to say. "Son, you will learn it doesn't do any good to get upset about every little thing. Pick your fights. My best advice to you is to just ignore it, do your job, and get the hell out of this man's army. It ain't for everybody."

Lloyd, emptying his duffle bag, joined the barrack discussion from his new west wing nest. "You mean it is okay, then? It ain't against army policy? Right here in the barracks?"

"No. It isn't against any policy."

"That's fucked up", said Green.

"How you feel about that, Sarge?" asked Ruffin.

"Son, it isn't a matter of how I feel about it. Listen, how long you been in the army?"

"I enlisted out of Detroit almost three years ago, but my ETS is in February."

"You ever heard the name Keith Clairborne Royall during that time?"

When Ruffin showed a blank face, Bolt surveyed the room to more blankness then continued, "Of course you haven't. You're too young, all of you. But when I was a teenager, we all knew who he was."

"Well, who the hell was he?" asked Ruffin.

"Well, you see, when President Truman ordered the integration of the military, Royall was Secretary of the Army. He refused to comply with the President's order and was fired."

"So?"

"Well, personally, that's when I enlisted. My old man even encouraged me."

"And you think that's good?" I asked. "Then why am I seeing what I'm seeing? This is 1968. President Truman's executive order was issued when? 1948? That's 20 years ago. Hell, I've been waiting for a chance to salute a black officer since I've been in uniform and that's a fact!"

"Well, I was agreeing with you young fellas for once. What I was saying, if you would let me finish, was that it turned out, even though the Secretary was forced to retire, it didn't mean nothing. His . . . colleagues remained at their posts. They're the ones who dug their feet into the ground. That's why nothing changed. I don't fight them. A man can still make a good life."

"Ah, man, that's a cop out," I said.

"I agree. That stinks," said Green from his bunk next to Lloyd.

"I'm out in February," said Ruffin.

"The flag is still there. People complain but it is not going nowhere. It's not against any War Department memorandum, Army regulations, or company policy. You may not like it, but as long as your ass belongs to Sam, there's nothing you can do about it."

"No black man with any consciousness of self should have to serve under that . . . symbol. It's just plain backward. It's like saying all our progress as a race means nothing."

"It is a fucked-up symbol of hate and I'm cuttin' bait!" announced Sgt. Wardell Tucker, one of the new troops. He was Regular Army. He made an immediate impression on me as a brawler and a handy man to have on your side in a barroom fight.

He took a pocketknife, cut the fishing line and the flag flopped onto Powell's bed.

"Whoa, calm down now, son," said Sergeant Bolt. But both men were of equal rank. Tucker only smiled.

"Well done," I said. "That flag is a symbol of our subordination! We have marched down a time-line from being niggers, niggas, niggras, Negroes, and coloreds to being Black with a capital 'B'. When I was home, on leave before I came over, I heard somebody shout, 'Black is beautiful.' And you know what? I like that."

"Yeah, we need to burn that mothafucker right here!" said another black soldier and set down his duffle bag. His eyes scanning the room, moved quickly from side-to-side as he reached into his fatigue pants pocket and withdrew a Zippo lighter.

"Now, hold it right there now, young soldier... Wellington!" said Sergeant Bolt, narrowing his eyes to read the nametag of the new arrival. "That is private property, this is an army barrack, and what you are about to do would be arson, a court-martial offense! I suggest you think about it."

Wellington turned and stared at Bolt, shook his head, broke into a wide, grinning smile, put the lighter back into his pocket, and continued on, dragging his duffle to his assigned cubicle.

Ruffin, retired to his own cubicle space, announced to anyone who didn't know, "I'm Luke Ruffin from Detroit. David Ruffin is my cousin and I just got the latest from MOTOWN!" He then chattered on about Berry-Gordy-this or the Temptations-that and pulled a record player from the top of his duffle bag. He plugged it in and set Otis Redding to singing "Dock of the Bay."

That was the beginning. Luke Ruffin would play Dock of the Bay until his record player needle wore-out. Then would go to the base PX, buy new needles and as time went by would play it some more, again and again for Uncle Sam.

After mess that evening, I trailed behind Johnson and three of the new bunch as they exited the barracks and headed for the NCO Club. "Oh, that. That's an empty ocelot tiger cage."

"Where da cat," asked Wellington?

"He's gone back to the real world with the captain," Johnson explained.

"Maybe we should put Wellington in the pen? How many Article 15 investigations and punishments are pending against your ass, man?" asked Green.

"Ha, ha, ha, you could serve your stockade time right here." agreed Lloyd.

"You ain't puttin' me in no pen!"

"Shoot, man, you aren't fooling nobody. You're in army jail now because the superior court gave you a break and the choice of military service or hard time," said Lloyd.

"So, what's wrong with dat? I ain't lettin' nobody cage me up if I can help it."

"Ah shut-up, fool. If you hadn't signed-up for three you'd be breakin' rocks right now," chuckled Green.

"Like I said, not if I can help it."

The replacements drove the average age of the company roster downward. Generally speaking the replacements were younger than the draftees, volunteers, and career soldiers and reserves rotating out. The new troops, men from the "fire zone," carried a totally different spirit than the soldiers they were replacing.

Particularly noteworthy was the more challenging attitude among the new black soldiers.

Getting to Know

The new boys were a mixed duffle bag, so to speak. Three days after their arrival Madson and Cak insisted that Bryson, three of the new guys, Green Darby Green, Raymond Lloyd, Robert Henshaw, and I join them after duty hours to meet a mutual friend.

Cak went ahead on his motorcycle, and we six soldiers shared two cab rides. From the base we traveled north on Base Road aka Paktagchai Highway #304, to perhaps a quarter mile from the juncture of east-west flowing Friendship Highway #2. There the cabs turned left onto a dirt pathway, and followed it 100 yards to an outcrop of buildings.

The cabs stopped, and Madson paid both drivers and led us to a building with a large, lighted, blue neon sign that read Royal Bar. However, in the window a second, red-neon sign screamed: CLOSED. Cak's bike stood parked in front.

Madson climbed the steps to the veranda and knocked on the door. It opened and a female voice shouted, "Stan! Mat-son! You come back?!"

A tall woman (tall for me; I measure 5' 5 ½") of 5' 7" or 5' 8" emerged. She wore black bloom-bottom silk pants and a white embroidered smock. Her long black hair had been gathered and pinned into a swirling crown. She embraced Madson, who in turn lifted her into the air before setting her back on the ground. He then began to introduce the rest of us.

"Dis is my friend, Mama-san Lucky. Lucky, dese are my friends..."

"*Muan gan pom duey!* Me, too! *See kon bpen pom puan duey.*" injected Cak, jointly claiming our friendship. He had emerged from the house and stood smiling on the veranda.

"*Chai krap, jing-jing.* Dese are our friends. This *puchai piu kao* white boy is my friend Henshaw. Him *baa mak-mak.*"

Henshaw nodded, smiled, and said, "Nice to meet you, ma'am. You can call me *Baa-Baa,* baby."

The enigmatic Private Robert "Bobby" Henshaw was easy to like, but a bit hard to know. He was all of six-feet-three inches tall but as thin as a rail. There was something about him that made you think of John Carradine.

Prior to his induction, Henshaw had been an English major at San Francisco State and had his college diploma taped to the inside of his wall locker door. He had taught the boys the outrageous jingle. A native of San Francisco, he was wild in a game kind of way — eager to try new things and was the rare white trooper that preferred the company of blacks. Sadly, although he smoked his share of *ganchaa*-filled water pipes, he had developed a fondness for the harder drugs during his three-month Vietnam tour.

"Dis is Lloyd." Lloyd's nickname should have been Smoke-this-and-Chill which was what he said in passing a joint during our common favorite pastime.

"How do you do, ma'am," he said and cupped his hands into a *wai*.

"Dis big, tall brotha here is Bryson, dis short brotha's name is Forest, and dis here brotha is Green."

Green, with a ubiquitous toothpick between his teeth, said, "Pleased to meet you, ma'am," and nodded his head.

He had quickly emerged as the elder spokesman and the voice of reason and sanity among the new arrivals. A draftee from Oklahoma, he was married and had two children. He was a decisive leader and often spoke with a turn or nod of the head, a hard stare, a raised eyebrow, or a barely audible grunt of affirmation or denial.

Bryson and I said, *"Sawatdii,"* and made *wai* signs.

Lucky smiled widely. "Oh, you speak Thai. Good," she said to Bryson and me. *"Dii mak-mak.* I like GI like speak Thai. Good." She looked at each of us and added, "You friend Stan, you friend me. Good *mak-mak."*

"But what happened? *Tom-arai, tamai bpen pid?"* asked Madson, looking around.

"We clote three mont now. Before you go we hab *choke dii tuk wan.* Den you leb. You go back we hab bad luck. Luckie *mai* lucky." She laughed at her own joke.

"But, we o-pen again. You see." She shook her index finger and nodded her head to emphasis her conviction. "We o-pen again." She paused and smiled. Then beckoning with her hands, she said, "You come in. You all come in. You want beera? I no hab wit-key. You want smoke *ganchaa*? I get water-pipe."

"Smoke?" I asked but was sure I'd heard correctly.

"Did you say smoke?" Lloyd smiled widely. "Right on the head."

"You don't even hafta ask," replied Bryson. *"Chaisi,' krap. Ao duut."*

"You just said the magic word," said Green.

"Jing-jing sa duey. Ao ganchaa," said Madson, translating our common desire. We all broke into happy laughter, then took off our shoes and entered the closed Royal Bar.

But that night in the closed bar, among other stories Madson told the tale of an unfortunate black soldier from Los Angeles who lost his composure and struck Sergeant Powell over the issue of his Confederate flag.

The next day at the motor pool in the midst of the morning first echelon maintenance Green, gnawing a toothpick, confronted Sergeant Bolt. "So did you hear the one about the California brother who went ape-shit upside a certain sergeant's head over a Confederate flag?"

"What in the world are you talking about, Specialist Green? Are you making a veiled threat?

"Not at all, it's a true story. The thang happened about six months ago. Brother got busted out. Look it up. I wouldn't want something like that to happen again. Would you?"

"Why would I? That's got nothin' to do with me. It happened under a whole different command. As long as he ain't violating any policy, why buck it? He'll be gone soon enough. Just live and let live."

"You act just like a uniformed Oreo Uncle Tom Tango."

"Young man, I don't even know what that is but youngsters like you can't begin to understand. I've been in this man's army sixteen years. You don't realize what that means. You young fellas want something for nothing."

"Nah, Sarge, it ain't that. Just grow a dick and stand up like a man. Just tell the lieutenant. We ain't going to allow them to fly that chicken-shit flag in the barracks!"

"Now, you just calm down. There is no use always complaining about something. Pick your fights is what I find is best."

"You just a Tom-Lifer like I said. The whole time we was in 'Nam I'm thinking, 'Okay, am I going to get a bullet in the head from Charlie or one in the back from some cracker?' You career, what happened to Lieutenant Edward Kitchen?"

"Now you wait a minute. I knew Eddie personally. He once served under me in Germany before he earned that battle-field commission! I know what happened to him and it wasn't right. But that was in a war zone. Things like that . . . happen.

"All I'm saying soldier is if you want promotion, then do your job and get along. If you want cherry assignments, just do your job and get along.

"You young troops always complain that the MPs harassing you. Hell, if you'd done your job and gotten along, nobody would have even noticed you one way or the other. And for your information, they're going to rotate Powell out early. So calm down, give it two weeks, young man. Just slow down and hold on."

In hindsight, it is easy to ask, just how in the world did he think that was going to happen?

A Dead King

It was a few minutes after 1700 hours; the fifth sun of April was in decline. My work day over, I had shaved, showered, and changed and, intending to spend the evening off post, had gone to Company HQ to the Sign-In-Sign-Out-Take-One counter. Sasse, finishing his own work day, tried to convince me to join him and his *tealot* downtown to watch the closing parade of an annual 12-day festival.

"We can share a cab. There's a surprise for my girlfriend I've got to get from my barracks locker first, but you'd like the festival. It celebrates Suranari, aka Khunying Mo."

"Khunying Mo? Who was she?" I asked.

"The wife of the provincial governor; she saved Korat City. The Thais, in fact, credit her with saving the whole kingdom," Sasse explained this as he cleared his desktop and placed a plastic dust cover over his typewriter."Khunying Mo, Suranari acted like a Thai Judith of Jerusalem facing the army of Holofernes."

"Holofernes? You going biblical on me, Sasse?"

"Yeah," he chuckled, "except Suranari led an entire village of women. Their men had fled the Laotians and the women of Korat were left to the designs of the occupying rearguard. So, following Suranari's plan, the fatal femmes of Korat wined and dined, then laid and slew the enemy troops in their drunken sleep. There were mass decapitations."

"Find 'em, feed 'em, fuck 'em, kill' em! Black Widows? Jesus, Sasse! Where do you learn all this stuff?"

"Oh, this is local. Haven't you seen her statue? Heck, you probably have and didn't even know."

"The woman with the sword in front of the town's white walls," I said, making the connection.

"That's her," he laughed.

"That's good stuff. I love history."

"Well, then that's nothing." We left the office and as we began the walk to our barracks, he spun an intriguing story about Bhumibol Adulyadej, then king of Thailand.

"I bet you didn't know he's the only king on the planet that was born in the United States?"

"I bet I do, now. Is it true?"

"Sure it is. His mother met his father, Prince Mahidol in Boston. The prince was studying medicine at Harvard."

"Really? That's kind of romantic."

"Really. And yeah, it was romantic because she wasn't a royal and they needed special permission. Well anyway, what I was saying was, the present king, Adulyadej, well, his older brother, Ananda, was king. They were raised in Switzerland and only came back to Thailand so that Ananda could perform certain ritual duties and ceremonies. Then the brothers were supposed to go back to Europe."

"Now when, again, are we talking?"

"It was just after the war. The visit was supposed to last six months, from December until June, 1946."

"Is it true that during the war Thailand had been an ally of the Japanese?"

"Yes, officially it was an ally of Japan. It was that or go the way of Burma and China. Relent or be conquered. They didn't have much choice."

"I wasn't criticizing. But in the three months I've been here, do you have any idea how many times I have heard it said, 'Thailand never been conquered, Thailand never been conquered!' Well, I guess, in a way, it hasn't."

"It's true. But despite the occupation there was an important Thai anti-Japanese movement. And that's why early in their visit, the brothers, Ananda and Bhumipol, accompanied by the prime minister visited a camp of the Free Thai Army. This was the group that had led the resistance against the Japanese.

"The king and prince participated in firing range target practice and obviously liked it, so at the end of the visit, Ananda was presented an automatic, gold-plated Colt .45; his brother—"

"The present king?"

"Right, but at that time he was still a prince. He was given a carbine, a Sten gun, and two automatic pistols."

"A Sten gun? What the blazes is a Sten gun?"

"It's a collapsible submachine gun. The British used them during WWII. It has a folding stock. Simple design. It's still the weapon of choice for rebels everywhere."

"Really?"

"Yeah, man. So, anyway, the brothers set up targets inside a garden of their Barompimarn palace compound and fired away from their second-story balconies. They had a virtual arsenal."

"Was it in Bangkok?"

"Yeah, it was, at Rattacosin."

"You tellin' me like they're shootin' machine guns off the balcony at targets below? Pow, pow, pow, pow, pow!"

"Yeah. What can I say? They were princes. So the morning of June ninth at 9 o'clock, everyone in the palace heard a single shot. Nobody thought a thing. They checked on the young king and the prince as a matter of course. But when they reached the king's bedroom, Ananda was slumped over dead."

From somewhere I seemed to hear, "Forest . . . ! Forest! Fuck, Forest!"

As I stopped and looked around, Sasse continued, "A single bullet had been fired from the gold-plated, 45 caliber pistol."

The Boys Are Not Refined

"Hey, Forest!" It was Madson. He was calling from the stairwell landing at the eastern barrack door and came bounding down the stairs. "Martin Luther King is dead! Dey done kilt Martin Luther King!"

"Oh, no," groaned Sasse. "I'm . . . sorry." He checked his wristwatch then said, "Really, this is crazy. Sorry. Look, I'm going to go. Are we still on?"

I shook my head negatively and hunched my shoulders in doubt. "I don't know, man. I don't know."

Sasse walked on but when he passed Madson, both men shook their heads in disbelief. Immediately, I thought of the inevitability of Dr. King's life ending this way and asked Madson, "Jesus, man, where did they do it?"

"In Memphis, man. In damn Memphis!" Madson continued as he quickly approached, "Dey done shot him down like a dog in da street in sorry-ass Memphis, Tennessee. Man! I 'memba when I first seed 'im in 1963 on live TV. Dey was marchin' on Washington. Brotha, dat was some incredible numba of peoples!"

"Yeah, man, I remember. I was home alone when I saw it. Probably was a good thing. My emotions were all mixed-up. I was so moved by portions of his 'I Have a Dream' Speech tears came to my eyes."

"Fuck, man, I 'memba. And now he done died! Dey done kilt 'im."

I felt a rush of anger. It was the same anger all America saw in the broadcast images of black inner-cities on fire in Newark, Detroit, and Philadelphia. It was "Burn, Baby, Burn" Watts Riot kind of anger all over again, as city after city came under dire siege and required National Guardsmen to restore order.

I began climbing the stairs to the barracks remembering how Dr. King had battled a growing irreverence in the black community over the new direction of his social and human equality movement. I stopped my ascent, turned back to

Madson and quizzically asked, "What the brothers back home going to say about him now? You know, man, just before my induction, Martin Luther King Jr. denounced the war?"

"He did?"

"You didn't know that?"

"Nah, man, I didn't know none of dat. I probablys was in the war already."

"Yeah, man. He was the main man behind that big San Francisco anti-war Mobilization Day. You don't remember that? " I asked reaching the top of the stairs.

"Nah, Forest, man. I don't 'memba none of dat. I wasn't into dat anti-war stuff. But ya know what? Now, he dead, just like Malcolm X. I betcha it was a goddamn government thang!"

I cursed it all and muttered, "Fuck, man, fuck it! I hope they burn it up. Burn it fucking up! Burn another damn dream-deferred!"

We entered the barracks 10,000 miles away from the mouth of the furnace, yet Madson and I were not the only black soldiers at full burn. At that moment, all the disharmony of America seemed housed in our loud, rowdy Camp Friendship army dormitory. We proceeded toward the rising commotion. Some of the Vietnam Fort Mead transferees could be heard chanting:

The boys I mean are not refined
They cannot chat of that and this
They do not give a fart for art
They kill like they would take a piss . . .

Another soldier watched the chaos repeating the phrase, "Burn baby, burn baby, burn baby, burn."

Soft-spoken Pvt. Carl Henry, who, together, with Johnson and I had checked into the 21st Transportation Company, was urging, "Cool it man. Everybody from the

South ain't like Powell. The flag don't mean nothing! I got one."

"Fire in the hole!"

"Yeah? Well, you don't advertise it. It's not hanging in our barracks," Green Darby Green responded.

A hole had been rent through the sheet metal on one side of Powell's wall locker, and an attempt had been made to burn the contents. The footlocker, too, had received an arsonist's attention. Both storage units were smoldering small billows of black smoke. Lighter-fluid fumes were palatable.

"Yeah, but I got one. It don't mean I hate you or any black or colored person. For me and I'm sure my friends back home it's just a matter of pride. It's just saying, 'Hey, ya'll, I'm from the South.' That's all it is saying, man. That's all it is."

"What's happening here?" It was Sergeant Bolt. He had apparently been summoned from the NCO Club.

"A fire," came a calm reply.

The sergeant turned, bolted toward the door, and grabbed the CO2 canister mounted on an adjacent wall. He sprayed through the hole that had been bashed through the footlocker side then he sprayed a sustained flow through the wall-locker rent and front slits, just as Johnson, the supply clerk, entered with a set of bolt-cutters.

Johnson cut the lock from the wall locker. Using a blanket from Powell's bunk to protect his hands, he removed the lock and opened the locker. The damage was not as complete as the arsonist had hoped. Powell's belongings appeared more smoke damaged than burnt and I did not see the flag.

The new second lieutenant entered and a voice shouted, "Atten-hut!"

"As you were, what happened here, Private?" There was a distinct element of shock in the voice.

Private Wellington smiled but said nothing, negatively shook his head, and walked away.

Private Henry saluted and spoke. "They killed Mister Martin Luther King, sir."

"What? These boys killed . . . ? What? Who killed King?"

"It's on the news, sir. Someone shot him," Bolt quickly responded in an effort to rescue the Luey from himself. "I believe they said it happened in Memphis, sir.

"You mean the colored . . . black soldiers did this . . . ?"

"No, sir, well, I'm not sure, sir. But I think something like that was said."

By now most of the observers had distanced themselves from the scene and were leaving the building.

"Who said it?" He looked at Private Henry, who had volunteered information.

"I don't know, sir. I just heard something like that."

"This is Sergeant Powell's locker?"

"That's right, sir," said Bolt.

"Where is the sergeant?"

"I believe he is either at the NCO Club or he's gone downtown, sir," Sergeant Bolt answered.

"But his ETS date is only a few days away."

"I believe you are right, sir."

★ ★ ★

I remember leaving the barracks with Madson, who was still wearing olive green fatigues, but, like a bad trauma, some parts of the evening remain hidden deep within my mind. Perhaps, the shock of loss? I do remember finding myself within a group of a dozen or so soldiers who, in Ox Bow fashion, decided all white Americans were guilty. In vigilante style we voted to storm Korat's infamous "white only" bar, and we took three taxicabs downtown.

As we reached the bar, a block away the *Suranari Festival* procession approached on its way to the town square and the statue erected in her honor near the ancient, white-washed, tenth-century city wall. We barged into the tavern as a Thai female singer beautifully wailed out the lament of loss carried in the *Ode to Billy Joe*.

That song! To this day, each time I hear it I think of the dead, broken, bloated Emmett Till, his barbed-wire anchor necklace still attached. The body being dragged from the Tallahatchie River, near one of those Choctaw Bridge bad places where nothing good ever happens, be you black, white, or indifferent. Bobbie Gentry knew.

Things are not always right, and that night her music brought me to my senses. I didn't hate all white people. Never did. I had just not been raised that way. But many in the room were not listening to the lyrics, or they attached a whole other meaning to the song.

Shouted out over the music I heard remarks spiced with the hot button tag names of "Shine, Spook, Spade, Spear-Chucker, Boy, Nigger" and one or two others aimed to encourage our hasty departure. But my mob had come for some blood, and so they gave as good as they got, with return volleys of "Chuck, Fay, Whitey, Honkie, Beast, Pig, Rabbit, Peckerwood, and Dude."

It should be said many of the whites sat silent or turned to their dates in vain attempts to ignore the gathered commotion. Furthermore, despite the racial slurs blurted across the room, no violence occurred until one soldier dared to remark, "They finally got the little black son-of-a-bitch!"

Then with blitzkrieg speed our aim became the striking of any and all white patrons we encountered. Was anyone concerned with being thrown into the brig or stockade? I don't think so, but it was only bare knuckles fighting. A few tables were overturned, but no bottles or short-timer sticks were used. The object was to inflict memorable pain but not to cause permanent injury. No cheeks were turned and no quarter given. It was just a good old-fashioned Donnybrook!

Although Dr. King would have been shamed, Malcolm would have been proud. Inside that bar, in a volcanic like eruption, our rage, hatred, and energy gushed, spilt, and was spent. Emotions had begun to recede to their normal levels by the time the girl in the song dropped her flowers into the swift moving current below.

We made a fighting retreat back outside just as the parade procession passed, with its horns, cymbals, chimes, and golden-costumed dancers. Leery of the Military Police, who had suddenly made their strong presence known, we darted through gaps in the procession, hired *tuk-tuks* and samlods and sang the 'Nam boys' marching song as we traveled to our next destination:

They speak whatever's on their mind
They do whatever's in their pants
The boys I mean are not refined
They shake the mountains when they dance . . .

Still heightened in fight and flight emotions, we retired to swap lies of valor and have the whores nurse our wounds and spirits at the Lucky Seven Club.

Bad Karma

Funny the way of the world, the day after MLK's death, two days before his rotation date, the gin gods or the devil delivered Sergeant Powell into my hands.

Intending to call it an early night, I entered the bathroom to pee, glanced into the mirror, then scanned the face basin counter and *voila!*—a gift from the gods, a week passed payday, a wallet bulging open with US dollar bills.

I looked at the ID photograph. The picture was that of Confederate-flag-flying Sergeant Powell, the previous evening's backlash target of the MLK assassination. Powell! The hard-drinking "Lifer" was an E-5—buck-sergeant—for heaven's sake! After 16-years of military service, the man had achieved one pay-grade below what the recently retired Sergeant Leggett had reached in his three-year regular army tour.

I looked around and saw no one, but heard the shower and looked to see Powell, sprawled on the tile floor. I replayed the obviously missing scenes in my mind: Powell returned to the barracks very near the proverbial drunken skunk. He hastily emptied the contents of his pockets onto the long counter running along the mirrored wall, some spilled into the wash basin. Unable to hold it any longer he soiled his pants, hurriedly staggered into a toilet stall and vomited his guts out for nearly ten minutes. He then staggered and stumbled, fully clothed into the shower, turned on its faucet head and slid down the shower stall wall to the floor.

And there he lay under the shower's waterfall. Faster than you can say Jackie Robinson, the urge to pee was gone and I began to act as I had been trained.

"What are the two types of soldiers?" The basic training drill sergeants had shouted in question again and again.

"What are the two types of soldiers?"

"The Quick and the Dead!"

"I can't hear your pussy asses!"

"The Quick and the Dead!"

That was our only acceptable response. I snatched the wallet from the counter, unbuckled my pants, stuffed the wallet into my underwear, re-zipped my pants, tightened my belt, and nonchalantly walked to my wall locker. There I thought for three clicks of a sand dial, grabbed a jar of Vaseline from my wall locker, and left the building through the barrack's eastern door three paces from my bunk space.

I had been a Boy Scout, a member of Troop 99. Our scouting rat pack adopted a mockingly serious survival code that succinctly shortened the Boy Scout Oath. Our more practical version pledged: "On my honor I will do my best to take what they give me and steal the rest!"

In my scouting hometown I had always found employment, and so I had not felt the kind of jealousy or desperation that drove one to steal. But my own outlaw days had come and gone in the autumn after my high school graduation. I had been lucky; the wild times had come to a fortunate ending.

To paraphrase a then re-arising Republican political star, "I am not, nor have I ever been by nature, a crook." And hell, locks are made to keep honest people out. There had been no locks.

I circled to the opposite end of the barracks. Adjacent the washroom on the western perimeter of our barrack compound, I spotted one of the large olive-green, recycled metal drums used as trash cans throughout the camp grounds. I emptied the wallet of its money, although 1 week after payday it seemed a considerable sum. It must have included his travel allowance. I tossed the empty wallet, I.D. and all, into the barrel.

I opened the jar of petroleum jelly and dug a large glob out, folded the currency into a tight wad, buried it in the excavated hole, covered the wad with the glob of petroleum jelly, smoothed the top surface with my fingers, and closed the lid.

I then entered the barracks to the immediate north. There I walked past the bunk of Bryson and using eye contact and a tilt of the head nonverbally signaled him to follow. He joined me outside and I hastily explained, "That racist, sharecroppin' Powell had a sayonara Camp Friendship night-out-on-the-town. He came back piss-ass drunk and right now, cannot tell his own ass from a hole in the commode. I hope he pukes shit—but he seems to have lost his wallet."

"What happened?"

"Finders keepers, Losers weepers," I said and held up the jar.

"What's that?"

"It's in here under the grease."

"Damn. Well, scored one against the good old boys. What you gonna do?"

"Look," I said, handing him the Vaseline jar. "Hold on to this for me for a few, will you? He'll be gone in a hot minute."

"Damn right I will."

"Thanks, Bry."

I re-entered my barracks. Three steps and I was standing at my bunk. I stripped off all clothing save my olive-green tee-shirt and boxer shorts and climbed onto my top bunk. The bottom bunk bed had remained unoccupied since my arrival.

I could hear Powell rising, somewhat recovered, shaking pickles from his brain, and taking account of things. He howled loudly upon the discovery of his loss. Loud swearing soon followed. I could not make out anything he said until I heard him say Forest, but the context in which he used my name was muddled and slurred yet the tone left no doubt. It was accusatory.

Powell apparently entered the dispatcher's cubicle and called the Military Police to report his loss and lodge suspicion and accusations. Twenty minutes later, from my bunk I heard them enter the barracks.

Two police officers stopped at Powell's cubicle and spoke softly with him. Powell raised his voice, and again, I heard my name. They left his bunk area, entered the east wing, and walked to my cubicle space. I slept.

One of the policemen softly said, "Private, Private 3rd Class Forest?" When no response came, one of them tapped his nightstick against the foot of my bunk.

One, two, three. I counted and began to roust myself. Slowly, I turned my head toward the MPs with a quizzical "what's going on here" expression as I lifted my body into a sitting position onto the edge of my bunk.

One repeated, "Private Forest?"

"Yes. I'm Forest," I said, continuing the frown. "What is this about?"

"Sergeant Powell has filed a charge that you took an item of personal property belonging to him."

"What? That's bullshit," I said, getting deeper into my character of innocence. "What the hell is he talking about?"

"Sergeant Powell called the station to report a missing wallet," the other spoke for the first time.

"I'm sorry. I have no idea what you are talking about. He must be drunk!" I indignantly protested.

"Do you mind if we look inside your wall locker?"

"I do mind, but go ahead." I continued the lie. Hell, I didn't care. They could search my locker until Hell freezes over. There was nothing to find! I continued to sit on my bunk and watch.

One unlatched and opened the wall locker door while the other aimed a flashlight inside. They spotted my own wallet sitting upon the top self. The MP who opened the locker door took the wallet from the shelf and opened it. They both noted the amount of currency and found nothing unusual there. They set my wallet back on the shelf and poked around some more but what was there to discover?

The Military Police were of no help to the poor soul. One offered me a weak apology. "Sorry, Private, just doing a job." And they left. Powell's wallet was still missing. The money was lost. Think what he wanted. Accuse whom he would. The wallet was gone.

Four days later I wrote my sister, Ruth, a letter. Her last correspondence had been distressing. Immediately prior to my induction, I had bartered a 1957 Fairlane-500 to have the engine of my 1959 MG Magnette rebuilt.

Ruth had three kids, my nephews Easley and Gilroy and niece Kendra. They lived in East Palo Alto and Ruth worked at Stanford University. She needed transportation so I had left the car in her care. In her letter, she apologized for having loaned the MG to my cousin Paul. He proceeded to push his rather large foot through the accelerator floor board and had blown the engine.

After completing the letter, I went to Bryson and he returned the jar. Oh boy! But I would have sworn I had counted $700 before burying the wad? Now there was only $500, and Bryson swore he had taken nothing.

Yeah, right. But what are you going to do, call the MPs? Why not ask Sergeant Powell how much it was? How much does a sixteen-year E-5 soldier make in this man's army, anyway?

I gave Bryson $50 for his aid and wrapped $400 in the letter instructing Ruth to use the money to repair the MG. "Boy," I thought, "where is the honor among thieves?"

Then a second, more noble perspective noted that, like General Sherman's troops marching through Georgia, I had, at least, temporarily crippled Sergeant Powell's ability to make his hateful race war.

But the act would also permanently remove the possibility of my becoming the Major's driver.

Mid-April Cookies

A mid-April mail call produced a box of chocolate chip cookies. They had been mailed from Pasadena by Starling.

At the time of my induction, although I was no babe-in-the-woods, I lacked deep knowledge of its varied tree species. The women I had known in the biblical sense comprised a short-list of three nameable multiple-time partners, two cousins who shall remain unnamed, and four one-time connections. One of these denies anything meaningful happened.

Starling was a good and eager kisser, but petting had been an exasperating pleasure, kindling fires of hope which could not be fulfilled under our heavily chaperoned conditions of engagement. It had remained an unconsummated romance, and now all bets were off.

Because like smart soldiers everywhere I had crawled into a protective shell against the outside world and any former personal relationship. There would be neither crying over spilt milk nor tears in my soup.

My best friend Vern back in Emeryville had been pounding the lonely wife of a soldier serving in Vietnam about this time last year, and I had considered him lucky. Life outside the army simply went on. People continued to grow, to move on, and to meet. The fact that you were not there was just tough.

One could only make light of the situation, send back photographs of fellow soldiers in the company Day Room, and attach a note reading, "Wish you were here!"

The beat goes on and like it or not every soldier knows the beat:

You had a good girl when you left
You're right
Jody was there when you left
You're right
Sound off, one, two
Ain't no use in looking back
Jody's driving your Cadillac
Sound off one, two

Each soldier had been duly warned. From the first day of indoctrination the drill sergeants had prepared us for the eventual arrival of a Dear John Letter. It gave a dual edge to mail call and the otherwise highly desirable correspondence that showed someone, somewhere cared. Mine had come in the form of a postcard. Sent by Misty it read: "Ours is a Platonic relationship, Plato for you and tonic for me."

Ha, ha. Get it? Yeah, I had to look up the word, but I got it. Right between the eyes I got it. I took it hard, but I took it like a man. I saw the next punch from a mile away. I stood at my bunk and read the letter in which she explained how "The stars are no longer in my eyes" in reference to our juvenile, high school ideas of glory, success, and fame in theater and the performing arts. After that I embraced the Jody Spirit, *et al.*

Let Jody describe his latest conquest and hear his tale of the yellow ribbon she had worn in her hair, day in and day out, during the first four months he had known her. Jody will laugh and openly admit he knew even before he asked the reason, she wore the yellow ribbon. He knew full well it was worn in remembrance of an overseas military person. He was hardly surprised and fully prepared to offer a concerned face when she told him it was for her lover who was far, far away.

Sympathetic Jody gave her first his ear, then his shoulder, and finally his bed on which to rest her bones and wait for her man's return. GI beware! There are few ties capable of binding young souls through the stresses of distance, time, and war. And it was a two-way street, wasn't it? No one seemed to be practicing celibacy except the Buddhist monks and a few Catholic priests back in the states.

At any rate, Starling had sent a box of cookies postmarked February, S.P.O. San Francisco. The deep chocolate chips were now light, chalky brown and the walnuts showed signs of aging, too. But the boys ravaged them as though they had just been freshly baked, drawn from the oven, and set before them.

G.T. Foster

Red River

It was an early May evening and the duty day was done. In the barracks, we were in various stages of showering, shaving, and dressing. Henshaw stood in the aisle before his bunk, naked beneath two towels—one draped around his neck and shoulders, the other wrapped around his waist, in a short sarong. He announced, "I have written a new poem." Then lifting a notebook, he read: "The House Girl—"

Her moniker, Miss Modesty she dresses
in horizontally stripped sarongs.
Hired to make beds and do laundry with
wisenheimer wide eyes of embarrassed
recognition, she lowers face cupped hands
quick turns and walks away to the washroom
shed shroud of giggle-cackle.
In the doorway the old one squats.
Her gums, tongue, and few remaining teeth
stained the scarlet red of the addictive betel nut
she stares into the space of time past.
Others pick up her slack, scrubbing, rinsing, and ironing.
They chatter-talk of the night before
in tones, pace, and idiom
too strange to follow words –
grab a sound and hold.
The two-cents of radio music adds
cacophonous pitch to rhythmic
human goings and comings.
Totters arrive with the unwashed

depart with the clean and pressed.
Camp followers, all.

"What ya'll think?" he asked, as he lowered the notebook then tossed it onto his bunk. He discarded the towel from his shoulder, lifted a fresh T-shirt from his footlocker and put it on. "Too long?"

"Nah, man, it was far fucking out," I said.

"Sounds like some of your California hippie shit. But I liked it. Especially that line about Mama-san out back in the wash house loaded. It was good man," Lloyd quipped.

"No bull, it was kinda cool. I liked the 'wizen wide eyes.' My wife has got those wise eyes, but where is the rhyme? I thought a poem had to rhyme," prodded Green.

"Not necessarily. Take 'Buffalo Bill's Defunct'; it doesn't rhyme." Half-dressed and fresh from my own shower and shave, I recited the short e e cummings piece:

Buffalo Bill's
defunct
who used to
ride a watersmooth-silver
stallion
and break onetwothreefourfive pigeonsjustlikethat
Jesus
he was a handsome man
and what i want to know is
how do you like your blueeyed boy
Mister Death.

"Say, what?" quipped a frowning, but smiling Green.

"Right. No man, it doesn't have to rhyme." Henshaw explained, as he stepped into olive-green boxers, discarded the second towel, and continued to dress. "You got rhyme, but then you got like iambic pentameter, blank verse, which is like 5 beats per line, non-rhyme; and like mine... free verse—"

Tornado like Ruffin came through the barrack's western door and asked in a loud voice, "Any you guys want to go to the base cinema?"

"What's playing?" asked Lloyd.

"Yeah, I'll go," said Wellington. "I ain't doing nuttin.'"

"You buying?" asked the usually muted Sergeant Tucker.

"Hell nah, not for you. Pay your own way. You make more than I do."

"You fuckin' cheapskate. You make more than all of us," added Henshaw. "How much did you get payday?"

"You get hold of some free tickets?" I asked.

"Nah, man. I was just checking to see if anybody else wanted to go."

"I'll ask you again," said Green. "What's playing?"

"You know, they're playing that new John Wayne *Green Beret* thing," informed Ruffin.

"Green beret? Find a hit and chill! I went to jump school. Was thinking Special Forces, but I almost fucked my knee up on my second jump. I transferred. Fuck the beret!"

"Fuck John Wayne! He never made a good movie in his life!" denounced Henshaw.

"What about that cowboy movie?" Green asked.

"They were all cowboy movies!" scoffed Henshaw.

"The one he's an outlaw," said Green.

"You talking about *Stagecoach*?" I asked. "What about *Stagecoach*?"

"Now, that was a good movie," Lloyd declared.

"My wife sure liked him in that," added Green.

"And old skinny Carradine," continued Lloyd in support of the worthiness of *Stagecoach*.

"Yeah, man, John Carradine." I agreed. "He's always good. He looks like you Henshaw. Did you ever see *Grapes of Wrath*?"

The Boys Are Not Refined

"Sure, sure I did. But I'm talking about how John Wayne can ruin a fucking movie. Even in *Stagecoach,* here comes... Ringo and all the action slows down," bitterly noted Henshaw.

"He was young," I said. "I think it was his first movie."

"Well, what about *Red River*? I loved him in *Red River*," said Ruffin in support of another worthy Wayne Western.

"Damn, that was good," Green said. "He was a gruff son-of-a-bitch."

"That was damn good," I said in echo of Ruffin's nomination.

"Good? Bullshit. That was great. They left his ass in the desert. They gave him his gun. But..."

"Gun? Nobody fucked with his gun," insisted Green, grinning and holding his privates. "They gave him his pistol."

"Okay, drill sergeant," laugh Ruffin. "They gave him back his pistol, but with no bullets. That was some cold-blooded stuff, man. That movie was great!" Ruffin proclaimed.

"Yeah, you're right. Well... that one movie was good," admitted Henshaw reluctantly. "But fuck John Wayne. I'm tired of his movies. I don't want to watch his gung-ho bullshit. Let's go to Mama-san Luckie's instead."

G.T. Foster

The Camaraderie House

During the months of May and June, when not on the road, evenings often began at Luckie's closed Royal Bar. Time there was filled with smoke, friendly banter, supposition, and even a level of thoughtfulness.

Luckie's inviting nest sat at the prime location and juncture of two important roads—Freedom Highway and Paktagchai Road. It was a small colony of bungalows and cottages. There was an L shaped building at the center. One wing of the building contained a large closed bar. The other wing held an apartment with an adjoining kitchen. This was the only part of the entire estate that was ever open during my tour.

When we revisited, a few days after our initial meeting, we met Luckie's husband, Pichai. He was a member of an elite Thai army unit, the Queen's Cobras, just returned from an active-duty tour of Vietnam. Both husband and wife were between 22 and 32 years of age. It was always hard for me to guess a Thai's age.

I didn't know why it was closed and not open to the lucrative base business so close at hand. I had never asked, nor had Madson explained its closure after introducing us to Luckie, the Thai owner. My superiors had not said the place was off-limits, but it must have been. It didn't matter that the place was closed, the two were gracious, willing hosts.

There existed a profitable trade-off: the camp Post Exchange (PX) was a virtual Sears and Roebuck catalogue. GIs were happy to fill Luckie's requests. She would ask, "You do me favor GI? Buy American cigarette at PX? I hab money" or "GI, buy perfume PX?" or "GI, buy camera PX? Can do?" or "GI can buy American whit-key PX? Johnny Walker, GI, Johnny Walker."

The husband, Pichai, never made requests but listened, often shook his head disapprovingly. Once he snapped, "You like any ting America, even America chit. Maybe, you want GI buy big box America chit! *Chip hai luui!*"

Perhaps, he was right. Luckie dreamed of America and her most cherished wish, she daily expressed: "Maybe one day Thailand be fifty-first state?" From her lips to Buddha's ears: *Suzerainty?*

What a strange idea for modern times — American born or not, a king's sovereign authority in kowtow to the US Constitution. The Thai military monarchy and American democracy are like water and oil.

Luckie's closed bar became our favorite haunt, a place to unwind or to meet-up. Seldom was the time one could not find a quick water pipe pick-me-upper. Most of the fellas would check by and post an oral message for later arriving friends before heading into town.

The place possessed a transformative quality. Sometimes it was a Wailing Wall. "No debate or comments, please. Just listen to my bitches and moans." Other times it was an un-muffled shouting rock of dialogue that gave no hiding place. Responses came whether you wanted them or not.

Evenings were full of ease, stories, and tease. Like the time Green, Lloyd, Madson, Bryson, Henshaw, Wellington, and I sat in a floor circle with Pichai and Luckie, and her brother Nod. Pichai placed two piles of chopped *ganchaa* before us. Then he took two water-pipes, but instead of water poured wine into their chambers, for flavor. He placed them both beside the chopped grass and said, *"Dut, dut."* (Smoke, smoke.)

The encouragement was unnecessary. Both pipes were immediately filled, lit, inhaled, and passed to other waiting hands on their journeys around the ring, as smoke curls and conversation filled the room. Luckie had asked, "*Tamai* black soldier, *piu dum* no like *piu kao*, white soldier?"

"White folk gonna be white folk, man. They wanna run everything." Bryson had tried to explain. "They can't help it. They operate under a haze. You think they conscious they racist? Hell, most of the time, they don't even know they've offended."

"I gotta agree, man." I said and gave supporting testimony. "The first fourteen years of my life, I repeatedly heard, 'You look just like Sammy Davis, Jr.' Collectively, they felt it was the highest compliment they could pay me."

"Come on, man. You know to ofay all brothers look alike," said Lloyd. He made the comment holding a lung full of smoke, then exhaled and gave his best, missing-front-tooth smile.

"Yeah, man, right-on to that," seconded Green, a ubiquitous toothpick between his teeth.

"Well, as a kid," I continued, "I sold newspapers on the street. So, I was out and about the town every afternoon; six days a week. They'd say, 'Hey, Sammy' or 'Hey, Sammy Davis.' I mean, they were buying the paper; it wasn't like I was gonna complain or give 'em some sass. I'm sure it was meant to inspire me as a kind of verbal pat on the back, but by that time Sammy had lost an eye. Remember that?"

"No shit, man."

"Yeah!"

"Man, everybody remembers that," affirmed Bryson.

"Folks still talk 'bout what a good lookin' man he was befo'," added Madson."But I only remember him in movies. He never looked no other way."

"Well, anyway, I was nine or ten. We were visiting in Victorville when it happened."

"When what happened?"

"Victorville?"

"The accident."

"Ha! What a hoot. Is that where it happened?" asked Henshaw.

"Sure, man. It was on Route 66. Just outside of town."

"I get my fix on Route 66," Henshaw sang in parody.

"Well, anyway, I have this uncle. He's got a fake eye. I've seen him with it in and I've seen him with it out. It's weird. And so, when I think of Sammy, I think of him. So, for me the pat on the back was like a slap to the face. Oh, but if for every time they said it, I had been given ten cents I would be a rich man."

"Wait, wait," interrupted Green. "Here Brother, here's a dime. It's a start. You know, you do kinda look like Sammy, chief."

"You tryin' tah signify, man?" Madson laughed.

"No, man, I'm serious. He does kinda look like a chubby Sammy Davis, Jr.," insisted Green.

"Sorry, Green, you're too late for the bandwagon," I said. "By ninth grade it had changed. It was like conjured magic. Suddenly, when they saw me, the entire white community began to see Dick Gregory."

The remark drew laughs and smiles. I continued, "But that effect did not last as long. By my senior year the white population had experienced a unified change of heart or maybe my face had changed during a growth spurt. And I had changed communities. But the resemblance, apparently, was obvious. When they looked in my face in collective voice, they proclaimed me to look just like Bill Cosby."

"Yeah? Betcha, 'gin, thought a dime be nice," chimed Madson.

"Here's another one Bro, but I think they were closest with Sammy." Green tossed another dime my way.

"I think whites still think we all look alike. Davis, Gregory, Cosby. It's whatever is put in front of their faces through TV, papers, magazines, movies...." Bryson left the series incomplete and shook his head in disgust.

"Damn, Bry!" said Green. "That's deep."

"Wow!" Henshaw threw his hands into the air, smiled and said, "Don't look at me!"

"Ah, Hennie, ain't nobody studdin 'bout chew," said Madson.

"We know you got a chocolate heart," assured Green.

"Yeah, we need to call you Vanilla Chocolate-chip," said Bryson.

"You know what I think?" I inhaled a deep hit from a passing pipe and made them wait.

"Well?"

"What?"

Exhaling I said, "I think they were trying to describe the 'it' factor. Pay me some kinda rare high praise. But instead they constantly managed to say the wrong thing. Like, 'Come on over. We fixin' to serve fried chicken, red Kool-Aide, and watermelon, in your honor."

"Dey said dat?"

"Nah, Mad Man. I'm talking about what they imply. The hidden...deeper meaning."

"Imply? Nigel Forest, you read too much," said Green

"Tell me about it, brother."

"So, tell me, you think it's all intentional?" asked Henshaw.

"Maybe, sometimes they don't know they're doing it," I said.

"Damn right it's intentional. You couldn't step on as many toes as whitey goes around steppin' on without it being intentional," declared Bryson.

"Right-on to that."

"You ain't never lied."

"The hunkies know dat, man. Every ofay know dat stereotype. Fuckin' red Kool-Aide, Forest?" Madson laughed and continued, "Dat way dey kin call you a nigga wid out usin' da word."

"That's right. It's just some kind of white folks' code."

"Fucking bigots. Hell yeah, they knew. You think Powell and Jenkins didn't know their rebel flags were pissing brothers off?" asked Bryson.

"That candy-ass Fisher. Why doesn't he just pass a company policy like Captain Jack did with the engineers?" asked Henshaw.

"Captain Cousin ain't had no policy! He just took care of it. Eben afta dat Los Anju-les brotha, what's his name? Sherwin? Yeah, Sherwin Forte. Well, after he went ape-shit on Powell, Cousin tried tah do da right thang. But I guess da brotha beat Powell so bad dey had tah bust him out. But yeh see, da brotha family was from Birmingham. He said his cousin was one of dem three little girls dey kilt in dat church. He said he didn't eben remember doin' it."

"Well, that ain't stoppin' Fisher."

"And why would he want to? The lieutenant is from Florida. Ray, you from Florida. How ya'll get along?"

"We don't."

"Is Florida in the South?" asked Wellington.

"We more like tropics, man."

"Tropics? Tropics. Come on now, Lloyd, Florida's south and he's a southern cracker," said Green, not giving his buddy any cover.

"If it ain't south my granny's a Nazi," teased Bryson.

"Well, he said it was free-speech," said Lloyd.

"Bullshit. What did that drunken dumb ass Powell know about free-speech?" I asked.

"It's just racist bullshit, man. Just bullshit," said Green with finality.

"Yeah, man," conceded Lloyd.

"Right-on, brother. Right-on."

★★★

Usually the conversation was lighter, but still (often centered on life in the Real World.)

"I had tried to enlist upon graduation from high school," Lloyd revealed one evening. "Hell, there was nothin' happenin' for me or no other brothers in Miami back then. So, I went on down to the Army Recruitment offices. They looked up my juvenile record and it came up dirty. They wouldn't take me."

"That's bullshit; Army take anybody."

"Well, you see, there was this one time, me and my younger brother had been chunkin' some rocks at these old abandon buildings, they were just some old shacks. Weren't no-body livin' in 'em. Kids were always throwin' rocks or bottles at 'em. But this one time, the security guard was around and called the police and me and my brother had to go to court. It was juvenile court, but they said we had to make restitution to the owner."

"What?"

"Yeah! They wanted us to pay for the damage. But we never did. Some of it we hadn't even done. But when I went to enlist, they said they wouldn't take me until I cleared up the matter with the court. I'm thinkin, shoot, to heck with that. And I got me a job in a Stan's Shoe Store. It was cool. The manager had these apartments.

"So, I was workin' there a couple of weeks and he comes to me and like he says he's got some apartments and needs somebody to like live in one and manage them. Would I be interested? Like the rent was going to be like $15 a month. I said, 'Hell yeah!' And I took it. It was slick, man. After a couple of months or so, I asked him if I could like work part-time, so I could take some welding classes at the junior college, thinkin' maybe I can play on the school baseball team, and he says, 'Sure.'"

"Ah, man, get out of here! So, what happened?"

"So yeah, man, I'm livin' in high cotton."

"Watch out!"

"Yeah, exactly. 'Cause that's like when Sam said, 'You know what? We changed our mind.' Fuckin' draft notice arrived in the mail bigger than shit. And that's God's honest-truth."

"Man, that's sad."

"Ain't that about a bitch!"

"Ain't it?"

"But, man, I swear that it's the truth"

"That's some stone-cold shit!"

"That's wrong. Man, that's plain wrong."

An easy favorite topic was our planned returns to the Real World. Ruffin had it all worked out.

"Just before I go back, I'm gonna go to Bangkok and have a Chinaman or one of those Indian fellas make me a bright-blue, tailor-made suit outta Thai silk. Then, when I get back home, I'm gonna walk from my house to the corner of Main Street and Broadway Avenue wearing that suit and a wide brim Panama hat also woven of bright-blue Thai silk. I'm just gonna stand there for about fifteen minutes. Then everybody gonna know I'm back.

"While I'm standing there, I'm gonna roll me a big joint. And smoke it. Smoke it like a cigar. Tippin' my brim to all the pretty-pretties that come by . . . all the time smokin', trippin', and tippin' 'til I smoke the whole thang up. Then for sho' everybody gonna know Jack is back, Jake!"

We all said it. It was said as if the current world were a dream: "When I get back to the Real World." Henshaw often poked fun at what we'd really find upon our return. He wrote a poem in which he would alter a line or two to fit the particular soldier's leg he was pulling:

> There ain't no use in looking back
> around your girl's a masculine pack
> sound-off the given names they carry:
> Tom, Harry, Dick, Jodie, Larry
> each wolf seeking to lay his claim
> to mutually shared shallow aim,
> a brief duet which she'll regret
> find, feed, fornicate, and forget
> you left, right? You left! So write!
> your one call home she balked
> on the phone in a breathy sex-laden voice
> still in bed she haltingly said can't . . .talk . . .
> right now . . . sorry . . . no choice
> and hung up! Your sweet buttercup, yet
> if upon return all that remain of her
> innocent eyes are thick jet-black lashes
> you shall resurrect, hoist, and heft
> what's left without an ounce of regret
> let phoenix rise from crimson ashes . . .

Green was often the poem's target, but his own return home version went, "Shucks fellas, I'm going home to my family. Heck man, I got two kids. I ain't seen my young daughter but once when they gave me leave just before—hell man, my boy be four, almost five years old. Then? I don't know. She wants me to go to school. But I don't know. School ain't for everybody."

"Well, I'm gonna go," I said. "Heck, my friend says they pay for almost everything with the GI Bill."

"Hell, I'm gonna buy me a crib with it. Why not?"

"Why not?"

"Why the fuck not?!"

★ ★ ★

The Boys Are Not Refined

Even Anthony "Tony" Baker, who had become Major Garrett's driver, frequented Luckie's. He was from New Jersey and before he became the Major's man, had been attached to the type A Company at Khon Khan. I remember one evening when conversation had, again, drifted to being back in the Real World. Baker, who I had considered intelligent, sounded a bizarre warning.

"Don't buy a new TV set when you get home."

"What?"

"Why? Rather why not?" I asked.

"That is how Big Brother's going to watch your ass."

"What are you talking about?" asked Bryson.

"Square business, Bro! I'm not kidding. They've got these cameras, built into the sets . . . like two-way mirrors. They can watch you, Brother. It's the new surveillance."

"Why would dey wanna do dat? I ain't done nutin' and I ain't no communist!" said Madson

"Then it's not you they are worried about."

"You believe that shit?" Bryson asked Baker. He turned to others in the room and repeated the question, "Come on, brother of mine, you believe that shit?"

"I don't disbelieve it. Just look at things back home. Things have heated up. Heck, we don't know who was behind Doctor King's killing. Was it a government plot?" said Green, in support of the admonishment.

"Yeah, man, that's right. And think about it, who really killed Malcolm X?" I added.

"Well, I'm not saying all that. But driving the Major around with my eyes open and my mouth shut? Hell, those 972s we thought were landmines? Well, they might be that, but they're also some kind of listening device, too. I know I'm not buying one. That's all I'm saying."

"You talkin' 'bout Russia, man. That's what they do in Russia. If they hear somethin' they don't like they send 'em off to some camp in Siberia," Bryson said.

145

"But we ain't talkin' 'bout no communists. Why would dey do dat in America?" asked Madson.

But Baker held his ground and countered, "I know none of you believe it, man. But they can do it. They got the equipment. They can do it." Then he slowly expressed each word of his admonition, "Don't...buy... any... new... TVs."

I didn't say anything out loud, but I thought, cynically, "Yeah, right."

★ ★ ★

On one strange occasion, a Thai police captain visited the compound. Three or four of us GIs were inside and someone—it could have been Bryson or Madson—was outside with Luckie. That person called to us to come join. When we did, I saw the captain, still in uniform, standing beside what had once been a drab, olive-green, American Army jeep. Now the wheels were shiny chrome and the jeep was painted a royal Thai purple.

Full of new owner pride, the captain lifted the hood and revealed the silver shine of chrome, the gleam of stainless steel, and polished aluminum sparkle reflected in after-factory upgrades to the head covers, exhaust manifolds, the radiator, distributor cap, and the carburetor cover. I marveled at the changes that had transformed a dull military vehicle into a snappy, smart, must-have ride.

I wondered, "Cost?" Then immediately flashed, "Oh, oh... Black Market!"

The Boys Are Not Refined

Gully Friendships

Over time a routine developed. Evenings began with a visit to Luckie's closed Royal Bar. There we'd sit, smoke, gripe, and recount the day. Then a chronic need for food, drink, and female sustenance led downtown where after dining, we spent a good deal of time at the Lucky Seven Club, the largest and most popular "Soul" bar in Korat.

Downstairs the tavern had a long dark hardwood bar counter with a huge mirror attached to the wall behind it that made the room seem twice its size. There were tables, booths, an elevated platform for live band performances and a jukebox on which at least twice each hour Otis Redding magically returned from the dead to sit on a San Francisco Bay dock and wail time away.

The upstairs bungalow rooms were rented by the bar girls for both living and working quarters. The rooms could be reached from either an interior stairway or by rear exterior steps that gave access via a long balcony walkway.

A percentage of the girl's earnings came from the sale of bar drinks. "GI wanna buy me drink?"

A watered-down drink for the lady and a conversation, long or short was part of the deal. If no agreement was reached between the GI and barfly, so be it. She simply moved to a new customer and asked, "GI wanna buy me drink?"

We became regular patrons of both the bar and the girls and after a while friendship became more important than pudenda and whoring (at least for me), for even after the most acrobatic and satisfying of sessions, nights were long and yearned to be filled with a deeper yin-yang interplay.

In what seemed a kind of quiet, modest embarrassment, the girls were not quick to talk of their lives before they had come to the profession. Much of what I learned about Nit's prior life had been supplied by Noi, Lek, and Toi and it followed that pattern with each of the others. Most all came from poor and/or abusive backgrounds and were from other areas of Isaan. None had grown up in Korat.

I sat with Lek at a table in the bar watching Noi gracefully move on the dance floor with Lloyd. Stirring the ice in her mixed drink with a plastic red stir-stick Lek explained, "Noi same same uder po' farm gurl. Her no from farm but her same same. Her po' villit gurl. Her family big. Her det-tiny be her be *gully*. Her no can chain."

She paused to make certain I understood. "Po' people Thailand hab same same det-tiny. Her want, her not want, no big ting GI. It be her . . . karma. Her det-tiny. Noi leb Udon goodbye apter her fadda tell her he goin' sell her to villit mama-san. He need to sab family hout."

"The house? You're kidding?"

"I no make joke. I tell you true. It be cheap hout. But him lut when him *kee-mao*. Lut all him money at night. Him bang bang *gully*, den him gamble. Lut *tuk baht*. Her own fadda! No goot."

"Damn. No good is right. At best he was a no-good father."

Many of the girls had been young orphans or adoptees. Some, like Toi, who had two children back in her village, were divorced or abandoned mothers and wives without other means. It was a short candle career in which product value was on a constant downward slide.

Early one morning as I dressed to return to post Toi lazily asked, "What you do when you go back State, GI For-it?"

Unlike many of her bar mates who read popular fan magazines, her room table top held Thai newspapers and copies of *The Stars and Stripes*. Of all the women that worked

The Boys Are Not Refined

at the Lucky Seven, she spoke the best English and was the only one that could read English.

"*Pom bpai roong riian*. I will go back to school *jing*, for sure. What about you? What will you do?"

Wearing a very thin silk see-through nightgown she sat up in bed, her drowsiness completely dissolved. "You tink I stay *gully* long time? *Mai mii tang*. No way. It neber happen GI. Soon I go Bangkok. I open chop. I teat *Angkit (*English*)*. You see GI? Din I no be *gully*." She had voiced the general whore's dream in a nutshell.

During daylight hours and without make-up they shopped in the marketplace for clothes and cosmetics and wore T-shirts, blue jeans, and a thin gold chain with a Buddhist amulet. But it was *haa-sip-haa-sip*, a fifty-fifty split as to whether they wore their religious icons during working hours. For at night, over sprays of alluring smells, they wore dresses and blouses. And they walked in flat or high heeled shoes or sandals with their hair swirled, stacked, or hung—mirroring the latest fashion of Petchula or some other glamour queen that framed the cover of the latest Thai movie or musical pop star magazine—not in pursuit of merit, but money.

At many of the bars working girls freelanced. They floated in and out and maintained their own, off-premise bungalows or apartments. Lucky Seven, however, was a house girl space. Soldiers and their dates were welcome, but freelancers were turned away by harsh words from Mamasan.

As professionals, the *gullies* shared a common attitude toward their GI clientele walking through the candy store sampling all the sweets: promiscuity was highly discouraged. The girls wanted to keep their health cards clean.

"We no like *kon jao-chuu, kon* butterfly. Why *mak-mak* black GI want be playboy all da time? *Kao len bpai puying-gapuying. Mai bpraat-ta-na. Kao mai sa-baai, mii rook-dtit-dtaw!*"

(Men play and go from girl to girl. Not good. Him not well, get contagious disease.)

"GI, want short time? GI, want all night?" If the answer was yes and the GI returned to the same bar, if the same woman was available, as a body-politic, the other *gully* girls preferred you continue with that woman.

The Boys Are Not Refined

No Red, White or Blue

The opening days of May delivered a heavy dose of heat and long hauls and was a basic grind. *Oh, what I'd do for one wild and free flash of an American girl's panties.* As I wiped the windshield of the five-ton truck, part of my daily maintenance tasks, that thought transported me back to Berkeley and the cool of the East Bay.

Sorry, GI, no can do. *Sia-chai duey kee.* Sorry about that shit! No pretty-pretties here in the motor pool. Only the heat, the bright sun, the blue sky, red hardpan earth, soldiers, Thai drivers, olive-green equipment, a choice of languages in which to listen to men gripe, bitch, and moan. And, just for laughs, more heat.

One day Lloyd obtained two buckets of paint; one white, one blue. During first echelon maintenance he painted the rear-axle casing of his tractor. First, he painted the entire canon-ball housing blue. After it dried, which wasn't long in the heat, he painted several stars onto this background.

It initially had gone unnoticed except for those drivers in the immediate area and his true company buddies. The next day, in an unescorted convoy to Phanom, it was a distinct hit. Upon our return to Camp Friendship, during the next morning maintenance other soldiers obtained buckets of paint to work their own magic. They painted the axles and rear-end housings in designs and combinations of white or red or blue. They were the only paints available, but all were preferred over the dreaded olive-green.

But our enthusiastic Sistine-Chapel like improvements came to an air-brake halt when Sergeant Bolt marched up to each soldier-artist and began to pee on his masterpiece. We should have expected it. Bolt was typically old school "Lifer."

The sergeant had a fondness for booze, with a preference for Scotch. A profound chasm separated him from us; he was a 1950's Negro soldier while we younger troops, culturally and psychologically were black. In response to all complaints he preached his favorite sermon: "Keep your nose to the grindstone is how one gets ahead in this man's army. The army has been a refuge to me and has always treated me fairly. I got no gripe."

If true, why, after sixteen years, was he only a sergeant E-6? He never explained. Nor did he respond to the question why there were no black officers in "this man's army?" Rather he pushed it aside, saying, "That is not my concern, soldier."

His current mission to bring spit-and-polish to our daily lives ran counter to any serious fun. "I will have every one of you up on charges of vandalism of government property," the sergeant now threatened.

"Vandalized? We done made 'em pretty," scoffed Madson.

Our laughter went unappreciated by Bolt. "The proper color is drab olive-green. Where did you get the paint?"

"The white, the blue, and the red, you really don't know their significance?" I asked. "Their meanings haven't changed since Boy Scouts. The red is for the blood we shed, the blue is for the heavens and—"

"Don't get cute with me, Private Forest. I don't care what they are. They're not the Army's colors! The Army colors are green! Green, drab olive-green."

"What's going on here, Sergeant?" asked the trailing Lieutenant English.

"This soldier... and as I inspect, several others, have vandalized government property, sir. I was on my way to inform you of yet another serious violation. It's just further proof of the extreme laxity within our company, sir."

"Well, what is it?"

Bolt squatted, pointed at my truck's rear-end and said, "Contrary to all army regulations some of these soldiers have willfully painted parts of their assigned five-tonners, sir."

Taking a closer look Lieutenant English asked, "How many are like this Sergeant?"

"I'm not sure, sir. But it looks like Forest, here, Lloyd, Madson and one or two others."

"Well, Forest, what do you have to say about all this?"

"Sir, there never was any intent to vandalize anything. That's ridiculous. We painted . . . at least I can say, sir, I painted my rear-axel to lift spirits, not to destroy morale, or trucks or any of that. The sergeant is either being dramatic or vindictive, sir"

"You will paint it back to its standard green at once."

"But, sir, they're patriotic colors. Heck, they're the color of the flag for which we fight."

"Immediately."

"Yes, sir"

"And the others! Sergeant, you are to see to it. They must all be repainted back to standard issue olive-green. Immediately."

"Yes, sir. I will, sir, with pleasure.

G.T. Foster

The Low-boy

A few hot and humid days later I was killing time playing Thai checkers against Lep, the company's Thai mechanic. My late return to Camp Friendship the previous day had allowed me to miss both the morning formation and a convoy assignment. Waiting with others who had not drawn morning hauls, we played under the shade and shelter of the corrugated steel roof erected over the concrete slab pit, repair and rest area.

In the midst of losing my fourth consecutive game, I was relieved to see Bolt exit the dispatch office with bills of lading in both hands. The late shipment orders included two choice, hurry-up-and-wait runs to Bangkok. The poor stiffs drawing these missions must patiently fight big city boredom and await the inexact arrival of a cargo, then shuttle the load to the Takli Air Force Base. 4 days minimum!

As usual, those juicy tasks went elsewhere. Favoritism and brown nose politics were always part of the equation. For me the sergeant seemed to be dishing out giant scoops of water buffalo chips.

★★★

"...I repeat, Sergeant Bolt, I have had absolutely no training or experience pulling a low-boy trailer. Everybody's warned me that it's different. The circle radius, the range of motion... you know?"

"You are assigned the haul."

"Come on Sarge—"

"Priivate Forest, you are assigned the haul."

"Hey, Sarge," injected Lloyd. "My load is going to Phanom. I'll switch with Forest."

"Sorry, soldier. It's his assignment and he's got to learn sometime."

"Why now, and why are you always on me, Sarge?"

"I'm not, as you say, on you. Private Forest, you are a soldier. Soldiers take orders. You think you should be in leadership? Leaders learn to lead by taking orders."

"I never said I wanted to lead—"

"Cut it. I read your file. You think you should lead. Learn to take orders. Rien is on a special assignment. You are to drag an empty to Phanom and then pull the low-boy load to the Air Force side of Camp Friendship; destination as per bill of lading. Do you understand the order, soldier?"

"Yes, Sarge. I'm hearing it loud and clear."

As crows fly, from Camp Friendship to the Phanom switching station, our destination eighty-five percent of the time, ninety miles would cover the distance. Aware of this inefficiency, the US Army Corp of Engineers were in 1968 completing a more direct north-south route into the eastern sector of Thailand's Central Plain. Carved through the forest jungle of Khao Yai National Park, and pre-named Friendship Hwy #2, the route, when opened, would give quick access to men and supplies from northern Udon, near the Laotian border to Thailand's south-central right flank bordering Cambodia.

But that roadway was not yet completed, and so, not being crows, we used the beaten path down the Korat Plateau via winding Friendship Highway #1. The highway had been so designated for the teamwork between the American Army Corp of Engineers and Thai workforces that had constructed it in 1965.

Basically, it was a western extension, an upgraded merger of several old east-west roads that connected the population centers of Korat and Ubon with the Thai-Laotian border region. The road, a 380-mile, modern, all-weather highway, ran through several bucolic villages where bicycle and ox drawn cart were the common modes of transport, and linked the northernmost Isaan cities with the central plain and Bangkok, the national capital and seat of power.

Although the trip from Korat to Phanom Sarakham was a hop, skip, and jump for crows, it was for us an easy 200-mile journey. The empty haul to the switching station was a no-problem piece of cake, but the next day on-the-job training return haul was anything but a joy-ride.

Twice I climbed intersection curbs while making turns. But at Nakhon Nayok I was wholly unable to maneuver the traffic-circle in the center of town. I literally parked the truck inches away from sideswiping an iconic fountain statue-hero. Lloyd alertly parked his own vehicle and came to my rescue.

At that point we made the practical decision. We jointly declared, "Fuck Bolt and Fuck The Army," then switched trucks.

About Face

So, now you should understand why I'd just about had it with Sergeant Bolt's power trips. On top of that, I was deep into one of those mornings when you just didn't want to hear anything from anybody. Period. We've all been there.

After echelon maintenance, while the Thai drivers mingled around the yard, we, American drivers stood in a second formation near the motor pool gate and guard shed awaiting instructions concerning a special convoy. Lieutenant English gave the command of relief saying, "Okay, men, stand-at-ease and smoke-'em-if-you've-got-'em." He then turned to Lieutenant French and the two officers huddled to make a decision on a matter in which they'd been unable to reach agreement.

The smoke order allowed me to break rank and walk to the edge of the formation where I lit-up with half the other American soldiers. As I smoked the cigarette with my right hand, I unconsciously jingled loose change in my left front fatigue pant pocket with the other. I had taken about four drags when Bolt shouted, "Fall-in!"

I clipped and extinguished the amber tip and put the unsmoked portion back into my cigarette pack. Still jingling the coins in my pocket, I moved to rejoin the formation. Bolt's voice rang out, "Soldier, remove your hand from your pocket and look sharp!"

I ignored him but ceased to jingle the loose change.

"Private Forest, I repeat, take your hand out of your pocket or I will file a charge of insubordination against you!"

I knew he had me and that I should simply remove my hand from the pocket. But once I had ceased the noisy distraction, what was the point? Power? A fight? Well, then to hell with the fascist Uniform Code of Military Justice! I felt like fighting.

Knowing many eyes of both my fellows-in-arms and the Thai drivers were upon me I mumbled, "Insubordinate this." I then shoved my right hand into its coordinating front pocket and stared into his eyes.

There was an audible murmur among the troops as he glared back then shouted, "A-ten-hut! That brought the formation to order. He made a sharp and snappy about face and waited for the end to the French and English conference. Then he filed his charge.

When Lt. English addressed the formation he announced, "We will convoy in two groups. The first group will be members of the first and second platoon and will depart with Sergeant Wardell and Lieutenant French. Sergeant Bolt and I will lead the third and fourth platoons. For the sake of highway safety and traffic flow, we will depart twenty minutes after the first group. Are there any questions?"

There were none. So he continued, "Company dismissed to your vehicles. Private Forest—."

★★★

Two days later, upon my return from convoy I was summoned into Lieutenant Fisher's office. He first listened to my point-of-view and then said, "Ultimately my only desire is for company harmony and to make the best of an untidy situation. You understand my hands are tied. Your insubordinate behavior dictates I assess an Article 15."

"Yes, sir."

"Very well then. In order to resolve this unfortunate incident and make the best of it, I offer a fine of twenty-five dollars or one-month loss of off-duty privileges. That would mean your off-duty confinement to post."

"Yes, sir."

Resigned and wanting to make the best of it, I opted to pay the ticket via 1-month payroll deduction!

G.T. Foster

May Day Goldbrick

Although the responsibility was solely mine, I was, nonetheless, thoroughly pissed. So, on May 15th, as Rien backed-up to hitch the fifth-wheel to an empty cargo trailer, in an act of goldbricking defiance, I intentionally left my only pair of government-issued, corrective prescription glasses on the ground beneath the dual-wheels of our assigned five-ton Kaiser Motor Works tractor. Since both my civilian and military driver's license stipulate: MUST WEAR CORRECTIVE LENSES, the powers that be weren't going to be happy with the situation but as it was, they were SOL (Severely-Out-of-Luck) and up the proverbial creek without the implements to navigate.

I reported my accident. It brought immediate relief. I was removed from the day's duty roster, and sent to the base clinic to arrange for a replacement pair of eye-glasses. As I sat across the desk from him, the medical officer examined my records. Then to my delight he said, "Unfortunately, it will be a while."

"Oh, really?"

"Oh, yes."

"How long?"

"How long?" he repeated. "Why, I would say, our best common practice has been five or six weeks."

"Why so long?"

"Well, it's mostly a supply problem. We lack any in-country replacement facilities. The closest available optometry services are in the Philippines. It is just a matter of course. Plan on a six-week wait."

Six weeks? Off the road? Days in the motor pool, nights in town. Why not? I hadn't actually planned on such a long term of protest. But now? Well, the dye was cast.

However, after two weeks of no-haul and hanging around the motor pool greasing fifth-wheels and fixing flats, my face became a bit too familiar. I was ordered by Lt. Fisher to purchase a pair of prescription eyeglasses in the downtown Korat marketplace, immediately.

After my eye examination, I ordered a pair of black-framed glasses.

"*Waen tah sai?*" asked the Thai optometrist.

"*See dum, kor see dum,*" Black, I want black, I had told him in choosing the frame color.

"*Koon tong karn waen tah see dum?*" He double-checked.

"*Chai si, krap. See dum,*" I said. Yes, sir, black."

When they arrived a week later, it was clear I had not understood all the optometrist had asked. The prescription eyeglasses were dark black lenses in a black frame. Night visibility was poor and night-driving difficult, but I was back on line and in the sights of Sergeant Bolt and his personal quest to make our company a spit-and-shiner.

G.T. Foster

A Swelling Edema

The company's young officer corps began to enthusiastically echo Sergeant Bolt's constant calls for discipline and a more garrison-mannered behavior from company members. One hot and muggy mid-day, pulling empty trailers to Camp Charoen Sinthrope, four of us American drivers — recently arrived Private Pride, a young black draftee from North Carolina; Private Johnson; Green; and me – along with our co-drivers, had stopped at the roadside diner in Sri Nakon Ayutthaya.

Pride, the new troop, was properly dressed in an olive drab green fatigue shirt. Although we all wore fatigue trousers, Johnson, Green, and I wore only our sweat-soaked olive-green T-shirts. Our long sleeve shirts were in the truck cabs. We sat at tables awaiting our ordered meals when Lieutenant French and Specialist Ruffin, his jeep driver, returning from Bangkok, parked and entered the diner.

My back was to them, so I did not immediately record their arrival, but the new trooper quickly rose and shouted, "A-ten-hut!"

No one else rose. I swiveled and turned around but remained seated. The lieutenant scanned the table and responded, "As you were." He paused briefly, then continued. "Specialist Green, you, Private Forest, and Private Johnson are out of uniform."

"Yes, sir. Boy, but it's hot, sir."

"For all of us, Specialist, for all of us. And yet, shirts are to be worn and tucked. The uniform must clearly display the

162

soldier's name tag and rank. It is not my policy, soldiers. It's army policy."

"Yes, sir.

"Yes, sir.

"Yes, sir."

"Then see to it, gentlemen. Another violation will result in Article 15 charges."

"Yes, sir. I'll go. No, no. Don't get up. I'll get them all," said Green.

"Mine is on the seat."

"Mine is draped over the seat," I said.

"Got it. Tell Mama-san to keep my plate warm."

We were standing in ranks but fully expected to be dismissed and perform the morning police-call litter walk of the yard. Normally, day-to-day management of the motor pool and drivers was left to the junior staff officers, specifically Lieutenants French and English. Perhaps, to show that he was fully on-board the spit-and-polish crackdown, Lieutenant Fisher made a rare appearance and addressed the morning formation.

"A-ten-hut!" shouted Bolt and we snapped into an attentive stance.

Fisher stepped to the head of the formation and spoke. "Stand-at-ease, men. Gentlemen, it has been brought to my attention that many of you are making a habit of leaving camp in the evening without signing in and out. This must stop."

There were audible groans of disapproval.

"Immediately!" He paused for effect. Then continued, "Many of you are failing to fill-out or get the proper signatures on bills of lading. Now, men every load has a bill of lading. That paper work identifies items, destination, and quantity. This is important information that must be accounted for. I stand before you to remind, but, also, to warn.

Continued failure to properly handle cargoes will result in immediate discipline."

Again, groans, but more quietly.

"And the last thing I must address is the failure to make morning formations. I am told some of you are being lax. The only accepted reasons to miss first formation is either sick-call or a later than 1600 hour previous-day return. These are battalion-wide policies. No other excuse will be tolerated. That is all, men. Sergeant."

Fisher turned to Bolt who snapped and held a salute. The lieutenant said something to Bolt, took another step, turned to face us, and stood silently.

"Company dismissed," Bolt said. "Private Forest, one moment, please."

Surprised, I stood in place as the formation broke and my fellows-in-arms gave me one darting eye of curiosity after another. Then both Sergeant Bolt and Lieutenant Fisher approached. I stood at full attention. Fisher, standing directly before me, moved his face into space that had not been occupied since Basic Training and ordered, "Soldier, remove those sunglasses so I can see your eyes!"

"These are not sunglasses, sir." I made no motion to remove them, but instead held attention, staring straight ahead. "They are prescription, sir. I am legally blind without them."

"You were ordered to purchase eye-glasses."

"I did, sir. I'm still waiting. They're coming from the Philippines, sir"

"Did I not order you to purchase a pair in downtown Korat?"

"You did, sir. I did, sir."

"And . . . ?"

"And there was a mistake, sir."

"A mistake?"

"Yes, sir. A mix-up; a miscommunication, sir."

The Boys Are Not Refined

"A miscommunication as you say?"
"Yes, sir. The optometrist made me these."
"Those?"
"Yes, sir. These.
"Well . . . those other glasses had better hurry up."
"Yes, sir."

G.T. Foster

Death by Friendly Fire

From the small, elevated band stage, a female in sultry voice sang the Thai version of *Sukiyaki* as though she bemoaned a soldier/lover who had gone far away. A drum, two guitars, and bass quartet provided musical support. We were sitting around tables in the Lucky Seven Club drinking beer from the bottles.

Madson reminisced, "When I was here befo' nobody fucked wit' yah. Long as yah pulled yo' weight and didn't kill nobody on the road dey just let yah drive. Now, dey got dey little peep-squeaks watchin' and reportin' yo' ebery move."

"Did you sign-out tonight?" I sarcastically asked.

"Dat's what I mean. Fuck Bolt! And yeah, I done fuckin' signed-out.

"Fuck Bolt, I didn't sign-out. If he says anything I'm going to say, 'Prove it'."

"That's how it's different, man. Tacky shit. Shit, man . . . I 'memba we was goin' up teh Udon befo dey built deh camp at Khon Khan. Well, dis brotha had bought dese chickens from dis farma. We had us a fire goin'. Water was boilin' so we could dip dem chickens in and pluck deys feathers. And da brotha had started in the wringin' deys necks."

"Goddamn!" exclaimed Wellington, as he apparently visualized a wholly unfamiliar scene.

"He done wrung two of 'em and dey was runnin' round and bleedin'. We was rollin'. Some of deh guys ain't neber seed no chicken runnin' 'round wit dey heads cut-off befo'. Well, Forest, up walks dis young, ofay Luey—wadn't even in our compney. Talkin' 'bout, 'Soja, I hab' watched ya'll kilt dem chickens and iffin' ya'll wring anotha onna dose animal's necks, I will hab yeh up on charges!'

"Well, de brotha just stood dere for a shoat minute, holdin' one a dem chickens. He just massagin' its neck, frownin', and registerin' in his mind what dis Luey done said. Den yah could see da light go on. And he smiled real wide, den opened his mouth wide open and put dat chicken's head in it. Brother didn't take his eyes off the Luey and just bit it off, den spit it out on da lieutenant's chest. Dat white boy turnt green, and started pukin—"

"Jeez Cripes, that musta been a crazy brotha," said Lloyd.

"You shittin' me?" I asked with my face in full-grin.

"If I's lyin' I's flyin' and I ain't got me no wings. We ain't neber seed dat ofay no mo'. We laughed. Boy, we laughed. And dat sho nuf was some good eatin' chicken. Dat brotha knowd what he was doin'."

"I'm going to go downtown, buy me a few little chicks and put them in that empty tiger cage. First time French or English come up to me says I can't do this, or I can't do that, I'm going to bite a live chicken neck in his face. I hope he just had his dinner," said Wellington in what I took for only half-jest.

Still chuckling from Madson's tale I turned to Green, noticed a contemplative look on his face. He seemed to temporarily have left the bar to visit some distant muse.

"Hey, man, what's up?" I asked. "Where are you, man? You still here with us, or are you back home somewhere in Oklahoma?"

"I was sittin' here thinking of war," Green said, gnawing a toothpick. "You ever think about the opportunities to get rid of an ally?"

"Jesus, man. That's dark," I said.

"Well, have you?"

"Well, if I'm honest, I guess I have."

"How can you not have thought about it? Hell, Nod's always talkin' about fixing problems with people. *Kaa mong! Kaa mong twenty dolla!*" said Bryson, laughing.

"I read this book once . . . Norman Mailer. *The Naked and the Dead*. You ever read that?" asked Green.

"Nah, I haven't read it. I think it was a best seller. Been meaning to, but nah, never read it."

"Me neither," said Bryson.

"Hey, that ain't my bag. I never was into that. Just throw me a high hard one and stand back and watch. That's me," said Lloyd in a literacy denial.

Undeterred, Green continued, "Well, there's this general. He turns out to be prejudiced against this captain or lieutenant. I think the guy was a Jew."

"A Jew? What's the difference?" asked Lloyd.

"I don't know, man, but that ain't the point."

"They are all circumcised!" I said.

"If he's got foreskin on his dick, he ain't no Jew," observed Bryson.

"Oh, yeah?"

"Guaranteed."

"I'm circumcised," announced Wellington.

"Are you a Jew?" asked Bryson.

"No."

"I didn't think so."

"Anyway," said Green, shaking his head but smiling, "the general sends this captain on a mission knowing it's impossible, figuring the captain wouldn't survive. And he didn't."

"That's cold, man," said Lloyd.

"That's some cold-blooded shit," said Bryson.

"Hey, that's kinda like in the Bible with David and Cleopat — no, no, I mean David and Bathsheba," I self-corrected. "David sent her husband, what was his name?"

"Uriah," said Bryson, causing all eyes to turn to him in silent surprise.

"Yeah, that's right Bry, Uriah. David ordered his commander to send Uriah to attack a heavily fortified city and then withdraw all support, leaving poor Uriah alone to the fatal consequence."

"But, why did he do that?" asked Wellington.

"Come on, man. He was banging the man's wife! Don't you read the Bible?" asked Bryson.

"Yeah, but I ain't never read the whole thang."

"Hell, they made a Gregory Peck movie out of it."

"Well, I didn't see it."

"I saw it. It was good," I said.

"I don't know why you are thinking about that stuff in the first place." Lloyd said.

"He was talking about flushing friendly problems down the drain," said Bryson.

"I'll name you one friendly nuisance I'd like to wave a wand at," I said.

"If you mean that Sergeant Bolt you guys are always complaining about," advised Bryson, "don't let him get to you, Forest. I told you, *Kaa mong, kaa mong*! Tell Luckie's little brother, Nod. He's always claiming to have friends who are . . . what's the word?" He snapped his fingers trying to remember. "*Muu-bun,* gunmen! Nod claims they belong to the Thai-Mafia."

"*Nuk-lang*: dats deh Thai name fo' deh mafia," Madson informed. "Green, ya wanna put a hit on da Sarge?"

"Nay, I wasn't thinking about that jerk. He wouldn't be worth spending $5. But you know what? Maybe I was. It's related. I was thinking about when we were in 'Nam and this one black lieutenant--"

"You guys had a black lieutenant?"

"Well, he wasn't in our company. Plus, he had come up through the ranks."

"Lieutenant Kitchen!" declared Bryson. He leaned forward, pulled a copy of a Jet magazine from his rear pocket and slid it into the middle of the table around which we sat. "It is from my sister in Seattle. I got it in today's Mail Call. Did you serve under him?"

"Only for a hot minute on this one detail. Bolt claims that he and Kitchens served together as NCOs in Germany." He paused for a moment then continued, "My wife sent me this and I got it in today's mail." He, too, stood and pulled a copy of the same April 4, 1968 Jet issue from his rear pocket and flipped it onto the table.

"If that's true then why is he such a Tom?"

"When I mentioned it to him, he accused me of threatening him. Can you dig that?"

"According to the article, they still don't know if it was a landmine like the Army says or a bullet to the back of the head," said Bryson.

"You doubt what it was?"

"Not for a minute. You?"

"Nah.

"Hell, nah!"

"Double-hell-nah!

An Odd Couple

Luckie's younger brother, Nod, was rumored to be a member or closely connected to the Thai Mafia, commonly known as the *Nuk Lang*. He had once presented an open offer to rid the company of Sergeant Bolt for $20 in US currency. He operated a small storefront in downtown Korat selling transistor radios, electronic devices, contraband Falling Rain packaged marijuana cigarettes, and anything else that passed through his hands, including, no doubt, many of the items Luckie received from the base PX as gifts or favors.

Henshaw, the company poet, had been medically removed from the driver's roster due to a severe hemorrhoid condition. He was reassigned as an assistant supply clerk. Most evenings found him at the closed Royal Bar; he and Nod quickly connected as a fellow travelers who smoked marijuana but preferred the harder drugs. Some company stockroom items could also be purchased from the shelves of Nod's storefront.

On one occasion Cak and Nod had taken several American GIs, Henshaw included, to a big Muay Thai boxing match at a gymnasium in downtown Korat. The match was both amazingly beautiful and brutal. A three-piece ensemble frenetically played Java pipe, cymbals, and drums. The music both mocked the action within the ring and intensified the adrenaline blood rush of all present.

We watched ringed pugilist compete following rules different than any we, as Americans had encountered. More like our street fights, it is boxing as a Thai art form and allows kicking, head butts, hitting below the belt, and unrestricted use of elbows and knees. The only thing similar between the competitive forms as practiced in America and Thailand is that unstopped bleeding ends the bout in a TKO.

To repeat an often-quoted critic of Muay Thai boxing, "It was enough to cause the Marquis of Queensbury to somersault in his grave!" But in the middle of all the action and shouts of encouragement from the many gambling happy Thai men and women present, both Henshaw and Nod sat quietly in their seats, nodding off the effects of their smack highs.

But despite the drugs, Henshaw was generally sharp as the proverbial tack. For example, one Sunday, all dressed in civvies, we took a two-hour train ride east to Surin—Green, Lloyd, Madson, Henshaw, Nod, and me. It was a kind of pleasure-sightsee-business trip. The train was straight out of the Hollywood of cowboy times. Clattering clackety-clack on steel wheels that vibrated over every gap between the track's iron rails, the box car coil springs produced a shimmery bounce constant enough to turn fresh milk to butter.

In Surin we became a special sight for the unsure eyes of local residents. The people were obviously not used to seeing black men and the children seemed never to have seen any man as tall as the 6'2" Madson. And to double the surprise, he spoke Thai! In answer to his question concerning the location of our destination, the children gave directions then followed him down the street in chattering awe.

The day's business belonged to Henshaw and Nod. They were to meet with a French art dealer in an out-door restaurant. The art dealer spotted us upon our arrival, waved us over to his table, then greeted and seated us. Green, Lloyd, Madson, and I sat at an adjacent table, drank cold Singhas, and watched the action.

"I'm sorry, but my English is not as good as I would like."

"Neither is my French," said Henshaw, "so forget about it. Speak Thai if you like. My madman friend will help me keep up." He moved his head toward Madson.

"No, I think English is best," the dealer nodded to Nod. Alright with you, Nod?"

"*Chaisi, krap*. You see? You look?" asked Nod, straight to the point of our visit.

"Yes, I examined the piece. Fantastic. It's Khmer. Where did you say the lintel came?"

"I no say."

"Go ahead, tell him, Nod. It's important. He has to establish provenance," said Henshaw.

"Oh, I see you understand. That makes it . . . easier."

"Yeah, I understand. Even if it's a hack and snatch you still have to establish the object's legitimacy; Art History 101. No one wants a fake."

"Fake? *Plom? Mai bpen plom!*"

"Oh, no, Nod. I know. An antiquity. But from where?"

"Nong Hong. But wat abandon, no use," said Nod.

The art dealer nodded and smiled knowingly, then asked Henshaw, "So, my friend, how do you intend to move it?"

"I have the custom stamps and Nod can get the Thai shipping licenses." Henshaw looked to Nod who shook his head in affirmation. Henshaw continued, "We ship on the 15th. All we need is the agreed payment and the address of the auction house where you want it delivered."

The Frenchman pushed an envelope to Henshaw. Henshaw picked up the envelope, stood and without counting, pocketed it. "The balance you pay Nod upon shipment."

"Agreed."

We all rose. Nod and Henshaw shook hands with the dealer, and we left. The art dealer sat back down, apparently, to dine.

It had been an interesting exchange. The only question it had left me with I asked Henshaw on the return ride to Korat. "How can you guarantee an exact shipping date on something, on . . . on anything?"

He laughed, "That's the easy part. On the 15th of every month a C-130 leaves the air force base carrying personal cargo of rotating military personnel back to the good ole USA. We will just tag and ship our load along with everyone else."

The Boys Are Not Refined

Cak's Wild Ride

It was the early evening of the last night in May. Madson, Lloyd, Bryson and I were at the closed Royal Bar. Luckie, her husband Pichai, and Cak were also present. We were smoking *ganchaa* through a water pipe and had all reached a very high state of "highness." In fact, I was personally deeply spaced and nearly passed-out when word reached the compound that Nod, who had escorted Henshaw to Korat in order to score, was, at that very moment, engaged in a street fight in the downtown marketplace.

Besides being Luckie's brother, Nod was Cak's closest friend. Upon hearing the news Cak, naked above the waist except for his broad gold chain with its multiple Buddha icons, jumped to his feet and rushed outside to his motorcycle. Still barefoot, he mounted his Kawasaki W2 650SS and roared away on the dirt path leading to Paktagchai Road (Camp Friendship Road). He left Madson, Lloyd, Bryson, and Luckie who had followed him outside, in a cloud of dust.

Cak reached the paved blacktop surface of Paktagchai Road and made an unhesitating northbound hard-left merge onto it. Failing to check, he never saw the logging truck on his right also heading hurriedly north on Paktagchai Road. The truck was moving about 55 miles-per-hour. The driver attempted to brake but his vision of Cak had come too late. The impact knocked Cak from his bike and hurled him several feet in the air. When he crashed to earth his body rolled, skidded, and scraped across the pavement before coming to a crumpled rest.

I was slow to rise from my stupor, but Bryson and the others had watched the entire event unfold. Having seen the crash that ended Cak's mad dash to aid Nod, they now ran quickly to the roadside. As they ran, they could already hear the chant-like murmuring.

Neighboring death-watchers had also heard the crash and gathered into a sizable crowd. They stood in small packs on both sides of the road and spoke in quiet voices using low pitch and register. It produced an *Ohm*-like sound of a repeated mantra, but they were only asking the customary questions of each other:

"Do you think he'll get up?"

"Good lord Buddha, I don't think so."

"Do you know him?"

"I know the family."

"He works at the American base."

"Nice motorcycle."

This was the essence of those deathwatch conversations. Only, spoken in Thai, the dialogues sounded strange and mystifying. It had begun with the first two of the death-watchers to reach the scene and would continue endlessly until . . .

We, American drivers, were all too familiar with death on Thai highways and the chant-like muffled sound of the gathering crowd's fatalistic and watchful chatter. No one was going to move to help! Not even Luckie moved to give aid or comfort.

This realization seemed to occur to both Bryson and Lloyd at the same time. They looked at each other and then with due diligence for their own safety made their way across the road to Cak, who lay moaning and bleeding. He had an obviously broken right leg. His left wrist and shoulder were apparently separated. The wrist hung from its forearm at a grotesquely odd angle. His whole body seemed fractured and bent.

In the meantime, Pichai, Luckie's husband, had appeared. He picked Cak's golden chain of protective and fortune-bearing Buddhas from the dirt along the road where they had landed. He held them up to his face at eye level and while inspecting them pronounced to no one in particular, "*Bung-ti, mai dii.* Maybe, no good."

While Madson and Bryson stood in the road to caution traffic and hail a taxi, Lloyd tried to tend and comfort Cak, who, although very badly hurt, remained conscious. A taxi stopped and as the stunned-faced driver and crowd of death-watchers looked on, Cak was lifted onto the car's rear seat. Lloyd sat in the back with Cak's head resting in his lap. Bryson joined the driver in the front seat. Madson squeezed into the rear with Cak and Lloyd.

They took Cak to the base hospital at Camp Friendship. Despite their best efforts, the severity of the injuries seemed to panic the Admissions Officer. Although Cak was an employee of the US government, the officer used technicalities to deny admission or treatment. "Did the accident occur on base property?"

"No. It happened, just now, on Paktagchai Road."

"Oh, sorry, but that won't help. But did it occur during work hours?"

"No. I said it just happened . . . minutes ago."

"No? Oh," he said in a disappointed tone. "No, no, but I'm so sorry."

It was never a question of injuries, anything but. Had Cak in fact been less injured—"We would be happy to bend the rules a little and help out," the Admissions Officer had admitted. It probably helped him swallow his own guilt, but he did not relent.

"But it would be a real mess and a nightmare of paperwork if he were to die on us. Look at him. Just look at him. He doesn't look too good. I'm sorry, my final answer is unequivocally no! Your best bet is to get him downtown to the Common Hospital. They will at least be able to give him something for his pain."

Out of options, they took Cak and his great pain and suffering to the downtown Common Hospital in Korat. Although gravely injured, he was admitted to the hospital.

The Boys Are Not Refined

He's Gone, Man

The second week of June the tail-end of a Southwest monsoon from the Indian Ocean swept inland and its headwind produced a news-release: "Henshaw has left the house," said Green.

"Hey, man, cool that," warned Ruffin.

"Loose lips sink ships," said Bryson, who had just come from his next-door barracks.

"It's okay. It ain't no secret," said Lloyd.

"Yeah, man, it's out of the bag. The staff sergeant made a comment and the Luey had to come clean. He has been placed on the official Absent-Without-Leave roster," said Green.

"Took the fucks long enough. His last poem was posted on his wall locker over a week ago. Green's got it," Lloyd said.

"Read it, Green."

"Shoot, Henshaw is in Laos by now. On his way to Kathmandu and horse heaven," said Lloyd.

"That's fucked," I bemoaned.

"Why do you care? Henshaw didn't give a shit," snapped Ruffin.

"Look, I just like the guy, that's all!"

"He's been on shit since 'Nam and he wasn't going back home," said Green.

"And he wasn't going to be without his horse. So, fuck it. That was the brother's choice," concluded Lloyd.

"Preach man. Teach. Read the poem, Green," Ruffin demanded.

"There are two of them," Green responded. He stepped to the end of his bunk, bent and opened his footlocker and withdrew the poems. "One he called 'These Sir What Are These.' The other is a little trippy piece he wrote about a banana, but I think he was talking about himself. He called it 'Banana Just Up and Split.' Which one ya'll want me to read?"

"Read 'em both."

"Hell yeah, read 'em both," I chimed.

"Nah, here Forest, you read one." Green handed me the banana poem and I quickly scanned the page. It was trippy.

"I'll read first," he said and began to read:

These Sir What Are These

Pvt. Moody,
Odysseus remembered
to smell the roses
Yes, sir, no, sir, three bags full, sir
A Saigon World of helicopter swirl
even in Bangkok
Sir, this cargo;
To what ship do I haul?
These bombs, sir
Is the whole consignment
for the base at Takli?
And those, sir,
what are those?
972 mines? that's funny,
My friend worked at station
number 972 in Berkeley
Sir, and those, sir
the big black barrel
with bright orange painted rings
Agent, sir? In English,
what kind of an agent, sir?

Road kill, movement stilled
must make traffic circle
by three or hell to pay

Lieutenant, captain
major hell to pay
Tie me to the mast
that I might hear the sirens play
Which jungle, sir?
Which jungle?"

There was a full beat of wordless quiet, then Bryson said it best, "Damn! Man, that Henshaw was far out."

"No shit!"

"Wait, wait a minute. Read the other one, Forest," directed Green.

I read, "Banana Just Up and Split by Private Henshaw."

Banana
rejecting a destiny buried
beneath fluffy dual whipped toppings
capped with a scarlet cherry and the pink stain
of a slain virgin under three
soft cream chosen frozen mounds
surrounded by stagnate streams
dripping flows of chocolate
caramel strawberry in syrupy cesspool
bunches of salty nuts in sweet
gooey crap world that eats cowards for dessert
split!

Casting fortune to blind luck
it became a chameleon
of its own slippery fantasy
walking along the least traveled fork
where the din of cars and people end
and a lone bird sang
Spying a smashed flower on the sidewalk
it froze betrayed by fear
for well it knew whether barefoot or shod
the smallest of humans would leave but mush

Yet casting its vision beyond the fork produced a thaw
Behold; a field painted in a rainbow tapestry
of wild flowers
Home and free to be
Perhaps here a song.

"Man, you're right, Henshaw was thinking about it the whole time."
"The poem is so obvious. The brother was already gone."
"The brother's been gone!"
"What about his family?" I asked.
"What about them?"
"Hey, I guess—"
"That relationship is dead, been dead."
"Well, I'll just stick to my weed."
"Me too. Just give me some grass to roll in."
"Right-on to that. Good old *ganchaa!*"
"Yeah, good old weed."

What Time Is It?

Between storms, a June afternoon sunbeam seemed to have dropped a strange cargo from the skies over Korat. "Check it out," said Green.

We had dodged driving assignments and were in the motor pool sheltered area killing the remainder of duty-hours. I spotted him entering the motor pool. He was new and young and walked in a kind of slow, practiced, bobbing-head, pimp swagger.

As he approached, he balled the fingers of his right hand into a fist, bent his elbow, raised his fisted hand and said, "Power, Brother. What time is it?"

I checked my wrist watch, made a quick military conversion and said, "In another ten minutes it will be 1400 hours, Brother."

"Nah, Brother. It's Nation time!"

"Nation time? What's that supposed to mean?" asked Green.

"It means, Brothers need to unite and work together."

"Nation time, huh? That's good. I'm Forest—"

"I get it. But that's kind of lame," said a frowning Wellington in a rather unfriendly tone.

" . . . Nigel Forest. This is Wellington, Madson, Green, and Lloyd."

"My name is William Childs. Friends back home in Chi-town call me Billy the Kid, ha, ha. You can call me Will or Billy or Childs or whatever. Just don't treat me like a kid. Ha, ha, ha. You get it?"

"You from Chicago," I asked?

"Does a tree have leaves?" he cracked.

"Dang, Bro. First thang dey gonna make yeh do, Bleed, is getta haircut," noted Madson.

"Yeah, dude, you tell them it's Nation Time and they gonna tell you it's barber time," said Wellington.

"They ain't fuckin' with me. I told 'em, 'Assign me in my MOS and I get a haircut.' They ain't done it, so I ain't had no haircut. Fuck it. I'm not here long. I'm leavin' this place soon as my general comes down."

"General?"

"General Court-martial?"

"Nah, Brother mine. It's a general discharge. I get it? Boom!" he snapped his right thumb and middle finger. "I'm back home in Chi-town. Hell, I get my papers, I'll get a haircut. Ha, ha, ha." He looked around the yard then said, "I'm supposed to be part of a pit crew. What the hell is that?"

"Repairs. You gonna work in the shop . . . and make mechanical repairs. I think? Hell, I don't know. I'm a driver," I said wanting to help the kid.

Lloyd pointed and said, "Look there. See those rectangular holes in the cement flo'? Dat's a pit. It's designed fo' inspection and repair to the truck's undercarriage."

"Undercarriage? Man, they ain't trained me for none of that. I ain't no grease monkey!"

"Tell it to the Chaplain! Or the duty-sergeant. He's in the dispatch room." informed Green. He took the current toothpick from his mouth, bit a small tip, blew it to the wind and return the remainder to his gnawing teeth.

"Alright, Brother mine. Power." Childs again made his fisted sign, then strutted off to the Dispatch Office. We watched in silence, struck dumb by the audaciousness of youth.

Billy Childs

That evening after chow, a group of us were flapping our gums in the yard area between the barracks and laundry shack. As Childs descended the barrack stairs, Wellington walked to the bottom step and extended his hand to the new arrival in a gesture of friendship.

"Hi. My name is Lark Wellington. We didn't really meet."

Billy reached as if to accept the gesture of welcome then jerked back his hand, leaving Wellington hanging. Billy then shook his head as if to say, *"No, no, no."* But he smiled and said, "Ain't nutin' no monkey man like you can do for me but bring me a Chi-town woman." Then he broke into a giggling kind of laughter and said, "Just kidding, man, just kidding. I'm Billy Childs." He re-extended his hand and Wellington took it. "What time is it?" he asked Wellington, still shaking his hand.

"Dang!" replied a stumped Wellington. "What you supposed to say?"

"You supposed to say 'Its Nation time'," cued Green.

"Right," remembered Wellington. "It's Nation time."

"Right-on, brother. Where you from?" asked the new troop.

"Spokane."

"Spokane? Where the hell is Spokane? Or better yet, where the hell is anywhere that ain't Chi-town?" He was young and brash but basically harmless, unless you took offense at not being from Chicago. "Well, don't nobody get too comfortable with me being around. I don't intend to stay... see? I'm getting' me a general as soon as the paperwork is all approved. Hey, I'm just here for the waiting," Private Childs re-announced.

"That's cool," said Green. "You said all that this afternoon. We's all just killin' time. How long you been in, Young Blood?"

"Me? Too long. Eleven-months too long. Not good. I came in just before my seventeenth birthday. My parents had to sign for me to join."

"Why the hell you join?" asked Wellington.

"Hell, I thought I'd like it. I got two older brothers, both of 'em serving. One in the army, one in the navy, but it ain't my cup-of-tea. No, it ain't for everybody."

"Damn, you sound like Bolt."

"Who's Bolt?"

"Our Oreo-cookie-ass duty-sergeant. You didn't meet him this afternoon in the motor pool? I'm afraid you will soon cross swords with that bootlickin', garrison, by-the-book jerk!" warned Green.

"Yeah, and he's gonna want you to get a haircut," added Wellington.

"Yeah? Well, wanting ain't getting."

Wellington and Childs began hanging out together and became an inseparable odd couple, daring each other again and again with an "I bet you wouldn't," or an "I bet you won't." One was stupid because he was young, the other, Wellington, was just stupid.

Childs, single with no dependents, had been born and raised in Chicago, Illinois, and had completed tenth-grade, dropped out of school, worked as an assistant to the assistant foreman in a dressmaking and design shop prior to his enlistment. Now, he wanted out.

"My MOS (Military Occupational Skill) is assistant supply clerk. But they transferred me from my unit in Kansas to Thailand after they gave me an Article 15 for three weeks absence-without-leave." (From day one, that was his constant explanation of his perpetual lack of funds. "Hey, Bro, could you let me hold a ten spot? They're deducting an Article 15 from my pay.")

Meanwhile, he insisted, "But I ain't no truck driver. They didn't give me new training. I never got no mechanical training. But now they telling me to work in the motor pool? Nah, man, I'm getting out. I've already signed my papers. But I'm going to keep on protesting to Battalion. They can't make me do this!"

G.T. Foster

Bridging the Gap

Throughout the month of June, in a fit of army gloom, I felt myself beginning to mark time. And you know what they say about the watched pot. Calendar days lost their meaning. Each was just another sweaty, hot day to be followed by another just as swelteringly hot. Each day pulled a prayer from my soul begging both God and Buddha to spare tomorrow from being as hellishly hot and unbearably muggy.

Otherwise, each rise and set of the sun was just another turned page in the monthly book of days. True-time, time memorialized, is marked by special events or something of note that occurred. When Madson announced, "Dey done kilt Robert Kennedy," I said, "Oh, well, if we're not safe, am I supposed to cry? Didn't they just kill the Right Honorable Doctor Martin Luther King, Jr.? Why should they be safe? Why should anyone be safe?"

From the beginning of the American presence in Thailand, the army switching station at Camp Charn Sinthrope, two and one-half miles from the squatters' hamlet of Phanom Sarakham, had been a key supply link and remained the 21st Transportation Company's main haul within the 19th Battalion mission to efficiently shuttle cargo from the Port of Sattahip to the eight air force bases under American lease.

Until June, Rien and I had made the journey alone or in tandem with one or two other driving teams and would

The Boys Are Not Refined

usually spend the evening across from the camp in Sombaht's home. Three events color my memory of that Thai June: first, the late May-June monsoon revealed a Thai delicacy.

Camp Charn Sinthrope was surrounded by chain link fence and coiled razor wire. Its perimeter floodlights, mounted high on tall telephone poles, made bright the night. Just beyond the motor pool fence and entry gate of Camp Charn Sinthrope, an enterprising Thai had constructed a refreshment stand. In order to conduct his business beyond daylight and gleam profit from evening traffic, a series of bright, white light bulbs were hung to encircle the top and illuminate the stand.

One twilight evening after the camp perimeter floodlights were turned on a sudden downpour began. In the middle of the heavy rains, giant winged water bugs, moth-like, began to fly to the bright lights. Tens of dozens, drawn to the floodlights, swarmed and hovered high in the air until driven by either exhaustion or wet wings, they fell crashing to earth, stunned but alive.

From nowhere three young Thai boys appeared. Each carried a bucket. The three boys rushed back and forth gathering the bugs. Although it was a warm monsoon shower, in anticipation, some men had built small campfires before the boys finished collecting the harvest. The boys then walked among the drivers hawking their goods. *"Haa baht, haa baht! Yaak mai? Haa baht!"*

Called *mang-da*, they were offered at 5 *baht* or twenty-five cents each. The entire catch was quickly purchased by the drivers as a stolen bargain. Some men ate the *mang-da* fresh-out-the-bucket. They merely plucked the wings and pincer legs and popped the rest into the old pie-hole. Others impaled the critters onto sticks and roasted them over the hastily constructed fire before consumption.

One of the boys, having sold Rien four of the seasonal snacks turned to me. "GI want *mang-da*? I give free to American GI! GI want?"

"No thank you. It is very kind of you to offer, but still, no thank you. *Mai ao nai, krap*"

There is another *mang-da* in Thai culture called a *mang-da song ka* or a two-legged *mang-da*. This is the term Thais have given to pimps and traffickers of human flesh.

Although no one was shocked by my pass on a serving of water bug, Thais were often offended, even pained, by the open refusal of many GIs to engage in Thai culture. Wanting to be the good guest often took me far afield and to places few of my fellow Americans dared travel.

★★★

"*Gin, gin,*" insisted Rien as he passed me the platter. Although the entre had apparently been steamed in preparation, it now sat alone, trembling on the dish, shaking like white Jell-O. Not Caucasian pink-white but white like a Spanish doily.

"*Bpen arai?*" I asked Rien. (What is it?) We were seated on the floor of an unfamiliar home, that of Sombaht's nearest neighbor, Achit, whom I had only met that evening.

"*Mai bpen arai. Gin, gin.*" (It doesn't matter. Eat, eat.)
"*Gin, gin,* Forest, *krap. Mii mak-mak bpan-yaa.*" (Eat, eat, Forest. You will have wisdom.)

I did not understand everything he said. I rarely did. I understood eat and that it contained much *something* and so I did, as I often had done. I used the serving spoon to cut and place a small chunk on my plate. Then I put the platter back into our communal center and took servings from two plates of mixed vegetables soaking in their brown sauces. I also served myself a scoop from the ever-present, stainless steel pot of steamed rice.

Using my chopsticks, I lifted and deposited the small chunk into my mouth. Usually, I was delightfully surprised. This time was different. My tongue registered it as a piece of cold, distastefully bland fat. Wholly without recommendation.

I lifted my plate and using my chopsticks quickly shoveled rice into my mouth to keep from gagging. Chewing very little, I swallowed as soon as I possibly could. Then I consumed the mixed vegetables and my remaining rice.

Rien took a second serving of the Spanish-doily, gagging dish then turned to me with an offer of more. "*Gin, gin. Bpen sa-moong kwaai.* (Eat, eat. It is water buffalo brain.)"

I placed my chopsticks at cross-swords on my plate and rejected the dish, politely. "*Mai dai gin iik. Em leeo.*" (I cannot eat more. I am already full.)

I chose the night of June 15th to make a first visit to Phanom Sarakham. It was a poor choice. It rained buckets and like small towns, villages, and hamlets everywhere that lack paved roads, gutters, and sidewalk drainage systems, the streets were a muddy mess.

There were, perhaps, fifteen buildings within the entire settlement, but most were two-story structures elevated above the street and flood plain. On each side of the pitted and flooded hardpan street, second-stories jutted outward to form awning-covered walkways.

A refuge constructed with forethought. The idea splashed across my mind as I stood outside a small kitchen stall on a spot along the walkway and watched a squatting woman, competing for clients beneath the awning protection, attend a wok and fire.

"*Gin kao yang,*" she asked?" (Have you eaten?)

"*Gin leeo, krap.*" I adjusted my wet cap and simply wanting to get out of the rain, I asked, "*Bar yuu tii-nai?*"

"*Bar yuu tii-nii,* she said pointing to the neon sign across the street and down the block.

The road was a series of puddle jumps that inevitably left my fatigues speckled in brown, splotchy splashes, but I managed to get across. Then with my head down, I quickly moved to the bar, stepped through the door, and stomped the mud from my boots.

As I stood in the doorway, I scanned the room and saw three women. The joint was dead. All three sat alone, one at the bar counter, the other two at tables. Otherwise, the intentionally poorly-lit barroom was filled only by empty tables, chairs, barstools, and the sound of a jukebox playing the lasts stanza of *Thai Sukiyaki.*

The shop's most pleasant eye-candy sat immediately in front of me as I entered. She was tall and slim with large, oval eyes, cupcake breasts, and the fair, creamy-white skin associated with Chiang Mai's northern region. Seated to her left—but on my right—was a short woman with cropped hair and a round face and squat body. Her dark skin screamed of Isaan origin. The third occupant, an older woman I correctly assumed to be the mama-san, sat on a high stool next to the bar counter. All three turned to the door as I came in.

The pretty eye-candy greeted me with venom. "*Ooii, mai bpai kup piu dum. Kon piu dam, mii kuuai yai. Mai dtong-gan nai leerie.* GI *tamai* you come here. We no want. Me neber go wit *piu dam.*"

Instead of a vinegary or a salty remark I made the "*taa-taa*" sound of disapproval and told her, in Thai, "That's not true or real." (*Mai tuk, mai jing*) Then I began to sing:

Yaak ja bpai bpai see chun bpai
puying muen Thai mii mak nak naa
Bpai len bpai laai mai-kurie huuang
Gaa paa gaa pon roong-rian bpai si . . .

The Boys Are Not Refined

"*Ooii, tamai* GI *piu dum puut Thai cham-naan?*" asked the dark Isaan woman, wondering why a black skin GI spoke Thai like an expert.

"Who teach GI Thai song? GI have Thai *tealok*." asked Miss Venom, softening to a surprised and curious tone.

"No, that's not true. I have no girlfriend," I said in Thai. "*Bpen pit, mai chuu. Mai mii tealok.* I have many friends and they teach me to speak Thai. (*Mii puan laai laai. Puan mii sorn puut Thai dai.*)"

Further calming her initial violent rejection, Miss Eye-Candy's venom-spent tongue placed a broad plank on the bridge of reconciliation and asked me my name; "*Kun chuu arai, kha?*"

"*Pom chuu* Forest, *krap*," I said. "*Kun chuu arai?*"

"*Pom chuu* Nuuan."

I asked her why the mean mouth nonsense and if she really thought blacks have tails ("*Tamai puut pit-plaat,* Nuuan, *krap? Kun kit kon piu dum mii hɛng?*"). I knew there was no way to explain such rubbish, but was willing to accept almost anything she said as an adequate apology.

"*Chan kor tort, kha. Chan mai kurie puut kup kon piu dum, na kha* (I beg pardon. I never spoke with a black person before, sir)"

I told her what she had said was untrue ("*Bpen mai jing, mai tuk*"). Then I requested an opportunity to demonstrate. She grasped my intended humor and laughed. A beachhead had been established. One thing led to the next. We became friends and I watched her inhibitions and racial discrimination melt away.

G.T. Foster

The Ride to Pak Thong Chai

I knew it was a mistake. Oh, how well I knew. After being in-country less than 24 hours I had learned that riding a motorcycle in Thailand was a bad idea. So...? When Madson, Green, Lloyd, Wellington, and Childs decided to rent bikes and ride to the famous silk factories 19 miles south of Korat why had I not followed my first instincts?

I should have said, "Thanks, but no thanks guys. I'd rather not. Instead, I'm going to rent a cab and go to Khao Yai National Park. I hear the *Haew Suwat* Waterfall is world famous. They say it's a not-to-be-missed sight. I'll have someone take a photo and call it *Forest in the Forest*"

But I hadn't said that. Instead I had gone along. To make matters worse, I cannot — to this day — navigate a motorcycle. Thus, I could only ride as passenger and the eventual pairings left me seated behind Madson.

The ride south was uneventful but pleasant. South of Korat, Paktagchai Road was sparingly travelled except for a few logging trucks. The roadway was a newly widened two-lane highway that had replaced the former road.

The widening and construction were a U S Army Corps of Engineer project. Although nearing completion, the road was not officially open beyond the village of Pak Thong Chai, where silk factories, including one owned by the American Jim Thompson, were located. Thompson is credited with the single-handed revival of the Thai silk industry during the 1950s.

Our stop in the village was brief. At one place we ordered chilled bottles of Coca-Cola and Madson purchased a small bottle of Mekong Lao, the strong Thai whiskey blend. He poured some into his soda as a spike and offered the bottle around. The offer was graciously rejected by all others except Childs.

We then walked to the factory district. There Green purchased a few yards each of different patterns of Thai silk to send his wife back in the world of Oklahoma. The clerk folded and boxed his selections and we walked back to the rented cycles to begin our return to Korat.

We had spent less than thirty minutes in the village, yet Madson had consumed the entire contents of the Mekong whiskey save the amount used to spike Childs' drink. I didn't like where this was headed, but I did have a helmet.

The motorcycles had been parked in a gravelled area. In pulling away Wellington and Childs went into a skid and crashed. They were moving very slowly and no one was injured. The others all hooted, including Wellington and Childs, but I found no humor in it.

"Funny? What's so fucking funny? You can be killed! Be careful!"

"Ah, Forest, relax," chided Green.

"Yeah, man. Take a chill pill," needled Lloyd.

"Ain't nobody hurt," giggled Childs.

"No, not yet!"

"Let's just go, man," said Madson as he revved the bike. I grabbed hold and we took to the road.

Sitting behind Madson with my hands clasped around his waist, tense, stomach racing, and heart pounding, my body would not relax. I felt like a helmeted member of the football team suicide squad, there to crash into as many members of the opposite team as possible. Vulnerable like the poor, impatient rider who had raced into the intersection looking straight ahead, only to be killed by us. Or was it our bus?

That fateful, second morning in-country I had become an instant convert to the idea—traveling a Thai road by motorcycle was inherently dangerous!

Coming down from a higher mountain elevation back onto the Korat plain produced a natural enough acceleration. But Madson insisted on even more speed, and unnecessary tilts and body shifts into and out-of the curving mountain passes. I watched the road ahead in an apprehensive state of impending doom. I expected a slow-moving elephant or stalled logging truck just around the bend.

Believing the devil does care but only awaits an opportunity, I felt a heighten concern for personal safety and yelled into Madson's helmet, "What the hell's the rush?"

But why would a man who cares not for himself, possibly care what becomes of anyone else? Madson, doubtlessly intoxicated, probably found added thrill in the hint of panic or fear. After I urged caution, he seemed intent on producing a perverse whine, scream, or cry. Instead, I clung and seethed in silence, replaying in my mind the story Madson had too often told of his triumphant, prodigal return to his "Real World" home in northern Mississippi.

He boasted of having taken a slow, night drive to the-out-skirts of his hometown, Tupelo with his best friend, Edward. They had parked on a slope overlooking the city lights where Madson pulled out a hand-rolled joint, lit it and said, "Dis shits from Thailand."

He passed the joint to his buddy and said, "Smoke-up." His friend filled his lungs and returned the smoking joint, croaking, "Here, Stan."

I swear I must have heard Madson repeat the tale three different times. Each time in telling, he had laughed until tears had streamed down his face. He says, he kind of puffed at it, but was really watching his friend.

The Boys Are Not Refined

"Eddie holds it in, den lets it out, real slow like, enjoyin' deh taste den ax, 'What's dis shit, man?' I tells Eddie, 'We's smokin' Thai Stick' and pass 'im deh joint. He takes anotha big, greedy hit and holds it all in, lookin' at da joint and den says, 'Dis sho' is some good shit.'

"But twenty minutes later Eddie done freaked. He cryin'. Callin' fo' his mama. Den he start swearin' I'm God. See, he been smokin' and smokin' but don't eben know what Thai Stick be."

"What is it?" I had asked upon first hearing the story.

"It bees some marijuana what done been cured wit opium oil. Man, it will fuck you up. But Eddie don't know nothin' 'bout none of dat shit," Madson hooted in laughter.

Each retelling of the story brought the joyous tears. It was sick, and I could not hear it without thinking of Art Linkletter's daughter who had jumped from the balcony of her seventh-floor Hollywood apartment fleeing short people with elongated heads during a bad LSD trip.

It was a violation of the rules of street drug use. The very purpose of a guide was that of a veteran escort. A guide did not manipulate a situation for sadistic glee. That ain't right. You don't spike the tea, then watch everybody freak-out! But if you do there is a deep psychological twitch down there somewhere.

Little of the return ride was in an upright, perpendicular angle. Rather, Madson would tilt left or right for no apparent reason other than annoyance. Alcohol reeked through the pores of his skin as I imagined, it was pickling his brain.

Paranoid? One-hundred percent.

One hundred yards from the front gates of Camp Friendship I pulled Madson's shirt collar very firmly and yelled, "Pull over!"

"What?"

Still tugging his neck by the shirt collar, I leaned closer to his helmet and shouted, "Pull over at the damn camp gates!"

He pulled over. The other riders noticed. They turned and circled back.

"What's up?"

"Change of plans. I've had it. I'm going in."

"Ah, come on, Forest."

"That's bullshit."

"The plan is to return these bikes and continue—"

"Bullshit is right! Fuck the plan! It's my ass and I've had enough stupid shit for one day, thank you. You guys act like you ain't seen shit the whole time you been here. If you wanna believe that marching song that you 'don't give a shit for wit or a fuck for luck', go ahead, but my life is too precious. I'm done. No hard feelings but I'm emotionally toasted."

"Alright, man."

"Yeah, man. See ya."

They rode on to Korat. I walked to the front gate, showed my identification, and slowly took the long hike to the barracks.

July Motor Pool Detail

The five-month North Vietnam Army siege and bombardment of the US Marine base at Khe Sanh revealed the weakness of the McNamara Line strategy. Hundreds of fighter squadrons from bases in Thailand and Vietnam dropped tons of munitions in combat missions against the besiegers to relieve the pressure.

Once the siege was broken, the July 5th closure of the base represented a shift from a fixed place defense to more aggressive *Air Mobile* battlefield tactics that made the land-based aircraft carrier—that was Thailand—even more essential.

As a result of the new strategy, there was an upward tick in cargo to be hauled. Both July and August witnessed an unusually high number of "special convoys." On those runs we were accompanied by a combined unit of Thai-civilian police and US Army military police as we moved shipments of secret and/or classified cargoes of latent danger, including 972 super-sensitive listening devices and highly explosive landmines.

Private log: The night of July 3rd I was on motor pool guard duty. A convoy was expected between 2000 and 2100 hours.

Since his arrival at Friendship, Private Childs had been an openly malingering malcontent holding hopes of a General Discharge. He had been removed from pit-crew and reassigned to stockroom as an assistant supply clerk but had found the minimal duties boring and had gone AWOL for 5 days. Recently returned, that night he was re-assigned to pit detail.

Childs came in early, about 6pm and I razzed him, "Hey man. I thought you were getting your discharge. What's up with that?"

"Brother-mine, I'm just marking time"

"Ain't we all? Mark time, mark."

"Look here, Bleed — let me borrow a jeep for a hot minute. I wanna go to the NCO Club. I won't be gone but for a few."

"No, hell, nah! Man, you know I don't have authority to let you do that."

He chuckled and said, "Alright, Brother-mine, alright."

"You want a coke?"

"Sure, unless I go to the NCO Club." Again, he gave his little giggle of laughter.

I left my gate watch and walked to the shelter and the coke machine and purchased two. But as I returned, I saw him leave the yard and walk toward the club.

The convoy came in on schedule. Wellington, Green, and Lloyd were among the drivers. As Green left the motor pool, he asked, "Where are Madson and Childs?"

"I saw Childs earlier. Quiet as it's kept, he's supposed to be on pit-crew. He asked me to loan him a jeep. I said, to hell with that, and he took off walking toward the NCO Club."

"What about Madson?"

"Madson? I ain't seen him. I think he went to town."

At about 2330 hours, as I was leaving the mess hall buffet assembly line with my food plate and tray, Childs came in. I told him, "Get your plate and join me. I'll find a table."

He did. "Hey, Brother-mine," he said, sitting down at the table I'd selected.

"What's shaking, Childs?"

"Nuttin' but the leaves on the trees, but they only shake because of the breeze. Boy, but Thailand's so hot ain't nothin' shakin' on the spot."

"Tell me something new. You get used to it."

"Tell me something true. When?"

"Green asked after you. Did he catch up with you?"

"I ain't seen him."

Throughout dinner Child's behavior was entirely normal. He seemed neither excited nor upset.

The next day it was all drivers, hands-on-deck as we headed back to Phanom Sarakham for another 972 shuttle relayed from Sattahip. I gladly took the assignment. Rien and I alternated the drive over the east-west loop south, while towing an empty trailer, to the Camp Charn Sinthrope switching station.

G.T. Foster

The Late Convoy

This cannot be happening, I thought as events, both known and unknown continued spiraling rapidly toward unwanted consequences. *This just cannot be happening!*

The previous night had been spent on the steps of nirvana. Nuuan, my young, beautiful, Phanom girlfriend had wondrously transported me there, twice. Then this morning she awoke early and with little effort aroused me. First, she slithered naked unto my topside and pecked kisses on my forehead, closed eyes, and lips. Having noticeably resurrected my interest, she served me a fantastic morning wake-up call, a most delightful "short time."

At 0600 hours I left the cubicle that had served as our bedroom and went downstairs and joined my three comrades from the previous night's revelry. We had plenty of time to make the morning formation.

Outside we hired motorized samlodes, commonly called *tuk-tuks*, to transport us back to the camp. There remained minor details to attend prior to the arrival of the morning's convoy.

Since the convoy was a cargo of 972 landmines it was assigned a special escort comprised of a joint squad of Thai civilian police and US Army military police. On these special convoys, they formed a front and rear-guard—the front, one jeep with three military police, one jeep with three Thai police. Two Thai policemen on motorcycles completed the forward detail. The rear-guard contained one Thai police car and one US army military police jeep.

The Boys Are Not Refined

We made the 0700 formation and were dismissed to morning mess. I ate breakfast with Green, Madson, and Lloyd, my previous night co-revelers. Leaving the mess hall Madson said, "I heard a ruma." He then waited until Green probed for deeper revelation.

"Well?"

"Somebody said dat deh dang convoy done been delayed."

"Who said it?" I asked.

"Hell, I don't know. It was when I was bussin' ma tray."

At that moment, Green sighted Sergeant Bolt on his way into the mess hall. He broke away from us, went to him and asked, "Hey, Sarge. Is it true the convoy's late?"

"Late? You ain't just a wolfing. The camp radio operator just told me they're at least an hour late."

"You kiddin' me?"

"Does a bear shit in the forest? No, man, I ain't kiddin'. Assemble in the motor pool and wait."

Green relayed this news to us. The day was beginning to look like one good old Army hurry-up-and-wait, Yogi Berra deja vu, all-over-again, morning. We knew the drill from experience. Usually twenty minutes needed to be added to any 972 convoy's travel time and there would be additional time needed to unhitch the trailers from one company and re-hitch them to the other.

"Anybody for going back to the village," I asked?

"Does a bear shit in the forest, Forest?" Green asked with a wide grin.

"Right-on," agreed both Madson and Lloyd.

We made the decision and informed our Thai co-drivers, then took a taxi back to the off-limits hamlet of Phanom Sarakham three miles away. There we tried to relight the night with our merry fucking, drinking, and smoking ways. Lloyd scored five pounds of primo *ganchaa*. It filled a shopping bag.

After forty-five minutes we cut our frolics and hired a taxi to tote us back to camp. As we approached the motor pool switching-yard on the camp's perimeter, Madson pointed and casually stated, "Dere dey is."

There was a long line of five-ton trucks hitched to trailers. Only—"No, they're not!" contradicted Green.

"The damn trailers are empty!" Lloyd simultaneously observed.

"Dem ain't our fuckin' trucks!"

"What? I'm confused!" I confessed.

"Those are 55th Company trucks from Sattahip!"

"Da fuckin' trucks is all facin' souf! Dat's deh wrong way!" noted Madson.

"Those are the trucks from Sattahib, alright. But where the fuck are ours?" queried Lloyd.

This cannot be happening, I thought. It had only been forty-five minutes. Okay, okay, an hour tops.

But it was happening. The convoy had, indeed, left without us. Our Thai co-drivers had obviously driven our trucks. We were a detachment of a United States Army transportation company moving a dangerous cargo of land mines though densely populated villages of a host country. We were the second link in the relay shuttle of a cargo of sensitive and classified, anti-personnel weapons on the way to the Thai-Laotian border. And we had managed to miss the hand-over.

I thought, Fuck, Forest! You hang around fuck-ups long enough and you will start to fuck up by natural habit. What are you going to do? You are busted. You are royally busted!

"This is bad," said Green

"No shit, Einstein," said Lloyd.

"We are royally fucked!" I said. "We fucked up!"

"That chicken-shit Bolt, he gave us bad information. He knew it," said Green with a contradictory smile. "That radio operator bullshit. There—"

The Boys Are Not Refined

"Yeah, dat bastard! Dere probably neber was no radio message."

"We should've asked Ruffin," noted Lloyd.

"Woulda, coulda, shoulda like a mo' fo," roared Green!

"What we going to do, guys?" I asked. "You know we are AWOL."

"And how!" Madson spelled it out. "A-W-O-L wid a capital A!"

"AWOL like a motherfucka, too." Green was still smiling but shook his head negatively.

"What we gonna do?" I repeated.

"Look, we pay this guy to take us back to Korat." Green motioned to the driver. "We'll take the new road. The highways complete."

"It's open?" asked Madson.

"Yeah, it's open."

"Why, didn't the convoy use it if it's open? It's shorter." I said.

"I don't know, man, but it's open. Baker, Major Garrett's driver told me. He took the major to Sattahib on it," insisted Green.

"Okay. So, he takes us? Then what? We still missed the convoy." I looked to each of the other three for an answer.

"We go to the motor pool and wait. When they come, we greet them like we never were in the convoy," Lloyd boldly suggested.

"That's fucked!" I responded non-pluses. "Just pretend we never left?"

"What good will that do?" Even Green had his doubts.

"Well, it's a plan. Anybody got something better?" asked Lloyd in defense.

"Okay. It's a plan," I agreed. "But, okay. Look, let's try to catch the convoy. If we can catch them before the dirt road turn-off we can rejoin the convoy before Korat. Okay?" Again, I looked to each of the others for assent.

"Okay wit' me."

"Me, too.

"Sounds like a plan."

Agreed, through Madson, we asked the driver to take us to Korat. We haggled briefly, then settled on a fare and began our pursuit of the missed convoy.

"Reo-reo, krap! Reo-reo!" ("Hurry, hurry!") We each took turns encouraging the driver to go faster. Faster, faster, we said, but in Thai. *"Reo-reo!"*

Then for the next few miles we rode in silence. We each knew we had only ourselves—collective or individual--to blame. The driver turned-on the radio and tuned-in a Luk Thung station, but Lloyd shouted out, "*Mai ao,* motherfucker. *Mai ao,* god damn it! *Mai ao!*"

Madson reached over and turned the knob. The radio went silent and he apologized to the driver. "*Kao mai ao fang arai, krap. Chan kam kor toot,*" he explained in a kinder tone. (I'm sorry. He doesn't want to listen to anything just now.)

But shortly thereafter Green lit a joint and the blue mood was quickly vaporized, banished in smoke.

"*Ao, krap, ao,*" said Madson and took the joint from Green. He took a hit. *"Ao mai?"* he asked.

"*Ao!*" I said. I took the huge joint that had been triple wrapped using three papers instead of one. I hit it and held it out to Lloyd. "*Ao mai?*"

His face brightened, and he said in a convincing manner, "*Ao.*"

I passed him the smoking wrap. After hitting the joint Lloyd gently bumped the driver's shoulder and asked, "*Ao mai, krap?*"

"*Mai yaak, krap,*" said the driver in polite refusal and continued his alert driving.

"*Reo-reo,*" Lloyd shouted, good-naturedly.

We burst into simultaneous laugher, then chimed-in. *"Reo-reo! Reo-reo!"*

After twenty minutes of a hurried ride Madson said, "Dere dey is."

This time he was correct. Plumes of dust could be seen off to the left as the caravan of five-ton semi-tractors pulled the hitched trailers' seventeen-ton landmine cargoes across the potted, bumpy, dirt road juncture to reach the paved roadway outside the village of Nakon Nayok.

Madson told the driver to turn left onto the dirt trail. "*Bpai saai, bpai saai.*" He did and we quickly caught the tail end of the convoy and its joint Thai police and US military police rear-guard escort.

"*Bpai reo!*" Madson instructed the driver to pass the rear-guard. We then overtook Lieutenant English, our company junior officer, who had accompanied the convoy. As we did so we realized we were dirty.

"Toss the grass!" Green shouted to Lloyd. "Toss that fuckin' bag!"

Lloyd was sitting in the rear opposite the driver. He rolled his window down and attempted to sling the five pounds of high-grade marijuana over our vehicle and unto the left-hand roadside. It was a difficult toss and he missed! The bag came up dreadfully short of clearing the roadway and landed smack in the dusty path of the trailing vehicles.

But the gods and Buddha find humor in ineptness and so they smiled upon us. The lieutenant's jeep driver was Specialist Luke Ruffin of Detroit. Ruffin quickly sized up what was happening and made witty work of distracting the lieutenant as he steered his vehicle over the abandoned shopping bag of contraband.

The dust and lieutenant's own eagerness to nail our asses to proverbial crosses might have ultimately allowed the dump to go undetected. For we were later told by Ruffin, that as soon as we passed the jeep, Lieutenant English grabbed the short wave and began yelling into the hand-held phone,

"AWOL GIs! A-W-O-L! AWOL GIs have entered the perimeter! Do not allow them to escape!"

Within minutes we crossed the dirt road. As the entire convoy of drivers pulled to the roadside and stopped for the standard equipment and cargo safety check, Madson told our taxi driver, *"Pak leeo, pak leeo!"* The driver stopped the cab in the middle of the road.

"Stan," I said to Madson as we exited the car, "Pay the driver and we'll settle-up later."

Looking around we spotted our respective drivers and trucks and walked quickly toward them. But a delegation of Thai and Military police swooped upon us. One shouted, "Halt!"

I turned to see a .45 caliber automatic pistol pointed at my head, as other MPs approached with weapons drawn. Almost in reflex, I had raised my arms into the air and could see Madson, Green, and Lloyd do the same.

"Extend your hands fully above your heads."

Having seen their weapons drawn, we were already in compliance. The Thai police, acting as backup, never unholstered their weapons, but noticeably rested their hands on their pistol hilts.

"Now, each of you, turn, and face the truck trailer!"

In this position, we were frisked. They paid notable attention to our cigarette packs hoping to strike pay-dirt and arrest any and all of us through the discovery of contraband.

Sorry. Too late.

When nothing was found they seemed at a total loss as to what to do next. After a long huddle it was decided we would complete the remainder of the convoy in our assigned vehicles. When we were finally released, the Thai drivers yelled our names and shouted loud cheers and several GIs joined them. There were also hoots of derision aimed at the MPs for having drawn their weapons on fellow soldiers.

Green, Lloyd, Madson, and I each drove or rode back to Korat wondering with what violation of the Uniformed Code of Military Justice we would be charged, expecting no less than Article 15s. That seemed to be the army express-lane catch-all punishment.

But the brass must have found it too difficult to charge us and shell out a just punishment without, also, smearing the service record of the officer in charge of the fiasco. Amazingly, we were never charged with a single act of misconduct. The entire episode was treated like a waste of time and swept under the table.

G.T. Foster

Uttaradit and the American Listening Post

A week after the adventuresome convoy Rien and I drew a special duty assignment into the Northwest. Three teams of drivers were to move separate groups of American intelligence operatives from outposts in Chieng Rai, Uttaradit, and Tak. Each of us American driver-soldiers was issued an M-16 weapon and ammunition. It was a statement noting an uncommon danger.

I drove first shift to the rest stop. From Sri Nakon Ayuttaya, Rien drove to our mapped location just beyond Uttaradit. We accessed the region on well-maintained roads that took us into areas of lush greenness alien to northwest Isaan.

Having located the rented bungalow of the American team we were assigned to move, I took the bill of transport inside for signature. Two of the Americans went outside to choose a spot for Rien to unhitch the trailer for loading.

The remaining agent, not knowing me from Adam, began to berate the Thais he had been sent to help. "These local villagers are nothing, if not lazy! And the proof is in the pudding. Just look outside this very front door. What do you see?"

To humor him I looked out the door of the hut. There a single fisherman stood in a pool beneath the stilted rental. "Looks like a fisherman."

As if saying, 'humbug' he scornfully repeated, "Fisherman? That man has spent the entire day dragging that net from one end of the pool to the other. Just out there swimming, instead of working in a field somewhere, why doesn't he get a real job?"

I hunched my shoulders in an "I don't know response" but thought, Didn't they say you were an intelligence officer? That looks like hard work.

There was absolutely no industry in the entire region. Where could the man hire-out? Even farm work is seasonal, and historically, Thai villagers nationwide have built stilted homes in preparation for harvesting the fruits of seasonal flooding. Their agricultural methods, too, use systems of dams and drains. When as designed their yards become ponds, they become fishermen.

This guy was no different. He was doing what he could to survive. It was a seasonal fishing pond constructed to put food on the table and a few *baht* in the pocket. But the agent saw only laziness.

"That is the reason this whole thing is a waste of time. They won't help themselves. They are ignorant. They don't know or care there is a war going on right next door. They don't participate in society. For Christ sake, they don't even have the right to vote or even seem to care. Listen to this. You want a beer?"

"No, thanks. Just had one with lunch." I lied.

His own beer in one hand, he turned on a reel-to-reel recorder that sat on a small table against the living room wall. "Sit down a minute and listen to this," he said conspiratorially. He pointed to a canvas folding chair. "You won't believe this. It was taped off a rebroadcast by Radio Peking. That's Communist China!"

I sat, and he adjusted the volume. It was a clear recording of an interview. There were two voices. (Years later the voices on the tape were identified as those of the black writer and journalist, Louis Lomax and Liang Chaiyakarn, at the time of the interview, a Bangkok lawyer. Chaiyakarn had been a member of Parliament during the days of representative government.) To this day, I am baffled as to why the agent shared the recording.

The first voice belonged to the interviewer, Lomax. He asked, "When do you think Thailand will have a Constitution?"

The second voice was Chaiyakarn, who responded, "There is no way of knowing. I have friends high in government and they say we should have a Constitution in about a year."

"What do you think about the Communist insurgency in Thailand?" asked Lomax.

"I cannot speak of that matter."

"Do you think your government is taking adequate measures to arrest the insurgency?"

"I cannot speak of that. The law does not allow it."

That was too much for the intelligence officer to bear and he stopped the recorder. "Get a load of that hoot. The law does not allow it! That's just what I'm talking about. It's a waste of time. Why are we here?"

I raised my hands palms up and frowned, but before I could say, "Well, for me it was the Draft," he took a swig from his bottle and pushed the restart button. The questions continued with Lomax asking, "What do you think of the American presence in Thailand?"

"I cannot speak of that. The law does not allow it." The agent again made a snorting sound of disapproval, but did not stop the tape.

"To what matters can you address yourself?"

"Other than to say I hope to run for office I cannot speak. The law does not allow it."

"Thai law does not allow it?"

"No. I must be silent and wait. I have friends who are in position to work for a constitution. Once it is promulgated, I can announce my candidacy."

"Is that all you can do?"

"Yes. I can only sit and wait."

"Is there any more you can say as of now?"

"No. The law does not allow it. But please, give my regards to the people of America. I was there as a guest of President Eisenhower. You have a wonderful country."

There followed only silence, save the hum of the reel-to-reel. The interview had ended.

"What do you make of that, soldier?" asked the talkative agent. He threw his head back to consume the final splashes from his *Singha*, the bottle still visibly frosted.

"Me? I would hate to sit across from that Thai in a high stakes game of poker. He doesn't give much away." It had been a throw away question, and although I had read *The Spook Who Sat by the Door* in high school and had been captain of the debate team the agent neither expected an answer nor cared what I thought. I wasn't the spook he was looking for.

With harsh and loud finality, the young, red-faced agent pronounced, "They are our ally, but this is a lazy, corrupt police state. Period!" and snapped off the power on the recorder ending its circular motion and hum, just as the other two field agents returned. I felt tension and saw glances of unease as he allowed himself to calm down. He seemed to have second thoughts about what had just occurred between us. But with the trailer unhitched for loading, Rien and I left. The agents would load. We were only there to haul.

We spent the afternoon in the small village of Uttaradit. Rather than sleep at the place designated as a hotel, Rien found us meals and lodging in a private home. And at the bargain basement price of an additional two dollars, I shared my bed with a local girl for the entire night.

The next morning Rien and I returned to the hut, hitched the trailer, and began the haul to the Air Force base at Takli where we would drop the trailer and complete our assignment. Despite the ample release found the previous night with the peasant girl, next day while driving, my solitary thoughts turned to Phanom and . . . I felt a flutter and wondered how soon I might see her?

It had been two months since we had first met on a rainy night during my virgin trip into the small village. Prior to that night I had always regarded the settlement as off-limits and had spent most nights at Sombaht's home about two-hundred yards from the motor pool on the camp's southwestern perimeter. At Sombaht's, Rien and I were often joined by other visiting Thai-native drivers and occasionally, other American GIs.

It was rare, but a couple of times I slept on post. GIs frequently complained of mites or body lice after stays in the log huts of Camp Charn Sinthrope. In contrast Sombaht's clean and polished floor was an invitingly wide bed.

But one night, in camp alone and bored, I'd visited the little hamlet and met Nuuan. She was very attractive and her manner was independent with only a hint of a willing subservience. Despite the initial encounter when she had venomously said, "It will neber happen between us, GI. I neber, neber date black GI!", she was actually modest and soft spoken. Our verbal exchange had been neither loud nor sharp.

Maybe it had been the implied challenge, but her words seemed to spring softly off her tongue, past her full lips, and out into the air space of the room. By the time they crossed distance to reach my ear drums they lacked the true tone of rejection.

She was left off balance by my Thai language skills. "Why you speak Thai so goot GI? You have Thai *tealok* GI? Most GI not learn speak Thai goot."

Perhaps it was as much her own vanity. She was pretty. And when I insisted that she went beyond pretty and was both lovely and beautiful, I was speaking from the heart and a woman, no matter how narcissistic, knows the difference.

It had been late. It was raining. There were no other prospects, white or otherwise, anywhere to be seen. So, she broke her own never-ever-happen rule and gave me a break.

We spent nights together on five occasions. Each time the nights were filled with passionate embraces of soft and steady coupling. Her fingers touched my fingers. Her arms wrapped around me, my arms engulfed her frame and her legs split or intertwined with mine deep into the night. Then come morning, my loins refilled and my blood boiling we would join in a Christian-Buddhist rebirth and resurrection instant replay.

She was great fun, had been to the city and was no hayseed. She had the normal prejudices but nothing insurmountable. I felt like Papa Bear after a long naked embrace with Goldie Locks. It felt just right. And on the road back from Uttaradit, I decided to ask her to move to Korat and become my *tealok*.

Rien and I stopped to check our cargo and tires and to stretch our legs. For privacy I went behind the trailer to urinate. I unzipped my pants, took my tool in hand and held it until I felt the flow begin. And then…behold! Horror of whores! Instead of urine my penis emitted a greenish ooze! Instantly it was obvious. She had lied.

Call me a fool. Call me whatever, but I had, except with her, always used protection. I do not consider myself reckless. She told me she was clean. She had shown me her health card. She told me all her clients wore protection.

Well then, who do I shoot?

It was really my turn to be shot and I reported to sick bay in the Camp Friendship Health Clinic. The medic gave my buttocks a shot of penicillin and issued me tablets of the same.

I was restricted to a two-week regime of no sex, no alcohol, no milk, no citrus, and no off-base passes. However, the full confinement to camp normally imposed with cases of venereal disease was impossible to impose on drivers.

When I returned to the village bar in Phanom Sarakham, I was told Nuuan had left for points north, perhaps her native village. Oh well, I guess she didn't really love me.

Good Buddhas

Most American GIs had no concept of the division in Buddhism between the Mahayana (The Greater Vehicle) and the Theravada (The Lesser Vehicle) paths. The defining belief, according to the doctrine of Mahayana, is that those who attain nirvana return to earth as bodhisattvas to help others reach the same state. Such is the Buddhist form and practice predominant in China, Tibet, Taiwan, Korea, Japan, and Vietnam.

The Theravada school is practiced in Thailand, Laos, Cambodia, Myanmar, and Sri Lanka. Although called the Lesser, it is the oldest of all Buddhist faiths and the only one to trace its origins directly back to the teachings of Siddhartha Gautama Buddha of the 6th century BC whose central doctrine was based on the temporal nature of life and the imperfection of all beings. Theravada is a mixture of Buddhism, Hinduism, and animistic beliefs.

Most Thais widely accept the idea of spirits everywhere—spirits of water, wind, and woods. There are both locality and tutelary spirits. Spirits are not so much good or bad as they are powerful and unpredictable and like Greek gods have many of the faults and foibles of humans—like vindictiveness, lust, greed, jealousy, and malice.

Enlightened Thai-Buddhist monks are deemed to have supernatural or magical powers. They are able to cast protective spells or counteract spirits and other potential dangers that lurk in life. These spells are kept in amulets worn by believers. Each amulet, or *pra*, holds the image of one of these enlightened monks.

Thus, there was a monk *(pra)* who was guardian of love, while another guarded fortune and others aided education, happiness, long life, and so on down the line. These are not so much your orthodox Buddhist beliefs as they are widely held Thai traditions, ancient faiths, and practices with Buddhism, a bright red cherry melded on top. And although a *pra* cannot be purchased, it can be rented at any local *wat* in the country.

At the end of July Cak came back. He walked into the motor pool with his head held as high as ever. His former brash spirit seemed calmer and he would forever walk with a limp but given the alternatives that seemed quite acceptable. Although nobody had given him more than an ounce of hope, Cak had become one of Thailand's rare survivors of a motorcycle accident.

His Buddhas were *jing* and held magnificent powers over fortune and fate. *Jing-jing*, fuckin' *jing*! Without a doubt.

The New Girl

With my health recovered and my privileges restored I spent the entire morning of my twenty-first birthday lying around one of the upstairs brothel rooms at the Lucky Seven Club in downtown Korat. We were such regulars both there and at the Kit Kat Club that our relationships with the female staff had morphed into real friendships.

While the dual-purpose rooms above the bar were often used for short-time or over-night rendezvous, they were also rented by the working girls for apartments. Like people everywhere, the women were different and much more pleasant during their nonworking hours. Outside the bar their interests were genuine.

Beyond the sex, Toi and I became friends. She often asked about America and the plight of black people. Thais knew of American slavery but most were uncertain about the timeframe. Even well-read as she was, she once asked, "When black people stop be slave?"

"*Lai-lai bpii gan,*" I said. "*Loy bpii.*" (Many years ago... 100 years). But the question actually made me realize just how recent that was.

Her husband had deserted her, but when I asked, if she was looking for a new one, she answered with a question. "For-it, you know *mangda song-ka*?"

"*Chai-si, krap.* Pimp," I said.

"*Jing-jing.* Some husband same-same *mangda song-ka*. He spend he money, he spend you money."

Toi also helped me with my language development and was forever trying to teach me the Thai alphabet with its forty-four consonants, twenty-two or so vowels and four accent marks. That morning being my *gert wan,* (birthday) I allowed her to give me a sponge bath and shave the hair from my groin—just for kicks. The act was wholly asexual. She thought it would be fun. I think it was the coarseness of my pubic hair that fascinated her.

★★★

Afterward I spent the entire day hanging around watching the women in their leisure. The previous night had produced a new hire. I wrote the following observation July 25, 1968:

No one wants the new arrival. She is a strong peasant girl with broad hips and round cheeks but she totally lacks sophistication and any knowledge of the ways of the city, if one can call Korat a city. In any event, her country ways make her stand out, even in a small-town crowd.

She is a bumpkin to the bone. Her flesh holds the smell of a rice field hand. But she is neither unwashed nor unclean but rather her soap is unscented, and she has yet to discover perfume. Her hair lacks the luster of constant shampoo and brush and comb. It hangs limp and straight. Her wardrobe is still farm girl but give her two months. She will be unrecognizable. Her hick-ness will have receded from the foreground and she will have learned to act the coy coquette.

But for now, she has no takers, poor thing. A soldier doesn't go to downtown Korat in search of a novice-whore. I'm sorry. Did I say she was a virgin? She was not. Nor was she *saao-saao,* a cute young thing. She was a country wife with two children. Her husband had abandoned her and gone off to who knows where. She did not lack experience, but it had been singular and shallow. What she needed now were the honed skills of empirical knowledge.

Poor thing! Lord knows you cannot make a whore a wife. But wives be warned, the transition to whoredom is no easy probe-grope-and-fumble task. A soldier doesn't hire a *gully* to just lie there like a wife doing her duty. He demands active participation from his paid partner.

Be a star. Get into the act. Put on a show. Make it seem like you enjoy it as much as your John. Bite your bottom lip and throw your head back while riding cowboy style. Moaning is always good, as is repeating your partner's name over and over. But be warned and be careful with the "Oh, daddy, oh, daddy" cries. Here, Freud and I have a parting of the ways.

The new girl has it tough, but it is only for the short haul. She will learn. She will figure it out. Heck, she holds drilling rights to man's most desired commodity.

G.T. Foster

The Wellington Riot

I was not there. I simply state what was told to me by the Chinese plate. In this case, Sasse acted as the Chinese plate and I herein report only what has since been verified.

He was a nut and on August 10th he cracked! It began calmly enough. The day was done and men had begun returning to the barracks an hour or so earlier. According to his own testimony, Wellington had showered and dressed and was leaving the barracks to go to the Non-Commissioned Officers Club to have a beer and from there he had planned to take a taxi to the market in downtown Korat.

As he walked down the aisle toward the barrack west door exit, he passed cubicles to both his left and right. Each contained a top and bottom bunk bed, two wall lockers and two wooden foot lockers. In most cases, given our company size, these spaces were occupied by a single soldier.

He stopped in front of the cubicle of Sergeant Bolt. On top of the sergeant's footlocker was an unopened bottle of Scotch whiskey. Without a word, Private Wellington lifted the bottle from the footlocker, then said, "Sergeant Bolt, give me a drink."

The sergeant had been tying his tie using a mirror mounted on the inside of his wall locker door. He stopped, turned around, stepped to Wellington and grabbed the bottle with both hands.

"The bottle's not open. Besides which you cannot drink in the barracks." He tugged as he said this, and Wellington released the bottle. He then held the bottle high to the light as if to examine its quality and added, "But I wouldn't give you a drink even if I saw you downtown!"

Wellington turned quickly and snatched the Scotch from the sergeant's hand. He then turned his back toward the sergeant to shield himself, unscrewed the cap and took a drink from the bottle. The sergeant was momentarily frozen in shock by Wellington's extraordinary level of insubordination and disrespect.

Then Bolt moved quickly and grabbed the bottle as Wellington began to take another swig. The two men struggled for possession down the aisle, then barreled through the rear door and unto the stairwell as Scotch splashed and spilled from the jostled bottle. Wellington seemed intent on imposing his will run amok while the lifer-sergeant was now willing to fight to the death to prevent such a thing.

Once outside on the stairwell, Wellington with his back against the rails made a sudden squat and recoil standup. Then with a hard jerk and sharp pivot, he used his left shoulder and hip to pry the sergeant from his bottle. Wellington now stood on the top platform; the sergeant stood a step below preventing his downward flight. Not taking his eyes off the sergeant, Wellington screwed the cap back onto the Scotch and then tucked the bottle in his left arm as one would a football, lowered his right shoulder and lunged downward into the sergeant's chest.

With the collision, he momentarily broke free and scampered past the sergeant but before he could reach the bottom of the stairs and safety an arm slipped around his neck. Nevertheless Wellington struggled downward, off the steel steps onto the ground even as the sergeant's arm, locked in a choke-hold, cut his wind.

It was then Stanley Madson returning to the barracks from the NCO Club a bit inebriated, observed the scuffle. He picked-up a discarded, long wooden plank from the ground, then "Shouting like a wild Indian," ran toward the two brawling men but was grabbed twenty feet from the scuffle by Private Childs. While momentarily restraining him, Childs growled, "Stay out of it, Stan. There are too many eyes."

Madson relaxed and stood down but hurled the long plank toward the combatants. It landed nowhere close—and came harmlessly to rest.

"Put down my bottle, punk," Sergeant Bolt hissed through clenched teeth, but Wellington stubbornly held on to it. The sergeant tightened his choke.

Wellington began to cough, and someone yelled, "Let him go, Sarge!" But Wellington still held the bottle. "Sergeant, Sergeant, let him go!"

"Let go of the bottle, punk!"

"Release the soldier, Sergeant!"

"Let go my goddamn bottle, you little bastard!"

"Release the soldier, Sergeant!" the voice repeated. It came from a soldier wearing a Military Police uniform just as Wellington relented and allowed the bottle to slide gently off his leg to the ground.

"Stand down, Sergeant!" said a second Military Policeman. Five or six other MPs could now be seen in the courtyard. Bolt released his hold on Wellington and from behind shoved him toward the military policemen.

What happened next, for that time and space, was not bizarre. Although the initial confrontation had been witnessed by only about ten men, as the scene played out it picked up audience. The crowd grew larger and louder as more and more soldiers witnessed, then urged others, "Come get a load of this!"

By the time the battle reached the bottom of the stairwell, over 60 spectators watched from ours and adjoining barracks. It had been first class, spanking good entertainment but now the fucking MPs had suddenly appeared to unplug the skirmish.

Hisses, hoots, and boos began to ring out from the onlookers. Many of the army rank-and-file soldiers see an MP as a mindless, faceless, cocky member of the force that all other soldiers dread and many troops hate. It is a fact that nobody likes a military policeman except his mother and another MP.

The MPs were now seen as referees in on a fixed fight who had stopped the event on a questionable Technical Knock-Out and must enforce their unpopular decision.

Wellington stood in the pandemonium, now free from the sergeant's death grip. With his fists held up in a boxing position, he pranced on the balls of his feet and cursed both the sergeant and the Military Policemen. He made a swift move toward the dropped bottle, picked it up, and hurled it at the sergeant. Bolt dodged, and the disputed bottle of Scotch whiskey shattered against the barrack wall. Wellington resumed his boxing prance and three MPs, night-sticks in hand, moved toward him.

Tossed from one of the upstairs barracks, a shoe struck one MP in his back. The stunned policeman turned and looked up as a barrage of all manner of objects—aerosol cans, Vaseline jars, boots, wire clothes hangers, pillows, and the like rained down upon them.

One MP shouted to another sitting in a jeep roadside of the courtyard, "Radio for backup support! Hurry! Radio for backup support!"

"Roger that," the sitting cop said and called into the hand-held radio transmitter.

It was unnecessary panic. The object monsoonal storm had passed. The remaining MPs were more than enough to box and pen a suddenly tame, weary, and worried Wellington and end the tumult.

The so-called Wellington-Military Police Riot carried immediate repercussions. Once peace had been restored Sergeant Bolt filed charges of assault against both Wellington and Madson. They were arrested and confined to the stockade pending a hearing under rules of The Uniform Code of Military Justice.

Beyond that, September 15th was set as the date the entire company was to be summarily transferred south to the Camp Charn Sinthrope switching-station boondocks. The brass had decided that someone would pay for the insubordination and total lack of control exhibited by some members of the 21st Transportation Company. Soon it would be off to the mites of Phanom Sarakham.

Gone would be the comfortable garrison barracks and its convenient running water and flushing toilets. That would be traded for four-man log cabin hooches. The latrine at Camp Charn Sinthrope was one large, narrow structure with twenty facing seats to accommodate our daily movements but would be severely tested by any mass emergency run from bad chow.

Whoopee! As a delightful by-product of our desolate move, all soldiers of pay grade less than E-6 could now look forward to an assignment on the rotating lime detail. Each day the lucky detachment must tilt the hinged outhouse building shell and expose its defecation harvest, then dump layers of a lime and lye mixture over the human body waste of the open sewage trench-pit—delightful duty!

The Faithful Soldier and the House Girl

Nathan had steadfastly refused to go to downtown Korat. He knew how most soldiers spent their time there. Not him. He would remain true to the girl he had left behind despite a mountain of scornful comments and jealous Jody taunts. Instead, he went to the base cinema or the NCO club.

In June, he relented. But he only went to the big *talot* (marketplace) so he could answer an inquiry in his correspondence. Once there he did not stray from the marketplace. He did not wish to eat and most definitely would not set foot inside the bars.

Yet, he seemed to enjoy the frenzy of the market, abuzz with people, sounds and smells all too unimaginable on the post with its piped-in Americana culture. But after the hour-long visit, he returned to the base and things safe and familiar.

The older house girls all teased him. Each in turn invited him to a home cooked meal and to meet their teenage daughters. He would invariably blush a bright red and politely refuse.

Many of the Spanish speaking soldiers asked if he were a *maricon*, while the blacks queried if he was still a virgin?

To the first, after receiving translation of *maricon*, he answered, "Of course not, I like women. What's wrong with a guy being true to his sweetheart?" And to the question of his virginity he simply answered with a question, "Why is that important?"

The brothers assumed from that, that he was. Their reasoning being that once a guy has had a little puntang, he develops a hunger. There is no contentment until his next serving. No, Nate was a virgin. There was no other explanation for his stalwart refusal to join them and chase the *gullies*.

Nonetheless, after his visit to the market, something had changed. His eyes sparkled and there was a beam upon his face.

Nom, a young and shy house girl, never looked any GI in the eyes. Alone, if not lonely, she and Nathan shared an empathy which neither was capable of expressing in the other's language. Yet, there developed, over time, a wordless communication between them and suddenly, after seven months in-country, Nate wanted to know how to say this or ask that in Thai.

He spent much of his free time reading alone near the washroom. A keen observer could not help but notice the rhythmic exchanges between Nate and Nom – their darting eyes rushed to greet, their smiling exchange of *"Sawatdii"* used in joyously soft hellos and gentle goodbyes, then followed their sad, quick turn away, as they returned to the gloom of loneness.

But when word of our impending September transfer to Camp Charn Sinthrope was made official they of necessity halted all pretense. Nathan begged and Sasse consented to bring his own Thai-girlfriend along and accompany Nate on a visit to Nom's home to meet her family.

Nathan and Nom were inseparable for the company's final two weeks at Camp Friendship. Theirs was a pure and simple love story.

The Death of the Elvis of Thailand

The morning of August 17, as I leisurely dressed to take full advantage of the previous day's late afternoon return, a radio blared in Thai, spoken too quickly to be intelligible, then segued into a song. Lem stood at the open door to the second-floor stairwell, his back to me, feet spread apart, body tilted, chin at rest on his upper fist as both hands gripped the handle of a dust mop. He stared into the distant blue western sky.

Walking toward him to leave and catch a late breakfast in the mess hall I asked his rear, "*Ja tam arai, krap?*" ("What is going on, friend?")

He turned to me with pained confusion on his face. There was deep sorrow in his redden eyes. "Dey kill him, Forest, *krap*. Dey kill Surapol. I not believe dey kill him."

"Surapol? Who is Surapol? Who are they? Who killed him?"

"Forest, *krap*? You not know Surapol? Him big in Thailand. Listen, dey play him song now."

From the radio the voice sang: "*Ter suay leer gern dum neearn kon pii . . . mai luum mai luum mai luum dum neearn.*"

Tuning down the volume Lem said, "Him make *mak-mak* song. Maybe more den hundred. *Chaisi,* easy more den hundred song, *jing-jing*. Him like Ameri-con Elbis Pretley. Him king. Eveb-body like. But now dey kill him. Him do..." Lem paused momentarily, to search his mind for the English term, then said, "*Gaan-sa-daang, gaan-sa-daang,* kan-saat. After kan-saat yet-ter-day dey kill him.

"Why, Lem? Why did they kill him?"

"*Mai luu, krap*. Him make great song, '*Sip-hok Bpii Hɛng Kwam-lang*', and now dey kill him, *chip-hai*!"

"Maybe they didn't like his song." I said and quickly added, "Just kidding, Lem,"

"No, Forest, maybe. Maybe, before. *Jing-jing*. Before some people no like *Luk Thung*. But him, him make people like. Him be in mobie, *duey*. Dey like him. Den him lat song, *Sip-hok Bpii, tuk kon chop. Jing-jing.* Dey *chop Grung-teep* (Bangkok), *chop* Chiang Mai, *duey*. Dey *chop* eveb-where. I tell you *jing-jing* Forest, eveb body like."

He paused, turned to a bunk bed and lifted a newspaper from the lower bed. "But now he dead. Dey murder!"

He handed me the publication. It was a copy of the morning's *Korat Dispatch*. It was front page news. Gunned-down after performing a concert, Surapol laying on the ground beside his imported Japanese sedan, its driver-side doors still open.

Somebody didn't like him! If he was as wildly popular as Lem just said, this had to be front page news on every Thai publication within the country! I said, "*Lem, pom luu suk kwam sia chai mak gcc tuk kon Thai*. It was an offer of condolence to Lem and the people of Thailand for such a grave loss.

He responded, "Don't worry, Forest, *krap*. Dey will be caught. In *bpra teet Thai kun mai dai kaa kon. Diiao dtam-ruuat jop!*"(In Thailand you cannot kill people; the police will catch you!)

The Boys Are Not Refined

A Morning of Many Questions

One-week later, on the morning of August 24, immediately after 0800 roll call I was summoned to the motor pool dispatch office. The Camp Friendship branch of the Army Criminal Investigation Department had sent two military policemen for my pick-up-and-delivery to Military Police Headquarters for questioning.

At headquarters they placed me in a corridor with a chair; uninstructed. After forty-five minutes the same two MPs returned and moved me to a room with carpet, a love-seat couch and a small coffee table. On the coffee table were single copies of two separate issues of *Stars and Stripes* newspaper. There was no other reading material. One wall held a large darkened glass window. *Probably two-way*, I thought. Another wall held a door to a closet sized room with a toilet and sink.

Undisturbed save my own racing thoughts, I sat alone for more than two hours. I picked up one of the military newspapers and read from the first page to the last. But the reading was un-focused and full of worthless information. I was on an emotional roller coaster. My mind rushed about dark, hidden, or forgotten corners trying to sort things out. I read the second newspaper. By noon I still had no idea why I was in Military Police custody.

What was going on? Knowing I had never trifled nor tampered with a single box of Uncle Sam cargo, I wanted to jump to my feet, kick over the little table, pound on the darkened glass window, and shout, "What are the charges?"

Then I would calm down and remind myself, *This ain't my first rodeo. What do the cops know? What do the cops ever know?* Hadn't they mistakenly shaken me down in the seventh-grade on Grand Thief Auto (GTA) charges simply on the coincidental fact of name? They were sweeping a net for the Briscoe Brothers, Neal and James, and my older brother's name is Neal.

I had been twelve, couldn't drive and did not even understand the concept of a joy ride. How many other times had I been stopped since? Too many to now be frightened or intimidated by a couple of MPs picking me up to ask who knows what. *So, calm the fuck down! Come on, man, take a few deep and slow inhale-exhales; breathe and calm down.*

Hurry-up-and-wait. About 1215 hours I was escorted down the hallway to the door of the adjacent room. The MP knocked upon the door and I was admitted. The room was occupied by a sergeant, a young second lieutenant, and a red haired major. Upon entering I came to a halt and raised my right arm in salute. "Private-Specialist 3rd Class Nigel Forest reporting as ordered, sir." I held the salute.

"At ease and be seated," said the second lieutenant returning my salute. He pointed to a table and I sat as directed. The lieutenant also took a chair and sat across from me. He lifted a notebook from the table. The major took an envelope from a desk and walked to our table.

Still standing the major began, "Soldier, do you know why you are here?"

"No, sir. I have no idea, sir," I responded.

"Son, you are part of an Article 32 Investigation. The Army has been watching you and your friends a long time. Do you have any idea the trouble you boys are in?"

"No sir, I don't. Like I said, sir, I have no idea what any of this could be about."

"Look at these pictures." He took several photographs from the envelope and placed them upon the table.

The Boys Are Not Refined

I picked them up and quickly shuffled through them. They were seven or eight, unremarkable, off-duty photographs of me, Madson, Green, Bryson, Tucker, Ruffin, Lloyd, Wellington and one or two others. Some of the pictures had been snapped at Dang's Lucky Seven Club in downtown Korat. All were candid and un-posed recordings.

"They are just pictures of us. Me and ... some of the brothers."

"Brothers. These aren't your brothers. Brothers," he derisively repeated. "Come on, son, wise-up. You are never going to see any of these guys again. You owe them nothing."

"Oh no, sir?" I asked. Repulsed by his statement, I completed a projected thought. *No? Not brothers? Not men? Not anything, but what?*

"You're going to complete your tour and go back home to your life." With rising anger, the major continued, "These photographs of you and your clique—"

He left the statement unfinished and hanging but I gave no response. While noting his accusatory tone I thought, *Clique? Is that what we are?*

"Did you know they were dealing black market?"

Whoa! Time out! Time out! In a single moment it was clear what this was all about. I felt both relief and dread. Relief, for I knew I did not deal in the Black Market. Nothing the major could possibly say throughout the remainder of the interrogation could in the least way harm me. Dread; because I knew others had.

"I have no idea what you are talking about, sir," I said.

During the full minute of silence that followed, the major's words, including the needle-jumping black marketeering charge, kept rushing through my mind. *They're not your brothers ...! You owe them nothing! They're not your brothers! ... dealing black market?*

The second lieutenant placed his notebook and pencil on the table, stood, crossed the room to a desk, and turned-off the reel-to-reel tape recorder, alerting me. We were being recorded! My stomach growled and fluttered but my bowels held.

The major raised his left arm to check his wrist watch and jarred me back into the moment saying, "It is time for the midday meal. You will be escorted to lunch. Think about the events on or around July 3rd and 4th. Sergeant, summon an escort to take Private Forest to his noon meal."

In Military Police custody, I was taken to the Mess Hall and ate my meal sitting with my escort. A couple of soldiers waved greetings but for the most part I ate in silence. It was the worst meal of my life. But as I ate, I realized that the major had made errors. He had attempted the old divide-and-conquer technique. It may have been tried and true, but at the time it was far too ancient and universally recognized for its shallowness. In my case, it failed to account for my blooming nationalism—a by-product of the new Black awareness awash prior to my induction.

When the major looked at me, he saw just another Negro soldier. He failed to see the Black soldier that had emerged after two years of pumping gas in the hyperspace of the Berkeley intellectual garden while attending a few classes at rebel-rousing Merritt College in North Oakland.

He looked but did not see the me who one afternoon, on the way to class parked his black 1961 Austin-Healey and entered the campus side-by-side to a fellow black male student. The fellow wore a snappy black leather jacket, a matching black leather beret, and carried books in one hand and a double-barrel shot-gun at rest on the opposite shoulder. The first Black Panther I ever encountered.

Although I earned few college credits, I had managed to pass a Negro History class with a mark of D. The joke of the final grade had been on me. College had found me unprepared for its rigor. The class, taught by the amazing, intellectually exuberant, Master George Daskorolis was an enlightenment. A great Socratic mentor, this Greek introduced me to the minds of Marcus Garvey, Malcolm X, Nate Turner, Booker T. Washington, and W. E. B. Du Bois while giving me a historical perspective of myself.

I chewed my chow and contemplated everything the major had said. Everything the major had said rang hollow. I owed them loyalty! A light clicked, and I thought, YOU KNOW WHAT? I KNOW YOU!

If the survival instinct is the first law of nature, then it is a natural consequence that humans use knowledge and position for self-advantage. A soldier once told me at Luckies hideaway, "I became an MP so that when I get back to Jersey, I can be a cop. Cops get all the goodies, kick-backs, and hook-ups."

I had hauled my landmines and general cargos up and down the roadways of Thailand, always keenly aware of the unfolding action. I had seen signs, scenes, and traffic of all types — gasoline station stops, roadway fruit and beverage vendors, lunch stops, traffic circles, bicycle riders, processions in village streets, celebrations in golden temples, walking saffron monks carrying silver rice pots for alms, coconut groves, rice paddies during both planting and harvest, and two American military policemen unloading boxed cargo from the back of a military jeep parked at the rear of a roadside lunch-and-dinner establishment.

And so, as I waited, I thought:

Why, yes, major, I know you. You are like Matt Dillon, that double-dealing, double-crossing, dirty sheriff who strongarmed himself into Miss Kitty's business as her secret and silent partner. In their busy little saloon, a man could get drunk, fleeced, or fucked —his choice. But if he squawked too loudly, he was either thrown into the clink or run out of town.

Yeah, I know you and your minions. Doc? That alcoholic, misogynistic fugitive from a botched Eastern abortion had travelled by both rail and coach westward toward new life in San Francisco. Weary from the journey, he only stopped in Dodge City for a short repose. Meanwhile, he treated a couple of Miss Kitty's gully girls. The bar seemed to have an infinite amount of good whiskey, so he had chosen to stay. The free drinks and free pussy kept him in a near blissful state.

And Fester! He was the marshal's stooge-pigeon, the snooping eyes and ears of the town. His blacksmith stable was used by all the out-of-town crowd. Each week he would limp-run into the marshal's office shouting, "Mister Dillion, Mister Dillion --" then spill his guts about this or that threat to public safety.

Who was the red-head major's stooge-pigeon?

After mess we returned to Military Police Headquarters and the CID office within. Before sitting at the table I looked first at the lieutenant and then the major and asked, "Am I being charged with something, sir?"

"No, Private Forest," responded the lieutenant. "You are not charged with any crime. This is simply an investigation to determine if anyone will be charged or if there is enough evidence to hold a formal hearing. We just want your cooperation."

"Yes, sir." I said.

"Look here, soldier, we need you to answer some questions," said the major. "We have lost 27 military vehicles within this command district over the last fourteen-month period. I have some additional photographs for you. We know that you and your boys frequent this location."

He slapped an 8X11, black-and-white photograph onto the table. It was a blowup of Luckie's hideaway, aka The Royal Bar. I thought, *more photographs.*

The Boys Are Not Refined

This one had apparently been taken by a camera with a strong zoom. A fleeting flash sent a vision of Baker, Major Garrett's driver. I first heard his admonishment, "Don't buy any new tee-vees." It was followed by a vague image of Baker with his PX purchased Japanese 35mm camera strapped around his neck. The thought was interrupted by the voice of my interrogator.

"We have the photographs!" he stated, again. He began to imperially pace the room like the Little Red Rooster. "This place was declared off-limits in October 1967."

"I didn't know that, sir."

"Come now soldier, who are you trying to kid?'

"I'm not trying to kid anyone, sir. How was I supposed to know that?"

"Let me be clear with you. Our investigation indicates that you are the head of a clique of soldiers very possibly involved in prohibited activities, including trades in the illegal markets."

"Sir, that is outrageous!"

"But you do know Private Childs, do you not?" asked the major in a switch to sarcasm.

"Yes sir. Of course, I do, sir."

"When the private was absent-without-leave, where did he stay?"

"I don't know, sir."

"No, of course you don't! Do you know if he had any unusual sums of money?"

"No sir. I did not notice anything unusual like that."

"Well, what about Private Stanley Madson," he asked after checking his notes. "Did Madson have large sums of money?'

"Honestly, sir, I never noticed anyone in our crowd with extra money. We all tend to live from paycheck to paycheck like all the other soldiers.

★ ★ ★

But it wasn't over. And around and around it went, unending, until I gave them a statement. They knew a lot. How they knew I didn't know. And although I hemmed and hawed to evade by pretended memory loss and semantic misunderstanding, the devil is in the details and they seemed to have them all.

I was going nowhere without a statement and in the end, they typed up a damning one which I signed. Then the interrogation ended, and I was returned to my barracks. I had spent nearly twelve hours in the custody of the Military Police.

The Boys Are Not Refined

Busted Brotherhood

What value, a friend?

In my unprofessional opinion, my family unit, by any measure, was damaged and dysfunctional. My father's obsession to somehow even the score in a never-to-be-ended war against his ex-wife, my mother Helen, led him on more than one occasion to commit human unkindness that was wholly out of character with the man he wanted to be.

For me, my friends became substitute extensions for all that was lacking in family. The role of big brother-older friend had been usurped by dynamics far beyond Neal's or my knowledge or control. In Neal's replacement I had found ace-boon-coons like Joe Patts, Albert Highcliff, Rudy Greenman, and Vern Fulway.

The major had said, "You are the leader of a clique of black soldiers." True or false the statement was cause for pause. I had been a founder, two-year team captain, and president of the high school debate and speech team. I had also been an eleventh-grade co-captain of the B football team.

But I was also opinionated and brash. In tenth-grade I was called the Merced Lip, a miniature Cassius Clay. My eleventh-grade English teacher had branded me a rebel-rouser.

Leadership? So, what's new? That had been the army's position since basic training. Or had I mistaken the significance of the probing Officer's Candidate School meeting that a few select recruits, including me, had attended. So why the accusatory tone from the CID? Hell, the Army had tracked me.

Still, I felt the major had gotten it seriously wrong. I was no leader of this rat pack. I was an individual spice finding space within the crowded mix. It was more a mutual admiration societal soup. Each soldier added to the group's final flavor. Green at E-5 was its binding ingredient while Madson, as the seasoned veteran, acted as chief chef on all matters of culture and taste.

But beyond that, I felt a bitter sting in the major's challenge to long lasting friendship. *Brother?* He had scoffed in a tone of dismissal. "You are never going to see any of these guys ever again once you get out of the army." He had been so cock-sure certain. "You owe them nothing."

Oh, but he was wrong. They were my friends and as such I owed them quite a bit. Friends and friendships had enabled me to survive the collateral damage done by the feeble efforts of divorced and unfocused parents. And I knew it.

At age thirteen my father proved it in the office shop of his thoroughly modern garage. "Son, your older brother Neal is not my child. He is not mine, but he doesn't know it. You must never tell him. If you do, I will deny it and never forgive you."

Although this hateful secret was safe with me, my father told far too many others to keep it secret for very long. That he should for any reason have felt a need to tell me still baffles and brings me to tears.

Along the way friends had become substitute family extensions. Friends were buttresses and supplied much needed adulation and comradeship. They were my buffers against the rocks, BBs, pellets, spit wads, and paper airplanes the world hurled my way.

It might have been the naivete of my youth, but I thought, *To hell with the major!* I fully expect to see Green, Madson, and Lloyd again, just as I expect to see Vern, Joe Patts, and Albert Highcliff when I return to California. Exactly what or who was he in the army to protect? Did he fight for a faceless flag? Was he an Automaton, just in to kill gooks? To hell with the ambitious prick!

The war was not something I thought of as separate from the rest of my life. Sure, we all used the expression "back in the world" or "back in the real world." But it was not as if we intended to slither back into society. Guys spoke of making flashy re-entries. They planned to walk down Main Street, USA wearing Sattahip tailor-made, iridescent, lime-green Thai silk suits as physical proof and loud declaration that Jack is back!

The war was part of our growth to manhood. A college boy does not think of losing contact with fraternity brothers or classmates. So why would the major denigrate military camaraderie? To hell with him!

Yet, the brotherhood had broken, and its individuals scattered like weasels, rats, and squealing cats. Someone had talked. How else could they know these things? Who had said what? They had kept me in their stinking custody for twelve hours. What was I to do? How long could I in good faith, nay, in the best of faith, have been expected to hold out against their threats? Should I have allowed myself to be implicated?

Someone else had told them things. Things they could not possibly have otherwise known. Then there were those photographs. Imagine, secretly watched. Under surveillance! Why? And who is the fuckimg snitch? It had to be Wellington or Stan or . . . even Baker?

The cops don't magically drop from the sky and say, "Oh, by the way, since I'm here, let me ask you a question that's been troubling me. Do you know anything about a stolen jeep?"

When I entered the barrack Green and Lloyd were at their bunks. Lloyd thumbed through a Sports Illustrated magazine while Green composed a letter.

"Do you guys know about Childs?"

They both looked up but neither spoke.

"Fuck! Who talked?"

"Loose lips sink ships," responded Lloyd.

"Just what the hell is that supposed to mean."

"It means we all talk too much, so shut the fuck up!" enjoined Green, as if on cue in defense of his buddy.

There was a moment of absolute silence. "I didn't mean anything. It's just that those fuckin' MPs kept me for 12 hours. Maybe I'm feeling guilty because I didn't know anything. They just snatched me up this morning." I paused, but the response came back in more silence.

"I sure didn't help that poor fool Childs none. God damn it! It might have been my loose lips but it was information shared among friends. I'm sorry, man, but they're going to hang that little bastard. On what, words that I said?"

"Look man, to tell the truth, the army CID people said for us not to talk to each other about this," reminded Green.

"And you're going to do that?"

"What can I do? What can we do? "He looked around the barrack and settled his eyes on Sergeant Wardell. Tilting his head toward the sergeant he continued, "Look man, I'm short. I don't want no trouble." He made the comment in a semi-humorous tone, mimicking the voice of the German Colonel Schultz character of the then popular *Hogan's Heroes* television program.

"You aren't going to say he did it, are you?"

"I didn't say that, man."

"Well, you guys going downtown? Let's share a taxi downtown," I suggested conspiratorially.

"Nay, man. Not me. It's late."

"Me neither, man. I'm gonna chill."

The Article 32 Investigation

After the case cracked, General Black appointed Major Garrett Investigative Officer. It was his responsibility to conduct a separate enquiry and if the facts so warranted, as prosecutor, to convene a hearing. His probe quickly led him to set an Article 32 Hearing which loosely parallels the work of the grand jury in the civilian judicial system. Scheduled for mid-September, the hearing would determine whether enough evidence existed to hold a court-martial.

With the company's impending move to Phanom Sarakham fully underway and disrupting contacts and habits, the time leading up to the hearing was nerve-wracking of its own right.

Whether by luck or design Rien and I essentially single handedly relocated both the company supply room and headquarters over the course of three loads.

The frenzy of events had scrambled things so much that people did not have to make special effort to miss one another, yet Lloyd and Green essentially stopped talking and virtually avoided me. It was as if they were afraid and were washing their hands of all connection to the matter. They also ceased their nightly stop and smoke at Luckie's hideaway.

Luckie on the other hand had been irritated with concern since Madson's August arrest. "Stan number one. Why he do dat? Him 'ber *nung jing-jing* (number one, no doubt) but sometime him *kon baa duey*." (crazy person, too*)*

On September 10, a week before the hearing she was doubly agitated. "Dey call me. Dey come here tell me. Me wit nit!"

"Wait, wait Luckie . . . they? Who came?"

"Merican *piu-kao*. Him come wit Thai 'terpreter. Him say me dey want me help. Who say dem my name? Not Mad-son. Stan, him no do. *Chip-hai*! It dat udder GI, him no goot. Him friend my brudder, Nod!"

"Wellington?"

"Him, *jing-jing*. He no like Billy, the udder GI. Dey like *muan-gan puying*. Same, same. Him *mii mojo* Billy stay wit' her, him AWOL, him stay here wit' her. Udder GI no like. Him look dem *tuk ti wai-laa*. Him see *puying* Billy. Him *mii mak-mak mojo* Billy. I know it be him say. I not truss. I no *chop*. Him *sip-loy!*"

"Are you going to testify?"

"Why not? I not afred!"

Meanwhile in downtown Korat on at least two occasions Green and Lloyd just happened to be rising to leave as I entered the Lucky Seven Club. They were behaving like short-timers who had suddenly lost their courage. They seemed to have made deals and were resigned to a position of every man for himself. They could care less what fate befell the kid, Childs. There would be no unified story on his behalf.

The Hearing

On the morning of September 16, I was called to the witness stand and was led into the hearing from an adjoining room where with other witnesses, isolated and watched, I had silently waited. I was sworn, seated, and ordered by Major Garrett to read my CID deposition into the court record as evidence.

Under questioning, I attempted to recant as much of that statement as possible. First, I suggested that the statement had only been signed from sheer weariness of the process. This was notably evidenced—the signed statement contained no-less-than ten places with my initials, points of restatement or paraphrase. And more importantly, I insisted the quotation attributed to me, *"Those fools done stole a jeep,"* was a misstatement of something said in playful jest between Private Childs and me.

"It had all been a joke. We often spoke of performing acts of extremism like hi-jacking an airplane and forcing the pilot to fly us to Cuba. Believe me we had no intention of carrying any of those things out. We would just be, just be . . . trippin'. You know, imagining?"

This strategy, however, ultimately led Major Garrett to suspect my own involvement. He attempted to entrap me with self-contradiction and perjury. But I held my own, and following my testimony I left the witness stand to return to the waiting room for the remainder of the day's procedures.

I was recalled the next afternoon. As I seated myself the Major began, "I must remind the witness that your testimony remains under oath."

"Yes, sir."

"Then let us continue. Did you or did you not on the 3rd of July at approximately 1900 hours while on guard duty at the 21st Company Motor Pool make the statement to the effect that Childs had stolen the jeep?"

"I made a statement to Lloyd. When he was walking out of the motor pool, I told him that Childs had been down earlier in the day and had said he wanted to take a jeep. When Green and Wellington came back out Lloyd told them that Childs and Madson had stolen a jeep."

"Did you tell Lloyd, 'The fool stole the jeep'? And when he replied, 'Who?', you replied, 'Childs'. When he said that he didn't believe you, you said that *he had stolen the jeep*. Presumably, 'he' meant Madson or Childs – and that in your opinion, 'they were crazy'?"

"Sir, I don't recall the full statement, but if you say those were the words I used—"

"Are they the words?"

"I don't know, sir. Well—" I looked at Childs, but he avoided eye contact, turned his head down and stared at his hands folded together and resting on the table.

"...yes, sir, they are."

"What basis did you have for making the statement?"

"I didn't have a basis for making it."

"Didn't you in fact see the jeep being stolen from the 105th Motor Pool?"

"No, sir."

"Didn't you know there was a plan to steal the vehicle from the Depot?"

"Childs had said he wanted to take a jeep, sir."

"Did he tell you which jeep?"

"He said Headquarters 1, sir."

"Isn't it a fact he said Headquarters 3?"

"No, sir. He did not say Headquarters 3."

"You said Headquarters 1 remained in its position? You observed this periodically throughout your tour that evening as guard. I believe that is what you said?"

"Right, sir. As I remember. When I came back, he was gone. I looked in the next yard and I saw Headquarters 1. It was still there, sir."

"Isn't it true that on the evening of 3 July you saw an empty space where Headquarters 3 is normally parked?"

"I guess so, sir."

"Isn't it a fact that when you assumed guard duty and Childs made his statement initially to you that he was going to steal a jeep that you in fact looked over to where those jeeps were parked and saw not only Headquarters 1 but Headquarters 2, 3, and 4 in their appropriate positions?"

"No, sir. I cannot say I did that, sir."

"You normally work in or around the 21st Motor Pool and you worked periodically as guard?"

"Yes sir."

"And are you familiar with that part of the 105th Depot Motor Pool close to what was then the 21st Motor Pool?"

"Yes."

"It is wide open, and you can easily see from one to the other, isn't it?

"Yes sir. They are side-by-side and wide open, as you say."

"Isn't it a fact that you know the depot vehicles are parked there at approximately 1800 hours including Headquarters 1, 2, 3, 4, and 5?"

"I never counted how many were there, sir."

"Isn't it a fact that you know now, and you knew then where those jeeps were parked belonging to the 105th Field Depot and you previously stated that you saw Headquarters 1 and you specifically looked for Headquarters 1?"

"Yes, sir."

"And isn't it a fact that you know that those jeeps are parked in numerical order? Parked in standard military fashion?"

"Sir, we don't park *our* vehicles in military order."

Contradicted, the major paused to read his notes, then continued, "Isn't it a fact that you conspired with Private Childs to steal a jeep from the 105th Motor Pool?"

"No, sir."

"Then what basis did you have for telling this to Lloyd?"

"I did not see him, sir. I don't know, I don't remember on what basis I told Lloyd."

"Who stole Headquarters 3 from the 105th Depot?"

"I don't know, sir. I cannot say."

"Did you see Madson steal the jeep?"

"No, sir. I did not see Childs steal the jeep, sir."

"I asked you if you saw Madson steal the jeep?"

"No, sir."

"What part did you have in stealing the jeep?

"I didn't play any part in stealing that vehicle, sir."

"Isn't it a fact that you know that Madson stole the jeep?"

"No sir."

At this point, perhaps sensing I had given my best efforts at shielding and withholding all damnable knowledge I possessed, Childs, without counsel from his Judicator rose to his feet and shouted, "Sir, I said I was going to steal Headquarters 1!"

For one moment our eyes met. In his there was a look of forlorn loss, then he turned away and continued. "I said it in a joking manner. When he left, I left and went back to the barracks. Me and Madson went downtown. I said it in a joking manner, sir, because we usually joke in that manner. As for stealing the jeep, sir, I don't believe Forest had anything to do with stealing the government vehicle. Forest would drop out of the conversation automatically when we started talking about stealing anything. That is the truth, sir."

To my surprise, Major Garrett turned to me, locked eyes, nodded his head, then said, "I know that. You are excused, subject to recall."

G.T. Foster

Billy Child's Court-martial

On October 12 we left Don Muang International and after a brief stop in Saigon and refueling at Anderson Air Force Base, were flown to Fort Buckner in Okinawa. This was the nearest and safest site the Army could gather enough brass to hold a general court-martial.

In Thailand, William (Billy) Childs had eventually been slotted in his Military Occupational Skill (MOS) as a company assistant stock clerk. He had been in-country less than one month when the crime was committed, or in this case when the vehicle had been inventoried missing.

Based upon information supplied by a stockade inmate and fellow company member, Lark Wellington, Childs had been arrested and confined to the camp stockade by Camp Friendship Criminal Investigation Department on a charge of black marketeering.

The Army does not hold itself to a high threshold of evidentiary proof for conviction. Unlike a civilian courtroom where the prosecuting attorney must prove guilt, under the Uniform Code of Military Justice it is the accused who is burdened with proof of innocence.

We were in Okinawa for parts of five days. Two days waiting, two days of trial, and a final day spent hurrying-up-to-wait for a flight and return to Thailand.

At the General Court-martial Childs was accused of the theft and/or aiding in the theft of a government vehicle. The missing vehicle, a jeep, had been parked in the Medical Staff motor pool. Our company motor pool was adjacent the Medical Staff's. The chain link lock on the gate had been cut with a large bolt cutter. As company assistant supply clerk Childs had access to large bolt cutters.

Again, I only heard my own testimony, but the trial was a perfunctory command performance of the same dog-and-pony-show we had undergone during the hearing in Korat. Only, this time it was performed in front of a collection of generals who would just as soon have spent the time filing their nails.

Childs was duck soup and taking the fall. Twenty-seven vehicles needed to be accounted for on US Army expenditure books. These officers were here to click their heels and sign-off. Yawn, yawn, the testimony be damned!

Child's defense was that he rarely spent time in the company motor pool and that the chief witness, Wellington, a volunteer regular army washout, was motivated by hate and revenge. The two soldiers were former friends engulfed in the frenzy of a love triangle. The argument failed.

Childs was found guilty, stripped of all rank and sentenced to five years federal prison at Fort Leavenworth, Kansas.

G.T. Foster

Black Marketeer

While maintaining ignorance, I must admit that Army supply clerks are notorious thieves. They frequently have connections to Black Market trading. But if that is enough to convict someone then they should remand all supply clerks to stockade confinement upon completion of Advanced Individual Training. If this were done prior to the individual's first assignment it would save billions of tax-payer dollars.

Maybe Childs stole the vehicle. Maybe, that hot, muggy evening he walked to the motor pool in a long trench coat. He would have worn a trench coat to conceal a very large bolt-cutter. Maybe, when he arrived at the motor pool, he saw the Thai soldier guarding the gate. Perhaps, he spoke to him in rudimentary Thai. Then, while still talking to the armed Thai guard, he removed the large bolt cutter from beneath the long trench coat and crunch! The chain was cut, and the lock removed.

Once inside the yard he selected a vehicle, in this case a jeep. Does a supply clerk have access to keys? Let's assume he had a key or did not need one. Somehow, he drove it to the gate of the motor pool compound. He got out of the vehicle to pull the gate open. He got back into the vehicle and drove it through the open gate and parked. He, again, left the vehicle and pulled the gate closed.

What say the Thai soldier?

And still, he now must exit Camp Friendship, without orders or with fake ones. He must pass the diligent Military Police guards at the entry gate. Succeeding this, he must then drive to the pre-appointed destination to consummate a sale.

That place could have been Luckie's hideaway. It was, in fact, off-limits. Why? I had never inquired. Black Market? Possibly. Luckie was enterprising. Pichai was a member of the Thai Queen's Cobras Special Forces and knew people of social rank and others with wealth.

Why not? It could have happened.

G.T. Foster

Krai Kaa Surapol?

The October morning of my return from Child's court-martial, as I walked through Don Muang International Airport, it was crystal clear. Today, Lem would be happy, the case had popped. The Thai police had their man. Rather, in this case, they had three men. Caught, cuffed, and carted off to jail in a police raid, they finally got the bad-guy killers of Surapol Sambatcharoen, and, apparently, had mounting evidence against several others. It was front page headlines of every newspaper given prominent display at the airport news-stand kiosks.

Surapol had been murdered on August 16, 1968. Yet, there was a lapse of time in which no one knew anything about the matter. That was especially odd, given Surapol's social status as a Thai megastar, and the Thai national conscience expressed in the dictum, *"Kun mai dai kaa kon diiao tom-loot jop,* or in English, you cannot kill anyone because the police will catch you."

One hundred plus times I'd been told or had heard this expression said by one law-abiding Thai citizen or another. It was often offered as calming advice against the escalation of verbal disputes into violent clashes. Well, in the military and police state in which they lived, perception was reality. The Thai police force, like the legendary Royal Canadian Mountie police-counterpart, seemed always to get its man. The lack of police capture of the brazen perpetrators stood in stark contradiction. So, what had been the delay?

In September, more than a month after his death, I had entered a roadside eatery. Mounted on a tall bamboo shelf, a

The Boys Are Not Refined

black and white television broadcasted news events. As I seated myself at a table I asked to no one in particular but everyone in general, "*Krai kaa* Surapol?"

Heads turned but there was no response. I smiled and asked again, "*Krai kaa* Surapol Sambatcheroen?"

Incredulous looks and glances spoke of unease and whispered hush-hush. "Did he just ask us, who killed Surapol? He, very obviously, is not Thai. Why is he asking? How could he, being *farang*, even know anything about Surapol?" Not a word had been said but it was all over their faces.

Then one brave soul did speak. "*Mai luu. Mai bpen kon luu.*" The tone was final and dismissive and came from a customer as he stacked his plate on a dirty-dish-bussing cart and walked out of the restaurant.

He didn't know, nor did anyone else. I hadn't expected he would and had only asked in friendly conversation, but the response had been telling. Who killed Surapol? At the time, only a few knew, and they were not talking. Not yet, not then.

But one had to admit the case had revealed a puzzling question or two. Who wanted Surapol dead? He had been shot after a concert. Were the gunmen disgruntled fans of his music? Hit men hired by a rival?

Yet the most bizarre element had been a particularly damning photograph that appeared in newspapers two weeks after the killing. It showed two Thai police officers sitting at an outdoor table set up near the crime scene within an hour of the actual shooting. The policemen had begun to interview witnesses. The photo showed a line of bystanders. Many were waiting to be interviewed. The point of view of the photographer had been from behind the assembled crowd. The police were most distant.

Oddly, standing among the bystanders and potential witnesses was a tall slender Thai wearing a Pendleton patterned long sleeve shirt. The picture captured his backside. He stood facing the officers as if waiting to be interviewed. That is what made the picture odd. He stood with his arms fully extended downward along his sides. In his left hand he held what appeared to be a Smith & Wesson 38 caliber revolver.

That had been late-August, but the case did not break until after a certain Thai police colonel of District 8 received a special package. The package arrived at the colonel's remote island home slightly before midday. Delivered by a courier, it had been signed for and received by the colonel's housekeeper. The colonel arrived home at 3:30 p.m. He took the package upstairs to the master bedroom. There he unwrapped it. It was a bomb! It exploded and sent his physical parts through the four walls of the room and beyond, and his spirit to the queue line to await its next incarnation.

You see, the Thai police had known who shot John. And it had taken the power of a high ranking Thai police district commander to keep the now-blown lid on. In this case, the police colonel had received a princely sum and the matter of who had shot Surapol had remained unsolved. However, friends, associates, and family had doggedly pursued the truth and discovered that Surapol's assassination had been a hired hit carried out by three members of the *Nuk Lang*, or Thai underworld.

Apparently, both Surapol and a village elder had set their minds upon having the same pretty young village girl as a second wife. The elder's intentions toward the girl were probably more honorable than the intentions of Surapol. But the power of fame and stardom in the minds of the young has a far greater attraction than that of honor and reasonable comfort alongside an old man long past his middle age.

But this was not a simple case of a girl choosing one lover over another. There was a contract and the girl's parents had signed and accepted payment to seal the deal. Although the girl had flippantly dismissed the contract and rashly chosen Surapol's bed, the old social pillar had other ideas.

It is not clear whether Surapol was warned off or whether the old man had gone straight to the *Nuk Lang*. At the time, the life of an American army captain held steady at twenty dollars US currency. In either event, a price was settled upon, a three-man murder team was hired, and the job was done outside the temple (*wat*) grounds after the Nakhon Pathom concert.

G.T. Foster

Return to the Phanom Boondocks

At our new base home in the outback, I'd hardly had time to move my belonging into the 4-man hooch I now shared with Green, Lloyd, and Madson. Although I still felt a need to resolve the differences that had developed over Child's court-martial, the evening of my return to camp I drew Charge-of-Quarters duty. This meant that I and a non-commissioned duty-officer were after-hours clerks responsible for contacting the proper personnel in case of an emergency. I had barely unpacked my duffle bag before the shift began.

Many of the black troops including Green, Lloyd, Ruffin, Wardell, and Pride had gone to the village that night to celebrate the liberation and return of both Madson and the incorrigible Private Wellington. Both soldiers had apparently resolved the charges stemming from the Bolt-Wellington skirmish, and had been released from stockade confinement and returned to active duty. But I considered Wellington a dirty, double-crossing snitch responsible for Child's fall.

As CQ that group's 9:30 p.m. return to post was duly noted by myself and Sergeant Bass, the NCO duty-officer. Their three-minute drunken ruckus of loud singing and laughter could hardly go unnoticed. I silently smiled as I heard them sing a song I'd helped write in an off-tune take of the Beatles' "I'm Crying":

Pom bpai talot (I go to marketplace)
Ja suu gadot (To buy paper)
Ja ken jote mai (To write letter)
Ja hai tii baan (To send home)

The Boys Are Not Refined

Gaa mia mai yuu (But wife not there)
Mia len jao-chuu (Wife plays the butterfly)
Pom leung hai (I cry)
Tamai (Why?)

Although the song was rambunctious, within twenty minutes the camp had returned to a slumbering silence and I was reading the *Stars and Stripes* newspaper when a loud and grievous cry of pain broke the camp calm. I grabbed my flashlight and with Sergeant Bass headed in the direction of the initial outcry. In seconds the company's sleeping soldiers were actively alert, as all around the camp lights-out turned to lights-on. Hooch doors opened and other soldiers emerged, conjoining our investigation.

We followed the sound of whimpering moans to its source. Four soldiers were already standing outside the hooch of Sergeant Bolt and pointed to its open doorway. Inside we found Specialist Fourth Class Johnson frantically trying to help staunch the sergeant's pain. But all Johnson's efforts seemed only to add to Bolt's misery.

"Mother fuck ... oh ... oh ... cocksucker," Bolt cussed in agony. "Asshole!" he howled.

"It was him."

"What happened?" asked Bass. "Who was it? What happened?"

"Oh ... it was ...Wellington! Oh, ooh ..." Bolt insisted between jolts of throbbing pain, "Cocksucker! My God ... ooh, it was him!"

"Did you see him?" the sergeant asked. "Did you see Wellington?"

"God damn you!" Bolt snapped. "It was him I tell you. Ooh ... oh ... I don't have to see the motherfucker, God damn it! It was him, I tell you, it was him ..." Bolt was on the verge of tears.

Sergeant Bass turned to those who had gathered and asked, "Did anybody see anything?"

"It was too dark, Sarge," said one soldier.

"I heard him scream. I looked out and saw a shadow running, but... it was too dark," verified another unenlightening witness. Company commander Lieutenant Fisher arrived just as Bass ordered me to inform him of the attack.

"Oh... I know it was him... damn it! Fuck! Goddamn it to hell!" continued the victim.

When Fisher tried to get more details, Bolt, sullen, between pangs of pain and discomfort, turned his rage upon the entire Army organization. Unaware there had been a change at the top, he began with General Westmoreland and the General Staff and denounced them all, distributing equal blame downward through our own company commander and his collection of greenhorn officers, with teat-milk still on their collective breath.

"It is all your motherfuckin' fault! Fuck! Our once great and proud military has deteriorated to a piss-ass, second rate, weak-kneed, fighting force that can't even fuckin' lick little fuckin' gook motherfuckers. You yellow-bellied officers allow a piece of shit like Wellington to wear the uniform. Well? No fuckin' wonder! No fuckin' wonder!"

He said these things with a quivering voice while vacillating his position from half-lying to half-sitting, only to switch back to half-lying upon his bunk. He moaned, groaned, and held his right knee as he struggled to find a comfortable position. He could not.

A soldier brought a bat into the room. "This was on the ground," he said handing it to me.

Then Lieutenant English and two medics from the camp clinic arrived. I left the bat in the possession of Lieutenant English and returned to the office of company headquarters. At twelve midnight, twenty-four hundred hours, there was a duty change and I was relieved.

The Exile

The next morning, at the zero seven hundred hour (7 a.m.) morning formation, Lieutenant Fisher was seething. His jaw clenched under a tightly closed mouth that twitched like a cow chewing its cud. Before almost the entire assembled company, he stood silent and staring. His olive-green fatigue shirt was already soaked in sweat.

When he finally spoke his eyes seemed to dart and focus upon either Madson or myself. He swiveled his head back and forth. Back . . . the eyes focused upon Madson, forth . . . they eyeballed me. "Sergeant Bolt has been transported to the base hospital at Camp Friendship with a shattered kneecap. The apparent weapon was a baseball bat. The bat has been turned over to the army Criminal Investigation Department at Korat. The assailant or assailants are at present unknown."

He paused for a moment and turned his back to the formation. He spoke to Lieutenant English, but only briefly. Then he planted the toe of his right foot, made a sharp, snappy pivot to reface us, as we continued to stand at full attention. Looking directly at me, Lieutenant Fisher said, "Private Nigel Forest!"

"Yes sir!"

"You are here and now being transferred and ordered to Sattahip. Immediately leave this formation, gather your gear, and report to the 55th company's First Sergeant Johnson. Company clerk Sasse will drive you there. Dismissed!"

Wholly surprised, I stepped out of the formation as Fisher continued, "Private Samuel Madson!"

"Yes sir."

"You are to go to Korat. You are to report to the 33rd platoon sergeant. Fall out and pack your gear. Specialist Ruffin shall transport you there immediately. Private, you are dismissed!"

I walked to the hooch I briefly shared with Lloyd, Green and Madson and I opened my footlocker and wall locker and began to repack their contents into my duffle bag. As I was doing so, Madson entered.

"Da lieutenant done flipped his lid," he laughed. "Forest, he done sho' nuff flipped. What da hell done got in tah him?"

"Oh, man, the army has suddenly branded us a menace. Did you know that you are part of a clique?"

"A clique? What da hell is dat, some kina gang?" asked Madson.

"Yeah, man, that's what it is. That's exactly what it is. Hell, you know what?"

"What's dat, Forest?"

"I think Mr. Dumb Ass Lieutenant Sir is just following orders. He was probably told by Major Lippman to do something. Do anything. Who the heck knows?"

"Well, shucks," snickered Madson. "What da fuck? Korat beats da hell outta dis shithole."

"What about Sattahip, man?" I asked.

"Where yeh gonna be in Sattahip? The 55th? Well, dey ova at Camp Vayama. It ain't bad, man. Not big like Korat, and deh army camp is separate from deh air force base. Dey ova at Utapao. It ain't bad, Forest."

"Well . . . hey, man, it's been fun." I had packed my duffel and was ready to walk to headquarters for my ride south. We shook hands and bumped shoulders.

"Yeah, it sho' nuff been dat all right. But, hell, man, I'm gonna see yeh. How long yeh got?"

"I got three more months. Take care, Madman."

I walked to company headquarters. Sasse was ready and waiting. We boarded the jeep and I left Camp Charn

The Boys Are Not Refined

Sinthrope in the rear view mirror. Upon my arrival at Camp Vayama I reported as ordered to First-Sergeant Johnson.

I was told by the first-sergeant, "Don't unpack your gear. My two platoons here are full. That CO of yours don't know his own ass. Now, look soldier, I got a squad in Bangkok workin' outta the motor pool. They're part of a platoon that was workin' outta the Royal Thai Air Force Base up in Udorn haulin' material to Nakon Phanom. I need you to replace one of those boys. He's goin' home. You go to Bangkok and report to the motor pool. You are TDY dere 'til further notice. Do you understand?"

"Yes sir, First-Sergeant, sir.... No, First-Sergeant I don't understand. I mean where do I billet in Bangkok? The American Hotel?"

"That's right. You see, soldier, you do understand," he smiled.

G.T. Foster

Bangkok Refugee

Now let's all cry. Boo-hoo, boo-hoo.

I arrived in Bangkok via company jeep transport and checked into the American Hotel as Temporary Duty Personnel (TDY). I was not obligated to report to the motor pool until next morning, so I didn't. Instead, I took a cab to the Chinatown district or *Charoen Krung,* so called because it was mostly built and populated by ethnic Chinese laborers and their families. There, I had been told, I would be able to find and purchase the album *Sip-hok Bpii Hɛng Kwam-lang,* the last recorded songs of Surapol Sambatcheroen.

After settling the fare I walked through a vibrant collection of shops, stalls, carts, and pedestrian street vendors. I took note of the jewelry and fine gold work. I was particularly stricken by a stall with an eye-catching display of "rental" Buddhas. I purchased, sorry, "rented" two, then stopped at a different stall and bought a gold chain on which to attach them.

I then focused my attention on finding a music shop and was directed to the many record shops that lined the *Saphan Lek* section of *Charoen Krung.* Once there I chose one, entered, and I asked the clerk, if he had the record. *"Mii pen-siiang 'Sip-hok Bpii Hɛng Kwam-lang' mai, krap?"*

His eyes brightened in surprise. *"Mii, krap. Mii jing-jing,"* he reassured me. The enterprising clerk quickly moved from behind the counter and fetched the desired album, but he also brought three other records by Surapol. He explained that these were earlier works and were at least as good as, if not better than, the album I desired to purchase.

The Boys Are Not Refined

I kindly thanked him but said no thanks, *"Kop-kun, krap. Mai, ao."* I paid for *"Sip-hok Bpii . . ."* then asked, *"Mii kruuang-len ja sur duey, krap?"*

"Mai mii, krap. Mai mii," he sadly said in regard to also having record players for sell. But he pointed to a nearby shop that sold radios, tape players, and other electronic devices. I went there and soon left with a reasonably priced record player.

I returned to the hotel and my room with my bounty and played the album. I liked it. Some of the songs I recognized as having previously heard and liked, including both "Mong" and "Snooker".

The next day, after quickly checking in and out of the non-bustling motor pool, I returned to the hotel and my music. I tried to listen and record the lyrical refrain of some of the songs into a notebook. It proved to be a difficult task and I feared rending my vinyl a stuttering scratch.

So that afternoon I returned to Chinatown and the shop where I had purchased the record player. This time I bought a reel-to-reel tape recorder-player that had a foot/second counter display.

It allowed me to pause and reset at will and greatly helped with the "What did he just sing?" problem I continually encountered while listening to my new *Luk Thung* album.

And that is how I began my Bangkok exile. It was a time of aloneness. I was truly on my own. It was a perfect opportunity for personal growth and reflection although, admittedly, I never stopped to engage in self-reflection. Perhaps too afraid of what I would see, or too dishonest to change. But I did make a big push in Thai language development. I committed to work almost exclusively on the album's title song, *"Sip-hok Bpii Hɛng Kwam-lang"*. It became the first Thai song I learned in its entirety.

Fortunately, the US Army's Ninth Logistical staff had entirely overbooked the necessary personnel for efficient coverage and operation from the Bangkok Motor Pool. The first three days I spent in morning trips to the motor pool to sign the duty roster, wait around fifteen minutes, and then I was dismissed for the day. It was tough duty, but somebody had to do it.

During that time, day and night spent in continuous practice produced a memorized, Romanized version of *"Siphok Bpii"*. It had been arduously learned, monosyllable by monosyllable, but I could now sing it. Unlike the snippets of Thai songs I had previous learned, I sang the song to no one. But, after the third day, I felt ready.

In 1968, each month, more than 32,000 of the American soldiers serving in Vietnam were given leave and free flights on commercial airlines to Bangkok, Manila, Singapore, Taipei, Tokyo, Hong Kong, Kuala Lumpur, Penang, Sidney, or Hawaii under the Army's Recreation and Relaxation Program, known more commonly as R&R. It meant everyday there were upwards of 3000 United States Government Issued personnel wandering the streets of Bangkok, radically spiking the local economy. They came to release war zone tensions and their stays amounted to five- or six-day alcohol- and sex-filled rages. In Bangkok these military money trees were herded and corralled inside the Patpong District's massage parlors, bars, and red-light houses.

In the bars, Thai rock bands blasted out covers to a thousand American and British tunes. I boldly walked into one with psychedelic strobe lights pulsating to the beat of the instrumental group of eight playing on the barroom stage. In a slick piece of advertising, a large, sky-blue satin banner proclaimed the band to be *Bpen Mai Dai* — The Impossibles.

I moved to the stage edge and waited for the song they were playing to end, then signaled the lead guitarist. He came with a quizzical look that quickly changed to one of bewilderment when I asked, "*Kun dai sa-daang pleeng 'Sip-hok Bpii' mai?*" (Can you play the song "16 Years"?)

"*Kun leung pleeng dai mai, krap?*" (Can you sing it?) He asked with a doubtful smile.

"*Chai si, krap. Leung pleeng dai.*" (Sure, man. I can sing it.)

He turned to his other band members for a brief pow-wow during which each member in turn popped his head from the huddle to take a peek at me. They broke and enthusiastically beckoned me on stage. The lead guitarist directed me to the microphone, then adjusted it to my height. I took a beat, signaled my readiness, and the trumpet sounded the opening dirge.

I sang:

Sip-hok bpii hɛng Kwam-lang
tang rak tang chang tang wan
le kom kuun
Sip-hok bpii muan Sip-hok wan
rak ur-ie chang san mai yang-yuun
Mii wan mii chuun mii kuun mii kom
Sip-hok bpii tii tur le chan . . .

It was a bar at 9 o'clock at night in the happy and gay district of a city that does not sleep and, yet, that place was as quiet and respectful as an empty Christian church prior to a funeral. But when I finished my song the place rocked and hooted back to life. The cheers were immediate and fulfilling. Each member of the band extended his congratulations and encouragement.

"Come back again, GI."

"What your name, GI? You stay Bangkok?"

But I was floating. I had finished the song, so I shook their hands, left the stage, and walked out the door, knowing there is magic in mystery. Leave them hungry with wonder.

"Where GI learn Thai song?"

"GI number one, *jing-jing!*"

G.T. Foster

The Bad Haul

The Bangkok Motor Pool yard was shared by various companies operating throughout Thailand under the command of the 19th Transportation Battalion. Refrigerated cargo was generally moved by the 13th or the 53rd company with an occasional assist from the 33rd platoon but on the day in reference, none of those units were in town and a shipment of frozen meats sat in the yard.

It was bound to happen eventually. Okay. I reported to the motor pool and was placed on the drivers' roster to move the meat. I pulled the detail with a 14-year buck sergeant (E-5). We left Bangkok hauling the cargo in a seal-locked refrigerated trailer. It was my first frozen shipment and my first assigned trip into the northeastern frontier beyond our battalion camp at Khon Kaen. The sergeant had made my role clear enough.

"Yeah, I'm Mike Stoller," he said by way of introduction. We had just pulled out of the motor pool and he was weaving his way through Bangkok morning traffic. "And, friend, we gonna get along just fine so long as you just take care of your own business. This load here? I got this. You just sit back and watch how it's done."

So, I was just along for the ride but nonetheless glad to get out of Bangkok for a change of pace. Signatures were needed at each of our two destinations. When we reached Khon Kaen we entered the encampment from the army gate and travelled through to the air force base. At our drop point the receiving stock clerk and Stoller jointly opened the sealed cargo, off-loaded the appropriate tonnage, resealed the trailer door, then signed and exchanged copies of the manifest.

Zip. Zap. The first drop had gone without a hiccup, and we were well within schedule to make Sakhon Nakhon by early evening.

At a village called Karasin, Stoller stopped the truck near a roadside diner. He said, "Wait here." He climbed out of the cab, removed a tire iron from under the seat, and walked to the rear of the trailer.

There was hardly a sound when he broke the wire seal. In the passenger side-view mirror the refrigerator door swung open. After a minute it closed. The sergeant took an arm full of steaks into the eatery. He came out shortly and we continued, as I sat tight-lipped, silently thinking, "Come on, man, don't you know I know what you're doing?" But I knew the answer. He didn't have to say a word. Obviously, he didn't give a good hot damn.

Next, we stopped for lunch at a well-situated kitchen in Somdet. Roadside. There were two Americans finishing their noon meal. We spoke briefly as we waited for our order. They were part of a three-man radio detachment embedded in the village.

Soon after they had left, a three-quarter-ton troop transport stopped and parked. From under the olive-green canvas-tarp rear Thai soldiers rose off facing benches, exited the truck, entered the kitchen-diner, and seated themselves at tables for lunch.

Sergeant Stoller purchased a bottle of Mekong whiskey for himself and ordered a bottle of Singha beer for each soldier and included a shot of whiskey for the captain of the expedition. Stoller consumed the bottle of Mekong with his lunch and purchased a second for the road.

It so happened the detachment of Thai soldiers were also going to Sakhon Nakhon. We finished lunch at about the same time. Somehow, between Stoller and the captain, it was decided, since we were all going to Sakhon Nakhon, one Thai soldier would ride in the truck with me while the sergeant (who was by the minute becoming more and more inebriated) would ride in the back of the Thai military transport.

This arrangement lasted all of five miles before the bewildered Thai officer and soldiers apparently could bear no more of this ugly, obnoxious, drunken, American GI. As I followed, their vehicle abruptly pulled to the side of the road and halted. I, too, pulled off the road and stopped. A single Thai soldier climbed from the rear of the transport, weapon strapped to his back and quick-time marched to the passenger side of my idling truck. Without a word, he tilted his head and signaled his comrade. The signaled soldier climbed from the cab and the two climbed back into the rear of the transport.

Meanwhile Sergeant Stoller ambled unsteadily out of the transport and staggered to our idling Reefer. He was, now not only drunk, but embarrassed and enraged to boot. He insisted on driving.

"Okay, Bud, I got this."

I insisted he not. "No, I don't think that's a good idea, Sarge."

"I didn't ask you for your opinion, Bud," he slurred.

"Yeah, but I'm giving it. I still don't think you driving is the best idea you've had today."

"Well, I'm a fucking sergeant and you're a fucking nothing. Move over, god damn it!"

Yeah. Like the wrong everywhere he pulled rank. And even though he far outweighed me, he was drunk. I could probably take him, but was it worth it? Left with the alternatives of fight or flight, I removed my rifle and travel bag from behind the truck cab seat and mockingly saluted him farewell. I slung my weapon over one shoulder and with my canvas travel bag in hand, walked the five miles back to

The Boys Are Not Refined

the village of Somdet thinking every step an incremental measurement of Sergeant Stoller's actual jackass size.

At the roadside restaurant I inquired of the American soldiers that lived somewhere in the village. When I found the three soldiers, I explained my situation. They formally introduced themselves as Kent, Joseph, and Michael, and cheerfully gave me quarter. They designated the living room as my space and the couch for my night's bunk and Joseph gave calming reassurance.

"There will be a jeep mail car from Sakhon Nakhon in the morning," Joseph said. "From here it goes to Khon Kaen. I'll call ahead. Don't worry, you'll be able to hitch a ride. Now, relax and make yourself at home, as we say back home." The men then left the room for other parts of the house.

As I looked around the room it was obvious someone had a sense of humor. On the walls were pinned the glossy newsprint covers from back issues of Life Magazine. Only one was framed.

It showed an anti-war protester stuffing pink carnations down the rifle barrels of elite Airborne Rangers.

The magazines apparently came regularly. Issues dating back to 1965 were stacked around the room. I put my gear down and thumbed through a few of the more recent editions of the weekly with its 1000-word stories of kitchens, balconies, Sirhan-Sirhan, heart transplants, Prague Spring, Soviet tanks, and Igbo warriors of the Biafra War. Jeez, black brothers killing black brothers!

The Great White Hope had opened on Broadway and how fitting that Muhammad Ali should star in the role of Jack Johnson. That was the least they could do! The government had taken away his passport, cutting his cash stream of multi-million-dollar Bum-a-Month fights. Otherwise, America, South Africa, and Europe could have continued their real-life search for a great white answer to him.

Oh, well. George Wallace was running on a third-party ticket. That should be interesting. And then there was that story of the US bomber carrying H-bombs, without their warheads. Crashed in Greenland. Thank God for small favors! Frigging Russian roulette! Wow!

The men rarely cooked and I was invited to join them for supper at a local restaurant. I accepted and was shown the wash area where I could shower.

Later we walked two blocks from their rented house to a large restaurant with a spacious dance floor. There was an eight or nine-piece band that played a mixture of Thai and American popular tunes. Of my three hosts, the soldier from San Jose, California, proved to be as obnoxious that evening as the drunken Sergeant Stoller had been that afternoon.

"Joseph is from New Jersey and Kent here is from Alabama. He don't like niggers," Michael informed me out of the blue.

"Knock it off, Michael," said Joseph. "Or at least get your facts straight. Kent is from Carolina . . . North Carolina, and you know it."

"Carolina, Alabama, what's the difference? They're both the South. I'm from San Jose. Colored, Negro? They don't bother me"

"California?" I asked.

"Sure. San Jose. I went to school with colored. I don't mind 'em. You ever been to San Jose? "

"As in San Jose State? Mexico Olympics, San Jose? Yes, I know the way to San Jose, do do do do do do do doo," I sang a paraphrase of the hit song by Dionne Warwick. "Man, I was just looking at Life Magazine and that photograph of Tommy Smith and John Carlos on the victory stand in Mexico City. Black Power! Wow!"

"That was something," agreed Kent.

Michael totally missed my humor and ignored my social comment. He continued, "Like I say, I don't mind 'em. They tend their fields and we tend to ours. You know what I mean? I know plenty of colored."

"Colored? Damn," I thought, "*He said it again, straight out of Jim Crow.*" Well, Black Power had jumped off the bus of the Student Non-violent Coordinating Committee and rushed onto the victory stand in Mexico City for a Cecil B. De Mille close-up, and not a minute too soon. I was now Black, but guys like Michael would never understand.

Joseph rolled his eyes to the ceiling. I looked at Kent. He was already looking back at me and shook his head in silent disagreement or disapproval of what had just been said. Throughout the evening Kent showed class and restraint, acting like a true gentleman. He made no off-color remarks. Neither Blacks, Thais, nor any other group were the victims of his tongue.

Yet, California-raised Michael had implied that being from the South, Kent was automatically a racist. Funny how we project. Truth be told, Michael, the San Jose soldier was the only bigot present that night.

Dinner came as a variety of dishes and we commonly shared them. As we ate, Kent asked, "What do ya'll think of all those Flower Children?"

"You mean the hippies?" I replied.

"Yeah, that's them. Those hippie Flower Children in San Francisco."

"What about them? I mean, I know about them. Hell, I know some of 'em. I used to work at this Standard service station at Ashby and Telegraph, a few blocks from the University of California campus. You'd see them there, thumbs out, seven days a week, 24-hours a day.

"Hitch-hiking?"

"Damn right, hitch-hiking. Ashby Avenue is a direct road to the Bay Bridge. The bridge connects the east side of the bay, Berkeley, Oakland, Richmond and the Walnut Creek bedroom communities to San Francisco and the west side of the bay. Most of the hippies were headed to San Francisco and the Haight-Ashbury District—or simply, the Haight, as they call it."

"Boy," injected Kent, "but I remember back home in North Carolina. I was living in Cherry Hill, going to school. But mostly drinkin' and partyin' with my frat mates. But I knew these three that just took off and left school. Went out there . . . to California."

"Man, the Haight was like the international headquarters for hippies. Our service station being where it was, I got a bird's eye-view of that . . . movement."

"Man, those three! It was two guys and a girl. They'd talk and talk of Berkeley as if it were some kind of Mecca. Like they were plannin' a holy pilgrimage to some Eureka-I-have-found-it sort of place. You know what I mean?"

"Yeah, man. I know what you mean. I tell yeh, there were kids running away to Berkeley, I mean young kids, teenage kids and even pre-teens. They were flooding into the Bay Area all the time."

"Them long-hairs," affirmed San Jose confidently.

"Long hair, short hair, no hair. It didn't matter. And many, unlike your college friends, were not even out of high school. They all came. Tripping . . . seeking the holy grail of Free Love, Free Speech. At the time of my induction I was hearing cries for free sex."

"Oh, yeah! I'm for that. But you know what? Even in Thailand where it gets mighty cheap, it always, always costs," San Jose said in noteworthy humor.

I gave a chuckled laugh and probed, "But all kidding aside, I don't get it and never got it. Free love and free speech I get, but if you have free love, why would you need free sex? It seems like a redundant request."

"Or a paradox," said Joseph breaking his silence. "That is, before you came to Thailand where, admittedly sometimes, it is practically free."

"It is, ain't it? But it does seem like a redundant request." said San Jose, continuing our across-the-races agreement.

"Ha, ha, ha." Kent sounded a begrudged laugher then asked, "You're not kidding me, right? Ha, ha, ha. Look, they're not talking sex like, like, fornicating! Excuse me. It's a pet peeve of mine. Why is sex such a taboo subject that it causes such knee jerk verbal response?"

"What do you mean?" asked Joseph.

"Say 'sex' and immediately stark-naked images, male or female, what be your pleasure, come to mind. It must be that cold northern puritanical guilty spirit being given far too much play. But ya'll stop it right there! That is not the road they are travelling when they demand free sex. They mean sex as gender. You know, male and female. Free-sex is considered a clarion call for gender equality. The equal rights of women, ya'll see?"

"Jesus, I feel stupid. Sorry, man. Heck, I just thought . . ."

"I didn't mean that as a personal criticism. It really is just a pet peeve, that sex thing. That's all."

"No, really. It really was…shallow, I should have solved that riddle in my own mind." There was a silent pause so I continued. "You know, I once met Mario Savio. He was working as a bartender in Berkeley at this place on San Pablo Avenue called The Steppenwolf."

"Really?" asked Kent. "No kidding?" He seemed impressed.

"That's kind of cool," said Michael.

"I often wondered what happen to him. They expelled him right? He can't go back?" asked Joseph.

"You got that right," I affirmed. "He cannot go back."

Kent said, "Maybe not to Berkeley. But he was probably one of those ten thousand protesters in Chicago."

"Chicago?" I asked.

"Sure, Democratic National Convention. There was a huge riot."

"Hell, the police went ape-shit. There's no getting around it," insisted Joseph.

"The first I heard about it. Hell, you know that is not the kind of story the boys in charge print in *Stars and Stripes*. How the heck you guys manage to get the news and all the Life magazines?"

"That was a gift from whatever officer established this outpost on the line. The issues just keep arriving like clockwork," said Joseph.

"Well, anyway, still speaking of sex, it seems this summer, back in the world, they all plannin' a giant Love-In at a San Francisco park," said Kent.

"Man," I said, "they had one of those the summer I was inducted!"

Kent continued, "I was just kind of thinking, kind of wondering what it all really is about. That's all."

"That'll be a great day for my personal all-time favorite lyric – 'Why don't we do it in the road?'" Joseph sang.

We laughed and joined in, "No one will be watching us//So we can do it in the road!"

"You know, I don't know?" I paused a moment. "There really might be something to the idea of a generation gap."

"Yeah, I know, but it is not always an age thing," Kent responded.

"Hell no, man. My grandfather is more in tune than my old man ever is," said Michael.

"I agree," I nodded. "Hell, there are things, if you are honest, that you have in common with your worst enemy. I believe it is about change and people."

"Smart people who come to realize that there are better ways to do things," concurred Joseph. "I think Kennedy got it. He understood."

"Yeah, maybe," said Mike.

"Too bad McCarthy didn't get the nomination," said Kent. "But the Paris talks are a start."

"I mean change in people," said Mike.

Admitting the point, I said, "Yeah. Change inside of people. But also more fairness. I don't know, man. Take the demonstrators and the so-called hippies. They talk about nature, and clean water, and pollution, and war and the harm we do to the environment. They make sense."

"I was thinking that, too," Kent agreed. "They make a lot of sensible arguments about things we should be concerned about yet never even stop to think about during the course of our day."

"Fuckin' long hairs. Hell, I say nuke 'em. Bury them all under a phosphorous cloud," said Mike.

The band played throughout the meal. When the waiter came to take orders for coffee or liquer I asked him in Thai, "Can this band play *'Sip-hok Bpii Hɛng Kwam-lang'*?"

Surprised, he asked, *"Kun luu-jac nii pleeng?"* (Do you know that song?)

"Chai si krap. Pom leung pleeng dai jing-jing. Puak kao len dai mai?" (Yes, and I can sing it, too. Can they play it?)

"Mai mii gohok?" he said, literally asking, "Do you have bullshit?"

"Pom mai gohok," I said, replying negatively to the question of pulling-his-leg, so to speak.

The waiter crossed the dance floor and went to the elevated platform that served as the stage. He spoke with the bandleader, then waved me to approach. The bandleader smiled and asked if I could really sing *"Sip-hok Bpii Hɛng Kwam-lang"* and I assured him I could. He beckoned me onto the stage and announced there would be a special performance of a special song. He then handed me the microphone and the band began to play.

After my first few notes a gasping silence occurred followed by a buzz throughout the building. The Thai restaurant staff flowed in to witness this strange event. The clients of the restaurant also looked on in stunned appreciation. Upon completion of my rendition there was a loud eruption of applause as everyone in the restaurant stood in ovation.

I returned to our table amid their thunderous approval. The owner of the restaurant soon came to our table and took the bill insisting that our dinner was free. Payment would dishonor him. Sweet! For me, it worked as a wonderful way to pay the other GIs for the ample American hospitality they provided as my overnight hosts.

That night I slept on the couch. The house began to stir about 0700 so I dressed and, with a Life magazine in hand, joined Kent in the kitchen area. He handed me a cup of coffee and said, "Good morning. Hope you slept all right and thanks again for last night's treat." He gave me a wide grin.

"You're welcome," I chuckled. "I never sang for my father, but I did sing for you," I said in a subtle reference to the play that I read had just opened on Broadway. I showed Kent the article.

Still smiling he said, "Your ride will be here in about half-an-hour."

He paused, then continued, but the smile was gone. "I've heard some rather disturbing news on our short-wave. It seems Sergeant Stoller had a bit of a problem getting that transport to Sakhon Nakhon. About ten miles from town he plowed into a buffalo-drawn cart. You've seen them. The Thais used them to haul farm produce to the local markets. He killed a farmer and his daughter. They were returning home from market."

"Jesus Christ," I said shocked into the present. "Crummy Christmas, how did he do that?"

But we both shook our heads knowing exactly why and how he had done it.

"Well, what's going to happen now?" I asked.

"That's the ugly part. Most Favored Nation status."

"What? Like he gets immunity?"

"Yes, sir."

"Even if he was drunk?"

"Drunk or not, what the brass is going to do to Stoller, they've already done. By now Stoller is on a plane headed for either Okinawa or the Philippines for a new duty assignment. Hell, he could already be seated in the Mess Hall having breakfast."

"That is messed up! It is not fair."

"In this case, it is certainly unfair. In cases like this, we are treated like diplomats. Guys are out of the country within 24 hours. And that's that. Sad but true. In all likelihood, nothing more is going to happen to Sergeant Stoller." Kent could only continue to negatively shake his head at the outlandish wrong.

I caught the mail jeep to Khon Kaen. By noontime I was in Korat. It would take me another two days to hitch back to my Bangkok duty station. No one ever questioned me about this incident, which only reinforced my notion that military justice is an arbitrary thing. It operates under the guise of the Uniform Code but where is the uniformity in a system that turns a blind eye to murderous drunken driving yet drums a soldier out of the service to be held in a military stockade or federal prison confinement for the suspected black marketeering of an army jeep?

G.T. Foster

Graveyard Shift

Upon my return to Bangkok I learned General Black or a member of the 9th Logistical General Staff had passed a disgruntled fart and a reshuffle of the entire battalion had occurred. Our company, 55th, no longer had shuttle responsibilities from the Bangkok Motor Pool. Our squadron's temporary duty assignment was terminated, and we were ordered to return south to our Sattihip company headquarters.

Back at Camp Vayama, I entered the NCO's crammed and cluttered office space and said, "First-Sergeant Johnson, Private Forest reporting for duty as ordered." I handed him my copy of the order.

"At ease." he said taking the papers. "You are no longer a private. Here is your promotion letter, Specialist Forest." He handed me the promotion order to E-4, looked over my papers, then picked up his duty roster clipboard.

I folded the promotion letter and placed it in my fatigue shirt pocket. He flipped a page, looked up and said, "See here, soldier, you can continue on the drivers' duty roster or you can work in the yard. I got a rotation hole to fill. The soldier assigned overnight charge of the battalion motor pool recently went back home. I do like to fill that spot with a permanent or at least, a long-term assignment. It's a headache rotating different staff through there. You think you might be interested?"

Somebody in heaven loved me and was cheating on my behalf. Or was it Buddha, hard at work on my dharma?

The Boys Are Not Refined

"Did you say it was overnight duty, first-sergeant? In the motor pool?"

"That's right, Specialist. You would be in charge of all entries and exits from the motor pool yard between 2300 and 0700 hours. The gate is locked. You're upstairs inside a watchtower. There is a P.A., public address system from the gate to the watchtower office. There is also a telephone. A Thai Army sentry circles and guards the perimeter. We just need…added security. What say you, soldier? You interested? Try it for a week."

"Yes, First Sergeant, I'm interested. What would be my duties?"

"Tell you what, it's great Monday through Friday duty. Your only responsibility is to be dead certain any late arriving or early departing vehicle, truck, trailer cargo, or whatever, be recorded. They are to be admitted onto the yard or exit from it on your authority! That's it. You get guaranteed weekends off. You are fully released from all formations. I can tell you like to read. As long as you are tending to the rest of it, you can read or write letters. And there's a radio up in the office there. Hell, you can listen to Armed Forces Radio all night, I don't care, so long as you do your job. Do you understand?"

"Yes, First Sergeant, I understand," I said.

"Are you still interested in giving it a try?"

"Yes, First Sergeant, I am. It sounds inviting."

"You won't regret it."

I took it thinking, "Free from all the daytime garrison spit and polish. No formations, no driving duties, not even those high-profile 972 landmine adventures. Motor Pool Watchman."

It was a great assignment for a loner. A soldier could read or catch up on long neglected correspondence. He could even do a little creative writing. And there was a radio, but it had poor reception. During those wee morning hours the US

Armed Forces radio and two or three Thai broadcast stations, all delivered weak, scratchy signals that faded in and out.

Mostly I listened to the recordings I had made onto my reel-to-reel in the Bangkok hotel room, or I slept from 2300 hours until 0500 hours. It meant my days were totally my own and I had weekends off! Jiminy Christmas, how can one guy get so lucky?

The Boys Are Not Refined

Pattaya Beach

The first Saturday after a week of such "rough and draining" duty I followed the suggestion of Medford, a barrack mate who said, "The beach at Pattaya, just up the road north, is a nice place to spend an afternoon. I have yet to meet the GI who didn't like it."

I hired a taxi and went. After exiting my cab I walked past the tables, benches, and crowds of the picnic area to the beach and its waters. Situated on the Bight of Bangkok, the beach at Pattaya can be very enchanting. It is a place of cool climes, silver-white sand, coconut palms, and brilliant waters of blues and aqua green hues beneath a shimmering golden sun.

But it takes a *saao-saao* to make perfection. And just like that, as I walked barefoot, shoes in hand, along the beach in shallow water, she appeared. Although time has undeniably enhanced the remembered image, in my mind's eye, she remains the most beautiful woman I encountered during my Thai tour. She possessed a dissimilar attraction spouted from her Thai-Australian roots. Her auburn hair and sharpened nostril line were instantly noticed. Yet, as I later discovered, hers was a world of Catch-22s. Because of her mixed parentage her unique beauty went unrecognized and she was ostracized to the perimeters of society.

"*Sawatdii saao-saao. Sabai dii luu-pao?*" I said. (Hello, pretty young sister. Are you well?)

"*Sabai dii, kop chai. Tharn lay, kha?*" (Fine, thank you. And you, sir?) She cupped her hands politely, gave me a quick glance, and continued her walk.

In Thai I responded, "I am well." (*Sabai dii mak*) Then asked, "Where are you going, young sister?" (*Kon saao bai tharng nai?*)

Bpai len dern noy, kha. (I'm taking a little walk, sir.)

I changed my direction and adopted her slow pace. She, too, walked with her bare feet in the clear water holding her sandals protectively. *"Kor toot lao, kun cheu arai?"* (Excuse me, but what is your name?)

"*Dichan cheu*, Marti, *kha. Kun puut Thai dai dii.*"(My name is Marti, sir. You speak Thai well.)

"*Kop-kun mak, krap. Bpen kon diiao, luu-pao, krap?*" (Thank you. Are you really, alone, Miss?)

"*Lam-pang? Pom mai bpen lam-pang, kha. Bpen kup wong don-dtrii dtrong-nan.*" (Alone? I'm not alone. I'm with that band over there.) She stopped walking, turned to the opposite direction, extended her arm and pointed.

I looked in the direction she pointed and I could hear a band. They were playing a Beatle's song. She smiled and began to walk, again.

I asked, "*Wong dom-dtrii dai len pleeng 'Sip-hok Bpii Hɛng Kwam-lang'?*" (Can the band play "16 Years of Our Past"?)

"*Bung-tii. Tamai kao luu-jak nan pleeng?*" (Maybe. How do you know that song?)

"*Pom leung pleeng dai.*" (I can sing the song.)

She laughed. Well, it was more a snicker or 'ha' than a laugh. "*Mai len kha. Kun dai leung pleeng?*" (Don't play, sir. Can you really sing the song?)

"*Chaisi, krap. Mai gohok. Dai krap. Leung pleeng dai.*" (Yes, it's true. No bullshit. I can. I can sing the song!)

"*Than chue arai, kha?*" (What is your name, sir?)

"*Pom chue* Forest, *krap.*" (My name is Forest, Miss.)

You cannot—yet, maybe you can—begin to imagine what it felt like to be able to say this to such a gorgeous creature. I felt like a proud, aggressive cock, strutting his stuff in flirtatious word play before a first date kiss. It was liberating. She was so *saao-saao*. Such a tender young thing. No more than 17 or 18.

She returned with me in tow to the picnic area where the band was in the middle of a number. When they finished the tune she spoke to the band leader. He then came to my end of the stage platform and spoke. "*Sawatdii*, GI. My friend Marti says you can sing Surapol Sombatcheroen songs."

"*Mai chai, krap. Tao-nan dtua nung 'Sip-hok Bpii Hɛng Kwam-lang'. Mai eek.* (Not true. Only one, "16 Years of Our Past". Nothing more.) Then I asked, "Can you play it? *Len dai mai?*"

He assured me they could. "*Diiao-gan, krap,*" he said. The maestro turned to his band members for conference then came back to me and said, "Come up, join nut. *Maa gan, krap. Maa gan*", beckoning me with his hand.

As I climbed the steps to the stage I could hear a buzz among the troops the band had been hired to entertain. The maestro handed me the microphone and I gathered my thoughts for the tricky introductory rhythm, then nodded for him to begin.

The guests at the beach party began to take note of the black American performing a Thai song. They ceased the inattentive chatter they had made throughout the band's performance of its repertoire and actually stood and listened. When I finished, they released bellows, hoots, shouts of "Right on" and loud clapping. They liked it.

Before the applause had died, the maestro-saxophone player in broad smile formally introduced himself. "*Pom cheu* Vinai. But you can call me Lucky."

Lucky, I thought? He did say Lucky. Well, Lucky it is. Another Lucky.

I didn't give it another thought. "*Pom bpen* Forest, Lucky, *krap*," I said and quickly agreed to stop-by his Sattahip address to become further acquainted. Then we could exchange vital information like band rehearsal and performance schedules, and discuss my own availability.

As it turned out, the band was one of the many local groups vying for entertainment dollars from the lucrative United States military base club business. It averaged three gigs a week between the Army base at Vayama and entertaining the airmen at Utapao. Although they also did private parties and receptions, the majority of the band's business was GI related.

I began joining them for their late afternoon and evening practice sessions. For the actual gig I would either travel to the site with the band and hang around or show up later, perform my special guest appearance and leave. This was the preferred method. It maintained the mystery. Word of these guest appearances spread, and the band received a significant spike in work requests, particularly in the Thai community. It seems the band had suddenly acquired a cross-over relevance it had previously lacked.

The band was *Tam Dai,* The Possible or The Can-Do Band. The name dove-fanned on the name of a then fast rising, widely popular Bangkok group called *Bpen Mai Dai,* The Impossible. Well, while that band ruled the city, we were hot in Sattahip and Utapao!

The Boys Are Not Refined

Welcome to Sattahip

The municipality of Sattahip, sixty-five miles south of the national capital was situated along the highway between Vayama, the US army base on the west and the US air force base at Utapao on the east. The community of greater Sattahip included the outcrop settlements around both the air force base and the army camp compounds. With its port on the Blight of Bangkok, Sattahip was located 3.5 miles south of Vayama at the curved bottom where the highway looped into a horseshoe and turned north toward Utapao.

Although my visits were infrequent, Sattahip left the impression of a small town when compared to Korat. Despite being a port, downtown had no hustle-bustle rush of any sort. I was, however, able to purchase a pair of bop-bop-baa-lu-baa green suede shoes, with brown leather trim, and to locate an Indian cloth merchant-tailor who quickly made me an outfit in a style similar to that of the Tam Dai band members. Later, from that same merchant, I ordered two suits consisting of two trousers, two jackets and a reversible vest.

Vayama Village, the small hamlet beyond the gates of Camp Vayama had only a few buildings on either side of the highway. The village had existed before the army settlement was constructed and, no doubt, survived the army's eventual departure.

Noot, the band's landlord, owned Paradise Club, the only bar in the little village. She also owned a colony of apartments and the adjacent apartment/studio used by the band, as well. These dwellings sat directly across the road from the bar, on the same side of the street as four or five other structures, including two different restaurants and their upstairs apartments.

Each afternoon, outside the larger of the two restaurants, Deeng, a young woman in her late teens or early twenties, choose the same spot, set-up a wok, copped a squat, and began her banter-squawked call to passers-by. "*Kao-pot, mii kao-pot, aroi mak-mak.*"

She sold her specialty of sizzling fried rice dishes through the late dinner hour and had acquired a noteworthy English vocabulary. I passed her daily as I walked to the band's studio and purchased a plate. We began to exchange friendly banter and laughter, even on days I bought nothing. She was curious and had deeply penetrating eyes that seemed to examine your face for falsity.

I do not know what his relationship to Deeng was, but the rise in my local fame caused the restaurant owner, probably in jest, to loudly question my intentions. One afternoon, immediately upon my arrival, he blurted, "*Mia noy, mia yai, mai bpen laai. Kwaam dtong-gaan mai. Oa mai?* You want marry?" Then, the crude jackass let out a cackle to beat the hens. But the insinuations bound within the marriage remark tilted things. The impact was instant. The comment made the situation awkwardly impossible for both wide-eyed Deeng and silently embarrassed me. The asexual intimacy of our verbal intercourse abruptly ended and stunted all growth in our relationship. I still bought her delicious *kao-pot*, but things were never the same.

The Boys Are Not Refined

The Hit House

My permanent work schedule created an entirely different rhythm to life in Sattahip as compared to what life had been in northeastern Issan Korat. Private John Medford of Bellevue, Washington, had the bunk next to mine. John was the soldier who had suggested the beach at Pattaya for a good time, for which I shall forever be grateful. The first week, he and I went to a place he called the Hit House. There a soldier was always welcome and could sit and smoke a few peace pipes of weed.

Two brothers, by the names of Witt and Nitt, lived there. Nitt, the younger, had been a professional Muay Thai boxer. Witt, the older and of noticeably brighter intelligence, had been his brother's manager.

In Muay Thai fighting, any unchecked bleeding results in stoppage of the bout by technical knock-out, aka, TKO. Wanting to win, over the years of his career, Nitt had habitually ingested a naturally grown, anti-coagulant herb prior to each fight. Unfortunately, after his retirement from the ring, Nitt became victim to the herb's frequent side effect. He chronically suffered extreme outbreaks of urticaria (hives). In search of relief, Nitt had become addicted to heroin.

Witt, once asked in a mixture of Thai-English, *"Tamai piu kao* (whites) not respect Thai custom?"

Surprised, I searched for words to explain as the question sadden and pained me. The inquiry, to my national embarrassment, was in reference to Private Medford. He had apparently never bothered to remove his boots or shoes during visits.

It was a common slight on the part of my fellow-in-arms. But we were both American soldiers. And like it or not, we were seen to some degree by the natives as reflections of each other. Why hadn't I noticed?

I saw the hurt in Witt's eyes and felt the insult as though I had committed it. But I felt just as badly for Medford and the unawares ill feelings he had caused.

I tried to explain to Witt that we were not all same-same as the Thais say. There are good blacks and bad blacks and there are good whites and bad whites. The good ones try to respect other cultures. I thought of Henshaw. Witt and Nitt would have liked him and he would have loved Nitt's heroin.

In regard to Medford, I replied, "*Mai luu, krap. Bungti mii nit noy bpan-yaa citee-waa kao mii huu-jai yai.* (I don't know. Maybe he's not very smart, but he has a big heart.)

On our shared ride back to Vayama, I told Medford.

"Look, I owe you for telling me about Pattaya, just like I wouldn't know about this place or Witt nor Nitt if it hadn't been for you. That makes it awkward for me to have to tell you." I stopped and waited for his response.

"For you to have to tell me what?"

"Witt asked me why do you always disrespect them?"

"What? Disrespect them? How do I disrespect them?"

"You wear your boots inside their home."

"What?"

"You wear your boots inside their home."

"Oh, man! But, but I come to buy weed."

"Doesn't matter. It's a private home. It's the same as a temple; no shoes."

Two days later when we returned to the Hit House, I removed my shoes and watched Medford sit on the porch and remove his boots. Witt watched, smiled widely and turned to me nodding yes.

Saved By the Belle

After the success at the beach party the question remained—what of the beautiful band groupie, Marti? Did I stop because she'd said she was with someone in the band? That answer falls within the vagaries of male-female glances and dances entwined in dating and mating games.

There was a problem-paradigm in the manner Marti had said, "I'm with the lead guitarist." It had been a mixed message, ambiguously delivered with twinkling eyes and a wide smile. It had wholly lacked finality and made me recall Susan moaning *No, no, no, nos* while she lustfully kissed back and helped me to take off our clothes. It was a beckoning challenge to change the two rejecting whines, d*on't* and s*top* to a unified plea of *don't stop*.

I was again, suffering through one of those Yogi Berra, *deja vu* moments. It was the old Misty Day, "Hello, Nigel" salutation and its alarming loss of orientation. The loss of way caused by a simple verbal exchanges made with the proper amount of fluttering and batting of the eyelashes, accompanied by a magical smile.

Once again, I was prepared to take a pathway not based upon any depth of forethought but solely upon love wrapped in lust and beauty. Good lord, help me. I was bewitched by her beauty and nudged forward by an urge to hold the butterfly. Choosing life-changing moments based upon — whims? Chinked and flawed!

Yet it remained honorable. You see, you don't always get what you want, but in this case, I got what I most needed. Something to calm the graceless sea of lust.

New on the scene and curious, I had stopped by the Paradise Club very late one afternoon as the neon lights came on. The entry doors were opened by Srisam. A student on break, she was visiting for one week. She was a refreshing sight.

That day, like the others of her brief stay, she helped her aunt, Noot, the owner, prepare for the evening wave of business. Ostensibly, she hung around the club before its opening, wiping off tables and chairs. But mostly she sat and conversed while Noot and a couple of her bar girls did the real cleaning.

At a time when hair was an important social statement of who you were, (Ain't it always?) she wore hers cropped short. Male and aggressive. We hit it off. She wanted to practice English and for six days I didn't miss an afternoon.

"What America like?"

"It is very big. I have only seen California, Arizona, and Texas."

"You say California hab many farm like Thailand?'

"Yes, but Thailand is hotter. In California in the desert it's hot, but Thailand is much hotter. Thailand is hot everywhere. And humid."

Her face was puzzled. "Hu-mid?" she asked.

"What's the word?" I reached to my rear pocket and pulled out my recently purchased best friend, a trusty *Quick Thai Handbook*. "Humid. *Chuun . . . . aa-gaat-chuun*. Thailand *mii mak-mak kwaam-chuun*."

"Maybe I study math and science in America . . . MIT. *Kun luu* King Bhumibol born in America?"

"Yes, I know."

The Boys Are Not Refined

"Many Thai student study America. Maybe I go to study America or I study Europe. Some say Venice like Bangkok. This be true, Forest, *kha*?

Ignorant of many things, the answer to that question I wish I had known. *"Sia chai, mai luu, krap. Pom mai luu."*

Srisam, on the other hand, was a great help. She helped me more clearly understand much of *"Sip-hok Bpii"* and translated the song for me:

Sixteen years from behind sees
the arrival of love and the arrival of hate
the arrival of sweet and bitter tastes
Sixteen years seem like sixteen days
Love! Oh, darn the maker of love that is brief
Not lasting it has joy and sweetness
within its bitter essence
Sixteen years, time for you and me
a poem about the love we shared
a brief happiness
an extreme lingering bitterness

Solace little sister
Thoughtfulness for each other
I never wished even a fraction of sorrow to come
The wind of heaven changed and
little sister birthed an honest cry
Goodbye dear
Big brother asks your blessing,
wishes you well and begs you forget
Sixteen wasted years
Little sister, a hidden dream within a nap
helped once awake
Big brother forgot the virtues taught
The opposite of love for one another arrived
Recite sixteen years
Sixteen years seen as an upside-down dream

about you and me finally ending our sorrow
Until then sixteen days shall seem like sixteen months
Sixteen months shall seem like sixteen years
And I shall be honestly good for fear of
mortally injuring fragile you

★★★

Like every other Thai, she had an opinion as to who was behind Surapol's murder. "Some say wife kill him. She pay *Nuk Lang.*"

"Why would she do that? Weren't they divorced?"

"Not yet. She hab *farang* lober. She afred she no get money."

"You believe that?"

"Maybe."

"Would you have a *farang* boyfriend?"

"Maybe. If he have big heart. Like you, Forest. He need big heart."

Can a woman, young or old, tell whether a guy really feels a like, fondness, or lust, and distinguish the difference? Ahh, but in the end she was a student on vacation and returned to Bangkok and school. After she left, I rarely went to the club. But I had my feelings toward Marti under control.

In fact, it had been while focused on a conversation with Srisam, that Noot asked and I had agreed to participate in the ill-fated *wat* affair, but first came a trip to Bangkok.

The Thai Tonight Show

In the last week of October, Lucky, bursting with joy, could hardly wait until I was inside the apartment before he blurted, "I have wonderful news. We go to Bangkok this Friday. *Kun* Forest, *krap,* you can do? Yes?"

"Friday? Bangkok?"

"Yes."

"Yes. Sure. Yes! The band is going to Bangkok! That's great!" I could feel a big grin widen across my face.

"No, not whole band. Only you. Only me. Rest of band, no. We go be on Thai teebee. They see us—you, me—all over *bpra-teet Thai.*"

According to Lucky he had once played saxophone in the Bangkok Orchestra and had used old contacts in the capital to gain an appearance on a popular, nationally broadcast talk and variety program.

"It like Thailand Johnny Carson. Like Thai *Tonight Show.* Some body sing, maybe dant, maybe tell funny story. I make contact. We go on teebee Friday nighttime."

Well, how about that? The Thai Tonight Show. *Da da da da da dada dada...*

Seemed like I'd been preparing for the event half my brief life. Ham had been my second name since my first taste of lime-light fame. That had come in the seventh grade.

During the Christmas program at Tanaya Junior High, the school chorus performed two Gene Autry songs. Both renditions highlighted solos. William Daniels was the son of a Baptist minister. He read music, sang in his father's church choir, and had an angelic voice. He was chosen to sing *Frosty the Snowman*. I was picked to sing *Willie Claus*.

I have never considered myself a singer but rather a performer. It was my job to stay on key, deliver the lyric, and tell the story. Later in high school, I further honed my skills through competitive speech programs and did in fact win the Victor Valley High School Talent Show Grand Sweepstakes Award in 1964. The following year rather than compete, I performed the duties of Master of Ceremonies. Hey, I've known that talent does not fall from the sky. It must be uncovered, shaped, and honed. I was prepared.

We hired a cab to take us to Bangkok, wait, then, make the return trip to Sattahip. We arrived at the television studio and were taken to the Green Room. An assistant to the host briefed Lucky on the nature of our introduction. We were told that although our host spoke both English and Thai, he would conduct the entire interview in Thai. I would be introduced with Lucky and would leave most of the talking to him.

The assistant then left us to wait. A large one-way glass window looked out from the Green Room onto the Thai Tonight Show set. We watched our host interview his other special guest, a very lovely beauty queen from a northern provincial village. She was in Bangkok to represent her village in the upcoming Miss Thailand Pageant.

She eventually proved to be the fourth most beautiful and lovely Miss of Thailand, finishing as the respectable third runner-up. But that night hope burned pure in her heart and she performed quite well at being demure, quiet, and lovely.

Her interview ended and we followed. As agreed most of the questions were directed at Lucky. I was asked, "Why are you in Thailand? What do you do here?"

I responded, *"Pom bpen tahon."* (I am in the army.)

We proceeded to chit-chat in the form of television journalism. I tried to explain that, although I was in the army, I was not an infantry soldier, but rather a truck driver.

He asked in English, "What do you think of your stay in Thailand?"

"I love Thailand. I believe Thai people have good hearts."

He translated my answer to his audience then, still in English, he asked, "How you learned to speak Thai so quickly?"

Before I could answer he chuckled in self-realization, then answered his own question with a second question, *"Ah, kun mii Thai tealok, chai mai?* (You have a Thai girlfriend, right?)

Not true, I have many, many friends, I retorted. "*Mai chai, krap. Mii puen. Mii puen laai-laai.*"

Finally he asked, "And tonight what are you going to sing?"

"*Pom ja leung pleeng 'Sip-hok Bpii Hɛng Kwam-lang'.*" This answer was met with applause. Following a beat of silence Lucky began on his sax. It was a smooth performance and went without a hitch. When we finished we were asked not to leave.

Our host wanted more. We, again, waited in the Green Room. About fifteen minutes later our host completed his program and signed off. He then asked us to join himself and the beauty queen for a second event. We unhesitatingly agreed.

Doo doot doo dom doo doo doo do do dom . . .

★★★

The television host, his driver, Miss Lovely, Lucky, and I climbed into a Mercedes four-door sedan. Our trusting host sat in the front with his driver, leaving the lovely Miss Beauty Queen alone in the back boxed between Lucky and me. No worries. We were gentlemen all the way in our travels across the city to a military installation.

After our admission unto the facility grounds, it was explained that we were headed to the Thai Naval Officers Annual Banquet and Ball. The driver drove us to the entrance of a gray, granite building. The bright lights and traffic activity said, "This is the place" and we were let out.

Thailand 1968 was nothing if not a military dictatorship operated by a junta of generals who rotated and occupied the office of Prime Minister among themselves. Yet the tensions and dynamics of power struggles and coup threats dictate that a military regime take an accurate accounting of power sources.

Although the Thai Army held the reins of power, it did not hold hegemony. The Thai civilian police, the Air Force, and Navy held important cards in the national power picture. They, too, were men with guns, men with whom to reckon.

We passed through a foyer and entered a magnificent ballroom with a large proscenium stage. The room exuded power and the party was in full swing. Officers and gentlemen of the Royal Thai Naval Corps sat at the various tables. Most seemed to have female companionship although many were out and about on their own. Had their dates declared, "Enough already," and taken flight? This seemed like the place to be.

We followed our host to front row center, an arrangement of large tables placed in a horse-shoe, so that no one's back was facing the stage. It was the celebrity table and these were Bob Ucker to-kill-for seats.

Many people were already seated. I was placed between two Bangkok cinema starlets whose names I did not catch. They twinkled with willingness to be next on the audition couch and were determinedly working all their glamour and charms. They only needed one break. One young hard, up-and-coming director or even an old hard-up and willing one, who could look deep inside and see the enormous potential and imagine the raw, naked talent just lying there and they would each be set.

What the heck. The food looked good! I put a couple of pieces of fried fish and some buttered, steamed crab on my plate and began to nibble away. But I soon felt a buzz as the focus of the room turned to our table.

On stage, the Master of Ceremonies had said something followed by *"Kun* Forest, *krap."* He was noting Lucky and my presence. A bright follow spotlight lit our table and he motioned for us to stand up.

We did, to warm applause. He then beckoned us onto the stage. We were both surprised. We had not known we would be singing for our dinner, so to speak. But on stage we went, accompanied by continued applause.

Lucky, showman that he was, pleaded excuses. Not knowing we were going to perform, he had neglected to bring his saxophone inside. Alas, it was back in the car.

No problem. "*Mai bpen arai,*" the Master of Ceremonies said, and rapidly fired off an instruction to someone off stage. As quickly as you can say "the Bridge over the River Kwai" someone was bringing out a spare saxophone with a fresh mouthpiece.

There was more applause.

Lucky took it, tested the finger-key and sound, smiled and nodded readiness. The M.C. handed me the microphone and I took a deep breath, then nodded to the director. Accompanied by Lucky and a full orchestra I sang *"Sip-hok Bpii Hɛng Kwam-lang"* for the second time that night.

The song has an odd opening measure and I must concentrate to catch the beat. Like always, the voice of Surapol played in my head, but the live audience made it different. I relaxed, caught the meter, and simply accompanied Surapol. We finished to a standing ovation.

As we left the stage, we were met by our television host. He led the way back to our chairs and paused at the table where the American Ambassador Extraordinary and Plenipotentiary Leonard S. Unger and his wife were seated. Our host said something inaudible to the ambassador. Mr. Unger turned his head to me, but didn't rise from his chair nor open his mouth. Rather, he lifted his wine glass in a faux toast. I nodded a return salute and the host led us back to our table, passing smiles and nodding heads in our full fame. Reseated, we wholly enjoyed a now well-earned meal.

Later, there occurred an even louder and more scintillating uproar within the ballroom when seven or eight fabulously dressed *katoys* entered. They were all gorgeous and each was escorted to a designated chair at what quickly shaped up to be the top draw tables. One sat at our table and another was seated with the American Ambassador and his wife. I have no idea who the other lucky recipients of the famed "lady boys" were.

The Boys Are Not Refined

Kon Baa

Two weeks earlier, back in Sattahip, Noot had asked me to participate in a local festival. I'd promised to give it some thought, then had quickly forgotten the matter. Two days before the event, she reminded me.

"Lucky is out of town. I forgot and didn't ask him. *Pom luum. Sia cha*i," I said.

"No problem, Forest, *kha*." She nodded her head and smiled.

"But you don't understand. I'm sorry. Lucky doesn't know. I don't think the band will play. Look, I'm . . . sorry."

"*Mai bpen arai*. No want band, only want you. Can do Forest, *kha*?"

"Oh...I think so."

"*Jing-jing* can do. You number one, Forest. You do for me. You met me marketplace, *talot*. Everybody walk wit monk to *wat*. Be band at *wat*, no sweat. You sing '*Sip-hok Bpii*', Forest, *dii mak-mak*."

She had me, so I agreed to do it. There would be a short procession from the central market to the grounds of the local *wat*. After the parade I was to sing.

The afternoon of the festival I stopped at the Hit House to shoot the breeze with Witt. It was along the way. A couple of bongs turned into six or seven, then I suddenly remembered. I should already be among those gathering in the marketplace for the march to the temple grounds.

I rose from my stupor, walked to the porch, put on my shoes, and ran to the roadside.

Within four minutes I hailed a cab. It was actually a very small Japanese pick-up with a cabin shell. Two benches had been bolt-mounted onto the truck bed. I paid the driver, climbed onto the back, and sat on one.

We arrived at the *wat* as the parade processional entered the religious grounds. I exited the truck and followed. Inside, the celebration was under way and the grounds were packed. I looked around and spotted a large pavilion-covered area where a stage had been erected for the occasion.

Near the stage, Noot stood scanning the crowd and wringing her hands, a worried scowl on her face.

The look broke into a wide smile when she spotted me approaching the stage. She came to meet and hurry me along just as I was beginning to feel a rare case of jitters. The whole thing felt wacky, off-kilter, and out-of-focus because I was buzzed and needed a "take-five" minute.

Ignoring my protestations Noot hustled me onto the stage and announced to the crowd, "America *farang*—*kao bpen ta-haan* — *ja dtong leung pleeng 'Sip-hok Bpii Hɛng Kwam-lang'*!"

Oh, would they had not applauded so enthusiastically. Accompanied by unknown musicians, I didn't hear Surapol's voice in my head. I twice falsely started. On the third attempt I lost count in the opening stanza, and even the lyrics were beginning to jumble in my head. Abandoned by my confident muse, I couldn't sing!

I cupped my hands into a *wai*, bowed my head, and said into the microphone, "*Kor toot, kor toot. Pom luum pleeng. Sia chai. Leung mai dai.*"

I left the stage feeling there was a giant stick protruding from my rear that all could see. The crowd, quite properly disappointed, murmured and hissed. I could not vacate the grounds quickly enough. I passed an ancient monk in a shimmering new wrap. Our eyes met so I slowed.

He said in crisp, clear English, "Your flesh shall be consumed by the worms of time. But what of your soul? Shall it follow the path of the Holy Spirit or fall off into darkness?" He then turned and walked in the direction of the festivities.

Outside the grounds I caught a taxi and rode back to camp with my spirits in a dark place.

Two days later Lucky returned. When he heard about the fiasco he was furious.

"You must never do again without band! *Tom pit,* make reputation black."

No argument there, I thought.

"No do, Forest, *krap. Jing-jing* . . . it kill magic *Luk Thung* music. *Mai dai. Mai dai.*"

I kept busy, but as part of the act, in Sattahip I maintained a choirboy celibacy. This was done by having all mating needs met outside of town in the big city. In Bangkok I had a steady woman. She worked the same bar and if I went there, no matter who she was with, it was the same.

"*Kun,* Forest, *kha!*" She called out. She always greeted me with a beaming smile. Then she turned to the person being dumped to say, "Oh, so sorry. I must go. See you later."

She was probably a couple of years older than me. She moved quite gracefully but always insisted on either walking before or behind me. Never alongside or holding hands. That kind of male-female public display of fondness or passion was a Western thing, wholly frowned upon in Thailand.

Men and women did not hug or kiss or walk down the avenue hand-in-hand. It was strictly taboo. Whether in outback Korat or Hicksville Khon Kaen soldiers found no advantage against this censure. And although in the Patpong district of Bangkok rules were broken, it was never by her.

We would ride in taxi to her *klong* (canal) apartment. She always rode in the rear seat while I sat in front, alongside the driver.

★ ★ ★

Once back in Sattahip, evenings were spent at the studio in rehearsal/practice, or more and more often working gigs. I wrote very few letters during my time in Thailand and the few I got from Stateside often said things I didn't want to hear. A letter from my sister Ruth caught up with me. Like the April cookies it, too, had been delayed, having first been delivered to the 21st Transportation Company at Camp Charn Sinthrope before moving on to me at Sattahip.

"Dear Nigel," she had penned. "I am writing a short note because I know how fond you are of Frank Charles Russell and I know you don't know. Well, I ran into his parents. They sold their house in Merced and have moved to Menlo Park to be nearby. Frankie is in the hospital in Berkeley with some rare form of brain cancer. It is already in the advanced stage and wholly inoperable. Jesus, Nigel! Do you remember the Ouija Board and that Christmas on 14th Street?" It was simply signed, "Love, Sis."

See what I mean? Ruin my night, why don't you? Of course, I remembered. But there was another sting in a postscript she thoughtfully added which read, "P.S. Do you remember the Padillas who lived next door, there on 14th Street? Ralph, the oldest, was killed in Vietnam in either June or July."

Holy mother of God! My old man would use that expression in moments of extreme exasperation and it was the only thing my befuddled mind could think to say that was not profane or totally blasphemous. *Holy mother of God. Why? Why Tache? Why Frankie?*

Ralph, like my brother Neal, was two years older than me. We had sold newspapers on the streets together for the *Merced Sun-Star* and when, upon entering high school, he had quit, I inherited most of his "regular" customers. When the new freeway uprooted the neighborhood, the family had moved to the west end of town, somewhere near Cone Avenue.

But now Ralph, or Tache, or just plain young Ralph Padilla was dead – killed-in-action during some soggy swamp ambush, or while defending some hopeless highlands outpost, or attacking a lousy lowlands Viet Cong unit of the enemy. Whatever the case, he was a dead casualty of this FFFFFing war.

But even before I could absorb the shock of that, she had told me Frank Charles Russell is dying in a Berkeley hospital. Damn, damn, double-dog damn!

It took me back to a Christmas ten years before. I was eleven years old and Ruth had gotten a Ouiji Board. That very night during a gathering in Ruth's upstairs parlor bedroom, Frankie had dared to ask the board, "What year will I die?" To this dare of knowledge the reckoning instrument eerily traced-out the year 1...9...6...9.

Mercy, mercy me, the night I read the letter, 1969 stood little more than 2 months away. For my money, you can keep those correspondences from home.

G.T. Foster

The Been Dead and Born Again

Late in October the band had a gig in the NCO Club on the Air Force Base at Utapao. I had accompanied them and was performing my one song when I heard Madson's distinctively Mississippi accent shout, "Go on man, go on! You sang it Forest! Sang it."

He had pulled a loaded petroleum tanker into the camp. We reconnected. You see?

What the 21st Transportation Company Commander, Lieutenant Fisher had done in his fit of frustration and fury by transferring Madson to a platoon at Korat and me to the 55th of Sattahip was blunder. His hasty verbal orders, given the morning after the attack upon Sergeant Bolt, had failed in their intended purpose. We had seemed to be having too much fun. The Florida officer looked at us and saw two free niggas.

He thought," My, oh my! But they are just too free!"

So, he planned. "Take that…"

And when we gleefully did, he thought, "Well, then take this!"

And when we smiled and saluted, he was angered. As a means of isolation, it was all a petty waste of time. Even after written orders followed Lieutenant Fisher's misplaced indignation, I saw Madson on several occasions. Shucks, we were unconquerable.

His very next trip to Sattahip we met at Noot's Paradise Club in Vayama Village, had a beer and crossed the street to Lucky's apartment. Rented for jam sessions and dormitory space, there were two large rooms. We referred to the entire quarters as the Band Room. Many of the band members lived in Noot's adjacent apartment colony and the bandmates usually ate supper together.

That evening Madson and I helped them consume a salad of very hot and spicy chopped chicken wrapped in lettuce leaves buried under crushed ice as we drank from cold bottles of Singha beer. It was dusk and the room was lit by candlelight. After the meal someone placed a water pipe and a box of *ganchaa* on the floor before us and we began to smoke. There was a sudden gust of air and the candle light flickered but did not extinguish. I looked at Madson and saw tears streaming down his face.

"Stan? What happened? What's wrong, man? What's wrong with you?"

Before he could answer, Songchai, the bass guitarist, spoke, "*Pi lok*." (Death walks)

"It was Lon," Suk, the drummer said. "It was Lon!"

Madson remained silent but tears continued to flow from his eyes.

"Who is Lon?" I asked

"Lon hang himself in dis room," Lucky said. "He be dead four munt, now. He play keyboard."

Madson seemed over his state. I asked, "What happened to you, man?"

"I felted real cold, man. Den I seed dis man. But it wadn't no man. It wassa haint."

"A what? A hank?" I asked

"A haint, man. It wassa fuckin' haint."

"A haint, a ghost? You mean you saw a ghost?" I asked doubtfully.

"Yeah, man. It wassa ghost. I done seen 'em back home in Mississippi. It wassa haint, a ghost, one of dose been dead folk. Dat's xackly what dit was, Forest. That sho' as hell what dit was."

There was no further mention of the unfortunate Lon that night.

The next day I arrived at the Band Room just before 11 a.m. Sithporn, Marti's boyfriend, was strumming and mixing riffs as I entered. I stood a moment listening.

Lucky came from the rear room. He looked at me, raised his eyebrows and said, "Come wit' me."

He led me through the room and out the rear door into the backyard. In the yard he stopped before what looked like a tiny house that people hang from trees to feed the birds, particularly hummingbirds. Only this miniature house was twice as large as a bird tree house and was mounted on a post. The post was buried in the ground. The house sat on the post about three feet above the earth. At the entry way to the small house someone had placed incense sticks and a pack of Falling Rain cigarettes. Some of the incense was burning.

"It is a…how you say…ghost house? No, no a…a spirit, yes, a spirit house. We build to make Lon spirit happy. He need drest here. Need drest, wait. We build so him drest."

Forgive me my twenty-one-year-old naiveté. I knew little of Thai Buddhism or their more ancient animism practices and beliefs. I nodded my head as though I understood, while superficially dismissing the whole thing as hocus-pocus, voodoo-like beliefs. I smiled and said, "I see."

But my shallow perception was saved by a memory flash when I recalled several times sitting in the front seat as my grandfather drove down an Arizona highway making a chirping "tut, tut" sound and pointing to crosses, candles, and flowers that marked a tragic spot. It meant death had occurred at that crossing, intersection, or patch of roadway for some poor Mexican or Indian.

"That my boy," my grandfather explained, "Marks hallowed ground. It's part of their culture."

"I have seen these on the road. Yes? I have seen them on the road where there have been...accidents. Right, Lucky?"

"Yes. *Chaisi.* You see dem on road. Thai people belieb you die accident, den you die early. Ip you die early you no be happy and you spirit stay. It cannot go because it not time be reborn oba again. Thai people belieb ip sometime spirit not happy, it do bad ting. We make spirit house so spirit be happy. Not do bad ting."

"I get it," I said, and I really did.

In the Pentecostal churches of my youth I had seen the power of belief. I had witnessed "the touched," sprawled and rolling on floors. Their eyes, too, had rolled. Their mouths foamed and they spoke strange languages they themselves could not understand.

I had felt the desire to be included and had yearned to be filled with this spirit. More than once I had silently asked, "Show me Lord, give me a sign." I had waited but it had never come.

Later, I stopped the watch. By young adulthood, religion had become a social thing. In Emeryville before the war, my friend Vern and I had attended Easter Services at St. Elizabeth Cathedral solely to sit near the two fine-haired, fair-skinned, private-school-going sisters. Real beauties.

Five months before my induction, Che, Vern's older brother, returned home after a stretch in federal prison for bank robbery. Vern has six brothers, so to be certain, I asked, "Vern, which of your other brothers rob banks?"

He responded, "They all do."

In prison Che had converted to the Black Muslim faith and joined the Nation of Islam. His chiseled herculean body quickly earned him a position in the organization's elite Fruit of Islam defense unit.

Out of curiosity, Vern and I had attended the mosque (referred to as temple) in San Francisco to hear Minister Majid speak. I was impressed with the Nation's Do-for-Self teachings, its rehabilitation programs, and the low recidivism of its largely criminal converts.

Yet religion had remained largely a social thing and although my initial GI dog-tags listed Islam as my faith, the declaration had been made more in protest than truth. Those tags, having been given as a keepsake memento of a meeting enjoyed and services rendered, were now in the hands of a pretty Mexican whore.

By November of 1968 my identification tags did not list a religion, but Buddhism and its system of merit and kindness had increasingly appealed to the kinder and eclectic angels of my nature. For me, the most refreshing and attractive aspect of the belief system is its attitudinally different point-of view of salvation (nirvana). It holds a more seductive, built-in salvation as opposed to the fire-and-brimstone of my religious past. The soul's final destination after a worthless life is not Satan's hot pits but rather the rebirth queue line for a do-over.

The Boys Are Not Refined

Bombs and Rockets

"Hell, I nearly shit my pants. They were fixing to go off, but who the fuck knew where they'd go?" Medford, my Hit House friend, had explained his early return to camp. "What a joke. There's going to be an investigation and some cage rattling. You watch."

There had been rare 3 a.m. activity in the motor pool. I had left my perch to open and close the gate upon the departure of 25 semis without trailers. From the yard, the American and Thai driver teams had gone to the harbor docks to attach to their freight trailers loaded with crates of bombs and rockets.

The drivers then assembled into a special convoy, with Thai police and MPs attached as usual with these highly explosive cargos. The truck line left the port and headed to the Camp Charn Sinthrope switching station, first stop for the crates on their way to the Laotian border, but drop point and end of shuttle duty for the drivers of the 55th Transportation Company. One-way?

Three hours, tops.

At 0500 hours I had opened the gate, again. A company platoon sergeant and another soldier came to the motor pool and left in a jeep, intending to catch up with the convoy. At 0615, on what had become the busiest night of my army graveyard watch career, Medford, driving an unattached semi, having left the convoy, returned alone to the motor pool. He told me the story.

"So, we had been driving about an hour and the truck behind me suddenly swings out of formation and speeds up alongside waving at me to pull over and stop. So, okay, I pull over and stop. The rest of the convoy behind stops with me, but the trucks ahead don't immediately stop.

"So we were strung out a bit. And Dix, the luey in the rear jeep drives up to me asking why I stopped. At the same time, Tom, the driver who had flagged me down had parked and came running back to my truck while the luey's all hot about me stopping, Tom's yelling, "Your tire! Your tire! I think your rear-tire's on fire! Do you have a fire extinguisher?"

"So, I look in the right-side mirror and see the smoke and climb out of my truck. I look behind the seat, but there ain't no fire extinguisher. I run around to the passenger side and asked the luey who had been balling me out about why I'd stopped, 'Hey, sir, let use your fire extinguisher.' But he looks, then asks his driver. The driver hunches, he don't think so, so the luey says something into the radio and the jeep takes off up toward the front of the convoy.

"So, I'm running toward the rear of the convoy asking other drivers. They all check and they don't have one. My Thai driver stayed cool. He started cranking down the trailer legs. I could see what he was thinking. Yeah, we had better disconnect our rig from the burning load. Man, that guy was right. It turns out, don't nobody have a fucking fire extinguisher. A convoy of 25 trucks, 2 MP jeeps and 2 Thai civilian police squad cars hauling highly explosive cargo through, at times, heavily populated areas and not a single fire extinguisher? Right. Not a one.

"So, by this time the trailer parking legs are cranked down. I get back into my truck, and while my Thai co-driver held the 5th-wheel latch, I pulled away and we detached truck from trailer. But by the time the 2 lueys had decided on a plan, the fire had moved from the tires to the trailer bed. I swear I heard the flames and crates began to hiss.

"Their plan was to do the only thing left, vacate the area. The Thai police went south to halt northbound traffic. The entire convoy moved a mile-and-a-half north of the site where we could safely wait. When the flames reached their height about 6 of those suckers shot out to fields on both sides of the road. Man, that shit was something! And now, I bet the shit's going to fly."

Medford was right. But in the army the buck is passed and sewage travels downhill. Even with my limited mixing on post with company personnel, I heard grumblings a couple of days later.

There should have been an investigation and overhaul of not only safety procedures but, equally important, trailer maintenance and repair—For want of greased ball-bearings a fire was had!

Instead, in true Army fashion, the two convoy platoon sergeants were rumored to have had poor performance letters placed in their files. But rather than cite the two convoy lieutenants for the same operational breakdown of standard safety protocol, the officers received letters-of-commendation for quick emergency response.

G.T. Foster

Loy Krathong and the Miss Thailand Festival

When you're hot you are hot! Lucky and I were asked to return to the capital to participate in the annual Miss Thailand Pageant which was held during the conviviality of *Loy Krathong*.

It would have taken far too long and demanded words we mutually did not possess for Lucky to explain to me, the eager but illiterate *farang*, that we would actually be participating in a 900-year-old festival, supposed to have begun at Sukhothai, the first Thai capital, during the 13th century reign of King Ramkamhaeng. In the initial celebration a court lady prepared a *krathong*, a float of 100 miniature boats crafted from lily pods. She then placed a small candle on each and let loose the entire fleet upon a pond to honor the king's birthday.

The event became a tradition embedded into the culture and is celebrated each year on the first full moon of November. These days banana-stem floats, beautifully decorated with flowers, candles, incense, and small coins are released on the waterways across Thailand.

Openly agreed to be the most picturesque of Thai festivals, Loy Krathong, as part of the Buddhist pantheon of celebrations, relies on the lunar calendar. Thus, its exact date varies from year to year. It is celebrated on the November night to pay homage to Mae Khong Kha, goddess of the country's life-bringing rivers and lakes. In 1968 the event was held on November 5th.

That evening we performed on the Chulalongkorn University campus grounds during the pageantry surrounding the crowning of *Nang Nop Pa Marol*, or according to Lucky, Miss Thailand. It was an efficient, business-like occasion. We showed up 30 minutes beforehand and waited backstage with other performers in a room next to that of the contestants for the crown.

Lucky elbowed me when he spotted our mutual acquaintance, the former co-guest on the television show and at the naval banquet. We waved and cupped our hands in *wai*. She smiled, made *wai* and disappeared. Later, she was the night's third-runner-up.

Our showtime arrived and the stage manager ushered us off to stage left to await the Master of Ceremonies' call. When beckoned, we entered to mild applause. I was handed the microphone and accompanied by a full orchestra, we did our thing.

There was a long walkway that jutted out from the main stage. Lucky, wailing away on his saxophone trailed behind me as I moved along the protruding pier. At one point I paused, crouched, and crooned down to my right and then to my left into sparkling eyes, and the waves of screaming, smiling, giggling Thais. Resuming my stroll, the long microphone cord coiled and forced me to jump rope and hop. I nearly mis-stepped and stumbled. But my near fumble went unnoticed, and we finished the song to loud, appreciative applause.

★★★

After the pageant, dinner, and a massage, I had returned by taxi to the hotel buzzing with adrenaline. Although it was after 3 a.m., sleep was the last thing I wanted. Even at that hour, a young Thai boy of ten or eleven walked along the sidewalk selling plastic bags filled with sliced pineapple and melon. I glanced his way as I exited the cab and his face lit-up in recognition. He pointed me out to his customers and shouted, "Surapol, Surapol!"

I smiled, waved, and entered the refuge of the hotel. What an electrical boost to the ego the kid had given me. It was as if I watched my own fame spread, carried on the image of me singing "16 Years Turned Upside Down", projected by television beyond the glittering city to light the hinterland village screens.

The after-hours coffee house was doing Gold-Rush-assay-office-like business. There was not a table to be had. The overflow had spilled out into the foyer and onto the wide staircase with its second-floor landing of shops, parlors, and salons. All were now closed. From the top of the stairs the landing rails served as a balcony. I ascended the steps to the second floor where two fashionably dressed young women stood by the stairwell landing. Chatting between themselves, they watched the action on the stairs and in the foyer below. When I reached the top I turned to them and said, "*Sawatdii,*" and cupped my hands into a *wai*.

"We are not Thai!" one of the women replied in crystal clear English that hinted annoyance.

"We are Philippina." The second voice was apologetic and kind.

"Please, excuse me. I absolutely meant no harm. I—"

My words were cut off and left unsaid. Along with others, the three of us were jerked from our conversation hub by a loud bellowing voice from below.

"You all want to see something weird?"

At the foot of the stairway stood two young, casually dressed white men. The buzz cut of their hair marked them as military. Unexpectedly, both men unzipped, unbuckled, and lowered their trousers and underwear to the naked ass. One then grabbed his ankles while the other performed the classic naval cornhole technique. It had the unsettling and hushed effect the two sought as they mercifully ended the act before its natural climax.

The two women were momentarily speechless. Then they began to explain. "We are nurses," one said, and they both nodded. "We, too, serve in Vietnam."

"We are on vacation-holiday," added the other. "But they are not like that."

"That's right. In Vietnam they are not like that at all. They are decent men."

"Good soldiers. They never act improper like that. Maybe, they are drunk."

"Maybe," I said, but I had my doubts that was the real problem.

Try as we might, the truth is, we (all three) were just too young to put into words what we all knew. It was the stress of war. An ancient dictum was at work—never use the best steel to make nails nor the best men to make soldiers. The best and the brightest, highest IQ students, had been shielded from the draft. The two soldiers below were not considered America's best or brightest.

We stood in an after-hours bar early morning the first week of November of 1968, the bloodiest year of the Vietnam War. Period. History would record that year's calendar days as long runs of deadly engagements between the forces of the Viet Cong and North Vietnam Regular Army opposing the Army of the Republic of Vietnam (South Vietnam) and their American allies.

Our side spun the results of these encounters with inflated enemy body counts and although the year-end sum was a battlefield deadlock, it amounted to a psychological victory for Uncle Ho, his Minh, and their communist allies. The American spirit had been daunted and we were probably witnessing behavior in 1968 that half-a-century later would be labeled Post Traumatic Stress Disorder.

G.T. Foster

★ ★ ★

"Our campaign is over and there is nothing come of it on one side or the other but the loss of a great many worthy people, the misery of a great many poor soldiers, crippled forever, the ruin of some provinces, the savage pillage and conflagration of some flourishing towns. Exploits these, which make humanity shudder."

Who said that, one might ask? US Ambassador Averill Harriman in the aftermath of the Tet Offensive and its American response?

No, Fredrick II, of Prussia, 1753.

That night, from the balcony, I had thought, "There, but for the grace of God…" But later, channeling Private Henshaw, the AWOL poet, I wrote the following:

SAY IT AIN'T SO, GI JOE

But the boy soldiers of war are not refined
Although they appear the all-American kind

I mean young troops who've tasted fear's attack
While weathering war's dreaded front-line combat

They down booze to drown troubles and cope
Then smoke their dope and abandon all hope

Under veneer of apple pie and Boy Scout law
They like wanton women to unscrew their awe

And prefer working whores—over the virgin lot—
Shedding goodie girls out their sexpot dreams

For wild bucking libertine delights who scream
And roar begging for more all night at fifty baht

Tender-age fighters are more volatile than vets
Dare piss one off and you will feel quick regrets

He'll break both your knees and allow none to aid
Or beneath your bunk roll a ticking grenade

The Boys Are Not Refined

The Mekong Lunch

Upon the death of Surapol Sombatcharoen, the Thai film industry had quickly gone to work in hopes of reaping box office *baht* from a story that, in reality, proved to be too true to be good. Two films were made. The first had been released to theaters within two months of Surapol's August murder.

The second was now also ready. Its budget had been larger and it featured Thailand's two biggest movie stars. The film was fittingly titled *16 Years of Our Past* and Lucky and I were to be part of the "pomp and circumstance" surrounding the movie release.

The first Friday of December, Lucky and I returned to Bangkok. I had given Madson the address for the agreed noontime rendezvous and had invited him to join us for the fun. He arrived at the restaurant before Lucky or our host. But he showed up with a bottle of Mekong, tipsy and sullen.

"Hey, man I'm glad you could come."

"Yeah, Forest, me too, but don't start on me 'bout da Kid," he slurred.

"Hey, Mad Man, what you talking about."

"It weren't nonna my fault what happen tah Billy Childs."

"Billy? What are you talking about, man? I didn't bring up the kid. What's eating you, man?"

"Bryson talkin' shit. Luckie all mad at me. Fuck it. Fuck it all tah hell, I'm da Mad Man, right? Den forget it den, Forest. Have a drink wit me."

"Nah, man. I can't party now. I got to keep my head straight. But come on, Mad Man, you slow down."

"Yeah, Forest, okay, man. Fuck it. Yeah, sho."

But by the time Lucky and our host arrived, Madson had only gotten worse. Throughout lunch he repeatedly used the rude Laotian *mung* instead of the preferred *kun* when addressing the other members of our party. This could have been overlooked or forgiven, but Madson well knew the difference, which made his slights intentional. Finally he started chant-singing "The Drunkard's Song":

Tung mee pii nii ja kee kao
Chan pii gin lao diiao kao mao mak

The two-line couplet translates, "My older brother drinks whiskey and gets very drunk." Madson sang the single verse over and over as though it were a power mantra. Each repetition was at a higher volume. He seemed sincerely wounded that it did not draw wild appreciation or mad applause. But this was Bangkok. Its inhabitants preferred *Su Tap* love ballads or at least *Luk Krung*, Child of the City songs. But never some disgusting, low-class, shit-face drunken *kee mao* song.

After the fourth repeat, I said in a jovial voice to mask my inflamed irritation and growing embarrassment, "Hey , man did you ever hear the other verses? I certainly never did, but, come on! Come on, Madman, cool it."

He stopped but, again, became rude to my hosts, lapsing back into Issan dialect, then began singing *"Kon Baa"*. It is a song I love, but it's also a *Luk Thung* song and about being loaded on marijuana. It, too, was totally off and inappropriate for the time and place. I closed my mouth, gritted my teeth, and shook my head.

Pom baa ganchaa jon huu dtaa laai
Hen moo to dtao kwai oo duan nai
Hen bpen duan kwam ok urrie
Dtat lurie kwam siia hai kom
Dut ganchaa naa ying dum--

The Boys Are Not Refined

Interrupting I said, "Sam, I hate to say it, but this is not working. We are fucking guests and you act like you don't get it. God damn it, Madman, if anybody gets it, you do! You are making me uncomfortable, and you are making our host uncomfortable."

He rolled his eyes and then scanned the room. To no one and everyone, he profanely muttered, *"Yet ma mong sot!"* (Fuck your mother, you animal!)

"Come on Madson," I pleaded.

"Ah, Forest," he slurred, then leaned forward to focus on my face. I had never known Madson ever to be as drunk as he pretended. He was a *ganchaa* man. Usually. He was edgy, but that was his attraction. But I knew he could be a nasty drunk and tonight the pint bottle of Mekong was nearly empty and he was the only one drinking.

"Madson, you are going to make me ask you to leave. It ain't right, man. But you ain't right! Not tonight, man," I said while shaking my head. "Not tonight!"

"Fuck it, man. I'll go. I'll go, man, Forest, man, I'll go. Yeh ain't gotta tell me tah go, man."

He rose from the table and turned his back to leave but turned to again face me and added, "Yeh gonna be good tah night, man. Yeh been doin' good. Keep-pon doin' it, Forest, my man. No bullshit. Hey, I'll see yeh later." He turned and walked away singing a tune he, Green, Lloyd and I had composed over time in Korat.

> *Pom bpai talot* (I go to the marketplace)
> *ja suu gradat* (to purchase paper)
> *ja kin jot-mai* (to write a letter)
> *hai tii baan* (and sent it home)
> *mia mai yuu* (wife was not there)
> *mia len chuu* (wife plays butterfly)
> *pom leung hai* (I cry)
> *Tamai?* (Why?)

G.T. Foster

It was the last time I saw Stanley Madson.

The Gala Premier

I returned to the business of the evening and beyond. The Thai nighttime television host was very much interested in future ventures. He really wanted a commitment from me. He promised continued engagements and support. "How long can you stay? Have you requested an extension to your tour? Would that be possible? Well, I have connections."

In fact, after lunch we rendezvoused with one of those connections, Prince so-an-so, the king's uncle. It was intoxicating and much of the encounter I only remember in blur. We were taken to the prince's estate outside the city and I was surprised to discover that the prince was much older than I had expected. Perhaps sixty?

Leaving the prince's palatial home, we switched from our host's car to the prince's van and rode back into the city to the event at the Queen's Theater. Along the way our host, interpreting for the prince, asked me, "Do you play golf? There is an upcoming celebrity tournament . . ."

Unfortunately, at the time I had yet to learn the game.

Nevertheless, that day's event was a very exclusive, invitation-only Gala Premier affair. It was auspiciously held December 6, the day following the king's birthday. Those present were a special, chosen elite, which seemed to heighten the glitz and revelry spirit of the occasion. The prince and our host joined the seated audience while Lucky and I went backstage.

When we were finally called to the proscenium arch, we shared the stage with the film's major star and starlet, Mitr Chaibancha and Petchara Chaowarat. The pair had remained on stage for our introduction. Idols of ten million Thai movie goers, both were at the height of careers that saw them co-star in 165 films together. Cookie-cutter film or not, that is a lot of time before a camera. Mitr, in those days, starred in half the 75 to 100 motion picture films annually produced by the Thai movie industry.

Lucky and I both *wai* greeted the two cinema legends and joyfully received their returned *wai*. It was a prideful moment and Lucky later said, "It like be stage wit like John Wayne, Lock Hutson, Dorit Day, Sophia Lo-ren. It be someone like dat."

Ah, but the ways of the world are strange. For who, besides Buddha, knew as we stood together on the Queen's Theater stage that Friday afternoon, Mitr Chaibancha would only complete two more important films in what remained of his career and life? One would be a parody of the life-style at the heart of *Luk Thung* and was entitled Magical Love of Luk Thung and the other, a sequel to two earlier installments of a crime fighter storyline, *Insee Thong*; The Golden Eagle was his very last movie. Both films were released in 1970.

No one knew. His domination of the industry was huge and has since caused undying speculation surrounding his demise. His last and fateful film was the first that Mitr had self-produced. It featured the return of his widely popular fictional character, Rom Ritthikrai, an alcoholic detective whose alter ego becomes a masked hero.

In real life, Mitr was very athletic. As a three-year high school Thai boxing champion he earned a college scholarship and was a trained Air Force pilot. After graduating he worked as a flight instructor at Don Muang Airport prior to his film career. He was the real deal and had always performed his own stunts.

During the final scene of the final day of shooting *Insee Thong*, our hero, having vanquished the villains, was scripted to fly off into the sunset by helicopter. As the camera rolled,

Mitr leapt from the ground to grab the rope ladder hanging from the aircraft but managed to grasp only the lowest rung. This was unknown to the helicopter pilot who engaged the levitation gear. As the craft rose higher and higher, Mitr was unable to gain footing. Finally, he could hold on no more, lost his grip, and fell eighty feet to hard earth.

The fatal accident was totally recorded and left in the final theatrical release of the film. The eagle had fallen and there would be no more sequels.

Boy! Talk about flying time. As we four stood together, there remained only one year, ten months and two days left of the grains in Mitr's hourglass. But we didn't know that, which allowed us to enjoy the moment.

We were artists and the stage was ours. For an artist, nothing compares to the spellbound reaction of an audience of strangers to your work. And we did our best to captivate.

G.T. Foster

Repeat Performance

Fame has an addictive quality, but the gala premier had left me with the feeling of having reached a pinnacle. I knew it would all end, but until then, it didn't matter. Enjoy the moment.

In downtown Sattahip I once exited a cab on my way to my Indian tailor. A young boy walking on the sidewalk widened his eyes in recognition, then jumped, pointed, and called out, "Forest, *krap*! *Kun* Forest, *krap*! *Kun bpen Surapol!*"

What a flushing boost. The famous love the rush and glow fans beam their way. The whole sunglasses thing is a fraud. Don't ever believe otherwise. Stars yearn for the beaming light of recognition. It's the same thrill the Lone Ranger must feel walking into a room with everybody eyeing and asking, "Who is that masked man?"

Oh, the famous be damned. Day or night they come out to walk behind shaded eyes hoping, nay, praying to be recognized. "I hope they do. God, I hope they do." But in return for that adulation the performer must continue to grow because greedy audiences always want more. The same old, same old just won't do.

I needed to feed the flame and Lucky had always known it. First he enlarged my part of the dialogue lead-in to *16 Bpii* ... In the back-and-forth of my introduction Lucky would ask if I was in the army. "*Kun bpen tahan, chai mai krap?*"

I would reply, "Yes, I am in the army." (*Chai leeo, pom bpen tahan.*)

"Are you not Laotian?" he would ask. (*Kun mai bpen puak Lao na, krap?*) It was a dual-edged question that played on my dark skin, comparing it to the darker, ethnic Laotian community while leaving unspoken the general Thai preference to *nuuan*, light skin.

"*Mai chai.*" It is not true, I would say. I am not Laotian. I am an American black person. "*Pom mai bpen puak Lao. Pom bpen American piu dum.*"

Still speaking Thai, Lucky would inquire, "If you are foreigner, why do you know how to sing '16 Years Turned Upside Down?'" Then quickly answer his own question with the over-used punch-line: "Ah! You have a Thai girlfriend, right?"

"*Mai mii tealot, krap.* I don't have a girlfriend."

"Then why can you sing Surapol Sambatcheroen's song? Are you Surapol?" (*Tamai kun luu jak pleeng Surapol Sambatchereon? Kun bpen Surapol, krap?*)

I'd milk the moment with a dramatic pause, while the audience imagined my response, then replied, "*Pom bpen Suraitan.*" Suggesting I was *suraa*—the spirit—and *tan*—overtaken; Surapol reborn.

In my mind, I was saying, "I have caught his spirit" and imagined it an edgy word play on rebirth, spirits, and ghosts. However it really translates or whatever it means, it worked drawing murmurs of shock or outbursts of laughter, and often, combinations of both.

But credit Lucky with also knowing the bit was only good for so long. He constantly cajoled me to expand my repertoire. So, throughout many otherwise idle pre-dawn motor-pool mornings, I pushed my tape recorder stop and start switches toward their planned obsolescence. I would write a monosyllable onto my notepad and restart the tape and listen. Stop. Rewind. Stop. Listen. Again, stop the tape, and write down another monosyllabic sound representing a Thai word. From these sessions two new songs emerged.

Memorized and practiced to the point of performance, I sang a 3-song set during a band gig of a private local wedding and finally fled the one-hit-wonder shed.

Shortly afterward, Lucky announced we had been booked for a January 5th return television appearance. This time the entire *Bpen Dai Band* would perform.

Extended Stay

After the success of the early November Loy Krathong Festival, I was under a constant barrage from Lucky and his Bangkok connections to extend my stay. I finally requested an application from the first-sergeant and filled out the Department of Army Form 4817 Request to Extend Current Tour. I had warned Lucky and his contacts that the likelihood of such a request being granted was very slim. I had honestly felt the chances were nil but lacked the language facility to go into that with them.

Within a week of submission the request came back. Denied. There was no explanation attached. I was left to fill in the blanks with my own whys. If I had been important enough to disquiet the army by my associations in Korat, they would certainly have taken an interest in my conduct and contacts in Sattahip and Bangkok. And not in a good way.

Yet, Lucky remained optimistic. "Don't worry. The prince will help. Him king uncle!" he insisted.

And sure enough, three days later, as I signed out in the office duty log, I heard, "Forest! Specialist Forest, would you come into my office, please."

"Yes, first-sergeant." I finished signing and went to his office doorway.

"Come in here." The first-sergeant sat behind his desk.

"Yes, First-Sergeant Johnson."

"Good morning. Close the door."

"Good morning, first-sergeant," I entered and did so.

"Sit down." I sat and he continued with his eyes fixed on me, "Is there anything wrong?"

"No, first-sergeant. Things are fine."

"I was just checking. You've been a good soldier with me." He looked down at an open folder on his desktop and fingered through some pages. "Very reliable. No problems, no complaints."

"Thank you, sir." I heard myself and quickly corrected. "Excuse me, rather I mean, first-sergeant. I know you work for a living." I smiled, not sure what the meeting was about, but not at all anxious. On the contrary, I felt very much at ease.

"I don't really know or want to know what the problem was with you and your last unit. I don't care why Battalion transferred you. I don't even know why they turned down your request for an extended stay. What I do know is you been a good soldier."

"Thank you, first-sergeant," I was still uncertain where this was leading but knew the sergeant was being honest. Had it been up to him ...

But finally he arrived at his point. "Anyways," he said, "you have an appointment in Bangkok, Tuesday morning. I'm going to fill both your Monday and Wednesday night slot in the motor pool. So, you will be rested and you can stay over if necessary."

"Thank you, First-Sergeant Johnson. But an appointment? With who, I mean, whom? With whom do I meet?" I asked knowing the only explanation possible was that Lucky's contacts had, indeed, acted.

The first-sergeant double-checked the order. "Well, with the military affairs officer. He's with the American Embassy. What do you know about all this?"

Despite what I knew, my heart skipped a beat upon hearing *American Embassy*. All I could think to answer was, "Nothing at all, first-sergeant, sir."

"You're going to meet him at this address. The Dunsit Hotel. It's on the New Road just up from the American." The first sergeant handed me the paper with the official who-what-when-and-where details. "You can hitch a ride to Bangkok on the jeep with the Tuesday morning mail drop."

Over the weekend I combated wave after wave of stage fright while drowning in the fearful thought I was way out of my depth, an amateur rushed to the big leagues. But my wiser angels in stern whispers counseled calm. "Get a grip. This ain't your first rodeo! Get a grip. Remember your three years of high school debate. Think about the benefits, the collateral training. You know how to hone an image. Buck up and act self-assured!"

With my spirit thus renewed, I recalled how my debate partner, Jim and I would enter the room, briefcases in hand, their contents of neatly organized files stacked safely inside, ready to be taken out and calculatingly set upon the table alongside a notebook and sharpened pencils. We came fully prepared to control as much of the subject, format, and venue as possible.

Debating the pros and cons of the forthcoming meeting, one thing was clear. I had been left alone with my own vices since arriving in Sattahib. The situation had been perfect. But I knew I would need to closely examine and question any change in working conditions under any offer to extend my stay.

The Ambassador's Man

Tuesday morning the mail driver dropped me at the American. I checked into a room then took a *tuk-tuk* to the Dunsit Hotel where I sat in the lobby and waited, playing mental games to calm my nerves. My emotions were again running wild, following the up, down, and shanked arch of a beach ball being volleyed during a boring one-sided baseball game. My mantra was a rendition of an elementary school cheer, "Be calm, be cool, and be collected." Waiting, my mind looped, "Stay calm, stay cool, stay collected, and stay focused."

Although, this time, he was wearing a light beige seersucker suit with a leather attaché bag strapped over the left shoulder, I recognized the cultural affairs agent from his do's and don'ts lecture on the airplane the January morning of my arrival nearly a year earlier. I stood to greet him. He extended his free hand, and we shook.

"Specialist Forest, I presume." It was a good guess since I was in uniform.

"Yes, sir."

"I'm Officer Deeds of the American Embassy here in Bangkok. Currently, I am both the Cultural Affairs Agent and the acting Military Affairs Officer." He tried to make a joke. "Sometimes the two hats get heavy."

I appreciated his attempt at ice-breaking humor and said, "I bet," and added a small chuckle sound.

"In fact, your problem has landed on my desk, twice, so to speak."

The Boys Are Not Refined

"I am sorry, sir, for any inconvenience that might have caused. I was reluctant to begin with. I tried to explain this to—"

"Let's slow it down a bit, why don't we. I thought we'd have a little brunch. The kitchen has a grill and I already have a table. Alright with you?" he asked, leading the way to the hotel coffee shop.

"Swell," I said and followed.

He showed me our table, pointed out the grill, then led the way to the buffet counter where pastries, fruit, and meats were laid for the choosing. I chose a warm apple Danish and a cup of hot chocolate and returned to our table.

"Well, Specialist Forest, it is a pleasure to finally meet you," he said setting his plate on the table and sitting. "Funny how these things work. Ambassador Unger had hinted I should contact you shortly after your initial meeting at the Naval Officers' Banquet."

It sounded like he had been given an order to read my file. "Really? What can I say? I'm flattered. I didn't really meet him."

"Perhaps, it would have been better for everyone if you had."

"Excuse me, sir, I don't follow?"

"Do you have any idea . . . ? No, of course you don't." He paused, then continued, "In some ways yours is a unique problem. But listen . . . Louisa Kennedy? Have you heard the name?"

I nodded in affirmation. "Yes, sir. Of course I have. What GI hasn't?"

"She became a cultural hot potato because of her song."

"'Little Strange Dog', 'Maa Noy Tamada'?" I asked.

"That's the song. Only the Thais call it 'Puu Yai Lee', Elder Lee. Although the incident occurred under Ambassador Graham, we certainly wouldn't want a similar occurrence, would we?"

"Sir, you've lost me, again. But what happened?"

"Oh, that's not important. What I'm saying is that these are problematic times. There are undercurrents of unrest. Hell, we've had our hands full trying to locate a missing American businessman. Went on vacation and vanished. Why, he had single handedly revived the silk industry in this country. How does a man like that go missing? You tell me. I tell you, it's the most confounded thing I've ever heard of. Then, there is Surapol Sombatcharoen . . . "

"Yeah?" I asked, pricked and thinking, "How is this a problem?"

"Well, this Surapol was an icon, created and controlled by the Thai Army through their broadcast network. You're singing his songs, and now the Thai Navy wants a piece of you. The Thai royalists and the cinema crowd are sizing you up to get their dibs in." He smiled and shook his head. "Son, you have become the object of a tug-of-war between two military factions and certain royalist elements. And for us, at your own embassy, it has become a bit of a headache."

"Come on, sir. No one is controlling me like that."

"You don't agree? It's not important. The truth is we have been asked by a person of influence to look into the matter of an extended tour on your behalf. Despite the ambassador's policy of non-interference in military operations, we have done so."

"I understand very little of that, sir. I assure you, I am only here because of friendships and good intentions toward Thai friends."

"That in itself is a rather sticky mess. The matter has been compounded by the fact that your contacts and performances were, apparently, a wholly private affair, made without knowledge or authorization. Not even your company commander was made aware of your involvement in these Thai domestic affairs."

The Boys Are Not Refined

That perturbed me. "I did not know it was required. No, I made no broad announcement, but I made no secret of my activities. I performed on at least four occasions at the NCO Club at Utapao. Where's the big secret?"

"Well, the performances alone are not the problem. In fact it's quite commendable—the ideal kind of Thai-American relationship. Wonderful. All American boys . . . To be frank, there was discussion of a transfer to a Chiang Mai USO unit, but the logistics . . . And that nasty incident at Korat will not go away. It was not isolated. Hardly. One of twenty-nine missing vehicles in that area of operation over the eight-month period of this year. No, hardly isolated. It amounts to an extraordinary drain of resources. It is an unusually sophisticated operation and your footprint has been left upon it. Your friend, Private William Childs has been . . ."

"Sir, he was a scapegoat!

"And you believe that?"

"Yes, sir, I do." The military affairs officer stared deep into my eyes and I returned the stare.

"The Ambassador has wisely chosen not to involve himself in this matter. You are entangled more than you know through relatives of a certain Chakri prince who resides in Korat and is a member of the royal family."

"Sir, I know nothing of this prince! What prince?"

"As I was saying, his family has large landholdings throughout the region. Apparently, your friend Srinual Priew Wan is a niece of Prince Mo. Although her business was closed . . .

"Are you talking about Luckie? The Royal Bar?"

"That's it, the Royal Bar. Well, it was declared off-limits about a year ago. She collects government rents for leases on the very land on which Camp Friendship sits."

"Humm."

"I reviewed your request but found no reason to overstep the decision of Major Garrett, your battalion executive officer.

However, if you re-enlist, that is, if you extend your service for three years you will be transferred to USO services in Bangkok and guaranteed an additional one-year stay. What do you think?"

I was able to chew and digest the offer much quicker than I managed to gobble the tasty pastry. It was a no go. I had come hoping the meeting could aid in my quest to extend my tour. I wanted to stay but only under conditions that would allow me the freedoms Sattahip had granted.

Trips and events had all been managed during off-duty hours without the involvement of any American official, military or otherwise.

Now that everyone was watching that conduct was branded "loose-cannon." It would not be allowed to happen a second time. But beyond that stood the idea of extending my military commitment.

"Re-enlist for three years? You're kidding me, right? No, sir, not today, not tomorrow, not ever. Thank you but no thank you, sir." The idea was too much. It was slapstick funny but to laugh out loud would have been rude. I could only smile.

"Well, I understand your decision. Nonetheless, should you wish to return to Thailand upon completion of your military service, despite that ugly affair and any splash of stain, this office is prepared to assist you in any possible way."

"Yes, sir. I do understand." I rose to end the interview and leave.

"One moment, Specialist. He turned to his leather shoulder bag and removed a legal sized manila envelope. "The Ambassador instructed me to give you this." He rose, shook my hand, handed me the envelope, and wished me good luck.

We went our separate ways.

Last Call

And that was the name of that tune. What was in the envelope? I wasn't staying. What did I care and why did it matter? But I opened it. Inside the envelope was a bound transcript of the William Child's Article 32 Hearing at Korat. Some kind of dead fish? I didn't get it. Tired of the entire incident I placed the envelope at the bottom of my Camp Vayama footlocker and moved on.

Over the next two weeks the band played at the army-base NCO Club, two air-base gigs, a wedding, a couple of private parties, and I continued to reap the fruit of minor stardom. The January 5th television engagement went well but was bittersweet, I performed knowing it was my last gig and there was something haunting and extraordinary in the way the band played.

After our television appearance we shared a group meal and I returned to my comfy, non-Spartan, government-supplied Bangkok hotel quarters. Sipping coffee and people-watching in its after-all-hours bar and coffee house, I met a nurse. She had worked a late shift and had stopped-by to unwind.

"I know you don't believe me but I have never stopped here before."

"I believe you," I said. "But why does it matter?" I asked, uncertain whether to believe her. I wanted to. Believe you me, I was so tired of *gullies*. Not as people, but as women who talked to you because they were working.

The nurse was shapely but not thin. More what one would call sturdy. Although she understood some English, our conversation was mostly in Thai. She had missed the buzz. She had never heard of me. She was Chinese-Thai, and that seemed to make a difference.

"But you are all Thais. Who would know?"

"People know. We are minority. I am minority. We are not really treated same."

Later, I told her, "I would like to go home with you."

"So sorry. I have enjoyed talking to you. But come on, I'm not a working girl, not like that."

"I know that." By then I believed her. That was the reason I wanted to go. "I would like to see how a Thai nurse lives. I really would." I had said something honest, and then continued, "No strings."

"Promise?"

"Promise."

We took a taxi to her apartment in a newly constructed eight or nine story building. It was a neighborhood in the middle of a building boom. There were many other apartments under construction. She gave the driver her *soi* (street) number but after three rapidly occurring turns I was left somewhere within the still-throbbing city, yet totally disoriented as to exactly where that was. I could not have given even a general direction.

Inside the apartment was clean, well furnished, and comfortable and she made us tea. As we drank, she admitted a sexual curiosity that was fortuitously mutual. For me, it was a psychological relief to be with a Thai woman who was successful in a normal profession. Most important, there was no money, no fame or other string attached. She liked me.

The next morning when it was time to return to my hotel, I was without a clue as to the long or short of it. I relied on the taxi driver to deliver me.

The Boys Are Not Refined

Good-bye Sattahip

It was time to leave and there were good-byes to say. If I'd had the facility of words in Thai I would have told Lucky and the other members of the *Bpen Dai Band*, "Look, Lord Buddha knows me. He sent Marti as a head-turning siren, an international girl from Ipanema, down the beach my way knowing I wouldn't care that she was someone else's girl and would be hooked through the nose and lost. However, my (open) pursuit of her had honorably ended with my introduction to you, the band members. All of you. My loss, our gain. And what a ride it has been."

In our actual goodbye, Lucky remained optimistic and sunny. It was not a question of would I return? For him, it was only a question of when would I return? He, therefore, wrote two songs for me to learn during the interim and perform upon my return for a triumphal Thai tour—my Douglas MacArthur moment: *"Gert Naa Bpen Kon Thai"*, "To Be Born Thai", and *"Pom Rak Muan Thai"*, "I Love Like a Thai". So, saying goodbye to Lucky was more like saying "So long" with a "See ya soon" attached.

With the other band members it was a combination of handshakes and *wai* with lots of smiles and hugs in the mix. There was a sense that we owed each other something unpayable. For me, the band had been heaven-sent. But its members had also reaped heaven as a reward for their open-mindedness.

The brothers Witt and Nitt of the open-door Hit House gave me a highly lacquered, bamboo water pipe, burnished with the images of various Buddhist icons, or more correctly, *pra*.

Other than Medford, I had made no close social or even military contacts on the American side. While in Sattahip I had gone native. There was but one more good-bye to give.

With Marti it was different. A sweet friendship of glances and occasional body brushes had been allowed to blossom because I had managed to smother my base desire to win her at all cost.

The degree or nature of her involvement with the lead guitarist, Sithporn, was never questioned or explained. Were they a couple in the biblical sense?

Things were complicated with Marti. She was a kind of band groupie, always around at our gigs. Delicious eye-candy. Yet, marked by her distinct, exotic look, she was an outcast. Unlike the present day, the Thai people in 1968 abhorred mixed-race children. They were ostracized and turned into social lepers.

Marti lived in an orphanage settlement on *Kilo-Sip*, a side street off the main road that ran into municipal Sattahip from Camp Vayama. She had drawn me a map to the settlement. Her cottage was plotted between two oak trees. One designated my turning point onto *Kilo-Sip* and the other marked her particular cluster of cottages. The taxi dropped me there.

She stood waiting for me outside her bungalow, and we walked around the perimeter of her complex. There were enormous moments of silence making the entire time electric.

"*Kun* Forest, *kha* come to future for Thailand?"

I modeled the correct syntax, slowly saying each word. "Will you come back in the future?" I corrected out of a comfort we had developed over time. All the band members, including Marti, had asked my aid in their English language development and had encouraged correction of syntactic error. I likewise requested correction of my misspoken Thai. We began to correct each other. Now it was an embedded second nature.

"Okay, GI Forest, *kha*, come back in . . . in future come back?"

"Honest? *Jing jing mai gohok*? I don't know. *Mai luu, krap.* I hope so. I want to. I want to come back. I want to . . . see you again."

"Me too, Forest, *kha*. I want see you again."

I recited words I had practiced for our goodbye. And although they held an element of humor, they were deeply felt. In Thai I said, "When I first met you on the beach at Pattaya, you immediately brought to mind the words of the Surapol song, '*Naao Ja Dtai Yuu Leeo*', ('The Cold Has Died, So Live'), and I didn't even know the lyrics. I thought, *To hug that girl would be like eating spicy duck roasted over red fire*. Marti, I think I love you. (*Maa gorn muu lai pom hen kun, gorn pon luu-jak pleeng Naao Ja Dtaai 'chan huua-ja bok hak men dai gort saao naang ga muan dai gin bpet yang fai deeng'. Pom kit pom rak kun krap.*)"

She laughed and said, "*I* understand. I know. *Chan luu - jak, kha. Chan luu.*

We hugged a full minute. It was warm. It was heartfelt. And it was good.

"Good-bye Marti."

"Good-bye, *kun* Forest, *kha*."

G.T. Foster

Who Really Killed Surapol

I signed off in the duty roster as a final checked-out from the 55th Transportation Company. Then I caught a lift on the 0500 hour mail jeep to the American Hotel in Bangkok and checked into my room. Later that same morning, I rode the daily 0900 Air Force/Army hotel shuttle to Camp Friendship in order to complete the required 9th Logistical Command's bureaucratic paperwork and get my travel orders, payroll allotment, and next duty-station assignment.

Arriving at the camp, but not wanting to "hurry-up-and-wait" on an empty stomach, I decided to eat before attacking the army clerical gauntlet and stopped by the NCO Club to satisfy a sudden craving for a hamburger and a plate of extra-crispy, practically burnt fries. My ordered plate in hand, and looking for a place to sit, I heard, "Well look what my pet ocelot tiger done dragged in."

I recognized the voice of Specialist Fourth Class Michael Bryson and it produced a flood of nostalgia. But he was not there alone. It was early afternoon old home week. Seated at the table with Bryson, enjoying a sandwich and beer lunch were two other good men; Sasse and Somchai completed the dining pack. I joined them.

As it turned out, freshly promoted to sergeant, Sasse had escaped the shit-hole of Camp Charn Sinthrope through transfer assignment to Battalion Headquarters. And Somchai had been elevated to battalion interpreter. We exchanged how-do-you-dos and how-have-you-beens and I caught up on news of old drivers and friends.

Bryson had successfully extended his tour and would ETS from Thailand in June, 1969. He had also continued his language tutelage. Mostly under Luckie. He proudly revealed he could now, on a rudimentary level, read in Thai.

"Green? Lloyd?" I asked.

"Green and Lloyd both ETS last month. They're home," Sasse informed.

"Madson?"

"I haven't seen him."

"I've seen him on post, but he doesn't come by Luckie's anymore. He lost his welcome," injected Bryson.

"What? How'd that happen?"

"I can't go into that right now. It's complicated. I'll tell you about it later." He raised his brow and made a slight head jerk that I read as a nod to indicate present company, then smiled and continued. "But right now, let's talk about you."

"Man, Bry, what a tease. But you're right, it would be rude. Okay, what about me?"

The change of subject quickly led to my song escapades and a discussion of Surapol in which Somchai had his own prime suspect and rejected the notion, accepted by the general public, that the singer's death had come over a second wife tug-of-war.

"So you tink still it be just simple? Little case of angry village elder, you tink, Forest? Hmm?" Somchai had almost taunted. "Nothing simple. Dis case not simple. Maybe look simple. But it not be simple."

"What's to doubt?" I asked, having my own, but not yet wanting to mention Surapol's wife.

"In Thailand? Everything. It's a redundant question, but, who killed king Rama VIII?" cautioned Sasse. He raising his beer in a salute to doubt.

"Yeah, who did kill King Bhumipol's older brother, Ananda?" asked Bryson clinking his mug against Sasse's. "I've always been fascinated by the story of the king's sudden demise. Come on, Somchai. What do you know about the royal mystery who done it?"

"*Mai luu jak,* I never study dis," replied Somchai in a plea of ignorance.

"Well, nine years after the fact they executed the Officer of the Day. A court lieutenant?" Sasse asked like a court attorney rising doubt.

"*Mai luu jing-jing.* Dis I not know about."

"Well, what does any of that have to do with Surapol?" I asked attempting to redirect the conversation.

"I am, as you say, spinning a precautionary tale. In Thailand they say, things are rarely as they seem," said Sasse in reserving his right to disagree.

"Well, get back to your story's theory," said Bryson shifting back to Somchai and his Surapol tale.

"You agree? I neber buy story of love triangle," the interpreter explained, looking to each of us.

"Okay. This is Thailand. *Haa mia mai dii gwaa.* You can always get a new wife," affirmed Bryson.

"Yeah, I don't buy it, either," Sasse concurred. "Big star like Suropol, no way."

"Okay, Somchai. Back to your theory. You mentioned the year, year-and-a-half prior to his death. You said Surapol had a continuing public argument with a long-time rival who was also very popular." I was trying to keep an open mind on this new angle but I needed facts and details.

"Bpen Ja Mon. He name Bpen Ja Mon," said Somchai.

"Yeah, Bpen Ja Mon. You said that he and Surapol sang songs of similar subjects."

"Yeah, but then you said that Bpen Ja is the real deal. What did you mean?" asked Bryson frowning in puzzlement.

"Him call Surapol fake, *Ploom Yai.* Big fake. You see, Bpen Ja Mon, him be a soldier in Korea. A sergeant." Somchai spoke in that slow clear voice that made him such a good interpreter.

"Him come back big hero. But he always get in trouble because he crazy. He do whatever he want. He kill a man. He go to jail but him get out. He *baa mak-mak* crazy. He say Surapol steal song, steal idea. Him *tom daa*, make threat, to Surapol."

"Come on," I said doubtfully. "Surapol stole his songs?"

"You see, Surapol have big sponsor, big support. He have regular army radio show. Broadcast from army base."

"But they say Surapol created a new genre," I insisted.

"*Baa.* Crazy," sneered Somchai.

I never felt more thoroughly dismissed.

"They say that now! Surapol dead. He hero. They be same-same, equal, peer. They both making music. Maybe, Bpen Ja Mon before, but they make same music. But Bpen Ja Mon bigger. He, he give many . . . interview. He very mad. I say, tink about it. Maybe right, maybe wrong."

The net effect of Somchai's story of revenge and copyright infringement was to create an additional mound of doubt. Although the official who-done-it police report named the village elder as culprit, many Surapol fans, like Sirisam, continued to point accusing fingers at Nuuan Sombatcharoen, Surapol's tearful widow and heir to his estate.

Assertions of affairs, theft, and infidelities only beg the question: Who really killed Surapol Sombatcharoen? Was it a case of stolen songs or stolen kisses?

Was it a conniving wife, a cuckold elder, or a cursed rival behind the three Nuk Lang gunmen? You want to bet? In Thailand, you pays yo' money and takes yo' chances.

G.T. Foster

The Betrayal

"Well, fellas," Bryson said as he slid his chair back and rose, "it's time I get the cargo on the road."

"What you hauling?" I asked.

"Gas-o-line. Our unit seems to do nothing but petrol these days."

"Well, I'm leaving, too," I said. I picked up my temporary orders and placed my cap on and mockingly saluted.

"Lunch is over, Somchai my friend, and we too must go" declared Sasse. He left a five-baht tip for the waiter and we all exited the NCO club together.

"Sasse, Somchai, it has been a pleasure to know you both. *Chok dii.*" I said and cupped my hands.

They both returned my *wai*. "Good luck, Forest," said Sasse.

'*Chok dii*, Forest," said Somchai.

"See you guys in a couple days," said Bryson.

The battalion interpreter and clerk got into a jeep. Somchai sat on the passenger seat and Sasse drove away. As the two men drove off, I turned to Bryson and said, "Okay, man, let's have the full skinny. What gives?"

"You mean Madson?"

"Yeah, I mean Madson. That's exactly who I meant. But what did you mean when you said he lost his welcome at Luckie's?"

"Your friend is a snitch."

"Whoa, now. Come on, man. That's deep. That's ugly. But that's deep. What are you talking about?"

"I mean it. Pichai is still pissed. His own military career was in jeopardy. Luckie feels like he threw her to the dogs."

"Well, they are not the people you want mad at you around here."

"But that's not the worst of it. Did you know he gave up the kid? It wasn't Wellington. I thought it was Wellington. But it wasn't, it was Madson."

"Wait a minute. You just all but admit Billy took it."

"Come on, use your head. Sure he took it. Where did you think the wire cutters came from? That night in the car? Come on Forest. But that ain't the point. Everybody's stealing. You want to argue whether the kid got justice or not?"

"No, man. Forget it. Justice under the Uniform Code of Military Justice? That don't exist. You and I both know the code is no more uniform or just than any other form of peeping, color-struck American justice. The real crime the kid committed was getting caught, and then not catching a break."

"But he never would have been caught if Madson had not snitched to save his own ass. That's the point."

"Mad Man!"

"Yeah, Mad Man."

"You knew all along they took it?"

"Well, nobody ever really said, but, yeah man. I ain't no fool. I pretty much figured it out when I saw the first bulletin posted in the motor pool."

"They were in it together?"

"Yeah, they were in it together."

"Who took it?"

"The kid. Drove it through to the air force side of the base and exited there. The flyboy guards saw it was an army vehicle and just waved him through."

"Jesus Christ."

"But Madson gave up Billy to save his own ass."

"But it was Wellington. Hell, we know he was mad at Billy."

"Be that as it was, it was Madson. Childs didn't give him the agreed-on cut. Billy kept putting him off. Billy was only a week away from his General, but he still owed Madson his cut."

"So Stan Mad Man cut himself a pound of flesh and called it all square, eh?"

"Yeah. Like one of those Shakespeare shakedowns."

"But Madson wasn't just running lines, he was playing with lives."

"Well, brother Forest, good luck with the rest of yours. If you are ever in Seattle look me up."

"Good luck to you, brother. I'm in Oakland. Well, Emeryville."

The Boys Are Not Refined

Karma Two

I had been stationed in Korat for eight months and there had been one woman that had burrowed her way through my heart into a special spot in my head, although we had only met on one occasion. Her name was Nong and that meeting had occurred during one of my first nights-on-the-town in mid-January. She was very pretty, beautiful in fact. But as it was, she was also six-months pregnant and unavailable, insisting, "I lub my baba fader."

And although I'd reminded her that the song says, "love the one you are with," she would not budge. Instead, she handed me over to a woman she claimed was her sister.

I had wondered if Jonesy or Smitty really was coming back? Would he ever? How many American service men held true to promises they made these women? How many really did return? At the time, she really believed her lover to be different. Convinced he would come back from Chicago, she had not been interested in any other.

Now, eleven months later, I returned to Korat on the tailwinds of fame and recent stardom.

I had left the late lunch and my enjoyable brush with old comrades to attend to the required business at battalion headquarters, part of my final clearance. I received my new orders which included travel and duty assignment. The Quartermaster also issued my monthly pay, plus an additional stipend as travel allowance.

Celebrity has its benefit and the encounter happened as Lady Fate would have it. Leaving battalion headquarters I met Nong. She was in the same section of the base because she had just visited the Administrative Office of the 9th Logistical Command in regard to a benefits claim for her son. Although we had met but once, she remembered me and seemed genuinely pleased to see me. I was in the jaws of ecstasy. I took her and her young son to the base commissary and happily purchased bags and bags of things.

Outside the commissary I saw a taxi driver I recognized. Although I didn't remember his name, I had met him once at Luckie and Pichai's closed bar prior to the company's transfer to the backwoods of Phanom. He also recognized me. See, what I mean about fame?

"*Sawatdii kun Surapol, krap,*" he greeted me by my new nickname, disarming my guard and making me feel at home. "*Yaak-tam taxi mai, krap?*" he asked, offering his service.

"Do I want a taxi? *Chaisi, krap. Dii gwaa. Oa taxi, jing-jing.*" I hired him to drive us back to Nong's apartment. She rode in the front with her infant son and I rode in the back seat. Once there I paid for the cab ride and unloaded the groceries. Oh, the fortunes of the stars! The driver even helped.

Inside, the child had fallen asleep and we were finally alone. The moment I had waited eleven months for had arrived. I was in the apartment of the most beautiful woman in Korat. I wanted to lift my head and shout praises and thanks, but instead, for some reason, I felt my right rear pant pocket. Hum, that's odd. It was empty. I felt the left rear and got that same empty feeling.

I felt my front pockets and looked around the room. But my wallet was not there. It was gone!

Stop!

Recall. The playback of my mind showed me clearly what had happened. I had taken my wallet out and paid the driver. Meanwhile, Nong was unloading the baby and bags. Distracted and wanting to help, I had put the wallet with my monthly pay and travel allotment on the rear seat.

The Boys Are Not Refined

The fast-thinking driver had seen the unattended wallet on the seat and had noticed my distraction. Cunningly, he had added to my confusion by quickly grabbing the remaining bags and whisking the three of us into the apartment. Then he had driven away.

Remember? Yeah, I remembered, but by then it was too late. Nong also understood what had happened and labeled the villain. "Him *luk jaw rakhe, jing-jing.*" Yeah, right. But by that time I'd already been bitten by the *luk jaw rakhe,* baby crocodile.

As for love? That moment was also gone. The night was lost. First in a vain search for the "little crocodile" that had stolen my wallet. Then in time spent returning to Camp Friendship to process a request for an emergency allotment.

Over time all things are worked out by dharma, but karma works overtime in Korat. My farewell plans were shot. I did not make a final visit to either Luckie and Pichai at the closed Royal Bar or to the *gully* girls of the Lucky Seven Club. The next morning, January 16th, orders in hand, I caught a military transportation van back to Bangkok.

Nuuan

Back in Bangkok and with a flight to catch the next morning, I hustled in and out of China Town shops looking for the perfect Thailand Remember-Me-Always. I ended up buying another buddha, excuse me twice. I rented-leased-purchased another *pra*. This one was said to aid in the achievement of one's educational goals. I also purchased a beautiful onyx sapphire ring. Its reflected star was brilliant.

After dinner, a bit pooped, I returned to my hotel. Of the 35 million Thais in Thailand, who should be standing before me inside the lobby but Nuuan? I had told no one where I was staying.

She smiled at me, but I did not return the smile. It was not that I did not recognize her; I couldn't forget her.

If not fate, then it was just plain bad luck. We had been heatedly entangled, so to speak, between time she had spent with some dripping GI and her mandated bi-weekly check-up. An unsafe period. A check of a health card is a valueless precaution. One of those wham, bam, bingo occasions of risk inherent during all acts of unprotected sex!

For two weeks I had taken the prescribed dosage and abstained from milk, sex, and alcohol and had sworn never again—without protection!

"How did you get my hotel name? How did you find me?" I asked as I walked past her to the elevator, headed to my room and most definitely not interested in stopping to chat.

"You very famous *kun* Forest, *kha*," she said picking up my step and pacing along.

The Boys Are Not Refined

Waiting for the lift the conversation continued. "I leb Phanom go back my home. When I no sick I get job U-tapao. Dere I see you friend work army. Him tell me you be Sattahip. I go Sattahip. I see you ban but no see you."

The elevator car arrived. We entered and she never stopped talking. "Dey tell me you leb, go home United State. But I know you hab go Bangkok firt so I here. I find you. You famous, *jing-jing*, Forest, *kha*. You easy find."

"I'm still mad at you!"

"I know. I sorry, Forest, *kha*. I bery bery sorry, *kun* Forest, *kha*. I no want do to you. I not know *chun bpen rook* (I was sick). Not know. *Jing-jing naa* Forest. I not know!"

We arrived on the fifth floor, I exited and she trailed behind. When I said nothing she continued, "I not know what do. Plead Forest, *kha*, tell me. What me can do?"

"Nothing," I childishly snapped. "You've already done it!" I unlocked the door to my room and entered.

She followed saying, "No, Forest, *kha*. No say dat. Nuuan sorry. Nuuan bery, bery sorry. I lub you Forest, *kha*. She began to sing what she knew was my favorite Thai-female-vocalist-sung song, the eternally haunting *"Thai Sukiyaki"*:

Oo sut tii rak gan chan ooi
Jer gan naa leeo naa kon dii
Duey bpla paa nii
Saabaa nii mii hai rak rao . . .

"Please, Nuuan, don't."

Tung tung tii chan
Sut jak rak tur
Roa duang haa Thai . . .

"*Mai gohok, kun* Forest *kha. Chan rak kun jing-jing.*"

"Please, Nuuan. You don't have to say all that. I believe you. And I believe you didn't know. But I am very tired and I must sleep. I'm leaving tomorrow. But I am not ready to leave. But even now, I am too tired to do anything more than sleep."

I said this while undressing. I was really tired and I was going to sleep. But Nuuan began to take off her clothes.

"No, don't."

"I clean. For chore *jing-jing*. I hab check-up two time dis week. I no be wit nobody two-week, Forest, *jing-jing*."

"I don't care! I'm going to sleep. I'm not interested." By this point I had removed every stitch of clothing as relief against the evening's wilting heat. So, butt naked, as if in preparation to bathe or breed, I flopped onto the bed.

"It okay, Forest, *kha*. I lub you. I want be wit you. Plead, let me be wit you. I promit no do nuh ting. I lub you, Forest, *kha*." She too removed all clothing. Naked, she crawled onto the bed beside me.

I awoke next morning cuddled in her nakedness. Does one ever dare trust a whore? There had been no sex. For my part I had prophylactics but anger and hurt had frozen all desire. Yet, as I lay there entangled, her body heat and the gentle rise and fall of her rhythmic breathing began to stir passions previously listed among the missing and killed-in-action.

"Nuuan," I said softly, and kissed her forehead. I repeated her name again, more urgently. "Nuuan, it's time to go. Get off me. Get up and I'll take you to a Goodbye GI Breakfast."

It roused her. We dressed and went downstairs to the hotel coffee shop. "I'm going to order two plates of bacon, toast, and eggs sunny-side up. It's an American tradition, reminding us to look up, look up."

"I no like sunny-up. Me like oba easy."

"Then it's over-easy for you. I'll stick to the sunny-side-up"

After breakfast I assured her all was forgiven. Then I bade her goodbye and returned to my room.

The Boys Are Not Refined

Leaving Bangkok

It was January 17th and back in my room I showered, shaved, and packed my duffle bag and handbag carry-on. I then began straightening the room as a final safeguard against things left behind. There was a loud knock upon my hotel room door.

"Who is it?" I asked, thinking it was Nuuan returned to profess more undying love.

"Military Police," came back the response in a duet of voices. Then a single voice asked, "Specialist Forest?"

Military Police? I thought, *what in hell? As* I opened the door, I cross-questioned, "Military Police? What can I do for you?"

In the doorway stood two army military policemen. "We are here on orders to escort you to the passenger boarding area of the Don Muang Airport to await your return flight to the good old USA."

"Escort? I don't need an escort . . . Sergeant," I said, noting the grade insignias of the two soldiers and addressing the senior ranking member of their police patrol. "I have already contacted the desk for a taxi to the airport. Thank you very much."

"It is not important. Private White," he said addressing the other member of his party. "Go to the front desk and cancel Specialist Forest 's cab ride."

"Yes, Sergeant," said the ordered soldier. He turned and left. The MP sergeant entered my room and said, "We are here on orders from Battalion Command. Are you ready?"

"As a matter-of-fact, yes, Sergeant, I am. I was just giving my room a once-over." I made a stab at humor. "I won't be back for a bit." I smiled, then said, "Excuse me while I check the bathroom."

I stepped in and gave the "necessary room" a quick look, then rejoined my waiting escort, all the time thinking, *So, the fools think I'm an idiot and would* . . . what? Miss my flight and go AWOL? No way! It isn't that important. Sure, I love Thailand like Odysseus loved Calypso. Undoubtedly, she flipped his lights fantastic, but when it was time to go . . . Thailand will probably fill parts of my heart and mind forever. But that is not what is important just now. Right now? This minute? The main thing is to finish my obligation and get the hell out of this man's army.

"Ready?"

We left the hotel and rode to the airport without incident except for my own silent memories of a year earlier as we passed through the fateful intersection. What a ride that had been. Red light, green light, driver error. We had killed the kid.

At the airport the MPs took full advantage of their police status and left their jeep parked in a loading-and-unloading-only zone. Close. From there, with the lower ranking MP carrying my over-night bag as I toted my duffle, they marched me to the boarding area, where, to my surprise, sat Major Garrett.

"Major Garrett, sir?" I said and held my salute.

He rose to his feet and with his right arm returned the salute. Then turned to the MPs and said, "Thank you and that will be all, Sergeant." The two military policemen saluted, turned, and made their exit.

"Be at ease and sit down, Specialist Forest."

We both sat.

"I really mean it. Be at ease. I simply wish to talk to you before your flight."

The Boys Are Not Refined

"Yes, sir," I said and waited.

"Totally off the record."

"Yes, sir."

"I am here in part because of William Childs . . . and in part because you puzzle me."

"I puzzle you, sir? I don't mean to puzzle anyone, sir. Billy? Puzzled? I'm puzzled by this entire morning. Do you think I stole the vehicle?"

"Not at all. And let me assure you I don't mean to trouble you. You have an hour before your flight. I will try to be brief. I said I came here because of Childs." He paused, but when I said nothing, he continued. "I am troubled there, too. Yes, I know to a degree, Childs was a scapegoat. Still, I have done all I can for that boy. I . . ."

The major hesitated as he seemed to second guess his choice of words. Then he continued, "He is a boy, you know. Barely eighteen. He came in at sixteen with parental permission." He shook his head as if noting it a poor decision, then continued. "Of all the soldiers in the 21st Company he spoke highest of you. He said you were constantly trying to calm down his spirit."

"Those sound like his words."

"Yes, that's what he said. I noted it. 'Calm down my spirit'."

"It was unfair, sir. How could someone in the country for only one month . . . ?"

"That is no longer a question. He was involved. He has admitted that. But you puzzle me with your protective loyalty and wasted abilities. Oh, I don't mean totally. Not by any means. Far from it. Do you know you were strongly considered for my personal driver?"

"Yes, sir. I must admit I had been . . . warned of such a thing." I smiled and continued, "Then things happened. Do you want to know the truth?"

"I meant it when I said be-at-ease. Our conversation ends here. I am here on my own behalf. Please."

"I understand my not being chosen. But you know, the way it worked out? I was enjoying the road so much that had the offer been made...? Who knows what I would've chosen? I still might not have become your driver." There was a brief pause, and I continued. "You know, sir, I have some, but very few regrets as to how things shook out during my Thai tour."

"I would think not. You seem to have made quite the adventure of it."

"Yes, I guess I did. I guess you can call it an adventure. But now the club is closed, and we good Mouseketeers have to go home. I was informed by the military affairs officer that the final decision was yours, sir."

"Yes. I thought it best. But not for the reason you probably think. I did not believe then, nor do I believe now, that you have any idea of the complex situation that was developing around you."

"That is probably true, sir."

"Do you have any idea who Prince Paripatra is?"

"Is he the king's uncle? Our host for the premier of *16 Bpii Hɛng Kwam-lang* was introduced to me as such. As an uncle, I mean. I believe he is connected to the Rama Movie Studio."

"A bit heady for an American soldier, wouldn't you say?"

"I admit, sir. It was a bit heady." We both smiled.

"Specialist Forest, there is a war going on in Vietnam. There are regional insurgencies that flare up within this country. There are politics too complicated to begin to go into with you. You're going home. You're smart. Use the GI Bill. Get your education. If you should return as a civilian, do so as an aware adult. Thailand is no plaything with which to trifle. Civilians do not have the same protections as American servicemen."

Finished, he stood and extended his hand. I rose and took his handshake of friendship.

"Good luck, Specialist."

"Thank you, sir. And good luck to you, Major Garrett." I released his hand, took a step back and raised my right hand in proper military salute. Then I smiled and said, "Good-bye, sir. I'm sure you'll make colonel soon."

He returned my salute and smiled. "Good-bye, son."

I watched as he walked away.

G.T. Foster

Taps: Last Call

Having once sung the songs of Surapol Sambacheroen, the Thai Elvis, there is a photographic print that hangs in my garage. Taken on the set of *GI Blues* in 1960, it is a picture of King Bhumipol and Her Royal Highness Queen Srikit while on holiday. The king and queen are seated between the film stars Elvis Presley and Juliet Prowse. Seen seated from left to right are Elvis, the queen, the king, and the South African co-star. I call the photograph "The Two Kings."

Elvis can be seen indicating something out to the royal couple. His right arm is fully extended in a diagonal point, his left hand rested on his left knee. However, in pointing, Elvis thrust nearly off his chair and, clearly into Queen Srikit's royal space. The photograph captures the queen's shy-away response to the invasion. Any mildly critical Thai is left to interpret Elvis' action as gauche, rude, and crude American behavior.

One can almost hear Elvis whisper under his breath in that rich Memphis drawl, "I always did like dainty little pretty thangs."

For me the photograph typifies and symbolizes the Ugly American. He is that love-it-or-leave-it guy who does not give a hoot for the other fellow's culture, customs, or traditions. For him it is all about the so-called American way of doing things. He never bothers to remove his boots and would rather fight than switch a bad habit.

It was the soldier I had chosen, that first day on the bus in Thailand, not to be. Instead, I had made an honest effort to do as a Roman or more lyrically as a Venetian would do while

The Boys Are Not Refined

in the Venice of the East. I had tried to understand and make ties. That is really all I did.

Along the way I met some brothers and a major who sneeringly implored me to betray them. He had snarled, "You are never going to see any of these guys again once you get out of the army. You are going to complete your tour and go back home to your life."

Well, although my soldier-boy acquaintances were not refined, by-and-large they are still defined as friends because I had their backs and they had mine. Yet, so far, so good for the redhead major's forecast. I have yet to see Green, Lloyd, Bryson, Madson, Ruffin, Sasse, Henshaw, Wellington, or any of the other brothers ever again. And don't correct me. Although both Sasse and Henshaw were Caucasian I consider them homeboys.

I did hear from ex-private William Childs via the American Red Cross, so technically the major has already been proven wrong. But I crave before the grave to sit down with a brother or two from those days, share a beer, pour a libation of forgiveness, and recount a time when we were young Yankee soldiers in a foreign kingdom.

Made in the USA
Middletown, DE
17 August 2024

59246650R00222